Lady of the Lake

The Adventures of W. W. Ronin
Book Two

By Gregg Edwards Townsley
Two Bears Books Saint Helens, Oregon

Cover design by Olivia Passieux
Cover photo by Josh Townsley
Video book trailer(s) by Bill Fogle
Published by Two Bears Books
245 N. Vernonia Road
Saint Helens, Oregon 97051 U.S.A.
www.twobearsbooks.com
Two Bears Books, First Edition
ISBN: 061585446X
ISBN-13: 9780615854465
Library of Congress Control Number: 2013947180
Two Bears Books, St. Helens, OR

Special discounts are available on quantity purchases by corporations,
associations and others. For details, contact the publisher at the address
above. Orders by U.S. trade bookstores and wholesalers, please contact
the publisher or visit www.twobearsbooks.com.
Printed in the United States of America

To my wife, Nancy, who is always my cheerleader and who remembers my song when I've forgotten where I've placed my keys. You are my muse, my best editor, critic and friend.

TABLE OF CONTENTS

The first intercourse between the white and red race in Nevada, of which there is any record, dates from 1832. In August of that year Milton Sublette reached the head-waters of the Humboldt River, with a company of trappers, among whom was the celebrated Joe Meek, long afterwards a resident of Oregon, of whom the following traditional story is told by Mrs. F. F. Victor, in her book entitled "Mountain and Forest." Within a few days after their arrival at that place, Meek shot and killed a Shoshone Indian. The unfortunate, though famous mountaineer, N. J. Wythe, who was also of the party, asked the trapper why he had done this, and was told that it was only a hint "to keep the Indians from stealing their traps."

"Had he stolen any?" queried his questioner. "No," replied Meek; "but he looked as if he was going to."

From Thompson & West's *History of Nevada 1881, with Illustrations and Biographical Sketches of its Prominent Men and Pioneers,* pp. 145-158

Lake Tahoe, Nevada
1880

Chapter 1

SHOULDER ROLL

Ronin rolled onto his right shoulder before standing and breaking into a run. The horse had simply stopped. It had halted like a freight wagon up against an immovable, and in this case invisible, rock. And the forward momentum — cushioned by years of rolling, wrestling and practicing fighting arts taught to him by a French fur trader a few miles south of his Kansas home — had carried him over Jackson's head, hand-first onto a sandy path just west of Spooner Meadow, a mile or so east of Tahoe, sometimes called Lake Bigler.

"Hand, forearm, shoulder, foot," the old man used to say. He stopped tumbling at the tree-line, where he fixed himself onto a tall ponderosa, slowed his breathing and waited.

The horse had obviously seen something, or maybe smelled something. But it wasn't like the damn thing had stopped because of a snake or lizard. *It would have reared up, right? Or whinnied or made some sort of noise?* Not this time. It had simply stopped.

Ronin had served a church for three years as a priest and whatever else was needed, then the Pinkerton National Detective Agency for seven years, more or less throughout the Midwest, and then for the last three years as a *private* detective, making his way through the American West. He no longer worked for the man, any man for that matter, except those he was temporarily seeking or serving for the possibility of a small reward. And sitting upon a beast had never seemed like anything other than a burden. He much preferred a stage, or a wagon, even a train despite the lingering outrage he still felt toward the iron robber barons who had stolen Wichita and so many other western cities.

In Biffle's 19th Tennessee Calvary during the War of Northern Aggression, truth be told, he was a teamster, a food wagon driver. You could ask him; he'd tell you. He was just a cook, though in the course of his duties, he'd killed more than a few men who needed killing. Fact is, the former reverend W. W. Ronin didn't understand the appeal of horses, except to occasionally eat horse meat. And that wasn't something he enjoyed, either. It had simply been necessary.

Clinging to the tall mountain pine for a good ten minutes or so, he watched his horse and hat, and noted that neither had moved all that much. Letting go of the tree (he hadn't realized he had been gripping it so tightly), he eased himself back into the clearing so as to ask his most dependable (though least understood) friend in the entire world what the hell had happened, when a still small voice whispered, "Did you see them?"

Ronin looked left and right, but not before he returned his left hand to the pine tree in front of him and his right hand to the black buffalo-horn handled gun sitting cross-draw on his waist. "Jesus Christ," he murmured.

You would have heard it. A stuttered and fearful prayer, he was annoyed that he was feeling either or both.

"Did you see them?" the voice asked again.

His head jerked to his right and then back again, looking this time over each of his shoulders. The tall ex-reverend grabbed his well-worn slouch hat with his gloved left hand, and picking it up, knelt down on one knee. He drew his gun and folded it into his hat, obscuring its view should a stranger make himself or herself known. His horse was a few yards off and hadn't moved, his lever-gun as well, its brass receiver gleaming in the late afternoon Nevada sun.

"See what?" he challenged. He wasn't sure he had heard anything, but talking to himself wasn't something he was strange to, having served as a pastor to a small and still emerging Episcopal church in Wichita, Kansas. "East Jesus," he called it now, ten years later because it had been in the middle of bum-effing nowhere until the railroad came and split the town in two, not physically, but spiritually. It would never be the same.

It had been Ronin's dream to be a priest, or perhaps his parents' dream if he were honest. After the war that hadn't settled damn near anything as far as he could see, save that black men and women were now free to be as lost, or as poor, or as frustrated as anyone else, he had picked up and headed to a Pennsylvania seminary. Not that he always felt that way.

It was his parents' hope that he'd contribute to the heal-ing of the war-torn nation, hardly understanding that it was two nations that were torn, and maybe his own soul as well. Though their dream had never really materialized — save for the three years he had spent on the Kansas frontier as a preacher — he thought Dorothy and Edwards Ronin were probably pretty good people to want what was good for their oldest son. He was glad that they were gone when he left parish work; that they were spared the knowledge that being a priest had been frustrating and unrewarding, and that he had wanted to leave as much as he wanted to stay from the very beginning of his pastoral ministry.

"See what?" he asked again, demanding something from the silence as if asking would matter. It generally didn't, in his experience.

He steadied his glance so as to look more keenly.

It was late afternoon in the Sierra Nevada. Long shadows were cast not so much by scrub trees as by the occasional ponder-osa pine or Douglas fir left behind by the timber companies and lumber mills, stripped for the Comstock silver and gold strikes, and the deep mines that were necessary to extract the ore. Trees used to be six-feet round in these mountains, he thought as he looked straight ahead, maybe even eight.

He found that his hands were sweating as he peered even more closely from the trees where he was hiding into the clearing, and then into the trees beyond the clearing, when he saw a small movement. A young Indian child, perhaps.

"See what, boy?" he asked, this time a little louder, a little more demanding.

Be gentle, you would have said. Don't challenge the child any further, you would have counseled. He looks scared.

Ronin waited.

"Did you see the babies, Mister Ronin? Your horse stopped because of the Water Babies."

"You've got to be kidding," W. W. Ronin laughed as he stood up.

Chapter 2

DUSTSUCKER

"So the Indian kid was just sitting there in the rocks, and you didn't see him?" Ronin's best friend asked, chuckling.

Three-hundred and fifty pounds, and a good couple of inches taller than any man should be, the Carson City lawman leaned back in his chair until it crumpled suddenly beneath him.

Ronin pushed the round cafe table aside and offered his hand. Both men were laughing.

"I'll never get used to how coordinated you are, Marcus," Ronin responded. The ex-reverend had taken to calling the deputy sheriff by his first name after their last adventure in Reno and after staying nearly three months at the American Gospel Mission in Carson City. Both had had a sobering effect on him, challenging him to live a more genteel and peaceful life along the Carson range and to pay better attention to the people he loved.

The man known as "Dustsucker" to his closest friends stopped smiling for a moment, as he hated to be the butt of a good joke even when it was delivered by people he liked. Six-feet tall and 180 pounds, Ronin was perhaps his only good friend. But being such didn't warrant his acting rude even if more intimate words between the two men were sometimes welcome. He stood there grimacing.

"Ah come on, Dusty. You know I'm kidding. I'm just saying that I've seen you ride a few gut-twisters in your day and it's never warped your backbone any. But put you on a chair, beneath a perfectly good table in a perfectly good cantina in the capitol city, and cock-a-doodle-doo if you're not done for the day!"

"Cock-a-doodle-doo?" Dustsucker asked as he brushed the peanut shells, dirt clods and other unmentionables that lived on the floor from his equally dirty canvas pants.

"And you call this a perfectly good cantina?" he hollered, twisting his neck so as to secure the glance of everyone in the Curry Street restaurant who didn't have their eyes already fixed on him. "What are you looking at?" he barked to a well-mannered group of businessmen and travelers sitting for their morning breakfast. "Don't be looking at me," he said to a young boy of not more than eight-years-old sitting at a nearby table with his father and mother. Dressed for a bank appointment or church, it didn't matter to Dustsucker as long as people stopped staring.

"Jesus, Dusty," Ronin whispered as he leaned across the table, tapping his right hand on top of his friend's left. An angry deputy looked back at him. A young man's fear soon faded to a grown man's embarrassment.

"I mean really, what's going on? I was just tellin' you a story about seeing Happy Hands' kid up on the mountain. I wasn't making fun of you."

Dustsucker relaxed back into a sturdier chair and, grabbing his red kerchief from around his neck, began stirring his eggs with a fork. He sat for a moment before picking up a piece of toast and slathering it with a spoonful of homemade strawberry jam.

The two sat silently as normal conversation and eating noises returned to the packed capital city café.

"I'm just not sleeping well, Ronin. I can't stand the widow Rogers' boarding house. I mean Mountain Street is fine, and a two-dollar room is adequate, but I'm just not suited for such a civilized place." Dustsucker said, looking up from his scrambled eggs, greasy bacon and pan-fried potatoes. Ronin had never seen him sit in front of a full plate of food for so long. If he wasn't sleeping he wasn't eating well, either.

"I miss the Warm Springs Hotel, Ronin, and the people who used to hang there. I'm speaking figuratively of course."

"Of course," Ronin laughed, knowing that quite a few of the hotel's guests had been hanged over the years, politicians some of them, crooks all of them after the Warm Springs Hotel had been torn down to make room for a much-needed state prison. Having been a great deal farther out of town, Dustsucker had liked the quiet out that way.

"I want to take a break from sheriffing, Ronin," he said. Dustsucker wiped his hands on his pants before shoving a second piece of toast through his beard and into his mouth. "I'm simply not ready to return to work."

Ronin smiled as he watched his friend shake his head from side to side, tiny grunts emitting from an intermittently satisfied customer. Was his friend shaking his head for simple emphasis, or profound joy? The still-warm strawberry jam had been made that morning from berries picked a few miles out of Placerville by travelers coming over the pass from California. Slade, Ronin, and the U.S. Marshal from Virginia City named Augustus Ash had been through quite a scrape a few months prior over the kidnapping of some kids from the Washoe Valley Indian colony while attending the Gospel mission school just south of Carson City. Folks were still sorting things out.

The Crestwell and Clancy gangs had suffered severely for the crime. Slade, a much-appreciated deputy sheriff with the Ormsby County Sheriff's Department had been wounded during a gunfight in Reno. He was still walking with a limp. Given his restlessness at the widow Rogers' boarding house, his breakfast time mood swing wasn't all that hard to understand.

"Well, Dusty," Ronin smiled, "that's why I asked you to breakfast, my friend. I've told you there's some curious goings on up at the lake. I've spent the last couple of weeks talking to settlers and traders from up that way. And I think it would be fun for us to do a little camping, if you know what I mean."

Ronin punctuated his sentence with a nod, stuck his thumb behind his right suspender and leaned back on his chair, smiling. The action wasn't missed by Slade, who thought briefly about yanking on one of the chair legs with his boot. "Jackass," he muttered under his breath. Instead, he made a point of wiping both of his hands on his kerchief and shirt and slurping some buttermilk. "If you're talking about an investigation, Ronin, you know that parts of that lake aren't in Ormsby County, right? They're in Douglas and some parts are not even in Nevada; the line between the two states is a little difficult to establish at times." Dustsucker wiped his mouth with his forearm.

"Always will be, I suspect," Ronin said, settling the chair on all four legs. "No, I'm talking about laying back on our saddles and blankets and having a couple of beers lakeside. We could be there by noon …"

The deputy stood up with such surprise that his second chair went flying across the room into a table of legislators. Unlike the other, it stayed in one piece. "I'm sorry, folks," the lawman said, looking about the room and tipping his hat to the Secretary of State. Leaning forward so that only his best friend in the whole world could hear him, Marcus T. Slade whispered, "Why are we still here if there's beers to be had?"

Chapter 3
SECRETS

Ronin placed his palms on the table and stood so as to get his friend's attention. "Whoa, buddy," he said, raising his hands. "We need to talk about this first. You've got breakfast to finish and I've hardly had a spoonful of this oatmeal."

Dustsucker nodded, and smiled as he slid back into his chair. There was no reason to let food go to waste, as he generally didn't know when his next meal would be. On the Comstock, assuming one could eat given the occasional quality of the water and the commensurate and bothersome evacuation that sometimes went along with it, it'd cost an arm and a leg to eat what he had set in front of him.

"I'll have some more bacon, please!" he shouted to a server named Jack, who when he wasn't serving breakfast, was working a bar on Carson Street. "And a biscuit as well," he asked, looking about. Ronin smiled. Slade liked to plan his meals because eating right and regularly had always been important to him. But the last few months he'd been troubled and his thinking scattered. After Reno, he'd had a hard time focusing on anything. Thoughts about his Ronin's friend Emma had daily crept into mind, and the pressing question of what he'd do if he didn't do what he was doing was a constant interruption to his daily discipline.

They had been friends since Ronin had arrived on the Carson Range two or three years back, he couldn't remember. He didn't ask why Ronin was no longer wearing a clerical collar and his friend didn't seem to be bothered by his back and forth on being a minor town marshal of sorts while rummaging around the hills just south of Virginia City as an Ormsby County deputy sheriff and occasional miner. A man needs to keep his own confidences, Dustsucker figured. While he was often accused of being a little too pushy about doing right when others were so easily persuaded to do wrong, he had a few things he didn't share with many. Hell, everyone did.

The son of a well-known Iowa pioneer family, Slade had left his home state when he was sixteen. While he'd given adequate warning to his father that he didn't see his future gathering corn cobs or cow droppings — a strapping boy was practically property in those days if his parents owned a ranch or a farm, and some were traded that way — he felt a certain amount of guilt for abandoning his family to the drudgery of prairie life, even shame.

Not that life along the Sierra Nevada had been all that much easier. He'd yet to find the kind of metal that other men had — precious metals that is. But speaking in another fashion, he had become the kind of man that few men ever became or wanted to mess with. And while he had certain talking talents that kept him employed with the Ormsby County sheriff as an occasional deputy, those same talents hadn't gotten him anywhere with a certain woman he had grown quite fond of just south of the city.

Emma Nauman was the prettiest woman he'd ever seen. The kind of woman he would have loved to introduce to his Iowa mother, had the distance between his mother and he been smaller and the love between him and Emma a good deal greater, or different anyway.

He'd been a good hand at times at the American Gospel Mission where Emma was the director — her husband Henry had fled the mission, but that was another story — and he didn't believe much of what was preached there, having not been raised among church goers. But he liked what they were doing with Indian children, moving them from dry, foodless places where they had no future to a place where that had both. While some folks criticized the mission for taking savage Paiutes, Shoshone, Washoe Indians and other heathens and trying to make them into white men and women, he thought the work was helpful and important. And if they turned out too white, well, he figured that was the downside, as white people weren't much better than red people. A lot of times they seemed a great deal worse.

He focused on his biscuit for a moment. An egg without biscuits wasn't much worth eating, he liked to say, unless there were a lot of eggs of course, in which case more biscuits were needed.

As interested and committed as Emma was to the children at the mission, what hurt most was Emma's lack of interest and commitment to him, not that words had been said. That had never happened, and likely would never. He glanced up at his friend, who had gotten the server's attention and secured some strawberries as well. Wild and succulent, they had been growing at various places along the trail from Placerville (formally called Hangtown) to Carson City. Only in recent years had anyone thought to save a few for the folks in the capitol city. They were worth a good deal of money, at least on his plate.

Even a three-hundred and fifty pound deputy sheriff had a right to live, Dustsucker thought as he sat there listening to his friend talk about Lake Tahoe, the Indians who were living there and the murders that had happened there just outside the Lake House Hotel.

"Look William, I'm all for going on a camping trip," he said, looking up from his food. "I got to get away for a while. And a case of beer sitting in the snow overlooking Lake Bigler sounds great ..."

"Lake Tahoe ..." Ronin interrupted.

Though Ronin didn't know John Bigler personally, Ronin and he were from neighboring cities in Pennsylvania, and southern Democrats during the War Between the States. But Ronin believed Bigler had been something of an opportunist in business and government circles, a trait Ronin was never able to accept, even among his closest friends.

Following a brief term as a California assemblyman, Bigler had been elected twice to the office of governor, serving at the same time as Bigler's brother William did as governor of Pennsylvania. Later appointed as an ambassador to Chile, Bigler had been unable to win any subsequent elections and was remembered for his anti-Chinese pro-mining industry sentiments. He had a significant alcohol problem prior to his death in 1871.

It was ancient history as far as Ronin was concerned — not that politics were important to him, certainly not those in California — but he didn't much take to naming Lake Tahoe after a slavery enthusiast who was also haplessly bent on abusing the mountain or its scenery. And Tahoe was an Indian name, despite folks not having any clear idea what it actually meant.

"Whatever," Dustsucker continued. "I'm just saying that it's going to be a tough one tracking down what's going on up there. Few people want to get caught up in figuring out what's happened to a couple Indians. Even fewer with what's going on with hard-drinking lumberjacks. It's what happens when you mix alcohol with assholes, if you ask me. People fall off the map. Some of them die. Funerals are a daily event in mining and timber camps, Ronin."

"I know," Ronin said, scraping the last bit of oatmeal out of his bowl and licking the spoon clean. He sat for a few moments appreciating a solitary strawberry still on his plate.

"You're not going to eat that?" Dustsucker asked, forking the berry into his mouth without waiting for a response.

"No ... I guess not," Ronin said, looking his friend in the eyes. Waiting for a moment to allow his mind to clear, he continued. "How other people feel about things has never meant anything to me, Marcus. A man needs to watch the 'gleam of light that flashes across his own mind,' Emerson said. He's an ex-preacher too, you know."

"There are more of you?" Dustsucker smiled. "Then we ought to get moving," he laughed. Dustsucker slid his chair away from the table, paying careful attention that it didn't fall over, and stood up. Ronin put a few bits on the table and they walked toward the door in silence.

"Goodness ought to have some edge to it, don't you think?" Dustsucker smiled, looking at his friend sideways. Ronin's steps stuttered just a few feet away from the door and stopped. *A Carson City deputy sheriff reading Emerson?*

"You've read his essay, "Self-Reliance?"

Dustsucker nodded.

Who would have guessed that a deputy sheriff would be reading anything at all? "Well then, we've got a lot to talk about, don't we?" Ronin said, opening the door.

Chapter 4

STREET PUSHER

Dustsucker was still smiling when Ronin stepped out onto Curry Street, just a few blocks away from the courthouse. Their eyes locked until Ronin sputtered, "What?" recognizing that Dustsucker knew what he was thinking and that a kinder explanation was likely due. The deputy was starting to explain his interest in Ralph Waldo Emerson, and his accidental attendance at a lecture of Emerson's in California entitled "Chivalry," when a tall, quick-striding, barrel-chested man knocked a well-dressed clergyman off the boardwalk a few yards away.

The Reverend George Davis, rector of the St. Peter's Episcopal Church stumbled face-forward into the street, barely bracing himself with his hands, and placing a small communion Bible he was carrying for a little girl in his congregation face-down into the dirt. Struggling to pick himself up, he straightened his collar, which had turned completely around so that it was now backward and shouted, "Hey! How about watching where you're going, son?!"

The rector's quickly-wheezed words were hardly a challenge. The nameless interloper didn't take them that way as he pushed past a couple of other folks on the wooden walkway until he stood squarely in front of the café doorway, facing the deputy and his friend, the former priest and detective who had just finished their breakfast.

"Get the fuck out of my way!" he said, his arms and legs still moving as if there had somewhere to go or something to get, and impediments along the way were something to be ignored.

Ronin and Slade looked at each other. They were both over six-feet tall, and while a case could be made that Ronin appeared slight in stature compared to his friend, neither were of the figure or frame of mind to be easily pushed around. It was Ronin who spoke first, having recognized the reverend and taken some umbrage over the barrel-chested man's attitude. He offered his hand. "William Washington Ronin at your service, partner."

The man grasped the hand because … well, that's just what people do when you extend a hand their way. You would have done the same.

"Fuck you, mister!" he growled.

The ex-priest levered the poor man's fingers downward while simultaneously punching upward with his palm on the man's right wrist, powering a great deal of pain into his fingers and forearm. The now angry, nameless, round-chested young man was immediately on his toes screaming at Slade who, with his deputy star on his chest, was standing in the doorway with his mouth open surprised by it all. "Help me! Help me!" the man shouted, as if something horrible was about to take place and a badge — even one that hung by a mere thread on the most worn and dusty of garments — was something that could stop the promise and pain. Ronin hadn't entirely decided what he was going to do yet, as an insult was simply an insult and didn't need to turn into an assault, at least as far as he was concerned, especially having just had breakfast with one of the town's constables.

"Sticks and stones will break my bones," the old man used to say as they practiced their martial arts in a field a few miles south of his Iowa church and home. "But words can never hurt me," the aging fur-trader used to sing while teaching the Wichita cleric the self-defense methods of French sailors called *Chausson* or *Savate*. The advice was still fresh in his ears, though his mother used to render the popular refrain a bit differently to him and his siblings, "Sticks and stones may break your bones," she'd say, "but words will hurt you deeply ..."

But Ronin didn't take kindly to obscenities hurled his way — he'd hurled more than a few foul words in his time, so they were no big deal even for a clergyman as long as the minister's mother wasn't present — he never liked the sight of a big man hurting others and had taken an iron pan to more than a few Southern soldiers who had moved similarly in and out of his chow lines during the war. And there was the fact, of course, that the man's actions had potentially complicated what had otherwise been a really good bowl of oatmeal.

Dustsucker was still standing there in the doorway wondering what was happening when Ronin relaxed his grasp on the man's fingers. "Friend!" he said, when the barrel-chested bully threw a haymaker punch at the deputy's face. "Whoa," Ronin exclaimed, stepping quickly to his left and standing the man up on his toes again. He slipped his left hand from the man's wrist to his elbow, and cuffing him on his right cheek ear, spun him around so that he now faced the street.

"Friend!" he said, though not with any particular tone of affection. He grabbed the man's gun belt with his left hand and, rocking the bully's hog leg out of his holster with his right, poked it into the small of his back. "Friend!" he insisted as he kneed the ignorant man in his buttocks, propelling him into the street, where he caught himself with his hands in the dirt in much the same manner as the reverend had a few moments before, though without a communion Bible to cushion his fall.

"Friend!" he repeated. "Dust yourself off and apologize to the folks you bumped into or knocked over, would you?"

The dust-covered, hairy bear-shaped young man stumbled to his feet, turned around to see who had assaulted him and, crouching like an angry 200-pound Sierra mountain lion, grasped for his gun, which of course wasn't there.

"No, really, I'm serious," Ronin said laughing, mirroring the same actions because they seemed so funny.

"Be the man your mother wanted you to be, would you?" he continued, his eyes drilling into the ignorant man's eyes, pleading that the violence should stop. "Apologize to the priest and the other people standing there, and go about your way."

A small crowd had gathered by the popular rector, whose ladies had just taken charge of the finances of the church due to very discouraging circumstances, all reports being that St. Peter's Episcopal Church was about to recover, though the priest's pride was no doubt suffering.

"Ronin, I'll take this," Dustsucker said, shining his badge so that it showed prominently on his chest. Touching Ronin's elbow, he gently pushed him to move aside. It wasn't good to grab at a man who was ramping up to do something awful. Things could get real bad real quickly. But Ronin smiled, and stepping away from the street, twirled the rusted Paterson percussion-style revolver and flipped it around so that the plow-handle sat forward in his right. He handed it to the deputy.

"Sir, this establishment is closed to you," Slade instructed sternly as he took the handgun from his friend and turned around. "Head home and pick up your sidearm when you sober up."

The man stood there listening, still grasping at his gun belt. Once, twice more, before he realized with surprise that his hog leg was no longer where it was supposed to be and the deputy's measured words sunk in. He nodded to Slade, looked briefly at Ronin and turned away.

Dustsucker turned toward his friend and smiled. He then shouted loudly so that those in the street could hear, "And steer clear of the nice folk in town, would you? Nobody should be messing with its reverends." The Reverend Davis smiled approvingly, and nodded as Ronin looked over at his friend.

"Yes sir," Dustsucker said, smiling as a large pile of brown corduroy in a crumpled black cowboy hat stumbled away, picking up two or three beer bottles he found discarded next to a nearby fence before tripping on a set of steps and laying down again.

The two friends stood in the doorway of the restaurant for a couple of minutes, appreciating the quiet and watching the barrel-chested man get up and saunter south on Curry Street toward the bawdy houses. The deputy looked at his friend and said, "Well, that was edgy, don't you think?"

"Not hardly, Dusty," Ronin responded, realizing Slade had been funning with him. "You'll be a two-fisted, do-gooder Episcopal church lady when you see what I've got for you up at Lake Tahoe, my friend. And I'm not talking just about the beer."

Chapter 5

EMMA

Emma stood by the front windows of her home at the American Gospel Mission just south of Carson City. She hadn't seen Ronin in days and wondered what had become of the situation at Lake Tahoe.

While there wasn't anything pressing or new at the lake, Ronin seemed interested in the possible connection between criminal acts on the old Bigler Toll Road and the recent drowning of a couple Washoe Indians just north of Cave Rock in a popular area called Glenbrook. It was his thought that perhaps they hadn't drowned, but may have been murdered. The oldest settlement on Lake Tahoe, Glenbrook provided most of the recent timber for the Comstock mines. The town was located on the eastern shore of the lake a few miles up and west of Carson City.

Glenbrook had been bustling with homes and businesses since 1860, when the area was first settled by Captain Augustus W. Pray. Pray built the lake's first timber mill on the south side of Glenbrook Bay. Twenty years later, Glenbrook was, more or less, a temperance town, swelling to five-hundred or so mill workers and tourists during the summer months, many of whom were intent on seeing the lake as tourists on one of four steamers that docked there.

Emma imagined what it must have been like to first see Lake Tahoe, to build the first cabin in the area, to harvest the grasses and to plant grain and vegetables and watch them grow. Legend was that when the lake was first seen by Captain Pray, the indigenous grasses were so high that a horse-drawn reaper had to be brought over the mountains from San Francisco in order to harvest them. Her hands on the sill of her living room window, Emma smiled, wondering what it would have been like to have been there.

The Carson Valley was still pristine when she and her husband Henry carved the first buildings from native sand and rock to begin the American Gospel Mission. Few white people had paused to consider the barren lands south of Nevada's capital as anything other than a place to hunt or through which to travel. But she had seen the possibilities. Ten years after the original Mormon settlers had left, it was as if God had spoken to her. Stopping their carriage a few feet from a small clump of Pinion trees, she claimed the sandy soil, and what little grew in it, for the kingdom of God.

Mormon missionaries had built the first non-Indian settlement in northern Nevada in 1855 in Genoa, and had done so as part of a similarly religious vision. But Mormon dreams of developing the area — evidenced by settlements in the Carson, Eagle, Washoe and Pleasant Valleys — expired quickly when Brigham Young, the second president of the Mormon Church, called church members home to stave off a possible federal invasion of Utah.

Emma liked the church's founder, Joseph Smith and, despite Protestant prejudices to the contrary, thought him to be a godly man and visionary. She didn't understand Brigham Young or the changes in the church after Smith's death. Though she had been a child at the time and a Presbyterian, it seemed to her that Mormons were forever different after the prophet's untimely demise by mob violence in Carthage, Illinois. Brigham Young, for all of his success in the Mormon Church, couldn't hold a candle to the original vision that had started the Mormon movement in Joseph Smith. And while it wasn't a matter of any personal consequence to her — she believed the Mormon doctrine of a new revelation to be a false teaching, and the origin of the American Indians to be a part of the lost tribes of Israel to be silliness at best — she didn't think that abandoning God's work because man's work had become too complex made any sense at all. She didn't imagine it would have made much sense to the prophet either.

Despite her prejudices, Mormons were often mentioned in prayers at the mission, as their failure to proselytize the valley for Jesus Christ had allowed the great American Gospel Mission to succeed. "God's ways are not always man's ways," she liked to say when an opportunity to testify to God's mysterious graces presented itself. The Mormon saints were just as much a part of "the mystery which is God," she told the conservatively-minded teachers and other workers at the mission when they met for devotions, "as was the disappearance of my husband, the abuse and kidnapping of Indian children from the mission while it was being run by my husband, and the mission's subsequent challenges and successes."

It is all God. Even the imagination and movements of this one curious and solitary man, she thought to herself as she stood at the window thinking of Ronin, sipping a quiet morning coffee and looking at the sun come up over the Sierra Nevada.

She hummed the tune to "My Faith Looks Up to Thee," by Lowell Mason, a bank teller whom she had met prior to leaving the Upper Ohio Valley with her husband to start their mission in Carson City. Mason had written over a thousand hymn tunes, many of which had changed the Presbyterian Church, deepening its faith and fervor. "My Faith Looks Up to Thee" was perhaps her favorite.

"My faith looks up to thee, thou Lamb of Calvary, Savior divine…" she began singing before breaking into laughter. A Presbyterian nearly all of his life, Mason had also set to music the nursery rhyme "Mary Had a Little Lamb," and was a very nice man.

It seemed like the Christian thing to do to invite Ronin to stay at the mission during the winter of 1880, though doing so had been misunderstood by darn near everyone in town, Amos Quinn had told her, the physician who had treated the ex-minister, most of the Washoe Indian men who worked the mission — that is, when they weren't fishing or hunting. Helping Ronin recuperate from a broken leg and surgery was the right thing to do, she reassured herself, despite the minor temptations that had presented themselves during his three-month stay.

They had once slept together in a bed all night after the disappearance of her husband, though nothing untowardly had happened. His visit had turned out to be so terribly timely.

She had met Ronin while visiting Amos after having been thrown by a horse and delivered into his care by one of the town's deputy sheriffs. Once assessed and situated, she had assisted the doctor during Ronin's surgery and was immediately intrigued by what had caused a former minister to work as a detective and bounty hunter along the eastern slope of the Sierra Nevada. It was strange that she had not met him previously, she thought, though her husband Henry had insisted on making most of their trips into town. What kind of man of faith would do such a thing, she sometimes asked in her nightly prayers at the mission. The questions were real to her, and focused not just on her new friend but on her now-missing husband as well.

Over the months Ronin had stayed at the mission, she had grown to understand that Ronin hadn't lost his faith as much as changed it. In much the same fashion as the father of all Hebrews, she thought: Abraham had left the comfortable surroundings of Chaldea, and Moses, the heart-string of the early Israelites who left the bosom of the ruling family of Egypt, if the Bible's stories could be believed. Both men had found new adventures, and had likely struggled in them as well.

She had done the same she thought, and not just since her husband had died or disappeared. Nevada's desert terrain was a rocky one, in more ways than one. Emma began humming the refrain, until the next set of words sprang from her heart, "Now hear me while I pray, take all my guilt away, O let me from this day be wholly Thine!"

Would she ever be up for the adventure God had set in front of her? And could she do it alone? She put her cup down thoughtfully, and clasping her hands in front of her began to sing quietly the hymn's second verse.

May Thy rich grace impart
Strength to my fainting heart, my zeal inspire!
As Thou hast died for me, O may my love to Thee,
Pure warm, and changeless be, a living fire!

Smiling, she nodded so as to signal invisible choirs of heavenly angels she was done singing. In a sudden change of mood, Emma looked to see if someone had brought the *Morning Appeal* in from town. Not seeing it, she sat down in her favorite chair, where she could continue gazing toward the mountains.

Someone had written in the *New York Times* a few years back, "Go West, young man, and grow up with the country." Henry had shown it to her, prior to their starting out on their journey west. "Washington is not the place to live," the editorial had said. "The rents are high, the food is bad, the dust is disgusting and the morals are deplorable." While the little Ohio River valley in which she and Henry had made their first home was nice, she had enjoyed every minute of their trip west, and nearly every moment since then. "Nearly every moment," she repeated to herself out loud, thinking back to the kidnapping drama that had involved Ronin and some of his friends. Perhaps that's why Ronin left his work as a priest, she thought, gathering up her apron and standing. He wasn't a farmer, so he wasn't interested in homesteading. He didn't seem much attracted to the often-heard, imaginative stories about plentiful game, or gold, or fur trading in the West. Perhaps he had simply journeyed west to start a new life. So many did.

She shook her head, thinking of her deputy friend, who seemed to flirt with so many things, and the darker, similarly conflicting motivations that often tried her husband's spirit some years previous. No, Ronin wasn't looking for riches, she thought, not like other men. He was after a secret that was even more important. The kingdom of God within, she imagined, a deeper sense of self. *The church could steal one's life away if a person wasn't watching.*

Emma stood and went back to the windows that faced the mountains she had come to love over the last dozen years. Perhaps Dustsucker and Ronin have already started up toward the lake? She closed the curtains to keep out the day's heat and, turning to head back into the kitchen, began to think of supervising breakfast for the mission's thirty-some children. Whatever the case, she was thankful she had met William Washington Ronin, and she hoped that God was keeping him safe.

Chapter 6
THE COURTHOUSE

Stepping out into the street, Ronin and Dustsucker walked a few blocks north along Curry until they hit Musser Street, where the Ormsby County Courthouse stood.

"It all seemed easier in the old days," Slade remarked, sitting down on a wooden bench in front of the courthouse to catch his breath. "I've been here since before the kidnappings, Ronin. I'm not talking about the case we just solved."

Slade was speaking of the Pyramid Lake War in 1860, when he had been a part of a rag-tag army of volunteers organized from Virginia City, Silver City, Carson City, and Genoa to punish a group of Paiutes who had burned the Williams Station Stage Stop after two white men had kidnapped a couple of Indian girls.

"Raped them, Dusty," Ronin corrected, "not just kidnapped them," listening to his friend speak of Major Ormsby's attempt to rescue the children and punish the Paiutes who were responsible.

"Well that may be," Dustsucker argued, "but we lost seventy lives trying to get those girls back."

In fact, the children had been rescued, in much the same manner that Dustsucker and Ronin had rescued the children taken from the American Gospel Mission a few months before. But the initial volunteer response and subsequent routing of the rescuers had necessitated a second military action by a much larger force of army regulars. With the Northern Paiute threat finally abated, Slade had settled into a series of jobs in Ormsby, later named Carson, county until Nevada's statehood occurred in 1865.

"Here's something for you," Dustsucker continued. "I remember when the *Territorial Enterprise* was printed on Carson Street, before it took off to Virginia City. Carson City was being built as fast as the timber could be hauled out of the mountains," he added, sitting back on the bench, resting against the walls of the county courthouse, formally Abraham Curry's Great Basin hotel.

Dustsucker drew in a breath and looked around thoughtfully. "You know, Carson City used to be made completely out of wood. Four or five blocks of tiny white-frame stores and houses packed close together, side by side. I think I preferred it that way," he said, looking at the Nevada sand stone which had become the new building material of choice. "There was talk at that time of replacing the courthouse with something more permanent as well, though I imagine it might take a great many more years until anyone thinks seriously of that."

"You liked the simplicity, Dusty. You're not fooling anyone. Drag a bad guy out back and thrash him within an inch of his life? Now, you've got to rely on folks like me to do that, what with your badge and all."

"Yup." Dustsucker looked down at his deputy star, thinking again how Ash in Virginia City wore a much heavier star made out of silver. "Hey," he said looking up at his friend. "Did I ever tell you that I met Mark Twain's brother?"

"Samuel Clemens." Ronin corrected, suggesting that "Twain" sounded pretentious. God only knew how long Clemens would be using the name, given that he'd used other names before it. Virginia City barkeeps swore that Clemens changing his name had more to do with Clemens' bar tab than with a leadsman's knot on a Mississippi river boat.

"I did." Dustucker said, proudly. "I saw him running around town one day waving a telegraph he got from Washington notifying us that we were now a state." He paused mid-stream before he continued, "I think that was the first time I saw him smile after his daughter's death." Orion Clemens' daughter Jennie had died a few months before statehood from spotted fever, but Orion had plodded on.

"'I, Abraham Lincoln do hereby solemnly swear that the said Silver state of Nevada is hereby admitted into the Union,' it said, or something like that."

"I imagine it all went downhill after that," Ronin replied, smiling. He looked around the city square to see what he could see. He was a relative newcomer to Nevada's capitol. Sitting back on the bench next to his talkative friend, he swayed back and forth as he considered the town's exploding population and its growing appreciation for clean streets, a better-behaved citizenry, happier merchants and businesses, and everything that went with it.

Slade's life was a good deal busier than it had been when they had met three years before during a bar fight at a Carson City saloon. Slade had grabbed onto the back of a chair and paused, so as to catch his breath as another man was hoisting his. Ronin's front thrust-kick had kept the deputy's skull from being shattered and led to a solid friendship between the two men.

"Dusty, are you really able to head up the lake with me?" he asked, thinking of how demanding his part-time job as an Ormsby County deputy must be. Neither of them had been quite normal since the gunfights in Reno and Washoe. It'd be a good thing to have Dustsucker tag along. Though he preferred solitude — chatty women and men were the bane of his existence, whether he was working as a clergyman or as a detective — it'd be nice to spend time with his friend.

"Let's do it," he nudged, glancing a couple of blocks west, where the Reverend Davis had stopped to talk to the Presbyterian minister, no doubt recalling the morning's adventure out front of the Curry Street café. He watched the Episcopal curate's arm-waving antics with interest.

"Sure, why not?" Slade smiled. "It will give me a chance to escape this fog I've been in since they stitched up that hole in my side. Tell you what," he said, "let me stow this shooting iron in a courthouse desk and I'll head over to the widow Roger's place to grab my bed roll."

Ronin winced. He found the widow Rogers a fair woman, but irascible since her husband's death, especially when it came to business manners. He wondered if Slade would be asking for a break on his rent. She could be as mean as a basket of rattlesnakes.

"I never asked. Where are you staying, Ronin? I've not seen you out at the mission." Dustsucker smiled and looked him square in the eyes. Ronin was uncomfortable with the inference.

He hadn't mentioned that he had moved from a small rooming house on Curry Street to more opulent space at Second and Carson. "I'm at the Ormsby House," he replied sheepishly. "Second story, with a balcony," he added, grinning.

Dustsucker dropped the gun into a drawer and turned sharply. "Then you'll be buying lunch, I suppose."

Chapter 7
SAINT PETER'S EPISCOPAL

Ronin told Slade he'd catch up to him at the widow Rogers' place, then stood at the courthouse for a few moments, thinking, before heading north on Musser to find his clergy friend.

He worried about Slade at times, and hadn't noticed the change of pace in Carson City as his friend had. He thought that Slade probably had his act together as a lawman, but was showing the strain. His weight, his general level of fitness, particularly after being shot in Reno, placed him at a higher risk with some of Carson City's shadier characters. And while there were fewer of them since mining had begun to wane, he didn't like the odds of one still-injured deputy facing the day or night alone.

Ronin had ended up in Nevada as something of an accident. He was tailing a Kansas City madam while working as a detective with the Pinkerton Agency after leaving his church in Wichita. The Pinkertons were impressed with his military service, although it was with a Confederate Calvary. They didn't much care that he had served as a teamster, sometimes food manager and cook, given his "fair share" of violent experiences in the war. Oddly enough, they also valued the rigorous ecclesiastical training he had engaged in after the war.

Madame Bovary was a woman of ravenous Spiritualist leanings — defrauding large groups of men and women throughout the Midwest in the course of conducting séances and other

Spiritualist business. Ronin had been one of three operatives who had followed her through a half-dozen states, finally bringing the former bordello owner in to face multiple counts of fraud, bigamy and other charges.

He found the woman utterly fascinating. He had initially maintained a professional distance in the relationship, though it didn't take long for him to begin wondering what might have occurred to her, him or them had they chosen different professions. One night, he wasn't wondering any more, and before he knew it, he was involved.

Despite it being a generally positive experience — he didn't really get the woman, but he enjoyed her if you know what I mean — before long, the Pinkertons and Ronin decided to part ways. The violation of his professional ethics was something neither he nor his employers were happy about, though Ronin wondered if there wasn't a certain wisdom to letting the heart find its way.

A book by the same name had been published in France six or so years before the Civil War began, and while Ronin wasn't aware of the book or its success, a Pinkerton superintendent had pointed to the similarities between the subject of their investigation and the book's protagonist. That's when he knew. A farmer's daughter who attempts to escape her ordinary life as a country doctor's wife, surviving multiple affairs but securing a suicidal amount of debt in the course of her adventure? Yeah, it was just a little too close to home. Its author, Gustave Flaubert, had been pursued by public prosecutors on obscenity charges but was acquitted, causing a subsequent explosion in notoriety and sales. Ronin thought he was lucky simply not being able to work again as a Pinkerton. The heartache he occasionally felt — women were a mystery, and strong-minded women seemed more mysterious than most — made it difficult for him to be with anyone since then, including his friend, Emma.

He walked quickly toward the Episcopal church, passing the Presbyterian and Methodist churches along the way. A large wooden building on the corner of Division and Telegraph streets, he found that he appreciated the chapel's quieter spaces. Like many religious buildings, the interior resembled the upside-down hull of a ship. Freshly painted Sunday School rooms and a library complemented the church's nearly spartan interior, though the sanctuary's lack of a center aisle always caused him to pause.

"Journeys should lead somewhere," he often thought while sitting quietly in the church's chapel, "at least to a damned communion table," he had insisted to the Reverend Davis during one very pointed conversation. Davis seemed intrigued, and wondered aloud if Ronin's center aisle fixation was more about his own lack of progress, rather than what Davis called Ronin's "Episcopal hysterics." Up until that point, he was under the impression he had left most of that behind.

"You've simply stepped off the path, son," Davis had said, regarding his leaving church work. "You can pick up, you know, right where you left off," he said. "The church has changed a lot since you took up whatever it is you're doing now."

The ex-priest found the pastor's words bothersome and let the conversation drop. Life was complex enough without re-introducing a whole new set of old voices into his head, telling him what he was supposed to think or do. He had hoped to find a singularly defining tone by journeying west, but so far, he hadn't found it. And the women he had met out west, Madame Bovary included, hadn't helped any either.

He sat in the silence for twenty minutes or so, considering what he knew about the murders at Lake Tahoe, and his interest in them, before Davis stepped into the sanctuary.

"I thought I heard you come in." Ronin looked up, mildly amused.

"Yeah, I wanted to see if you were okay."

"I am, how about you?" Davis replied.

"As good as it gets," Ronin frowned. The rector's redirection was anticipated, but not appreciated. "I hear you're still having problems with your bell," Ronin replied, hoping to set the conversation back on track.

"We are, William. It's got a significant fracture, I'm told, and that doesn't get better by doing nothing." The priest paused as if to consider whether he should continue. "It will only get bigger, you know?" He paused again. "We all need to be recast sooner or later, Ronin. Don't you think?"

Ronin looked at Davis sharply. He hated clerical doublespeak. It was pretentious to speak about one thing while hinting about something else. Why were pastors into such baloney? The rector's moment was wearing thin.

"Sometimes a bell is just a bell, reverend," he said. Ronin didn't believe that the three years he had spent in ministry were anywhere near as consequential as the time he had spent being a detective. He hoped he hadn't done similar harm to people seeking an honest conversation when he was a priest.

"That it is, Ronin, forgive me. You have a good day, you hear?" Davis exited into the sacristy, where the church's wine and wafers were kept, which was exactly what Ronin was hoping to do at the lake that afternoon, if he could get his friend Dustsucker to hurry.

Chapter 8

THE WIDOW ROGERS

The widow Rogers smiled as Ronin approached the porch of her home on Mountain Street. "William," she shouted, or at least it seemed that way to him as he opened the gate to the front yard. She appeared a great deal more enthusiastic than usual. "I wondered when I'd see you again! You did a wonderful thing for the people out there at the American Gospel Mission. We're all quite proud of you!"

Ronin looked the length of the porch and seeing no one other than Mrs. Rogers decided that she was speaking in the "royal we," an annoying habit at best. He liked Samuel Clemens' comment that "only kings, presidents, editors, and people with tapeworms" had the right to use the word "we," though he wasn't sure which of the categories Mrs. Rogers fit.

"Mrs. Rogers, how are you doing?" He gritted his teeth while kicking the dirt off his boots on the porch's first step. "I've been meaning to stop by," he said, knowing that his statement was a lie but was the lesser of two evils as he genuinely disliked the woman.

"Well, I'm doing fine, Mister Ronin. Gillom and I were just talking about your rescue of those poor Indian children from the mission. I wish you would talk to him about it. Hearing that a reverend might leave the church to do some actual good would do him some good, if you know what I mean."

"Still worried about how he's doing, Mrs. Rogers?" Ronin was consistently surprised by the nasty edge of the widow's comments. He wondered how awkward the relationship must have been between her and her late husband. He noted that the widow's graying hair was pulled back into a pony tail, a sure sign that she was working and that non-working folks needed to watch out.

"He has a habit for profanity, Reverend Ronin."

"Bond," he called her by her first name to make a point, "it's just Ronin. I've told you that before. I no longer work for the Episcopal church."

"Well sure, William, but a priest is still a priest in my eyes." She smiled. "And a boy should learn that a man should choose his words and work wisely." The widow, in her early forties he thought, maybe younger, made an effort to get up. "Would you talk to him, Mister Ronin?"

"Please don't get up, Mrs. Rogers."

Ronin took a seat on an unusually clean, white bench on the front porch. He gazed out at the yard, noting the roses she had been cutting before his arrival. Fresh trimmings laid in the sandy soil of the front yard, amidst patches of rye grass. A pair of scissors sat on a flowered cushion beside her.

"They're beautiful," he said, nodding toward the front gate where a dozen rose bushes bordered a white-washed picket fence. A darker-colored soil had been piled up beneath each bush. "Soil amendments," he said, as they reminded him of his dead mother's efforts in western Pennsylvania.

"The Nevada state flower," she replied, with a smile as grand as the red blooms she had been trimming. They were striking.

"Ought to be the sagebrush, from what I've seen of Nevada, Bond. Some of them grow twelve feet high, you know."

"Ronin, the sagebrush isn't much of a state flower," she argued, picking up the cut flowers from her lap and removing one glove.

"Well, I suspect not," he replied, "when you're just looking at the bush. But there will be yellow and white flowers on them in another month or so." He figured that August or September was the time the sagebrush usually bloomed, though he wasn't sure. He wondered why he didn't pay better attention to such things.

"Not enough I'm afraid, Mister Ronin."

He sat silently, wanting to compare Gillom's uneven growth as a man, at least in his mother's eyes, to the uneven beauty of the silvery grey-green bushes that flourished throughout the state. But thinking it would be too obscure a reference and too unkind, he said simply, "Perhaps not." After a moment's thought he added, "Though I've come to love the bush, with and without."

The widow Rogers picked up her sheers with her ungloved hand, placing the roses she had cut into a small blue jar filled with water. "The with and the without, Mister Ronin? Hmm ... that's exactly how I cared for Mister Rogers when he was alive, you know. And I guess it's how I will treat Gillom as well. Well said, reverend, very well said."

Rogers and Ronin sat on the porch of her Mountain Street rooming house, he making sure that nothing he might say could be construed as a sermon, and she admiring the roses until Slade finished moving about in the back room.

"Couldn't find my fishing rod, Ronin," he exclaimed as he pushed the porch screen door open with his foot. "Excuse me ma'am, I should have used my hands," he said as he threw a woolen bedroll over his left shoulder. Turning to his friend, he continued, "I imagine I'll be able to fashion one when we get to the lake."

"We'll make do, Dusty. Folks always do," he said, smiling at Mrs. Rogers. He paused as he stood up. "It was a delight talking to you, Mrs. Rogers," he said, thinking he probably meant it this time.

"It was my pleasure, Mister Ronin. Do stop back. I'd love for you to talk to Gillom."

"I will."

"We'll only be a couple of days, ma'am," Dustsucker said as he swung his leg up over the horse, kicking it into a trot. "Save my room!" he shouted. "You know how I love it back there." Dustsucker had a room at the back of the house, on the first floor looking out toward the wood shed and yard.

"Mister Slade, there's the issue of your rent," she shouted back as he galloped down Curry Street, waving his hat. "Don't expect any discounts!"

Chapter 9

KINGS CANYON ROAD

Neither man spoke until they turned right onto Kings Canyon Road by the Presbyterian Church. Ronin and Dustsucker caused quite a stir on Mountain Street, as folks didn't generally gallop through town any more, and certainly not in the more residential sections. The Methodist minister had shaken his fist at them as they dashed past his street-side vegetable garden.

"What was that about?" Ronin asked, catching his breath and making sure that he hadn't lost anything from his bags or bedroll.

"What was *what* about?" Dustsucker asked. Ronin drew up his reins until his horse came to a full stop.

"You know what I'm talking about. Galloping down Mountain Street like we had just finished a cattle drive! And why so quickly away from the rooming house?"

Dustsucker lowered his head and paused, so as to carefully put his words together. "Mrs. Rogers is showing some unusual attention my way, Ronin. And to be frank, I'm a little uncomfortable with that."

Ronin began laughing. He kicked his horse in the sides and slapped the reins to the right flank so that Jackson began walking. "Hell, I thought you didn't want to talk to the woman about the rent, Dusty! Here it's not about rent, it's about romance!"

Slade sat up tall in the saddle, his face changing colors until he appeared about as red as the long underwear he wore year-round beneath his torn and dirty blue checkered shirt. "Ain't talking about romance, my friend! I'm merely pointing out that I can't trust the woman's intentions, not since I got back from Reno."

"She's taken an interest in the rescue, I assume?" Ronin smiled.

"Exactly. She wants to me share the details with her and the boy. And has asked me a bunch of times to help clear the table after supper, to linger in the kitchen while she cleans the dishes, or to take a brandy on the porch after others have headed to bed."

Ronin nodded.

"I'm not used to all of this attention, W. I mean, I wouldn't mind a little bit more from other women in town, but the widow Rogers is my land lady, not my love lady. And while beggars can't be choosers, I'm sitting this one out. Know what I mean?"

"Got it." Ronin nodded as he always did when people asked if he understood, and began to wind his way out of the city to climb a subtly steeper grade into the Carson Range. If a man was to have a woman, to choose to be with a woman, or to involve himself with a woman, he figured a man ought to give the sort of woman he was hooking up with some thought — and be thinking about the kind of woman, but maybe the actual woman. He could see no harm in getting to know someone.

His experience with Madame Bovary made the point. Tailing Bovary had brought him to Nevada three years ago. The heart goes where it wills, he learned. But the head, "or any parts south of it" as they used to say in his Episcopal seminary, didn't need to go with it. It might have been a man who first bit into the apple, but it was a woman who made him do it, or suggested he do it, anyway.

"Ever just sit with her and talk?" he asked, hoping that Slade had seen the human side of the widow Rogers, the piece of her that was simply worried about raising her boy, or making her way in the world without her man.

He looked over to see if Slade was listening. The look he got would have startled his horse. They trotted along silently until they came to the base of the mountain. "Look, we don't need to talk about this, Dusty. I was just trying to help." The deputy turned his face toward the canyon road and leaned forward as the road began to climb.

Ronin hadn't been to the lake by the Kings Canyon route as Clear Creek Road had become better traveled in the last five years. While Clear Creek was less direct in some ways, it allowed him to stop by Emma's place. Heading past the timber yards south of the city also helped him prioritize what was sometimes an awkward visit and do it anyway.

Ronin smiled to himself as he leaned into his horse. The grade up Kings Canyon seemed steep, though Dustsucker said it wouldn't be more than eight percent or so. This would easily wind a man who wasn't used to the altitude, or riding on a horse.

Looking toward the south, he thought about Emma's mission and its easy view of the Carson Valley. He loved the woman, at least he thought he did, though he didn't know what to do with his feelings, given he had business to conduct and she had a mission to run. And there were always the religious differences — Jesus, were there differences between them.

"What are you smiling about?" Dustsucker asked.

Ronin looked up, realizing that he had begun to grin and shake his head. "Nothing Dusty, least not anything about you."

"Better not be grinnin' about me, Ronin. I don't care how much of a rough and tumble guy you are." Their eyes met; he had never seen his friend look so stern. "I'll kick your ass if you're laughing about me, reverend."

Ronin hated when people called him reverend.

He looked back toward the road. He was smiling because he couldn't believe that the fundamental truth that was standing between he and Emma was faith, or his lack of it and the clear looniness of what appeared to be her faith.

He didn't know much about Presbyterians. Despite being from western Pennsylvania, he'd spent too little time in West Virginia and Ohio to know if that's what he was looking at. To put it simply, he didn't know if she was normal or not, and he wasn't about to get involved with a woman until he did.

"I'm thinking about women, Dusty. There's no explaining them, my friend." The road turned into a series of switch backs, with expansive views of the Carson Valley below. Sparsely blooming beds of red, purple and blue flowers contrasted with rabbit weed and sagebrush, reminding him that he was still in the desert, though the climb was primarily through grass and forest lands.

"Know what the *Bible* says about women, Dusty?"

"No, can't say I do," his friend responded, clearly annoyed they were still talking about it.

"'Three things are hard for me,' Solomon says. 'Four of which I am utterly ignorant. The way of an eagle in the air, the way of a serpent upon a rock, the way of a ship in the midst of the sea, and ...'" he paused so as to emphasize his point, "'the way of a young man with a woman.'"

"Well, we're not all that young anymore, Ronin. You'd think we might understand a few things by now."

"Yeah, you'd think so." He turned to look at a heavy rock wall held in place by a masonry embankment. "How long did you say this trip would be?" Ronin hated heading anywhere on a horse. He had simply never gotten used to riding one, preferring a carriage or even a train, though the latter was still a great source of heartache to him.

"Seventeen miles to Glenbrook, my friend. In the old days, seventeen miles of heavy ox-carts hanging ass-ended over the edge of a cliff!" Dustsucker laughed.

Ronin winced, pulling his horse away from the edge and closer to the tree line. "Don't imagine that we'll make it by dark then, Dusty."

"Might not, my friend. You doing okay?" he asked, noticing that Ronin's usually ruddy appearance seemed blanched, an odd color given they had been out in the sun for a couple of hours. "There's some water up ahead. We'll stop for a while."

"Sounds good," Ronin replied. A patch of sunflowers, or "mule's ear," Dustsucker said, appeared along the side of the road. The yellow and orange flowers were beautiful. His friend mentioned that a similar hill full of the flower blossoms could be found in a couple of hours up toward Marlette Lake. From there they'd be able to see Lake Tahoe.

It had been a hour or so since they'd seen anyone else on the road, which seemed odd given that Kings Canyon connected Carson City with the rest of the nation. "Endless masses of people traveled this road in its heyday," Dustsucker explained, "moving people and product back and forth from California and the mining areas you and I call the Comstock." Lumber moguls Bliss and Yerington had ridden it, as did governors, presidents, publishers and other luminaries. Slade explained that there was a time when some five-thousand teamsters were moving goods up and down the road, until a few years ago when travel on it began to decline.

"How so?" Ronin asked.

"I don't know," Dustsucker said, suggesting that the condition of the road might be part of it. Ronin moved closer to the inside of the hill.

He'd only ventured into the Sierra Nevada a few times, more recently toward the lake looking for Glenbrook, given the murders. He preferred staying out of the mountains, enjoying the smaller communities at the mountains' base: Genoa, given that the Mormons had left. Carson City, though he felt the capital was getting a little too toney for miners and ranch hands. Virginia City, particularly the hills to the south where settlements like Gold Hill and Silver City reminded him of what the West originally had been like, if one could look past the sometimes empty machinery and mines. Even Reno was nice.

The mountains were a bother to him once he discovered the rigorous rape of landscape just beyond the tree line. Business was business, but the monumental efforts by more than a dozen timber and lumber companies had supplied not only the silver and gold strikes of Virginia City with construction materials, but also removed most of the trees from what was otherwise a pristine lake and landscape. At times, it just didn't look normal.

"Six-million board feet of timber were taken from these hills, Ronin, and put into the mines. And God only knows how many more million feet of trees have gone into construction and firewood." His friend gestured to the right and left. "From the Truckee River to the East Fork of the Carson River some sixty miles south in Alpine, California, the mining industry has taken much of the timber. And most of it, my friend, sooner or later flowed by barge, train or flume through the tiny city of Glenbrook."

"Maybe we ought to camp up ahead," Ronin suggested. He was tired — and given the emotional toll of the journey. It wasn't only that he wasn't a fan of the timber and mining operations, but that they reminded him of similar changes brought on by the railroads in Wichita some ten years prior — he was hoping to clear his head.

"You bet. No reason not to take it easy," Dustsucker replied.

The first train in Wichita had arrived in 1872 in the middle of the night. While the ache was primarily personal — large numbers of folks were happy to see the town grow, and see Wichita be included in the boom — Ronin felt the bond issue in

1871 and the subsequent service lines brought to the city tore too severely at the social fabric of a community in which he had hoped to settle permanently.

To the surprise of his congregation, he was happy to leave the state two years later. His congregation confused, they rallied to give him a much appreciated gesture of love — a Colt .45 caliber revolver when they learned of his desire to head west. He had wandered the frontier since then, continually running out of room and settling, more or less, along the Sierra Nevada, hoping to find a more permanent peace.

He didn't know what he was looking for, and sensed at times that whatever it was, it was more archetypal than anything else: a "promised land" he joked with his friends, an American mecca of sorts, where simpler times might be appreciated and the kind of life that people seemed to be looking for — though he wasn't sure everyone was looking for the same thing or that it had ever existed — could be caught and celebrated. He regularly reminded himself that he was at the outer edge of the American frontier. Except for California, Nevada was as far west as an American might journey, and the West, as he had hoped to discover it, was practically gone.

Chapter 10

BANDITS

"Ho there," a voice shouted. "You folks look like you could use a break! How about getting down from your horses and sitting a spell?"

Ronin looked to his left, expecting to find a well-hidden stage station or hospitality house. But seeing six men on foot and two others on horseback behind what looked to be an abandoned log house, the short hairs on the back of his neck bristled. He realized he should have been paying better attention, not that it mattered now.

He glanced over at Dustsucker, who seemed equally surprised. Their eyes didn't meet and the deputy was not smiling. This was clearly not the water stop Dusty had promised. The men weren't there to offer any traveling considerations or kindnesses.

"Ho yourself, gentlemen!" Ronin shouted, turning back to his left while hoping to gain some distance or time. He pulled up the reins of his horse so that he faced the man closest to him, who he took to be the leader in that he had drawn his piece and pointed it their way. Slade's horse bucked to its right and circled behind Ronin's, momentarily hiding Slade's right flank. Ronin took the movement to be purposeful, allowing the deputy to scan behind them before bringing his horse up to Ronin's left side. Hard eyes looked both ways.

The bandit's lead man wore a clean, pressed yellow shirt and black vest, complimented by a gold kerchief as if he were going to a Sunday meeting. The man's gun belt hung low on the waist of his blue jeans and chaps, fastened by a half-dozen silver buckles and conchos. His dark hair was long and swept back.

"I'm thinking you should keep your hands on your horses, señors," he said with a Mexican accent, "as you might make my men nervous."

Similarly dressed men stood in a more or less straight line facing them, the silver and nickel work on their jackets, gun leather and rifle stocks suggesting a certain southwest familiarity or extraction. Had they been Caucasians, they might have been thought to be dandies, if road agents generally portrayed such an appearance, which they didn't.

"We're not anxious to dismount señor, unless you need us to," Ronin offered. "We'd be just as happy to continue on if you like," he said in an effort to escape what was quickly becoming a potentially lethal moment.

The lead man held his glance, cocking his head to his right as if to further consider the situation. His mouth opened into a large, toothy grin. "But that is what we need you to do, gentlemen," the lead man repeated, his eyes sunken and unblinking, suggesting a practice and parlance not to be trifled with. "You see, we've lost our horses," he smiled. "We would very much like to borrow yours." The threat was real.

A taller man in a black waist coat to Ronin's left smiled toothlessly, cocking what looked to be a '73 Winchester. He leveled it so that it pointed at Ronin's left side. The man's action made Ronin's reaction awkward, as a rifle shot would certainly blow him from his horse, and braced by two other highway men, Slade would have to shoot *across* Ronin's horse to kill the lead man and the two cowboys to his right.

"Whoa, buddy," Ronin said to the hard-driving man with the rifle, raising his right hand so as to offer further consideration. "I'm not trying to cause any trouble, compadres. I'd be happy to give you my horse if you'd allow me to dismount?"

The two gunmen separated until there was a distance of twelve feet or so between them, leaving two pairs of gunmen standing slightly behind them. Save for the silver and nickel studs decorating their clothing and guns, they were hard-looking men who appeared as if they'd been riding for days. Hungry and unshaven, they looked dangerous and desperate.

"What do you say you boys back away and think about this instead," Slade said coldly. Ronin was startled by his friend's redirection and looked at him. He couldn't figure a defensive action where one of them wasn't going to get shot if the situation devolved into that.

"Dusty!" he raised his eyebrows. "Mind if we sit this one out?" Ronin asked, hoping Slade would read his mind.

The lead man cocked his firearm as if to make a point. Dustsucker met the man's escalation and raised him one. The deputy's scattergun, a Remington 10 gauge, was still secured to his saddle when he fired a load of buckshot at the taller man with the rifle, lifting him into the air and folding what was left of him over the stump of a tree. The heat of the steel on his horse's neck caused Dustsucker's horse to scream and immediately begin bucking. Its hindquarters lifted the surprised deputy a dozen feet into the air and propelled him forward, feet over head, into the same stump.

Hearing the scattergun's loud rapport, Ronin dumped his four-inch Colt Army Revolver out of his holster with his right hand, thumbing a charge into the lead man's head. The man spun counter-clockwise like a Washoe zephyr until he collapsed into the sandy soil, his six-gun still cocked. He let go of the reins of his horse, and gripping his ride firmly with both legs, raised his left hand so as to slip-hammer four additional shots toward the remaining men, before spinning his horse and drawing his long Colt and thumbing four more charges at the men who were still standing and the two hiding on horseback on the leeward side of the cabin.

All four were on their knees or faces when Dustsucker rolled onto his side and, drawing both of his sidearms, laid a barrage of protective fire toward the cabin in the event there were others inside. Ronin was off his horse, standing next to the six footmen with his rifle, when Dustsucker "clicked" empty.

"Jesus, God!" he shouted before turning to put a large caliber bullet into the chest of one of the injured footmen, who was reaching for a gun. "What the hell were you thinking, Dusty? We could have been killed!"

"We would have been killed in any case, Ronin. Those were the Banderas brothers. They've been wanted from Hangtown to Virginia City. I suspect we're lucky to be alive. And we're going to have to trail those other two who got away."

Chapter 11
BANDITS AND BOWELS

"Hell if I am!" Ronin replied, leaning his rifle against a tree and pulling five .45 caliber brass cartridges from the side of his belt. He lifted the four-inch revolver from its holster on his strong side, opened the gate and began emptying the cylinder's contents onto the ground. He loaded one, skipped one, then inserted the remaining four cartridges before cocking the hammer and releasing it so that the firing pin sat resting on an open chamber. Then thinking better of it and anticipating further trouble, he opened the gate again, spinning the cylinder until he could insert a sixth round.

"You're telling me that you know these guys?" Ronin asked, looking up at his friend.

Dustsucker was dusting the dirt off his chaps. Reaching into his vest, he pulled a shotgun round out of his pocket before discovering that he had fired both loads from his horse. No wonder she had thrown him. He reached for a second 10 gauge shell. "I'm telling you they have as big a reputation in these parts as Black Bart does holding up stagecoaches.

Ronin shook his head firmly. "Bart hasn't been seen this far north, Dusty."

Slade scolded his friend, "I'm not talking about Bart, Ronin, though you might want to keep up with things if you're going to make a living trying to catch some of these guys. Bart was last seen in Shasta County, my friend. The word I got from a Wells Fargo detective the other day is that he's headed to Oregon."

"I don't speak much to Wells Fargo detectives," Ronin replied, remembering a few arguments he'd been part of when working for the Pinkertons. "Nor am I much interested in bandits who write poetry."

"Maybe not. But I'm talking about the Banderas brothers, my friend," Dustsucker replied, shaking his coach gun shut and beginning to look for his horse. "Imagine I'm going to have to buy another shotgun scabbard," he said, before looking over at Ronin to see if he'd be willing to help look for his ride.

"Imagine you're going to need a new horse first," Ronin laughed, pulling the 7.5-inch Colt Calvary model from its resting place. He placed it in his left hand, opened the gate and up-ended it. He spun the cylinder with his left thumb and watched as four spent cartridges and one live one dropped to the ground. He stooped over to retrieve the live round. "Don't think Winnie liked your cavalier ways very much. You're lucky you didn't blow the damn horse's ear off! You likely deafened her, you know."

"Hope not," Slade responded, figuring he'd had enough derision for the day and would look for the horse on his own. "She's been a good mount, Ronin, but what was I to do? We'd been killed for sure. Don't know that anyone has survived their heists, at least the ones I'm aware of."

"...and look at this, Dusty!" Ronin exclaimed, picking up a hand-tooled piece of brown leather that had obviously come from Slade's shotgun scabbard. "You not only blew a hole through that rifleman — and while I'm at it, let me say thanks — but you blew a hole through the leather as well."

Already a ways up the path in search of his horse, Slade stopped and turned around. "Like I was saying, I'm going to need a new scabbard. I shot that one to hell just trying to say a simple howdy."

"Well, maybe you may want to make sure it has an open boot next time!" Ronin paused, looking at Slade struggle to climb the hill. "Want some help?"

"Thought you'd never ask," Slade responded, grimacing. A generally happy and uncomplicated man, he didn't know why he had been so sensitive lately. He didn't like being so upset. He looked toward the tree line, where he saw Winnie grazing on a small plant next to a patch of cheat grass. Winded, he bent over and rested. She'd eat five or six pounds of feed if left untended, and there was the pressing issue of the two bandits who had gotten away.

"I see her," Ronin shouted, pointing up toward the trees.

"Got it handled," Slade growled, standing up and trudging toward the tree line.

"Good," Ronin replied, "because I think I shit myself."

Dustsucker turned around to look at his friend and simply stared. Ronin was standing there smiling. "It's not real bad."

Dustsucker could always count on his friend to bring a lighter side to a harsher moment or mood. The deputy had been in more than a few gunfights in his life, the down-side of which wasn't any easier than the event itself. It took days to regain one's focus, more than a couple of hours to find one's breath, and at least a couple of minutes to make sure one's pants were clean. "A lot of us do, Ronin," he said laughing. "When the bullets are flying, a bowel movement isn't too far behind."

Chapter 12

SIT A SPELL

"Why don't you take a moment and clean yourself up?" Dustsucker said peering over at his friend, who had paused for a moment as if he didn't know what to do. "It happens to the best of us. Don't worry about it. I'll grab the horses and maybe we can sit a spell."

"You bet," Ronin responded, looking for a clump of grass or trees in which to hide. In the ten years he'd been wandering the West, he'd seen more than a few men simply drop their drawers where they were and take care of business, but he'd never gotten used to that. And while the shit-slinging of church folk wasn't much different, pardon the expression — Ronin regularly wondered how otherwise well-behaved people were so indifferent to keeping their more intimate and excitable thoughts and moments private — taking a dump in the presence of one's friends seemed like the wrong thing to do if one was ever going to learn to truly love one's neighbors.

"Rule number one," he said to no one in particular after finding a clump of scrub pine on the windward side of the house, "ought to be keeping oneself unstained by the world." Looking around for something with which to clean himself, he laughed quietly. Funny how easy it was to apply the more obscure passages of scripture to one's life. The text came from his Bible, the author of which — James, the brother of Jesus by all Protestant accounts, a man thought to have spent more time in righteous prayer than righteous practice — more than likely never would have thought of so hygienic an application to his affirmation.

He squatted for what might have become a very private moment when he was suddenly alerted to gunfire near the tree line. Looking up, he was surprised to see Dustsucker with the two missing horsemen. Dustsucker's mount was lying on its side, dead, and the deputy was on one knee handing his sidearm and shotgun over to the bandits. He watched as the two men holstered their own guns so as to grab Dustsucker's.

"On the dodge, are you boys? Or just traveling the lonesome places?" Dustsucker shouted. He was clearly nervous.

"It doesn't much matter now, does it?" one of the bandits asked. Ronin dropped the pine cone he was considering and re-buckled his pants. The man speaking didn't appear as Mexican as the taller bandit next to him. It was unlikely they were brothers, but both men were well armed and clearly angry.

The taller man in the sombrero spoke next. "Where's your friend, lawman?" He was looking beyond the deputy toward the front of the house where the other bandits laid crumpled and dead.

Ronin considered the options. Dustsucker was closer, but had given up his size advantage by remaining on his knee and on the downside of the hill. Short of his Bowie knife, still tucked into the back side of his gun belt, he was unarmed. Ronin looked over at his horse tethered to a tree forty or so yards away. He needed his rifle. A couple of 216 grain bullets would certainly solve things as his brass-framed Sporting Rifle could put twenty-eight rounds down range per minute, once he got it going. But there was no way to cover the open ground without spooking the two bandits, and it was likely they'd kill Slade while attempting to kill him. Immediate action seemed to be the obvious course. He hoped that Slade would be as quick to respond with his knife as he had been twenty minutes earlier with his shotgun.

He slid the 7.5-inch Calvary model out of its cross draw holster and took careful aim with it, figuring they were at least fifty yards away. For a moment, his mind wandered, wondering what a longer barreled gun, and consequently more accurate gun, would cost in Colt's custom shop before placing the front site of the firearm on the bandit farthest from his friend. He'd take that man, but Dustsucker would have to handle the man closest to him with either his bare hands or his knife. He slowed his breathing and waited to see if either of the bandits would make a careless move.

A bead of sweat dropped from the tip of Ronin's nose onto his right knee where he had braced his firearm, his left hand cupping his other hand and the trigger guard so as to still the weapon's recoil. His right knee and elbow provided a stable base. He didn't have to wait long.

"Hold this," the bandit closest to Slade said, raising the barrel of Dustsucker's shotgun so that it no longer was pointed at him. He then reached for his friend's revolver, tucked into the front of his belt. It was now or never. There wouldn't be a second chance.

The Colt rocked backward, hitting the right side of Ronin's hat as the man farthest from his friend crumpled into the dirt. Ronin cocked the revolver a second time as it fell into place, searching for a target, but Dustsucker had already begun a deadly dance with the remaining bandit. Deflecting the gun, he spun the bandit into a bear hug and pulled the gun into the bandit's waist. Burying it into his assailant's belly would mean he couldn't fire it. An accidental discharge would put a round through the bandit's belly or leg. Dustsucker took a deep breath and pulled the man's arms and gun hand into a deadly squeeze.

There was no place to breathe, the bandit thought! The deputy's size and weight made it impossible to escape. The bandit's hat fell off as his head fell forward. His eyes began to bulge reflexively for lack of air. He began to turn blue. He had no choice. There ...was...so...little ...time...to...do...anything. He cocked the hammer, nudged the gun as far to his side as he could and made a calculated choice. He'd shoot, hoping to miss his own internal organs while hitting his opponent's. He'd bleed a bit, for sure, and likely would be missing a huge chunk of flesh. But... there... was... no... other...

He fell limp into Dustsucker's arms. The bandit had run out of breath and time. The three-hundred and fifty pound deputy grabbed the firearm, jamming his thumb between the hammer and frame and, de-cocking it, placed it into his own holster before looking over at the man's companion. The other bandit was dead, with a large bleeding hole in his chest. He allowed the unconscious man to fall to the ground and, kneeling on his chest, looked up to find Ronin.

"Finish your business?" Dustsucker asked, smiling. He noticed how much he was sweating. Grabbing his neckerchief and wiping his forehead, Dustsucker bent forward to catch his breath. They were a good thousand feet higher than Carson City's 4,800-foot altitude. Despite riding the Carson Range regularly, he wasn't used to the thin air, not while struggling anyway.

"Yeah, not exactly my friend," Ronin replied, noticing how spent his friend was and feeling grateful he was uninjured. "I was kind of finishing yours."

"Well, why don't you finish up after binding this son-of-a-bitch," Dustsucker wheezed. "We'll head back into town in a few minutes and find out what we can about today's events. And maybe we'll send a crew up to bury these jackasses."

Ronin smiled. The word "jackass" was his term. He hadn't heard Dustsucker use it before. While he had never used the word in church — there were other words he liked better — he thought it descriptive of the people he was sometimes involved with. Ronin was appreciative that he was having some influence on his friend, who had had such an influence on him.

"Maybe I'll wait with that. I don't seem to have made much of a mess of things. Let's get you back to Mrs. Rogers' place after we drop this guy off. It can't be all that important to be clean-up right now, when being careful better serves my friend."

Dustsucker smiled. The former reverend W. W. Ronin was a good friend, even when he was making jokes at someone else's expense. The day had been long, but his mood was improving.

Chapter 13

RIDE BACK TO CARSON

It was close to sundown when they got back to Carson City. "You saved my life back there, Dusty," Ronin said, happy to have returned to town. He was enjoying the Ormsby House's hospitality. Despite the lure of the lake and pressing business still unattended to, a warm bath, a hot meal and a tasty beer sounded like the perfect evening.

"Well, I imagine we're kind of even then." He looked for a spot to tether Ronin's horse outside the courthouse. "You saved mine, too. A pretty good shot for someone who doesn't particularly like guns."

Ronin noted a friend sitting across the street from the courthouse. It looked as if he was sleeping. "I never said I didn't like guns," he responded, thinking of the nickel custom-engraved revolver given him by his former congregation in Wichita, "I said that I didn't have much use for them." He slipped the rope's hitch from the saddle horn of his horse and began to coil it. "Not that I don't find them pretty." He smiled. "A violent man is not someone to envy," he said, quoting the Bible though he wasn't exactly sure where. "I'd much prefer to handle things with my hands, Dusty. You know that."

"... and your feet, Ronin? Don't forget your feet." Slade always found his friend's foot fighting, as Ronin called it, to be girly at best, though he couldn't argue with its outcome. Too busy to notice, Ronin missed the inference. "Not that it matters much, I suppose, whether you use your handgun or your feet."

"If I have to shoot someone," Ronin added, taking his Yellow Boy rifle from the scabbard attached to his horse's saddle, "I prefer to do that with a rifle. A handgun is a poor excuse for a long gun when what you need is a rifle, right?"

"Heard it said, my friend, many times," Dustsucker replied, noting that for a man who didn't like guns, Ronin certainly seemed to have a lot of opinions about them. "Wanna untie our friend and drag him into the courthouse?" he asked as he dismounted and tied the Jackson's reins to an iron horse tether.

Ronin smiled, jerking the line to let his prisoner know it was time to move. The two of them had walked nearly a dozen miles down Kings Canyon Road, allowing Dustsucker the horse. They hadn't been able to locate the two horses ridden previously, and given that the deputy had been breathing pretty hard on the mountain, it was an easy agreement to put Dustsucker on the only remaining mount.

Larry Banderas, he had learned while walking down the mountain, maintained he was Mexican. He wasn't a brother to anybody, or anybody they had met anyway. He didn't particularly want to share what he was doing in the mountains though he lit up, so to speak, when Ronin had asked him about a couple of Indians killed on the eastern side of the lake.

"The holy place," he had said before clamming up, causing Ronin to question what he had gotten himself into when he had invited his friend to help investigate the slayings. He wasn't up to visiting a Washoe sanctuary or "thin place," as he understood such places to be. It was widely known that some men weren't welcome in such places, white men in particular. Given Emma's thinking that maybe he and Dusty should take it easy for a while, he wondered whether they were ready for what might turn out to be something far more complex than previously believed.

The Bovary case had taken him close to a year to solve when he was a Pinkerton detective, and while elements of the alleged murders seemed a great deal simpler, it might be easier to settle the nature of his relationship with Emma than to invite a whole new set of friends and felons into his life.

Ronin drove a foot up between Banderas' buttocks when the bandit hesitated mid-way up the courthouse steps. Banderas squealed and then stood, jumping up and down on his heels. Ronin had clearly caught his testicles, as he had intended. It took a few minutes before Banderas was able to begin moving again.

"Ronin, let's do what we can to keep this guy breathing until we can get him into a cell, okay?" Dustsucker asked. The ex-priest had a surprising habit for causing people pain at times. But he'd been a good man to have around the last few years, helping to detain some of the more difficult or dangerous criminals and solving some mysteries local law enforcement hadn't been able to nail down.

Ronin nodded. "You bet."

Scoop-kicking his prisoner had perhaps been a little enthusiastic, given that a shove could have done the same thing, but his hands were full and he wasn't quite finished winding the rope. "Hold on, Larry," he said, shifting the rope to his right hand. "Don't move, I want to leave the rope with the horse."

Larry Banderas, a lanky man with a penchant for dressing as dandy as his now-departed partners, looked over his right shoulder at Ronin and stopped. There wasn't any question in his head that the man might cause him more pain if he took off running down the street. And where was a man to flee without a whore's help or a gang to hide behind?

"Si, señor," he responded, smiling and pretending to be submissive.

"Cut with the Mexican crap, Larry. We already established you speak English," Ronin barked before placing the coiled rope onto the horn of his saddle. "It's time to be talking too, my friend. There's a lot more that I want to know about Cave Rock and those murders before I stick you away for the evening."

"Si, señor," he said again, dropping his eyes to gaze at the wooden boardwalk outside of the courthouse before looking up to see if Ronin had noticed. Dustsucker smiled. It could take a couple of days before Larry Banderas was willing to speak, what with the threat of a noose around his neck and all.

Chapter 14

HAPPY HANDS

The man who had been sitting across the street was now standing on the boardwalk by the courthouse entrance. His sudden appearance surprised Slade, who was peering in a large window to see if someone might come out to assist them. "Excuse me, mister," Slade said without noticing who it was, "I didn't see you standing there."

Happy Hands broke into a fit of laughter. "How long does a man have to stand in a doorway for you to see him, deputy?" Slade looked up, his hand reaching for his gun. Familiarity wasn't always a good thing for a lawman and sometimes brought rude surprises on both sides.

"Whoa, my friend," Happy Hands said, waving his arms in front of the deputy as if his friend were walking in his sleep. "It is I," he bellowed in as low a voice as he could summon.

Neither Ronin nor Dustsucker had seen their Indian friend since the shooting at the Bowers mansion in Washoe Valley. Happy Hands had lived on the edge of the Washoe Indian colony for at least a dozen years. Squatting in empty buildings and apart from the rest of the tribe, he and his son Little Wolf found trade and income by assisting travelers through the valley or the occasional tourist or business owner who was interested in seeing what was left of Washoe City. It seemed a bit marginal to the two of them — who were occasionally concerned with what was correct and lawful — but members of the Washoe Tribe had had it hard since white men had come into the valley, and neither man could think of a Washoe man, in or outside the colonies, who had done any better than the two of them. Most of the Washoe men served as seasonal ranch hands or worked in timber mills or the Comstock mines.

"My friend!" Dustsucker exclaimed when he recognized who was blocking his entrance to the courthouse. "Where have you been? I thought for sure you would check on my healing after Reno." Overhearing the exchange, Ronin looked over in surprise, figuring that Dustsucker was teasing, given that neither of them had much use for Washoe magic men, if in fact Happy Hands was one.

"I didn't think you welcomed my 'mumbo-jumbo,'" the Hands responded, taking Slade's exclamation as something more serious. "You didn't welcome it when ..."

"That was me, my friend," Ronin interjected. "I'm a bit uneasy when folks begin asking for heaven's help when a heart-felt expression or hand will do. It's taken me a while ..." he said, speaking of the seven or so years he had been absent from the Episcopal ministry.

"... to trust again?" Happy Hands embraced the ex-priest. Ronin hadn't remembered telling him of his time as a man of the cloth. It made him uneasy to think that the Indian might have some real gifts. Still, it was good to see the old man.

"Little Wolf told me you were down this way," Ronin said, remembering the week prior at Spooner Meadow when the child had spooked his horse while warning him of Washoe spirits called Water Babies.

"Did he tell you that I wanted to go to the lake with you?"

"He did not, my friend," Ronin answered, "or I would have looked for you." He wondered if he was telling the truth. As much as he enjoyed the old man, the Indian had cost them some time by directing their attention to a rogue gang of Paiutes north of Reno rather than speaking of the men who had taken up residence in the valley's mansion.

"I had hoped to catch you, Mister Ronin. There is great danger ahead of you — ahead for both of you," he said, looking over at Ronin's friend and then at the man in their custody.

"Perhaps you found this man on the mountain?" Happy Hands asked.

"We did," Ronin and Dustsucker answered simultaneously, looking at each other and surprised by their synchronous answers.

"This man is not from the mountain, my friends. He is from the valley. And he has much to say."

Ronin and Dustsucker looked at each other. Happy Hands' arms had stopped moving.

"We figure he's got something to tell us," Dustsucker said. "Are you saying he has something *important* to tell us?" he asked, making sure his emphasis was clear.

Happy Hands had not only stopped moving while he was speaking, his colorful hand movements being the source of the name he was known by. He was also suddenly silent, and looking intently at Ronin, ignored the question. He then asked quietly, "Perhaps the two of you would like to get cleaned up?"

Dustsucker looked at Ronin, who looked at Happy Hands, who was still looking at Ronin. It didn't appear as if a hot meal or tasty beer was in Ronin's future, at least until he had had a warm bath.

Chapter 15

VIRGINIA CITY

"That's just plumb ridiculous. You're telling me that a man on horseback shot six men, without himself being injured?" Versal McBride was incredulous. Marshal Ash shifted in his chair and started to perspire.

Ash and McBride, the owner of the Bucket of Blood Saloon in Virginia City, had breakfast together every Thursday. One of a hundred-plus saloons in town, McBride took a unique and unusual interest in the Comstock. The Virginia City fire had destroyed nearly a thousand buildings six years prior, include the Bucket of Blood. The weekly meeting was Ash and McBride's way of keeping tabs on things as they kept an unofficial account of the comings and goings on the Comstock and encouraged others to do the same.

"Not six men, Versal, eight if you count the two on horseback, and I can't say that he killed them all. Deputy Slade was involved in the gunfight as well. Apparently, he fired the first shot, setting off both barrels of a 10-gauge shotgun and blowing one of the bandits nearly in half!"

"Jesus," McBride responded. "We're talking highwaymen, right?"

"Exactly. The kind of men we haven't seen up this way in some time, Versal, I mean never in such numbers," Ash clarified. "Slade says he's got one of them at the county courthouse, and that a bunch of these guys have been robbing people up and down the road from Placerville to Virginia City for a couple of months now. They're particularly good at stopping stagecoaches."

"Really?" McBride asked.

McBride hadn't heard of any stagecoach hold-ups in Nevada, though there was a guy by the name of Bart in California who was said to be building a career by stopping Wells Fargo coaches. The bandit was always neatly dressed and wore a long linen duster and bowler hat. Save for hating horses, wearing a flour sack over his head and leaving a couple of poems behind, the gentleman bandit's work was thought by law enforcement to unremarkable, though the poetry of the man's actions hadn't escaped McBride's interest.

"You don't think Black Bart has gotten this far north, do you?" McBride asked, remembering that most of the bandit's work had been in Calaveras, Mendocino and Shasta counties.

"Doubt it." Ash responded. "Slade says the group is calling itself 'the Banderas Brothers,' though it's unclear they're really brothers. The guy he's holding in the Ormsby County Jail speaks perfect English, he says, and may be the last of them."

"Maybe," McBride said, noticing that his bartender had stopped serving a group of miners who had spent the whole night in the saloon celebrating somebody's new claim or birthday — it didn't matter which as long as money was changing hands. He shot the bartender a curious glance and, raising his glass, gestured that they be served no matter how drunk they were or how noisy they were becoming.

"Word is that Hank Monk knocked a few bandits off of the Placerville Road a couple months back when they attempted to stop one of Doc Benton's stages."

"Likely not the first people Monk lost over the side," McBride said, smiling while nodding to the bartender, who had resumed serving the men.

"So this Ronin character, who apparently has an eight-shot revolver…"

"They don't make an eight-shot revolver, Versal," Ash interrupted.

"Yeah, I know. It's a figure of speech, Augustus," McBride replied, dropping his left eyebrow. "This is the guy who ramrodded the recovery of those mission children, right? And wasn't there some shooting involved with that?" he asked while looking toward the door of the saloon, where a young couple and child had come in to seek breakfast but immediately turned around and left.

"Yup, that's the guy. I tried to arrest him at one point last year for killing two fellows in your saloon. You might remember that. The fellows had killed his dog or something like that."

"No," he said, "I don't remember." Pushing his chair away from the table so as to chase the young couple down the street, he couldn't think of a reason why a nice family couldn't have a nice breakfast in a nice saloon. It was Sunday morning, for God's sake, and the bar business was slow. He paused, patiently waiting for the marshal to finish.

"I bring the whole thing up because I think you ought to get to know him, Versal. He was quite handy in Reno and apparently is making a big name for himself in Carson City. One never knows when one might need some extra outside help, if you know what I mean."

"I imagine one doesn't," McBride said, while shooting another glance toward the bartender, mouthing silently to keep the place open while he pursued the couple down the street. "Listen, Augustus," he said, pushing the saloon doors open. "Why don't we talk about this later this afternoon? I've got to catch me some business first, but sooner or later I'd like to meet this fella."

"He's a former pastor or priest, Versal." McBride skidded to a stop just outside the double doors, which had opened onto an already busy C Street.

"I don't know that I need any more clergymen in my life, Augustus. We've got too many padres padding the streets up here already, and most of them ain't doing anybody any good."

"I know, but ..."

"Exactly. If he's good with a gun, then maybe I ought to meet him. Have him and Slade stop by. I'd like to talk to them both."

McBride turned around and left. And the Bucket of Blood's saloon doors swung both ways.

Chapter 16
HOLY MAN

Happy Hands sat back on the bench outside the Ormsby County courthouse, a seat he believed by the simple feel of it to be one on which his friend Ronin had sat a day or two before.

He didn't believe he could always "feel" things that others couldn't sense or see, but he suspected that all of life was connected in some way, and that perhaps his most complex friend, "the former reverend," as he sometimes called himself, had sat there and been part of the creation around him.

If there were three aspects to the reality he knew beyond the one in which he lived, and he believed there were, the most precious was where only the Creator lived. And yet that essence, unknown and untouched by even the holiest of men, could be found in everything that was alive: rocks, trees, water, sand, the sky above and the children of man.

He sat on the wobbly concrete bench for a while, feeling the sharp aggregate of native rocks and listening to the brush of sand when he moved. He stood suddenly and shook his head. Surely this seat was a part of the meaningless nonsense white men made and lived with. Touch a tree and one could sense his ancestors. Stand next to a rock or a stream and one could feel the generosity of the Spirit that fed and dwelt in all things. But sit on these benches — Happy Hands paused to rub the pain from his behind — well, perhaps Mister Ronin had sat there before, but there was no knowledge to be gained by his sitting there any longer.

He brushed his hands against the soft grey trousers he had borrowed from a white man he had met on the path to Sacramento.

He'd noticed a great decline in visitors to the valley over the last couple of years. It had made his acquisition of white men's cloths more difficult. Happy Hands pushed his long-sleeve cotton shirt back into his pants, and continuing to shake his head, walked over to a cottonwood tree near the Ormsby House on Carson Street. He sat down underneath its shade.

He understood that changes would come to the white man's culture. He'd seen a great many of them already. It was said that the Spanish had come to these valleys before, though he hadn't seen any. And then the California gold rush, as the white men called it, had brought thousands of white men. But none of the transitions had been more profound than what had happened to his people. Areas that previously belonged to the Washoe tribes were now "owned" by others. They were fenced and protected by angry men, women and children even, who didn't understand his people's desire to access streams they had fished in or fields in which they had hunted throughout their lives. The natural rhythm of the tribes — summer at the lake and winter in the valleys — was upset by the diversion of streams, the deforestation of the mountains and pinyon groves and the general distrust white people had of the peoples who had lived between these mountains for thousands of years before their coming.

A priest had once told him that the great "white father" Thomas Jefferson's intent was to give Indians "a space to live undisturbed by white people as they gradually adjusted to civilized ways." Yet he wondered how a white man could give to an Indian what he did not own?

In time, the game perished. The trout they had pulled out of the area's lakes, rivers and streams were no longer there. Even the rabbits, berries and pine nuts they once thought were so much a part of the Creator's abundance couldn't be counted on. What the Paiute Tribe hadn't done, in frequent skirmishes and full-blown battles, the white men had finished. Now, his people, never a proud people but a happy people, were forced into colonies where they couldn't sustain themselves save for the jobs provided them by white men: maids, hunting guides, farmers and laborers. All of it made him sad. Everything he had was influenced by the white man.

"Even these clothes," Happy Hands said to himself quietly, "even this name."

"What are you murmuring about, my friend?" Ronin asked as he walked out of the Ormsby House in a fresh set of clothes after a delightfully warm bath. "And how do I look, if I might ask?"

Happy Hands rubbed the sun from his eyes and, replacing his hat so that his eyes were shaded, said "You look like a man."

"And that I am," Ronin answered, "a rather good looking man, don't you think? And much cleaner, I might say."

"Of course," Happy Hands responded, moving to one side. "Should we sit until your friend returns?"

Ronin said, "Sure, let's sit up here, though," patting the concrete bench by the door to the courthouse. It's so much more comfortable than sitting in the dirt."

Chapter 17

AS LONG AS
IT'S TRUE

"I had a dream last night," Happy Hands said.

"You had a dream?"

"A bear came to me."

"A bear came to you?"

"Why are you asking me questions, Mister Ronin? I'm trying to tell you something."

"I'm sorry, I was trying to listen."

"Then listen to me. Don't speak so much." Happy Hands sat silently and then began again. "A bear came to me last night and told me that you needed a holy man to go with you to the lake."

"Why are you telling me this?"

Ronin stared at the man he was beginning to regard as a friend. Except for the occasional gibberish and gobbledygook, Happy Hands was easy to endure, a quality he typically had difficulty with and one that caused him occasional embarrassment. Relationships, he had come to believe, should be much easier.

"Because you wanted to know," Happy Hands continued.

"I wanted to know what?"

"... if I was a holy man."

"I never said that."

Ronin was getting a headache with the back and forth. He figured that sitting on the bench with Happy Hands would be a good thing. They'd get better acquainted. They might grow to understand each other. They might even become friends.

"Did Dustsucker tell you that?" he asked.

"Dustsucker never said anything."

"Are you sure?"

"What does it matter?"

"What does what matter?" Ronin pursed his lips.

"Who said what, Ronin. What does it matter who said what, as long as it is true?"

Chapter 18
STRAWBERRIES

Happy Hands sat smiling, straddling the concrete bench and sitting a great deal closer to Ronin than the gunfighter typically permitted a man or woman to sit. He was uncomfortable sitting so close.

"Look," Ronin said, hoping to gain some distance between the two of them. Intimacy wasn't something he regularly practiced, and when asked for wasn't something he did well. "Why don't we begin again? To be frank, I'm thinking we're just sitting here waiting for our friend to come along and have supper. We're just passing some time. You and I are talking to get better acquainted. I'm not really up for anything deeper, if that's okay with you."

"I'm thinking the same thing," Happy Hands responded. He sat there for a moment, looking into Ronin's face, before he asked, "How is it you are so uncomfortable with me?"

"I never said I was uncomfortable."

"Yes, you did."

"Okay, maybe I did." Ronin grimaced. He was feeling uncomfortable so maybe he had said that. Whatever the deal was between them, here or weeks before in Washoe City, he wasn't enjoying it and desperately wanted to lighten the moment. "Why don't we chat about this holy man thing, as you put it?"

Happy Hands fidgeted, as the space between them seemed too tight to be talking with his hands. Sitting as he had before on the aggregate bench had only produced an irritation on his buttocks, and not one that was easily eased by rubbing his buttocks. And yet straddling the bench so that he faced Ronin seemed to be making his friend uncomfortable.

Why did white men need to be so detached from the earth — their buildings, their footwear, even how they sat? He would never understand such things, he thought as he threw his right leg up over Ronin's head, dismounting the bench as if it was a horse. Happy Hands sat down on the grass a few feet away. He looked up at Ronin, who had leaned backwards and practically fallen off of the bench so as to avoid being touched or kicked.

He searched for a way to say what he wanted to say. He believed Ronin to be a good man, even a spiritual man. The deputy had told him that he had once been a priest in the white man's church, that he had left his church on the plains many years ago and traveled a great many miles away from his home so as to live on the eastern slope of the Sierra Nevada.

Happy Hands had heard of people traveling long distances: white men on railroads, so as to look for gold and silver; families who had come west in order to conduct business or farm; Native Americans who, at the urging of soldiers and settlers, were no longer welcome to live in their ancestors' lands, moving hundreds, even thousands, of miles to make other people happy.

He cocked his head as he looked into Ronin's eyes. He didn't understand a person leaving one place to live in another, unless survival necessitated his moving. A man's life didn't change much because he altered his location. While he hadn't traveled much — Pyramid Lake to the north, the great desert to the east and south, the great lake to the west — in each of those places he was the same person. Wherever a person went, there he was. How is it that white people didn't understand such things?

"Ronin, you know the lake is important to us, right?"

"I do," Ronin replied, noticing that Happy Hands had stopped fidgeting once he'd moved to the grass. "Your people travel there in the summer when the valley becomes too warm, and return to the valley when the mountains become too cold."

"Well, that is true, though the warmth or cold is not the reason. We hunt and fish where we can. Without the Paiutes' horses, it takes some effort, I think." Happy Hands looked at Ronin to see if he understood.

"Okay," Ronin responded. He had heard that the Washoe tribes' traditional enemy did not allow the Washoe to own or ride horses.

"When I say it is important, my friend, I mean in a spiritual sense. Tahoe is the center of our life together. Some tribes camp on the tips of the lake, others on each side. But all of us know the lake to be our mother, in the sense that it's where we come from. The streams and rivers are sacred to us. The Creator provides these to us so we can live."

Ronin listened as Happy Hands explained how important Lake Tahoe's fish and game were to the Washoe Tribes and other Native American tribes as well. While the Indian was talking, he thought about how similar certain places were to people of his own kind.

Reelfoot Lake, for instance, in northwest Tennessee — he had played there as a child. And later as an adult, he had camped along the lake's shoreline. Primarily flat lands, an earthquake during his father's lifetime had produced a bayou-like swamp, where natural ditches and basins filled with brackish water and balding cypress trees suddenly now coexisted.

The New Madrid earthquakes, as they were called, in 1811 and 1812, had redefined the area. The quakes were so significant that buildings had fallen in Ohio, Kentucky, Missouri and Tennessee. Some folks had actually watched the Mississippi River flow backward for nearly a day, creating a lake where no body of water had previously been. The change had taken some getting used to. Change was a part of everyone's life, Ronin thought as he listened to Happy Hands explain how the sudden appearance of white men in northern Nevada had altered Washoe life forever.

"I was an antelope shaman," Happy Hands continued. "I would sing the animals to sleep during our annual hunting trips. With the white men depleting our game, there are now fewer antelope to sing to, my friend. There were many of us in those days. But the white people's farms and ranches have made it difficult for us to hunt and the animals to roam.

"It's a sad story to be sure, Happy Hands. But we make the best of our lives, do we not? We get by with what's given to us." He looked at the Indian to see if he was listening. It was perhaps the longest conversation they had ever had with the man. "I don't read this book much anymore," he said, tapping the New Testament and Psalms he kept in his right vest pocket. "But the white man's holy book says that 'Life is short, and then we are gone, so we must count how few days we have.'"

Despite what their back and forth, Ronin didn't know what to think. The Washoe's way of life was surely over. Everyone could see that, certainly Happy Hands could. Should the Indian be taught to live and act as white men? He didn't know, though Emma apparently did, and thus the Indian school she had built on the south side of town. Ronin shook his head. Whatever the case, there was no hope in pursuing past dreams when present realities argued against them.

The two holy men sat in silence for a few moments, the Nevada sun beginning to ebb its way back over the Carson Mountains as the temperature started to drop.

"There used to be more of us, my friend," Happy Hands said quietly.

"More of your people? Or more holy men?" Ronin asked.

"Both."

"That's got to be hard," Ronin said, not knowing what else to say.

"Now I grow strawberries," the Indian said.

Chapter 19

CHICKEN DUMPLINGS

"Sorry boys," Dustsucker announced as his boots clicked hard onto the wooden boardwalk lining Carson Street. "Hope I didn't keep you long!"

"You did not," Ronin replied, happy to have the interruption and standing to place his right hand on his friend's left shoulder. Happy Hands made about as much sense to him as Emma did when talking passionately about her mission. He was uncomfortable with the feelings they expressed, and the emotions their expressions created within him. "We were just talking about the lake. I'm afraid we didn't get too far, except to hear that Happy Hands fashions himself to be something of a holy man for the Washoe Tribe. Ever hear of such a thing?"

Slade shot Ronin an angry glance to let him know that a little more respect might be in order. "Imagine I have Ronin; imagine you have too," he said, shaking his head. He gestured past the livery at the Ormsby House, toward an open door where he knew food and other refreshments were available. "What do you say we get us a drink and some supper, gents? I had to push past a table full of house guests at the widow Rogers' place to meet you guys, and they were just sitting down to a supper of chicken and dumplings. I'm famished!"

Dustsucker patted his belly to make the point, looking at Ronin once again to make sure he was going to behave should they decide to have supper indoors. Mixed groups weren't always welcome in Carson City's saloons. Chinese laborers, rowdies who had infected parlor house girls with venereal diseases, and respectable women of a religious or temperance bent weren't always welcome in such places. Dustsucker looked up and down at Ronin and Happy Hands before figuring their entrance into the Ormsby House Supper Club was a sure thing. He pushed open the door.

"Any chicken floating with those dumplings?" Ronin asked, having eaten once at Bond Rogers' table and swearing he wouldn't do it again. "I remember plenty of carrots, celery and onions in the broth, but I don't remember much chicken."

"Whoa, partner," a large, dark-haired, mustached man said, pushing back on the door as Carson City's biggest deputy pushed the opposite way. "Sorry friends, but this is a private club. And we don't allow injuns in this place."

"Funny I haven't seen you before," Dustsucker said, noting the badge on his vest and a brace of Patterson percussion pistols carried Hickok-style beneath a bulging belt line. He stepped back so as to allow the man to exit, except that he wasn't exiting — he was blocking the doorway. "Excuse us, my friend. I didn't know there was another law enforcement agency in town," he said, stressing the word "agency" while looking at the silk vest staring him in the eyes. "Pinkerton," he said out loud. "I'm sorry friend, I didn't realize your badge only said 'Pinkerton.' Mine says "Ormsby County Sheriff." Mind if we step inside?"

In reality, Slade's badge didn't say anything other than the word "deputy" on it, a constant embarrassment given the attention, value and weight accorded badges in other venues and locations, Virginia City in particular, where the badges were made out of silver — actual silver, not just silver plate — but the point was the same. Dustsucker was a sworn deputy sheriff in Ormsby County. And whoever the large man was in the doorway, he was simply a private officer or guard. And he was standing in Dustsucker's way.

"Excuse me deputy, I didn't realize you had a prisoner with you," the Pinkerton said, placing his hands at his belt line, closer to his guns, and filling his huge chest with air so as to appear larger. "We've got policies about bringing jail birds into this place. A goodly amount of respectable people ..."

Slade pushed an open hand to the left side of the Pinkerton's face, knocking his head against the doorway so that both sides of the Pinkerton's face had been struck heartily. The Pinkerton tottered for a moment before falling forward, straight as a board onto the timbered walkway outside the hotel entrance. Dustsucker had to step back so as to allow the man's head bounce a third time on the wooden boardwalk outside the supper club. He emitted nary a word or groan.

"A little more respect might be had for Pinkertons, my friend," Ronin said bursting into laughter. He had mixed feelings, having been a Pinkerton Detective, but the scene somehow struck him as humorous. Happy Hands knelt in the street to see if the man was seriously hurt.

"Did you see how he put his hands on his guns?" Dustsucker asked, looking at Ronin and wondering why it seemed so funny. "He squared off at me, Ronin! Can you believe that?"

"Dusty, I don't imagine he knew you were a deputy at the time, or maybe he did. But hitting him upside the head with that huge palm of yours wasn't the kindest thing, either." Ronin smiled. It wasn't natural for him to be laughing at someone else's pain.

"No, I suppose we should have waited for him to shoot us and then offer us an explanation, William."

"You're right. I'm sorry for laughing, Slade. It's just that you're usually the one to be arguing that people get a listen to before a punch in the ribs. And I'm the guy usually flying off the handle to protect the two of us." Ronin knelt by Happy Hands' side and asked how the man was doing. Happy Hands nodded, suggesting he seemed fine, though he had been knocked unconscious. Both noticed that he was beginning to come to.

"There is that," Dustsucker said, pulling a pair of double-lock handcuffs from his belt. He reached into his vest for a key, and not finding one, patted a second pocket before retrieving it and inserting it into the cuffs. Rotating it to the left, he popped the cuffs open and tossed them to Ronin. "Put these on the guy, would you? And pick him up. I'm going to stick my head in the doorway to see if I can find a manager, then we'll lock him to the horse post until we're finished with our meal." Slade peeked into the doorway and, seeing no further reason to pause, entered the Ormsby House saloon.

Chapter 20

SUPPER CLUB

The saloon wasn't actually a saloon. It was a real fashionable dinner house with a display of derringers on the wall. Dustsucker had never been there before, and seeing that it was so nice a place, wondered how Ronin could have secured a room upstairs. From what he understood of the man's finances, he didn't know how Ronin could afford such a place. He pushed past a half-dozen people who had risen from their tables in order to see what the commotion was at the door when he was met by a man who identified himself as the manager of the supper club, Victor Goodwin.

"Mister Goodwin, thank you for identifying yourself. I'm Marcus Slade, an Ormsby County deputy sheriff, and..."

"I know who you are, deputy."

"Well, as I was about to say, your man was blocking the door a few moments ago and wasn't about to allow my party to enter."

"That is correct, sir. We do not allow Indians in this place, out of respect for Major Ormsby, of course."

"I see," Slade responded, glancing toward the door to see if Ronin and Happy Hands had entered yet and then back toward the man who had identified himself as the manager of the property. "You are aware of course that Major Ormsby is dead," Slade said.

"Of course sir," the manager huffed. "He has been deceased for twenty years or more. I don't follow your point, sir." Goodwin heard one of his diners laugh, and noting that he had the attention of a good number of the club's diners, added with a smirk, "Frankly sir, I'm not amused by your violence or your argumentation."

"I'm merely pointing out, Mister Goodwin, that Ormsby's being killed during the Paiute Indian War was an unfortunate thing. I know, as I was there. He was a good man and he deserved better. And while I applaud your wanting to venerate your former employer by not allowing Indians to sit for supper in your fine dinner house, I'm troubled on three points."

"Three points, deputy?" the manager asked.

"Yes, three points, Mister Goodwin." Dustsucker was on a rare roll of erudition. He noticed that his friends had finally entered the restaurant, having left the Pinkerton door guard fastened to hotel hitching post outside. He was aware that most everyone in the tiny establishment was enjoying the exchange between the two of them.

"First, Mister Goodwin. Mister Ormsby was a fine man. It is a shame that you never met him and that he never had the privilege of meeting you. I think he would have enjoyed you. Second, it was the Paiutes who killed Major Ormsby, sir, not the Washoe. This man is a Washoe chieftain, and is historically an enemy of the people who killed our friend. If there are Indians that you should keep from entering this place, he is certainly not one of them. And third, the William Ormsby I knew wouldn't have suffered a minute of confusion over whether to take a share of a man's purse for supper, or any other business endeavor he was offered. He was a businessman and entrepreneur if I have ever met one. And you, sir, are not his friend if you are not willing to take our money."

The dinner house exploded in applause and hollering, some individuals clearing their tables and standing on them so as to gain a better view of the man who had bested Victor Goodwin at debate. Hearing noise above him as well, Ronin noted that his neighbors who had rented rooms on the hotel's second floor were heard to be expressing themselves as well, either in annoyance over the unexpected interruption to the evening's peace and quiet or enthusiasm over its sudden champion. The *Morning Appeal* noted that a more impressive performance had not been seen or heard in the capitol city since Mark Twain had left town fifteen years prior.

Goodwin waited for the applause to finish before seating the three near a window on the hotel's east side, where they were able to view Carson Street and a certain young woman and doctor strolling toward the Supper Club's entrance.

Chapter 21

EMMA AND THE DOCTOR

"Well look at that!" Dustsucker said, peering out the window.

"Look at what?" Ronin asked, as a sharply dressed young man and woman pushed past the crowd, still gathered in the Supper Club doorway.

"Sir," the woman said to Goodwin, "you have a man tied up to a hitching post outside. Free him this instant. It is hardly a Christian thing and he is certainly not a horse."

Ronin spun around, recognizing the voice. "Emma," he shouted, "Come and join us if you would." Emma and Ronin's eyes met, as did the doctor's eyes as well, before their looking at each other so as to consider the invitation.

"Why not?" Quinn said to his date. "I don't believe I've seen Mister Ronin since he fell in a hole and broke his leg."

Ronin found the doctor's tone oddly disconcerting, but concluding nothing by, it pulled a chair over from the table next to them and gestured for them to sit. "I believe you all know Mrs. Nauman," he said, looking around the table. "This is one of our city's finest doctors, Amos Quinn. Dr. Quinn, this is Marcus Slade, with the sheriff's department."

"I believe we've met."

"We have, sir. And Miss Emma, I apologize, but that's my prisoner outside of the Ormsby House. He won't be there for more than a short while."

"And this is our Washoe friend, Happy Hands," Ronin said. "Happy Hands lives in Washoe City, doctor, but is traveling with us."

Quinn extended a hand toward the Indian. Happy Hands stood with his hands at his side. "You are a doctor?" he asked. "What kind of doctor are you?"

"A medical doctor, Happy Hands." Quinn kept his right hand out in a gesture of friendship, waiting patiently for it to be returned.

"As long as you are not a dentist." Happy Hands laughed, shaking the young doctor's hand. "I won't shake the hand of a dentist."

"Few people will," Quinn responded. Everyone laughed and took a seat.

Amos Quinn had been a physician "all of his life," he often said when questioned about his youthful appearance and medical training. He had attended the University of Pennsylvania, an institution Benjamin Franklin had founded in 1749 as the Academy, College and Charitable School of Philadelphia. Prior to studying at the university's medical school — the first medical school in the country, Quinn often commented, when challenged by older more established physicians in Carson City — he had shadowed his father and other talented physicians in the practice of allopathic medicine.

Quinn's talent, background and occasional blabbery about the University of Pennsylvania had separated him from the affection of similarly-minded professionals in the city, though the town's law enforcement types had taken a liking to the man when someone needed patching. Fact is, Quinn did better than most on those corpse-and-cartridge occasions, and his lifelong interest in learning, particularly the insights of European practitioners, had given his medical practice a distinctive edge. Plainly put, Quinn believed in washing his hands prior to surgery. And the fact that he was doing so seemed to contribute to a higher surgery survival rate than that of those who did not.

"Excuse me, Emma," Quinn said while getting up. "I want to wash up hands before supper."

"Sure thing, Amos," Emma said smiling.

As the doctor pulled away from the table to use the Ormsby House's indoor facilities, Ronin reached over to touch Emma's left hand. "Amos?" he said.

Emma pulled her hand back. Neither Dustsucker nor Happy Hands commented, though the implication was plain. "Amos is his name, William. Why wouldn't I call him that?"

"I don't know," he replied. "I'm just asking."

Uncomfortable with the silence, it was Happy Hands who broke the stillness first. "Dustsucker, this may not be the best time, but I wanted to tell you that I am not a Washoe chieftain, as you put it."

"What?" he said, taking his eyes off Ronin and Emma, who were locked in an angry lover's gaze, though up until that point he wouldn't have called it that. "I'm not following," the deputy said, trying to refocus.

"You told Mister Goodwin that I was a chief. I wanted to point out that I am not a chief. I am a holy man, as your people put it."

"They've got other names for your kind as well," Ronin interrupted, breaking away from Emma's gaze. "Most of them are not nearly as generous."

"William!" Emma said. "Don't be so unfriendly to our guest."

Ronin looked at Emma and then at Happy Hands. *"Our" guest? How was there a "we" when the "we" had obviously left the table to wash his hands?* He would never understand this woman, or the relationship they had or didn't have. "I'm only saying that some folks have some real trust issues when it comes to Washoe holy men, Emma. I'm not saying anything unkind."

"Next you'll be talking about the Chinese," Emma responded, referring to the thousand or so Chinese living in Carson City at that time, though not always comfortably.

Once again, there was silence at the table.

"I once blew the craziness out of a woman by walking around her and blowing a whistle," Happy Hands said, looking at Ronin.

"What?"

"You heard me," the Indian said.

"I guess I did," Ronin responded looking around the supper house to see if Quinn was anywhere to be found. "I wish it were so simple, my friend," he said standing up. "I'll be in my room. The four of you have a pleasant supper."

Chapter 22

SECOND FLOOR VIEW

Ronin climbed the wooden steps to the second floor, noting an uneven stain to the pine stairway and wondering how a hotel eatery with such a sterling reputation could employ such a surly manager, though it wasn't the manager who was uppermost in his mind. A limited number of rooms with a second floor view of the front avenue had been available when he had signed in. While for safety's sake he didn't favor a chamber at the very end of the hallway, he was happy to be accommodated there. Now he wasn't happy at all.

He keyed his door and slipping quietly inside took off his gun belt, hanging it over the far bedpost. He propped a chair up against the ornamental brass door knob, pausing to check how sturdy it was before sitting down on a crimson-colored, cane-back upholstered side chair next to an ivory ornate dressing table by the door. He took off his coat.

Maybe it wasn't Goodwin who had gotten him upset. Perhaps it was Emma, or maybe Quinn. Or possibly it was the relationship between them. Or then again, as Emma had said numerous times after the shootings at Bowers mansion, "Give yourself some time." It would probably take a few months to get over that kind of violence. There had been a lot of it, in Reno and Washoe City, and now on the road leading to the lake.

It wasn't as if the men didn't deserve to die. *I'm not the final magistrate in such matters. I'm not sure God is either. The community is, whether it's Carson City, Virginia City, or a spate of gold and silver-digging hole in the walls all the way back to Placerville. What reasonable community can tolerate such men without harming itself?* Ronin didn't imagine that any reasonable person or persons should. Some men needed to die sooner than others. Helping those men die is what he sometimes did. Someone had to.

He took off his boots, taking a moment to inspect his socks — a man needs good socks — and then climbed onto the bed thinking of Remy and Clem Crestwell, whose lives had been taken by the U.S. Marshal in Reno.

The two boys probably hadn't started out bad, though it was possible they had been born into a long line of mean women and men. Clem's apparent mental disability — God, he was slow — had likely contributed to Clem's being the sorry son-of-a-bitch he was. Killing Clem and his brother Remy might have been a good thing, remembering the time he had side-kicked the poor dumb bastard through a Carson City saloon's door frame. Though Clem might have turned into the kind of person an ex-Pinkerton would have enjoyed having a beer with, he doubted the decent-minded ex-clergyman side of him could ever have stomached his brother.

Ronin removed his New Testament from his vest pocket and put it on the table by the bed. He thought about reading it, but instead patted it. His years in the church had been few, but narrow. The time he'd spent preaching and teaching hadn't en-couraged him to have friends like Remy, whose friends called him "a jackass," and Clem, perhaps the slowest thinking outlaw he'd ever met. Maybe that was a good thing. Maybe living a narrow life wasn't living a bad life after all.

He leaned over the side of the feather bed and peered out onto Carson Street. The Pinkerton man was still shackled to the hitching post, looking every bit as surprised as he did when he first greeted them at the door. Dustsucker must have tossed him into the water trough before hitching him there, as he was still soaking wet though not nearly as angry as he previously appeared when Carson City's biggest deputy sheriff boxed his ears into the side of the Supper Club doorway and slammed him face down into a muddy capitol street.

Ronin made a mental note to wire Chicago to see if he actually was a Pinkerton; something his friend would probably forget given that he'd be dragging him to jail for interfering with a police officer, or some such thing. Lucky for the Pink that he hadn't actually battered deputy Slade before he had his ears cuffed. He smiled: never stand between a hungry man and his dinner.

Remy and Clem Crestwell were dead; the possible moral differences between them were now clearly unimportant. The same could probably be assumed of the Clancys, who had wasted the formative years of their mother's love to become kidnappers and killers.

He shook his head and sat back against the Ormsby House's brass bed, a considerable improvement over the ill-equipped slab he had slept on above the Curry Street saloon. He had slept on worse, he guessed.

Peter Clancy was likely sitting in the new state prison with a pillow under his head, or soon would be. He didn't generally follow up on such matters, preferring the simpler life of an outdoorsman, though the Ormsby House and its hot and cold water privy was a nice break. So too seeing his friends.

After leaving the church in Wichita and signing on with the Pinkertons, he had met very few people who were tolerant or interested in his inner thoughts and judgments. Say what you want to say about church folk looking toward heaven when they could be doing some earthly good, church people were at least interested in discussing the questions, some of them anyway. And it was pleasant to pass an evening or two over a glass of beer or wine blathering on about such things.

Emma had enjoyed those moments, he thought sipping from a glass of water, especially before the children had been kidnapped, though neither of them drank much wine except for medicinal purposes, and Quinn had suggested a glass or two would be a helpful thing while his leg was healing. He turned onto his left side and propped himself up, putting his hands behind his head so as to have a better view of the doorway.

Not all of the Clancy brothers were dead. The oldest brother had seemed like a caring man, in some deep down sense, Ronin thought, though the U.S. Marshal for the Nevada District, Augustus Ash, had caught him dragging a young child in front of a window at the mansion and chose to eliminate what he thought to be a potentially lethal and imminent threat to the child's life. Who knows?

While he didn't know Peter as well as he had gotten to know Paul, the boy had spoken of his older brother's desire for them "to no longer be involved in criminal pursuits." Their late mother hadn't approved of such things and had hoped for something better, and Paul had promised to keep them out of trouble, as weak as that promise turned out to be.

Patrick, the youngest of the Clancy brothers, had been a problem all his life, according to Peter who seemed strangely obligated to tell the entire Clancy family history to Ronin, prior to him Peter in one of the few Ormsby County Jail cells available. He couldn't help wondering if there wasn't something similar to the way the two families had been raised, particularly the youngest boys. Remy and Patrick were both troublesome loudmouths and had likely experienced their fair share of fists trying to shorten their and everyone else's pain. Opting for the lower bunk because of his injured arm, Ronin apologized to Peter for breaking it after discovering him in the mansion's kitchen. A big man, he'd hardly flinched when Ronin swung the Yellow Boy's heavy octagonal barrel onto Peter's right arm, snapping the radius bone and preventing him from drawing his sidearm. A perfect *chasse marche croise* drove his head into the kitchen's hard plaster lathe walls and knocked him unconscious. "It's probably the only reason I'm still alive," Peter said, having missed all the shooting.

Grabbing a small mirror from his saddle bags, Ronin touched his lips. They were chapped. His beard was rough as he hadn't shaved in a couple of days. With Emma's attention elsewhere, and not having a congregation to stare at him wondering if the young reverend was old enough or wise enough to really be their pastor — "Jesus was only 33," he'd said, when braced by the women of his congregation — it really didn't matter. Maybe he'd grow a mustache and beard, he figured. He looked over to the sink to see if they had replaced his towels and toiletries and wondered if he had a razor. Like Quinn, he'd always had a youthful appearance. Maybe the fresh-shaven look was attractive to Emma. Ronin sat up and stroked his chin as if he had a beard, pulling his cheeks into a point and smiling. Perhaps he would grow one. Pushing the mirror to the top of his head, he wondered if his hair was beginning to thin.

There was no reason to be upset — a woman did as a woman wanted to, and a man should do as he wanted to as well. He pulled boots on and got up to take a stroll over to the livery before walking to the courthouse and speaking with Banderas, who was likely standing at the front of his cell entertaining everyone. A chatty man was a worthless man. And what kind of a name was Larry anyway? Certainly not Mexican.

Chapter 23

IT WAS HOW I WAS RAISED

"Once I healed a minister who had headaches," Happy Hands said, carefully crossing his right hand over his left so as not to disturb the crystal water glass and the confusing pile of silverware by his right hand.

"A minister, you say?" Quinn asked, thinking he may not have heard the Indian correctly. The doctor leaned in, amused by the Indian's awkward efforts to control his hands and arms while speaking.

The Supper Club's table was set formally: a china soup bowl and dinner plate sat directly in front of Happy Hands, with three forks to his left, a tea spoon, soup spoon and a knife to his right. To his left, a bread and butter plate and a butter spreader hovered above the forks beside a cloth napkin. Three glasses to his right, as tradition dictated, appeared directly above the knife: one for water (the largest and already poured), another for red wine and an additional goblet for white. The Ormsby House did things right, Quinn thought, remembering his parents' frequent dinner parties in Philadelphia, where multiple courses where the norm and the evening's place settings presented a dilemma to even the most practiced of diners.

"Yes, a minister here in Carson City," Happy Hands replied. "The white man served refreshments at the end of his sermons." He paused, as if choosing the right words. "I've never heard a sermon, but I assume that his teachings were lengthy or tiresome because they needed such a repast." He smiled as he had never used the word "repast" before. "You see, he did not drink the tea or eat the cakes he was provided."

"So?" Emma asked, turning her attention away from the second floor stairway where Ronin had disappeared, suddenly interested in the suggestion that a Christian pastor had submitted to the ministrations of a heathen holy man.

"That is why he had headaches," Happy Hands responded. "I saw this in a dream."

Emma sat back in her chair, taking a water goblet with her, calmed by the thought that the minister's misdeed had never really taken place. Realizing that Happy Hands was waiting for a response, she asked to be sure. "This was a dream then, right?"

"No, this was a minister here in town. But I saw why he had headaches in a dream."

Quinn and Emma looked at each other, wondering what to say next. Emma's upper lip beaded with perspiration, as it often did when presented with a moral dilemma. She remembered the gospel imperative: we are to live in the world, not to be of the world. She touched her hands to her mouth and began anxiously rubbing them. Quinn broke the silence, hoping to repair the breach. "Have you always been a holy man, Happy Hands?"

Happy Hands looked at his dinner companions. He had never understood the white woman, uneasily wringing her hands. She seemed like a nice person, but he was confused by what he had heard about the children's religious training at her mission. Rather than allowing the children to follow their own paths, to know their own powers — or spirit helpers, as his people called them — they were being forced to follow the white man's religions. The Episcopal service he had observed on a Sunday mornings seemed sedate enough, the breaking of bread and the pouring of wine a good thing he figured, no matter what the significance. But the regular harangues at the mission by teachers and preachers from other groups in the capitol city greatly troubled him. They were killing the Indian in order to civilize the man, Ronin had explained. And while he appreciated the thought that the white man's path would ultimately become the way of most Indians, the men and women they were converting didn't belong to either culture. They seemed hollow inside. A hollow man wasn't a healthy man.

"It was how I was raised," he answered, hoping to make a point. "It's how all of us were raised."

"Your parents brought you up to have visions and dreams?" Emma asked, stuttering at the thought that a red man could be a religious man, without the discipline of a Christian minister or missionary. Dustsucker looked at Quinn asking for help and, not seeing any, was about to say something when Happy Hands responded.

"Not my parents, Mrs. Nauman, but the tribe. Our whole tribe knew that I had my own path. There were a lot more of us before the white man came to the valley. And while all of us were not holy men, each of us was different than the other. You must understand that, with so many children under your care."

"I believe the Great Spirit calls all of his children to express their gifts, in obedience to Christ," Emma said. "I have simply never thought of an Indian as having those very special gifts as do Christ's ministers and priests."

"I wouldn't know about that." Happy Hands thought about the men he had known who were Christian clergy. None of them had seemed special to him, though a few of them had been good people. "I do know that I had many dreams as a child and that one night a bear came into our family's lean-to and stared at me. This happened many times, and sometimes I would fly up into the sky."

Emma nodded, listening. Quinn and Slade relaxed, noting that Emma seemed genuinely interested in the Indian's story, even if it differed from her own.

"Sometimes I would see shapes in the sky that other people didn't see. Or hear the flapping of a bush that other people didn't hear or feel. These things told me I was different. And that the bear was calling me." He sat silently, with his hands in his lap so as not to disturb the pretty objects set on the white man's table. Perhaps the woman wasn't so narrow after all. Perhaps she had simply reminded him of his wife, whom he had left when he was younger so as to move to the nearly abandoned village known as Washoe. Who could live with a contentious woman? He sat, wondering, when Emma interrupted.

"Do you pray, Mister Happy Hands?"

He looked in her eyes and recognized the woman to be, despite her reputation, an honest person seeking to find the right way for herself and for those she cared for. He decided to answer.

"Of course I pray, Miss Emma." He felt more comfortable with the woman, and called her the name he had heard his friend Slade call her an hour or so previously. He could not call her "mother," a name other Indians had recently taken to. "A holy man must always pray. Sometimes I pray for three or four days in a row for someone. It is what I believe Ronin calls 'ritual.' Praying, smoking, washing, sprinkling, it depends on the person's needs or on mine. A holy man must always pray."

Emma thought of her friend and briefly glanced at the second floor stairway. She caught Amos looking at her and blushed. She wondered if the good in Ronin had been washed away by the killings in Washoe, or others in recent days. She looked back at the Indian and said, "On that we agree, Mister Happy Hands. A holy man must pray. If he does not pray, he is no longer holy."

Dustsucker turned to see the waiter walking toward them with a couple of steaks, bowls of potatoes, beans and a large corn salad. It was Tuesday, so it was Basque night at the Ormsby House. He could tolerate the wine, though he preferred beer, and enjoyed the family style dining, as it reminded him of his Iowa home. What he didn't like were the beans. Basque beans were still beans, and he had eaten plenty of them riding high desert trails and washes throughout northern Nevada. But Basque eating was hearty eating and he loved the fact that there was no end to the food.

The waiter put their plates down at a table next to them and summoned help to clear away extra dishes and silverware from their table setting. He looked at Goodwin, before returning his gaze to the deputy, who still had his hat on. Dustsucker braced himself. He rarely removed his hat and never did if he was told to. A simple plainsman design, Dustsucker's hat was, except for Ronin, his daily confidante and friend.

"Sir, what would the Indian have to eat?"

Dustsucker relaxed. "I imagine he'll eat what we eat, won't you Happy Hands?" Happy Hands nodded. The server grimaced and Goodwin shrugged his shoulders. Heaping, hot dishes of food were placed before Dustsucker, Quinn and Mrs. Nauman.

"I'll return with the Indian's food in a moment," the server said.

Dustsucker immediately slid his steak across the table to Happy Hands' place and looked into the server's eyes. "You can return in a few moments with my food, sir. We'll not tolerate any more rudeness at this table, or at this establishment," he added, looking over at Goodwin. "I don't treat others that way; neither will I allow my friends to be treated that way."

Happy Hands saw the server smile as only a white man smiles, and watched him return to the kitchen.

Chapter 24

WOOZY

Ronin kicked an empty can of beans from the back entrance of the Ormsby House on Curry Street all the way to the county courthouse, a couple streets north at Musser and Carson. He sat down on a concrete bench, being careful to brush the petal-less flowers of the capital's cottonwood trees from the bench's surface.

A flurry of cottony seeds blew by. It was June to be sure. Pulling a cloth handkerchief from his vest pocket, he sat down, and finding a clean space on it blew his nose. Cottonwood trees could be pretty, adding appreciable shade along riverbanks and creeks throughout northern Nevada — the silvery green color was a nice contrast to the otherwise monotone sandy coloring of a Nevada summer — but he hated the springtime sneezing that went with them. If he were to drag any of the cottony hairs back with him to the hotel, he'd be miserable the rest of the night.

Satisfied that he had cleared a clean seat for himself, he sat down and cast a weary glance up and down Carson Street, for safety's sake. He then stood, adjusted his gun belt and entered the courthouse, climbing the steps to second floor offices and jail.

Larry Banderas couldn't be nearly as miserable as he was, after seeing Emma with Amos Quinn, the town's most talented surgeon, ruining his opportunity to plan the next week's travel with Happy Hands and Dustsucker.

The Indian seemed intent on heading to the lake with them, and as Ronin wasn't generally in the habit of running across the grain with people when they were insistent about something, he figured things couldn't get any worse if he included him. If Happy Hands was a Washoe holy man, whatever that was — in all his travels he'd met few medicine men who were even worth speaking to — he might have some skills or insight into the men or the murders. But it was a maybe and time was quickly moving on. If they waited any longer to get up there, whatever clues there were might be long gone.

"Larry Banderas, please," he said to the deputy parked behind a desk full of keys and six-shooters. "Make a habit of counting your shooting irons every night?" he asked the boy, who couldn't be more than sixteen.

"Excuse me? Who did you say you were?"

"I didn't say, son," he responded, putting his right hand down on the desk to steady himself. His left hand was stuffing the handkerchief back into his lower vest pocket when the young man's hand came in contact with his right, pinning his ungloved hand to the desk.

"Son, I'd be careful who you pick a fight with, if you don't mind me saying." He smiled briefly, waiting for the deputy's response, but was unexpectedly distracted by the sudden throbbing in his forehead. It was if something inside of him had shifted, making one side of his head feel heavier than the other. Whatever it was, it briefly obscured his vision. He reached to touch his left eye, noting the deputy's anxiety and looked up, suddenly dizzy. Was it the cottonwood trees? Or the long flight of stairs he had climbed to access the jail?

"I'm W. W. Ronin," he said, patting his upper pocket for an announcement card, the carrying of which had continued to be a habit even after leaving the Pinkertons and the Episcopal Church before that. Visiting cards were not generally used in the West, but he'd found them to be a handy introduction when calling on members of his church or when involved in an investigation. Finding none, he began to apologize when his right elbow suddenly gave out and he toppled onto the desk. The deputy was startled and released his grip. Ronin immediately slid to the floor.

"What the fuck?" the deputy yelled, standing so quickly that his wooden desk chair bounced off a full sheriff's rack of rifles and shotguns on the wall behind him, emptying the lower drawer, tumbling ammunition and six-shooters to the floor. Two deputies sprinted into the room from the jail, having heard the commotion. Deputy Mort Spinnaker stood there with his eyes and mouth wide open, his guest appearing to stir while still on the floor.

"What the hell?" Ronin murmured, pulling his right leg under his backside and leaning forward so as to stand. "I'm not feeling so good, deputy. Would you mind… would you mind getting me a chair?"

Spinnaker and the other deputies looked at each other before the older one put down his shotgun and barked, "Get Mister Ronin a chair, sport! We don't need any more trouble tonight!"

"Trouble?" Ronin whispered, though barely loud enough. The room was spinning. His stomach was grumbling. He felt like he was going to throw up.

"Slade is going to be pissed when he hears that his prisoner somehow snuck out of here between shifts."

"You think that's what happened?" the younger deputy asked as Spinnaker pulled his chair away from the sheriff's rack drawer and began pushing at Ronin's backside.

"I have no idea what happened," the older man barked. "But I do know that he's not going to look lightly on the fact that this Larry guy is out the door while his friend, the eminent detective William Washington Ronin, is sitting on the floor."

"He's not on the floor anymore," Spinnaker said, having pulled his visitor up onto the chair so that he sat facing the front door, the chair back braced by the front of the desk. Ronin leaned forward, grabbing his head with his hands and moaning words that were indistinguishable from a cow in heat, except slower and lower, but just as personal and troubled.

"Jesus, I've never heard anybody moan like that," the older man said, grabbing Spinnaker's wrist. "What the hell did you do to this man?"

"I didn't do anything," Spinnaker reacted. "I don't even know who he is!"

"You must have done something," the older deputy quipped, looking around for a basin or bucket in case their visitor wretched. "You young guys just can't do anything right!"

"Oh Jesus ..." Ronin said, rolling forward on to the floor and hitting his head. And that's where he was laying when Dustsucker came in.

Chapter 25
MISSING PRISONER

Slade's perfect supper came to its less than perfect end when Ormsby County Deputy Mort Spinnaker interrupted the flaming dessert. A fine crème brulee for four had been served tableside when the short, wheezing youngster of a lawman heaved out the words, "Your prisoner is gone and there's a private detective laying on the floor in the sheriff's office!"

"What?" Dustsucker exclaimed, looking up at Mort Spinnaker and then back down at the wonderfully fancy dessert Victor Goodwin's staff had prepared for them, "so as to make up for the previous misunderstandings." Dustsucker had commented that the custard was rich and creamy, and silkier than he had experienced anywhere before, though it had been some time since he had enjoyed the delicacy. "Someone taught the table server how to caramelize the turbinado sugar in just the right way," he'd said, impressing everyone at the table.

"Who knew?" Emma asked her friend.

Emma, Amos Quinn, Happy Hands and he were about to take their second spoonful of the burnt crème when Spinnaker bent forward and widened both of his eyes, blinking like railroad lanterns so as to make his point even more urgent.

"Well?" he asked, nervously nodding his head as if listening to the brain-piercing whistle and clickety-clack of an out of control steam train.

"Alright, alright, I'm coming," Dustsucker said angrily, struggling to stand upright while trying to fold his napkin in just the right way so as to not insult his friends. His cross draw holster and revolver caught the table's edge. "Excuse me, please," he said. "Miss Emma, my apologies. And would you mind watching this for me?" he asked, attempting to smile. "If I don't return in a couple of minutes, maybe you'd like to take my dessert back to some of the children?"

Emma nodded, surprised and ruffled by the clatter of guns and table top. Quinn met the deputy's gaze. "Marcus, we'll take care of all of this. You go tend to Mister Ronin or whoever it is. If I'm needed, you know where I am."

"Of course, doctor."

Dustsucker ran out the front of the Supper Club with his young deputy, trying to catch up.

It was widely known by other officers in the department that Mort Spinnaker had other issues than his sometimes poor and insolent attitude. He had a problem with his breathing, for instance. His aunt had once stood him up against a tree on the family farm, when he was nine or so, and driven a nail into a tall elm tree hoping that he'd outgrow his wheezing when the young man grew tall enough to pass the nail's height by a full inch. The folk remedy hadn't solved his asthma any. Lengthy moments of exercise sometimes left him wheezing or winded.

Spinnaker hurried past the hitching post outside of the Ormsby House, spun around and yelled to Deputy Slade, who was a couple of yards ahead of him, "Is there any reason this guy is cuffed to a horse rack?"

Dustsucker stopped fast in his tracks and shouted back, "He's a giant pain in the ass, Spinnaker. Let him loose. We've got more important fish to fry." A few seconds later, Dustsucker braced himself on the courthouse railing so as to catch his breath, wondering how the Banderas boy had escaped the county's new jail. Waiting for Spinnaker to catch up, he bellowed up to the second story, "Deputy Slade coming up. Come ahead?"

"Yeah, but bring a doctor!" a voice returned. "There's something wrong with your friend Ronin!"

"Jeez ..." he said, shaking his head and turning to head back to the Ormsby House. He didn't go but a few steps when he saw Dr. Quinn and Emma running toward him.

"Trouble, Slade?"

"Sounds like it, doc."

"Well, let's take a look," Quinn replied, sprinting up the steps three at a time. Miss Emma, Slade and Spinnaker entered the second floor office area a few seconds later, where they saw a couple of lawmen leaning over their friend Ronin, and Quinn, who was trying to keep Ronin from sitting up, holding on to his head.

"William!" Emma said, running to him.

"Emma, what are you doing here? I thought you and Quinn were having supper?"

"He's here with me, William. Did you fall?" Quinn knelt down beside her, taking Ronin's radial pulse, which seemed unusually slow. "What happened?"

"I don't know," he said holding his head with his left hand. "I blacked out," I think. "Must have been the stairs."

"Ronin, you seem a little warm," Quinn said. "How have you been feeling?"

"I'm feeling fine," he said, shaking Quinn's hand from his wrist. "I fainted, that's all, nothing to worry about. I wish you people would give me some room to stand back up," he barked, counting six people around him and wondering who was guarding the prisoners. He slid into the chair and began to brush the dust from his tan canvas vest and pants.

"Maybe I should have eaten more," he said, looking at Emma, and Quinn who was grabbing at him, still trying to get a measure of Ronin's health.

"You didn't have *anything* to eat, William," Emma responded without thinking, "unless you had something in your room."

"Yeah, well I guess I wasn't hungry." He slapped at Quinn's hands and wondered what he had to do to get him to stop touching him.

"You seem fine enough to me," Dustsucker growled, bursting into the room from the cell area. "Spinnaker, where the hell is my prisoner?

"I'm…"

"The cell is locked. The bars are in place. But the Banderas boy is gone."

"Banderas is missing?" Ronin jumped up, patting his gun belt to make sure everything was in place and looking to see if there was a broken or open window. "How could you lose Larry Banderas?"

"I didn't," Dustsucker argued. "I was sitting for a nice supper you might remember, or maybe you don't remember because you were laying on the floor here!" He turned back to Spinnaker, who seemed at that moment to be the most vocal. "I'd like to know who did lose him?"

Spinnaker nodded to the older man with the shotgun, Jim Garrett, who was beginning to chew on his lower lip. "No relationship," the older man had said, to Patrick Floyd Garrett, a New Mexico saloon owner who told Ronin, as a Pinkerton Detective, he hoped one day to be a U.S. Marshal. "Jim, were you sitting back there?"

"I was, and I don't know what happened. To be honest, I may have dozed off. But what I do know is that about fifteen minutes ago I heard the outer door click and, looking up, discovered Banderas' cell empty."

"Spinnaker, were the two of you out here? Didn't you notice anything?" A heavy door divided the jail from the sheriff's offices.

The younger deputies shuffled their feet. "We didn't notice anything either, Slade. Might have been napping as well, I guess …"

"Jesus, guys!" Ronin popped. "This is amazing. I stick a nearly dead Mexican into your jail and you can't seem to remember what happened to him. Is there any surprise that there are outlaws running all over the Sierra Nevada when the capitol's jail and prison cells can't seem to hold them?" The rapidity of Ronin's speech took a toll on him. He sat back down in Spinnaker's chair, facing the door, pale, tired and out of breath.

"He isn't Mexican," Happy Hands said, entering the room with a shy smile on his face. "And he isn't 'running all over the Sierra Nevada ...'"

"Hell, you say," Ronin interrupted, bracing himself to get up.

"He's sitting on the bench downstairs."

"He's what?" Dustsucker bellowed, angry that three white deputies couldn't hold a near dead man, whatever his national extraction.

"He's actually lying on the bench," Happy Hands responded. "He was hiding in some bushes on Curry Street when he collided with the butt end of my rifle."

"Hell, you say!" Ronin repeated, looking around the room to see if he had brought his rifle with him.

"I can't stomach a man who says he is one thing when he is in fact another," Happy Hands replied, looking at Ronin.

Dustsucker took a deep breath, as others stood gawking at each other, wondering what Happy Hands meant. And then he took off running down the courthouse steps.

Chapter 26

LARRY BANDERAS

"Well hell, Happy Hands, you didn't say you had cuffed him! I wouldn't have run if I'd known that."

"I'm sorry, deputy. But your younger friend dropped his cuffs a few moments ago, while running to your aid." Happy Hands stood there grinning, having knocked the fugitive off his feet, and secured him to a nicely painted bench outside a business on Sixth Street. "Mister Spinnaker," he continued, "I believe I can help you with your breathing difficulties. I'd be happy to dream about it ..."

Spinnaker stood next to a tree wheezing, his left hand steadying himself as his right hand brushed rhythmically across his chest. "Whatever," Spinnaker replied, having never spoken directly to an Indian before, let alone a Washoe, and hoping never to speak to another again.

Taking a key from his vest, Dustsucker unlocked one cuff. "Mister Banderas," he said. "You've broken out of my jail and that displeases me. Wonder if you'd mind accompanying me down the street a ways and back upstairs where we can shackle you more securely?"

Banderas had apparently paused long enough in leaving his cell to grab his poncho, a blue and yellow blanket with red diamond designs. Ronin couldn't place the pattern, though he had seen something similar, he thought, when traveling through New Mexico nine years before with the Pinkertons. Certain he wasn't Mexican, he had guessed by his tall hat and even taller attitude that Banderas was a Texan. Now he wasn't certain.

"You heard the deputy," Ronin said. "Slade, what happens to men who break out of your jail? They get an extra helping of supper?" he asked, grinning as he put his hand out to take the key and unlock the other bracelet.

"Not exactly," Dustsucker replied, motioning to Garrett who was already pulling rope from Dustsucker's horse.

"Want to drag him up the street a bit, Slade?" Garrett asked. "Maybe we take him straight to the new penitentiary?"

"That's a bit far, Jim."

"Señor, please do not hurt me."

"Cut the Mexican crap, Larry!" Ronin interjected. Ronin handed the cuffs back to his friend and watched him loop them over the back of his gun belt.

"Well then, how about to an outhouse up by the Indian colony then? He's so full of shit," Garrett continued, feeling some responsibility over the man's getting away, a trait Ronin admired about Garrett, he thought as he watched Spinnaker and another deputy come around the side of the building and stand there, watching.

"Larry, last chance. None of us speak Spanish, and I'm thinking you don't speak very good Spanish either, so what do you say, wanna talk American?" Ronin began tapping his boot, to the tune "Mother Is the Battle Over?" a Civil War song his mother used to sing to him and his brothers when they couldn't sleep. He began humming the first line.

"Okay. I'm speaking, alright?" the prisoner responded. "And the name isn't Banderas, it's Crum. 'Banderas is Spanish for 'flags,' moron."

Ronin threw a right whipping kick, or "fouette" in Savate, to the side of Larry's head, but instead of making contact with the toe of his boot, which he thought might really hurt him, he hit him with his instep. The kick knocked Crum off the bench and into the street. "That's my friend you're talking to," he shouted, before grabbing his own head and stumbling toward the bench Crum had been sitting on. "Jesus, this pain in my head is awful ..."

Emma ran toward him, and sitting down, pulled his head into her dress. "I'm so sorry you're hurting like this, William." Dustsucker shot a concerned look his way, before saying, "I can handle this Ronin. Why don't you and the doctor focus on your own situation?"

"I don't need a doctor," Ronin replied, noting that Quinn was nowhere to be found. It seemed that Emma was surprised, too.

"Well, Larry Crum or whatever your name is," Dustsucker said, grabbing the man's arm, "how about you and I go back upstairs? We'll find some extra locks to put on your wrists and ankles, and then maybe in the morning we can take you on a trip up the mountain. I'm guessing the Crum brothers, or Banderas brothers, or whatever you call yourselves, will be happy to see you again. Think you'd be up for that?" he asked, pushing his prisoner toward the two deputies who were watching. Crum stumbled, at which point all three deputies took appropriate hold of the man.

"There are more of them?" Ronin asked.

"Banderas is plural, moron," Crum yelled, as two deputies attempted to control his arms and a third his collar or neck.

Ronin jumped from the bench and, with a short hop, delivered the same right whipping wheel kick this time with his toe knocking the man out and propelling him into the street.

"Ronin!" Dustsucker shouted.

"What?" Ronin exclaimed. "I'm tired of this man's nonsense. I won't be treated poorly and I won't allow my friends to be made fun of, either."

Dustsucker looked at the ground, wondering if he should take Ronin to the doctor or the hoosegow. He was tired of it as well, but abusing a man in custody wasn't something he wanted to explain to his sheriff.

Emma spoke first. "Happy Hands," she asked, placing her hand on Ronin's forearm, "is there anything you can do?"

The Washoe's head turned quickly, surprised by the Christian woman's request for assistance. Perhaps she was a good person after all, he thought, smiling. "There is much I can do, my mother. But most of what needs to be done is up to Mister Ronin."

Chapter 27
CRUMS AROUND A TABLE

Leonard Crum stood eating a sandwich alongside a flat rock on the south shore of Lake Tahoe. The gray, table-like slab of granite was situated in the midst of a lakeside boulder field just a few feet across the California-Nevada state line, if a reliable line could be drawn, which Crum didn't think so. Leonard had been told it was the very rock on which Mark Twain had penciled the famous words, "The fairest picture the whole earth affords," though he didn't know how anybody could know that, given that Twain had written a great many things about places he had visited and he wasn't there to say so.

Though Leonard's brother Larry could be trusted to know the value of a horse, tool or piece of jewelry — skills that had made them more than a little bit of money when they lived on a slide above the eastern slope towns of Franktown, Washoe City and Galena — it had been a while since the brothers had traded on the misery of folks in northern Nevada. Burglaries among the broken-down houses and businesses in the Washoe Valley had been strong enough to support the Crums in a manner they thought their parents would have been proud of. But as the valley's mills began to close — the Virginia and Truckee Railroad skirting the east side of the mountains *through* the valley instead of *to* the valley — the people who could afford to moved to either end of the line. Carson City for some, Reno for others, the point being that the Crum brothers' opportunities for economic gain became fewer and farther between.

Leonard didn't mind, especially since Larry's intuitive sense of where the money was turned out to be correct. Folks traveling to and from the lake from points east and west posed a new and better opportunity. Sightseers and other travelers typically carried cash, and cash was king.

The younger Crum brother sat down to think, tossing small bites of what was left of his sandwich to seagulls that were attracted to his food.

Before coming to California, the Crum brothers had owned a bakery in Logan, Utah, just north of Salt Lake City. The bakery had actually been owned by their parents, Bill and Diane, who were proud of their boys and had hoped that someday the two of them might take over their enterprise. "We Make Good Bread," the sign said, just above their names, "Larry and Leonard Crumb." The brothers dropped the "b" from the spelling of their last names, as it had been the butt of jokes by customers who tried to imagine what it meant to have two toddlers making bread in the early hours of the morning, when "the children ought to be sleeping" they said, which of course they were. It was the hope and dream of their parents that the two boys — the older boy, handsome and the younger one, not so much — would someday work in the bakery and pastry shop that bore their names. The mere mention and repetition of the saying, "crumbs don't fall too far from the master's table," a thoughtless Biblical proverb that entailed the little crumbs being eaten by a much bigger family dog, was enough to drive both boys away from the family home and dreams. They didn't stop until they hit the Sierras.

Now, Larry was likely sitting in a Carson City jail, booked under the last name of Banderas, the result of a ruse they were playing in the mountains above Carson City so as to keep their identities secret.

Larry had read that on more than a few occasions, early settlers in Nevada had pretended to be Indians by dropping arrows by and into the bodies of their victims. "There was nothing new under the sun," Larry said when suggesting that they darken their faces — already dark enough due to living outside in the Nevada sun — and dress as Mexicans so as to be better bandits. "It doesn't take a military man to figure out how to get away with murder," Larry said, arguing that the reference was a fair one given that it had been white soldiers who had done the murdering in the Mexican-American conflict that had resulted in six new American states, including Texas, which neither of them had ever visited but instinctively disliked.

Whatever the case, as the particulars didn't much matter to him, Leonard liked the big hats and silver conchos they got to wear, and occasionally left behind, so as to make people think Mexicans were doing the robberies and killings. The money was good enough for Larry to continue being a member of the Masonic Lodge *2 in Washoe City, a part of "Grand Lodge of Nevada," as it was called, given the distance from their sponsoring brethren in California. Larry had been raised to the sublime degree of Master Mason a few years back, and was due to become the Most Worshipful Grand Master of the lodge. Eighty-some men were still on the rolls, though it had been a while since anyone had counted the active ones, and Larry was one of the few who had received a lambskin apron. Most of the men wore canvas.

"The Holy Bible, square and compass," Larry used to say, though Leonard didn't understand what any of that meant. "They're our guide," he often explained when they weren't out robbing and killing or wearing Mexican clothing. "Someday I might sponsor you as a member," he'd say, not being able to invite Leonard to join without his first asking.

It was beginning to get dark and Leonard needed to figure out what he was going to do. Picking up his saddle bags, he headed over to the canvas fly he and his brother had tied between two pine trees to protect themselves from evening breezes that sometimes blew across the lake. He had seen what had happened to his brother and had stood by the bodies in amazement after the lawman had left. Figuring out what to do wasn't what he normally did for the seven or so men who were riding with them — the numbers went up and down, depending on the job — but standing over their bodies and taking their firearms and other valuables before heading back to camp to think was what he had to do. It was what his brother would expect him to do.

"The compass doesn't just remind us of God's unerring and impartial justice," Larry had said on more than one occasion, "it reminds us to measure and to plan. Good things come to those who think before doing," he'd said. "It's also one of the ways we honor our parents," he'd pointed out, having heard that his mother and father had perished in a bakery fire shortly after their leaving Logan. Indians had burned the bakery to the ground, though there was some question whether Indians or Mormons were responsible, given that there were so few Indians in Logan and that their parents were a religious minority in an otherwise saint-filled town. "Might have been Paiutes," someone had said, "or Shoshone, or maybe even the Ute tribe," they had been told by members of the church. "It's hard to say," Mormon elders in Carson City had told the boys, when they had inquired. "Stranger things have happened."

In any case, it was important to plan before heading into Carson City to find Larry. Leonard had buried the seven men by a stand of trees behind the old way station, "good men," Larry had said about the out-of-work logging crew from Alpine County. It was something he knew he should do, after removing valuables and particulars that might give their identities away.

Leonard didn't know what he was going to do until the sun came up the next morning, and the saw mills at Glenbrook began to whine and hum.

Chapter 28
DOCTOR'S OFFICE

"Well, it seems to me, Emma, that Ronin ought not be going anywhere until we have some sense of what's going on." Quinn quietly put his examination instruments away as his patient, the former Reverend W. W. Ronin, rested on an examining table. He had only seen the man in a professional sense a couple of times, initially when the ex-reverend's leg was broken, and then on a follow-up visit at the mission, when his patient had refused to leave the mission to visit him in town.

"It's too cold outside," he had said, or so Emma said, it being the middle of winter though she had come to understand that Ronin simply didn't like doctors, or better stated, what doctors did. "I don't get involved in people's lives willy-nilly," he had subsequently explained, suggesting that doctors, dentists and pastors as well seemed to make it a point to offer their ministrations so as to feel good or to make money. "If somebody needs my attention," Ronin pointed out, "I generally give it to them. The bad ones end up with their bodies broken or their lives shortened."

Despite her look of surprise, he had continued, "I don't string things along and I don't understand why these men do, either," he said, speaking about the Reverend George Davis in particular, who had come to visit him from the Saint Peter's Episcopal Church while he was at the mission recuperating. "I don't need the attention," he had told Davis. "And I don't need the doctor's attention either," he said. "And if there's a dentist lurking nearby, tell him to go to hell also." He hadn't really meant to say it that way — the words seemed cruel when considered alone — but when they came out of his mouth, they had a certain weight to them. Over the three months he was mending at the mission, Emma had learned to give him space as well.

"He's not a man who can be controlled, Amos," Emma said, before noticing that Ronin had fallen completely asleep on the wooden exam table. She put her hand on his arm and shook him. "Did you give him something?" she asked, surprised, as he had only been resting a few moments before.

"No, of course not," Quinn responded quickly, putting down his equipment and grabbing a small vile of ammonium carbonate from his medicine closet. Emma looked at him sharply. "These are only smelling salts, Emma. I'm going to wake him."

Happy Hands, who had been sitting quietly by the office window, watching Ronin sleep, jumped to his feet and grabbed the bottle from the doctor's hands. "Would it be so wrong for the man to sleep here for a while?"

The whole situation made Quinn anxious.

Dinner with Emma Nauman might be a nice evening, he had thought earlier that afternoon when she had suggested they give the Ormsby House's Supper Club a try. They hadn't been out before, and while the dinner date might cause some people to talk, it wasn't as if he was cavorting about with loose women like a certain rich banker on the Comstock.

Taking the brief stroll from his office to the Ormsby House on Second Street, they ran into Ronin, on whom she so clearly had a crush, not that it was any of his business, and not that dinner was any kind of commitment. Then, sitting there with Ronin, the portly deputy whom he had counseled many times to lose some weight. "It will help the pain in your knees," he had suggested over many appointments where the deputy had sought his advice, to either lose weight or to fix the advancing symptoms to which his being overweight had contributed. Then to sit there listening to the Washoe man — not that he had an issue with Indians, he simply didn't understand them — telling him about being a Washoe holy man, whatever that was, while flustering over all the extra utensils the Supper Club typically provided. Well, he was simply finished, done, over it all and didn't want to hear anything more about any of it.

"I'm fine with his sleeping here," he said to Emma and the Indian, "as long as I don't have to stay here too." he said. "In fact, I'm not feeling all that well myself, Happy Hands, if you'll excuse me. If you would lock the office when you're finished, I'll pick up when I open back up in the morning." Then nodding to Emma — who he didn't understand either, except to note that she was an attractive woman who didn't wear a lot of extra hoops and bustles in a western city where woman seemed to think there might be a need for a fashion show now and then — he closed the door behind him and breathed a quiet sigh of relief.

He walked out onto Carson Street. It was about a half hour after 10 p.m. If he hurried, he might be able to enjoy a solitary cigar and brandy on his back porch before turning in for the night.

Chapter 29

WHILE SNOOZING

Emma watched the doctor leave and wondered what she might have said to have gotten Quinn so upset. Things had gone so well earlier in the evening, she thought, looking at Happy Hands, who in response simply shrugged. Maybe Quinn had misunderstood. It wasn't as if they were keeping company or courting, though the cup of coffee she had offered him a few months back at the mission might have been taken as an invitation. Perhaps the simple stroll from Quinn's office to the Ormsby House stirred him to thinking there was something more between them.

Ronin's jaw dropped open as he began to snore on the examining table. Happy Hands seemed pleased with himself, though she couldn't understand why. What was the big deal about rousing him with the smelling salts? They had been used since Biblical times.

"Happy Hands," she whispered, "what are we doing here?"

"We are watching the man sleep, my mother. He is dreaming. Do you not see his hands moving?"

She walked over to the window where Happy Hands was and sat down beside him. Ronin was lying on the same table he had been when she had first noticed him nearly a year before. She had fallen off her horse out front the Ormsby County sheriff's office and deputies had brought her to Quinn's office to see what was wrong. It was the day, or day after, her husband's leaving. She was confused and not at all feeling well, and was fortunate to meet a physician who understood that not everything that bothered people was physical in nature. Some of it was spiritual, or emotional, she thought, though she didn't know where Quinn stood with the such things. Someday she'd ask.

"How do you know that he's dreaming?" she asked, watching Ronin sleep.

"His hands, Mrs. Nauman. They're moving as if he's being pursued, which of course he is," he said smiling, though he didn't expect her to understand.

"Pursued?"

"Surely you know this," he said, though he didn't think she did. Helping a student save face while learning the deeper things of the spirit was an important aspect of mentoring someone along the journey. "When a power or spirit comes to a man, as he has come to Ronin, he becomes ill. It is nearly always this way, though it was not this way with my uncle," he said smiling. "When I was first called, a bear used to come and stare at me."

"A real bear?" she asked.

"Who can say?" Happy Hands responded. "What is real to you is not necessarily real to me. This happened many times," he continued, "and sometimes I would fly up into the sky."

She remembered flying in her dreams as a child. Jesus would come to her and take her by the hand, and sometimes he'd even speak to her. "It's not your time," he'd say, a phrase that had stuck with her over the years suggesting that maybe some things were planned out, happened as they were supposed to happen, though she couldn't fit all of her life in that frame of mind. Her husband's leaving, for instance, and the difference between what she felt toward Ronin and he, apparently anyway, didn't feel toward her, at least not in the way she wanted it to be.

"Do you think Ronin is a holy man?" Emma asked.

"Only he knows, my mother. But this I do know. Something is troubling him. And if it's a spirit, he will need to find a spiritual friend to help him find his way."

Emma swallowed hard. She had attempted to be his spiritual friend. But too much came between them, she thought, not the least of which were her feelings. If she had her way, he would become her husband, and they would work to fulfill the dream that God had first given her when she and Henry were perched on a knoll overlooking the Carson Valley. Ronin was a hard man to get close to, in every sense.

"Perhaps you are that friend, Happy Hands."

"Perhaps. Only Ronin knows."

Emma sat for a few moments, considering the evening's events and what Happy Hands had said, as Ronin continued to sleep and dream. She heard a clock chime in the front room of Quinn's office. Realizing it was an hour short of midnight, she stood as Dustsucker appeared, knocking at the front room's door. "Miss Emma," Dustsucker said, entering, "it occurred to me that you might need someone to accompany you home. May I?"

"Of course, Dusty. Happy Hands, are you able to remain the night if he takes that long?" Looking over at her Indian friend, she found him curled up in a chair, already sleeping.

Chapter 30
CONVERSATION

Ronin woke choking from a nose bleed. Sitting up, he pinched his nostrils shut and held them together briefly before looking around the room for a towel or cloth. He found a green hand towel on the table next to him and, picking it up, was immediately aware of the Washoe holy man staring at him, smiling.

"What's so funny?" he asked, folding the towel in half and wiping the blood that was clinging to his nose.

"Nothing," Happy Hands said quietly, having tucked himself into the shadows of Quinn's examining room, sitting on the floor with his back against the short wall behind one of the glazed glass double doors. "I put that towel there, hoping that you would need it. The fact that you do is a sign that your dream was real."

Ronin opened the towel and looked. Not seeing a great deal of blood, he folded it again and began to dab at the sweat beads on his forehead. The bleeding was no big deal, he figured. It was the sweating that concerned him, as the temperature in the room felt chilly.

"I've had a lot of nose bleeds, my friend. In fact, there have been very few nights since coming to Carson City that I haven't had to clean up a bit upon wakening." He looked around the room before continuing. "It's a dry climate, you know. This looks like Quinn's examining room," he said. "Where is everyone? And what time is it?"

"It is the middle of the night, William," Happy Hands replied, never having called him that before, but having heard the mission woman refer to him in that way. Ronin shot him a surprised glance. "Miss Emma has gone home. The deputy sheriff accompanied her there, as it was late," he said as Ronin winced. "The doctor has left as well. He too seemed upset."

"Upset?" Ronin asked, looking for a place to toss the towel before settling on a corner of the floor by the physician's medicine cabinet. Happy Hands watched Ronin slide off the edge of the table and steady himself with his left hand. It took a few moments before he was able to stand unaided. "I'm still feeling woozy, my friend. How about you?" he asked, thinking that maybe he had eaten something that had made him ill, before remembering that he hadn't had anything to eat that evening. Perhaps that was the issue.

"Ronin, you should sit down. We have much to talk about. You should tell me about your dream, for instance."

The man tracker couldn't remember dreaming, though when he wakened, he was convinced he was being choked. "I wasn't dreaming," he said, "and you still haven't told me why we are here."

"You didn't ask, my friend." The words had a nice ring to them, and Ronin seemed to use the words freely. It was important to use a student's words instead of one's own, especially when attempting to explain something difficult. "You were kicking a man when your face grew bright red, my friend. The man everyone thought was a Mexican. He really lives in the valley, you know."

"Stop calling me your friend."

"Am I not?"

"Does it really matter?"

"The truth always matters, Mister Ronin, and facing it may be the most important thing a person ever does."

"Jesus, Happy Hands. Go see if you can find the doctor. My head is spinning again ... and I don't know ... what I'm ... going ... to ..."

Ronin crumpled at the base of the examining table. Happy Hands leaned forward and pulled Ronin toward him. He set the ex-reverend's head in his lap and began to stroke his heart. "This is an important journey you are going on, my friend. It is not to be taken lightly," he whispered, not expecting Ronin to hear him. But he knew that the spirit, or spirits, that were troubling Ronin would hear him. Happy Hands held him closely throughout the night and continued praying, so as to put them on notice.

Chapter 31

MULLER'S FOR BREAKFAST

It was about 10 a.m. when Ronin stirred again. Looking out Quinn's examining room window, he saw Happy Hands and Dustsucker sitting on the porch of the Muller Hotel a few buildings north eating breakfast. A tall man had his back turned to him. It appeared to be Marshal Augustus Ash from Virginia City.

Lena Muller set down a loaf of bread. "Mister Slade, we may not be the nicest hotel on this block, but we still don't tolerate a man sitting at breakfast wearing his hat."

"I'm sorry, ma'am. I plumb forgot," he said, looking around the porch where a half-dozen wood cutters from Glenbrook were enjoying their meals with their hats in their lap. "You run a nice establishment, Mrs. Muller. I've always enjoyed it," he said, hoping to mend the proprietor's opinion of him.

"It's not the St. Charles, Marcus. And the prices probably reflect that. But we like it this way. You know I don't tolerate a messy room."

"No ma'am, you don't."

"Who do you have with you today?" Lena asked, noting the Indian but thinking nothing of it.

"This is Marshal Ash, of course."

"Good to see you again, Marshal."

"Ma'am." Ash tipped his hat.

"And this is Happy Hands, a Washoe friend from the valley."

"Mister Hands, nice to meet you," she smiled.

Happy Hands smiled.

Ronin exited the St. Charles Hotel, where Quinn and another physician had their offices next to the Pioneer Stage Company, and tipped his hat to his friends, who were seated next door. "Good morning," he said, taking his hat off when Dustsucker motioned toward it with his eyes.

"What can I get you, Mister Ronin?" Lena Muller asked. "The flap jacks are good this morning."

"That'll be fine," he replied, smiling meekly at Happy Hands and Dustsucker and nodding toward Marshal Ash.

"Your horse is in the St. Charles' Carriage House, Ronin. I didn't know what arrangement you had," Dustsucker said, pointing with his thumb to Third Street, where the hotel's proprietor George Tuffy had built a reasonable livery and Chinese laundry.

"It's typically at Benton's," Ronin said, "I guess I left Jackson tethered to a post at the jail, is that right?" he asked. "I don't know what happened to me last night. I wasn't feeling good at all. Thank you."

"Don't mention it," Dustsucker and Happy Hands said simultaneously.

Ash looked up from his food. "Something happen last night?"

"Well, yes, actually," Dustsucker commented before saying "the same" to Mrs. Mueller, who now had all of the orders from their table. "You'll remember I was telling you about picking up a man named Banderas up the mountain a ways. Some of his friends had tried to rob Ronin and me. We killed six or so ..."

"Eight, I think is what you told me last."

"Right, eight. Six of them standing in front of us and two others who came up to us afterward," Dustsucker continued.

"Well, the ninth man we put in the hoosegow here in Carson City, for attempted murder, robbery and so on. He got loose somehow last night."

"And?" Ash asked, looking concerned.

"And I found him," Happy Hands interjected, "hiding in some bushes."

Ash looked over at the Indian, who he didn't have any personal issues with but whose views he'd generally discounted, even before the Washoe kidnappings. Happy Hands liked to spin a good story and, like Ash's German relatives, typically left the important parts of the story until the end. It was aggravating. "You found him?" he asked, sighing aloud.

"I did."

"Well, good for you, Happy Hands. Kind of makes up for not telling us about the Clancy brothers living at the Bowers Mansion." Ash wasn't one to forget.

"I wouldn't be too hard on the man, Ash. He's come in handy, you know," Dustsucker responded. "So, as I was about to say, we caught up to the guy, and found out his real name is Larry Crum, not Banderas, and we re-situated him in the county lockup before telegraphing you last night.

"I appreciate that," Ash said. "I took the train in this morning to help out. In fact, Mister Ronin, I was talking to one of the businessmen in Virginia City a couple of days back and he'd like to meet you. He thinks we might be able to help each other."

"Don't know much about Virginia City businessmen, Ash, save a couple of bankers, that is and a crystal ball gazer or two."

"Ball gazers?" Ash erupted into laughter, struggling to regain his composure. "Well, I'm hardly talking big time here, Ronin. But he'd already heard about you, after you plugged a couple of men in his saloon a few months back, and given your performance at the Lake House in Reno and Bowers Mansion getting those kids back, he thinks he and you might have something in common."

"Don't know what that might be and I don't suspect I'll be getting up to Virginia City very soon, given what's gone on at the lake. I've made a personal commitment to look into that, Ash. While you're here, can you tell us anything about that?"

"Just that I heard there were two, not three men as first reported, and that they were Washoe. Slade, I'm assuming your agency has taken an interest?"

"Not hardly, Augustus," Dustsucker said. "Sad to say, the sheriff drags his feet a bit when there are Indians involved. There's been some discussion of the Washoe having their own police, but there are so few of them and the federal government doesn't seem to be much interested."

"Not that I've heard," Ash responded. "So your office hasn't done anything with this yet?"

"No," Dustsucker said, looking embarrassed. "When Ronin said he'd be heading up that way to have a couple of beers lakeside and maybe look into the matter, I'm afraid the sheriff figured it was taken care of."

"Jesus ..." the marshal responded. "Well, how about the three of us head to Glenbrook and poke around. If someone is killing Indians up the lake, they might just as easily begin killing white men," Ash said. "No offense meant, Happy Hands."

"None taken, marshal."

Ronin's hotcakes arrived first.

The St. Charles and Muller's hotels sat adjacent to each other. Both multi-story brick structures on Carson Street, Muller's catered more to the working class. Food was cheaper and the pancakes were bigger, Dustsucker had pointed out, when Ronin and he had first eaten there a couple of months before. Besides, Muller's wife was a professional cook and baker. And while the St. Charles offered "the finest saloon in Carson," as one of the original proprietors had said — some still believing that — both Dustsucker and Ronin had found it pretentious. George Haswell, a former deputy sheriff from Sacramento and proprietor of the establishment, could be counted on to fill them in on what was happening with the capitol's legislators and losers, both of whom seemed to congregate there. When violence took place at the St. Charles, Haswell could be counted on to lend a hand.

Everyone else's food arrived shortly after Ronin's when Happy Hands said, "Mister Ronin and I have been discussing about my going along."

"I have?" Ronin asked, remembering that the matter had come up, though he didn't recall their having come to any agreement.

"We have."

"And why is that?" Ash asked, remembering that the Indian hadn't been of much help when the children were recovered at the Bowers Mansion. The damn Indian hadn't even noticed the children living there.

"Where you are going is holy land, my friends," Happy Hands spoke. Everyone's eyes looked up.

"Holy land?" Ronin laughed, thinking the Indian was initially talking about Glenbrook. The Comstock's New Jerusalem, the new development around the lake had become quite hoity-toity. "Glenbrook? Hardly, my friend," he offered.

"No, Ronin. Cave Rock."

Ronin felt suddenly nauseous. "Excuse me, everyone," he said, abruptly standing. "I'm not feeling totally well yet, I guess."

"Sit, Mister Ronin," Happy Hands said. "You need to hear this."

Chapter 32

CAVE ROCK

"There were never many of us," Happy Hands said, picking up his butter knife and spinning it on its tip. The knife fell over after a few whirls, but not before it caught the attention of everyone at the table. "But the Washoe people were special in the Creator's eyes," he continued, looking at Dustsucker, whose attention seemed to be glued to the butter knife, which was now balanced precariously, almost magically, on its spine. "When the white man came to our valley, our people scattered. Some traveled north; some traveled south. Now there are very few of us."

"I'm sitting, Happy Hands," Ronin interrupted, unimpressed by the Washoe man's butter knife trick. He grabbed it, put it to the right side of Happy Hands' plate and picked up the Indian's napkin, gesturing that it should sit in his lap, not on his plate. "But I've got to tell you, my friend. I'm wondering why I'm listening to this."

"Because we are not so special now," Happy Hands chipped back, raising his voice. "Did you know that when land was handed out to all of these people," he gestured to diners in the restaurant as well as passerby on both sides of Carson Street, "we were not given anywhere to live?"

Dustsucker thought of the ruling in 1866, a couple years after his arrival in Carson City, where the Superintendent for Indian Affairs said there weren't enough Washoe Indians to consider giving them reservation lands. A couple more years, he said, and the Washoe would likely not exist. Dustsucker began to mumble that he had talked to the Bureau of Indian Affairs at one point, and that the two of them were thinking that in time something might be done to give the Washoe ranch land south of the city. He didn't believe the story, circulated by many in the valley that Genoa had first been traded to white men for a couple sacks of flour. Ash opened his mouth first.

"Happy Hands, please get to the point. None of these people had anything given to them." Ash nodded to people walking on Carson Street. "What they have, they worked for. You could have just as much if you worked for it, Happy Hands!"

"What they have, Marshal Ash, they took, from people like me."

"Okay ... " It was clear Ash didn't want to argue. He regarded Happy Hands as lazy, evidenced by the fact that he was wearing someone else's cloths — the Washoe had long given up wearing traditional dress — and was squatting in someone else's house outside Washoe City. It didn't matter to Ash that the house was abandoned and that many other dwellings in the valley were just as empty and aching for new occupants.

"We did not own these things, my friend, but we used them. This valley was a part of our stewardship," he said, picking up a cup of tea and blowing on it. Ronin noticed he was more at ease with the table's accoutrements than he remembered him being the night before. He gained a little more appreciation for the knife spinning act and wondered if Happy Hands had used it purposefully to get everyone's attention. "When the white man streamed through this valley on their way to the pine nut mountains and beyond, he didn't only take silver and gold out of the hills, he took our way of life."

"That's true," Dustsucker said, "and maybe someday someone will be able to do something about that, Happy Hands. But I'm with these gentlemen; I don't know what you're getting at."

"We were here thousands of years before the white men came," Happy Hands continued, "and in less than a dozen years, maybe even a half-dozen years, our way of life was gone. We were driven off the land. Our forests were cut down. Our fish and game were killed, and much of what was done was not even used," he said. "It still lays littered across the land." He paused and made sure he had caught Ash's attention. "Then you employed us as servants, farmers and tour guides," he smiled. The Indian's eyes suggested certain sadness. Happy Hands was just getting started, when Emma Nauman unexpectedly walked onto the restaurant's patio.

"I heard you were here!" she exclaimed, nodding to everyone. She locked her eyes on Ronin and curtseyed, holding the folds of her dress out to either side. She waited for a response.

"Um ... we are at that, Emma," he stuttered, before Happy Hands interrupted the interruption.

"I was just about to tell everyone a story," he said, patting the chair beside him. "Why shouldn't a beautiful woman sit beside me?" Happy Hands smiled.

"Certainly, I'm happy to see that you noticed. It seems Mister Ronin made it through the night," she said coolly. "Did everything go well?"

"It did," Happy Hands replied. "Mister Ronin had many dreams, but hasn't shared any of them yet, and I believe he's beginning to feel much better. Aren't you, William?"

William heard his name being spoken and wondered for a moment what he'd have to do to convince Dustsucker's Indian friend to stop using it, when he noticed that he was, in fact, feeling better. The nausea that had caused him to suddenly stand a few moments ago had passed, and his headache seemed almost gone. He nodded briefly, before turning his attention back to Emma.

"You look radiant today, Miss Emma. I believe that's a new dress," he said.

Dustsucker looked up, hearing the name he always called Emma on someone else's lips.

"I mean, you seem refreshed and ... what a lovely dress," he stumbled, staring at its bodice, which seemed more bare and bigger than he had noticed before. "It's blue, isn't it?"

"Yes, Mister Ronin, it's blue," she said, giving up hope that the man she couldn't help thinking about might have something more endearing to say.

"Ronin," Happy Hands began. Ronin looked away. His face was flushed.

"There was a day, before the many days, when the Maker of All Things was counting out seeds that were to become the different peoples of the world. He spread them out in a large winnowing tray, setting so much to one side and an equal amount to another. The Creator made other piles as well," he continued, "counting them out equally. But suddenly, the west wind — which is always a trickster — waved his hand and scattered the seeds everywhere."

"Jesus," Ronin complained, "I've heard enough. I don't like to listen to these stories in church. I hardly think I have to listen to them over breakfast."

Emma looked at him, sternly. "Go on, Happy Hands," she said.

"Most of the seeds fell to the east, where a great many peoples now live. But the seeds that were to have been the Washoe people? They were scattered, blown away by a mischievous spirit. That is why there are so few of us."

Happy Hands finished, placing his tea cup down and his hands into his lap. He looked over at a server, hoping that he would notice that he wanted more tea.

Ash broke the table's silence. "And your reason for telling us this, Happy Hands?" he sighed. The Washoe man turned and looked at the marshal. It wasn't as if the marshal was always sneering at him; it was simply that he discounted him. It didn't appear to be personal. He treated him as if he was any Indian, which of course he was, which was perhaps the point.

"That is why you have not done anything about our people, marshal. We are too few, too unimportant and because of that, there are two men at Lake Tahoe, laying dead and unburied."

"You know these men?" Ash asked.

"No, but I know their spirits. They want us to meet them at the Standing Grey Stone."

Ash looked at the Indian for a moment, while the three others at the table conversed about the rock most people called Cave Rock. "For thousands of years," he thought he heard Dustsucker say, but his mind was elsewhere. It wasn't a careful thing to reveal details of a crime to individuals who might later turn out to be suspects. It ruined the chain of evidence, Ash had told Thomas Kelly once, who was acting as his deputy in a difficult investigation in Gold Hill. Kelly at the time was Police Chief in Virginia City. Kelly's department hadn't preserved a crime scene's details adequately enough. People outside the investigation, even the damn newspaper, had picked up aspects of his investigation that might have been useful later in identifying the crime's perpetrators.

Ash looked at Emma, the missionary lady. She clearly she hadn't been involved, given the amount of time she spent talking about "someday getting up to the lake and riding on one of those steam ships." He imagined she was fishing for Ronin to take her there, not that it mattered. Similarly, Dustsucker was too honest a man to say one thing and do another. Then there was Ronin — the son of a bitch was simply too mean to be killing Indians. If a trail of dead men were to appear, they'd certainly be white and they would deserve their fate. Could Happy Hands be trusted? Happy Hands' guilt seemed unlikely.

"Happy Hands, that's just pure malarkey!" Ash exclaimed. "No one was killed at Cave Rock. The men were murdered elsewhere!"

Happy Hands looked again at the marshal and wondered if he had misjudged him. How did the marshal know where the murders had been committed? He knew, because the men had told him so in a dream. Could he trust the marshal to keep their confidence? Did he have the right to share what he knew? Would their spirits be pleased? He decided he could trust the man.

"Since we're talking marshal, the murders occurred at Glenbrook. The men told me that. They were murdered at the end of the pier. They were beaten and then drowned. Furthermore, I am not the only that knows this. You know this as well."

No one knows that, the marshal thought, except himself. Not even the Ormsby County sheriffs understood that the examination of the men had been sent via telegraph from Glenbrook, directly to his office in Virginia City, and that the remains of the men showed bruises, despite being fished out of the lake. "You are under arrest, my friend, for the murders of ..."

Dustsucker erupted, "Whoa, whoa, whoa! Are you kidding me, Ash? This guy hasn't done anything! Look at him!"

Happy Hands sat with his hands clasped in his lap, a horrified look on his face. He hoped the marshal wouldn't utter their names as speaking their names would call their spirits. His nighttime dreams were already a mess, and Ronin's even more so.

"You can be sure of that?" Ash paused, taking his handcuffs from his belt and placing them on the table before facing the deputy.

"As sure as I am that my pancakes are getting colder every minute this damn story goes on!" It was rare that Slade cursed, Emma thought, wincing. Ronin held his breath, noticing Emma's pain.

"Deputy," Emma whispered.

"I'm sorry, Miss Emma," Dustsucker replied. Ronin looked over at his friend, relaxed his shoulders and smiled.

"Marshal Ash," Happy Hands continued, "I only tell you these things because their spirits told me to. And as for where and how they were murdered, you and I, and the man called Bliss, are the only ones who know about it. He was the one who told you, my friend."

Marshal Ash was not Happy Hands' friend and Happy Hands knew it. But he used the word out of discipline. It was important to know the truth. It was also important not to hate those who were part of the truth.

"Okay, that's spooky," Ash replied, wondering how an Indian would know about the telegraph from Bliss' Glenbrook home. "I'll tell you what," he said, pausing a moment to check his feelings and think. "How about the four of us head up to Glenbrook and have a conversation?" he said, looking at Slade who was beginning to shovel the remainder of his breakfast into his mouth as fast as his mouth could accommodate.

"The souls of the dead travel south, my friend. And they are waiting for us to meet them at the Standing Grey Stone."

"Then we'll head to Glenbrook first, to visit with the vigilance committee who found the bodies. And then if we need to, we can ride over to Cave Rock."

Ronin's stomach groaned loudly enough for everyone to hear.

Chapter 33
BENTON'S

It was 8 a.m. when Ronin rolled out of bed and crossed the street to the Lake Tahoe Stage Office at Benton's Livery and Stable. The plan was to meet a few minutes earlier than the Glenbrook coach's departing time, and to spend those moments interviewing Larry Crum. The marshal wanted to question Crum regarding any possible involvement in, or knowledge of, the Tahoe murders. As he had been uncooperative thus far, Ronin suggested that a fresh face, in the form of a certain U.S. Marshal, might cause Crum to take a more conversational tone.

"Ronin," nodded the marshal as he stepped onto the boardwalk on Carson Street. Ash was seated on a wooden bench just north of the two-story stone building's doorway, shadowed from the sun just cresting the Carson range.

"Marshal," Ronin echoed, tossing Ash an apple and taking a toothpick from his mouth so as to take a bite of his own. "No time for breakfast, I guess. I thought you might appreciate this from the Ormsby House lobby."

"Now you're sounding like Deputy Slade, William," the marshal quipped, pushing his white linen duster back behind his gun to grab a handkerchief, "or should I call you 'reverend'?"

Ronin bristled, looking up from beneath his hat. "I thought we covered that a couple of months ago?" He spit out his toothpick. "It seems to me I had my thumb in your eye at the time."

"Yeah, or something like that," the marshal responded. Ash took a small bone-handled knife from his gun belt after wiping his apple, and began to whittle. "I appreciate it, Ronin. We all have our pasts," he said laughing. "I'm a bear to be with until I get something to eat in the morning. I'm sorry about that."

"Yeah, I'm the same," Ronin replied, taking a bite out of his apple while looking for the toothpick he had spat.

"What do you think is going to come from talking to this Crum fellow?" Ash asked.

"Well, he's perhaps the most contrary man I've met, Augustus," he replied, locating the toothpick on Benton's plate glass picture window. "I've hit or kicked him everywhere but Sunday in the course of getting him into the county lock-up ..."

"Hit or kicked him?" Ash asked, surprised to hear that the prisoner had been beaten.

"Yeah," Ronin responded, looking at the marshal. "Maybe you have a problem with that?" Ronin waited before continuing. "As I said, he's quite the contrarian and doesn't seem to want to let go of anything." He took a step toward the window and raised his hand as if he was going to remove the toothpick from the window, but hesitated. "He mentioned Glenbrook, you know."

"Yeah, I heard," Ash said. He slipped his knife back into its sheath and threw a perfectly cut spiral peel into the street. "Funny how neither of you said anything."

Ronin turned, leaving the toothpick where it had landed, underscoring the letters "Bent," just under the name "Benton's." Ronin smiled. "I figured it wasn't my information to share, Augustus, and you didn't ask. One of us would have gotten around to it at some point," Ronin said, thinking of the marshal's sudden disclosure to the Indian that the dead Washoe men were killed at Glenbrook. "Why tell everyone where they were killed?"

"Vigilance Committee fished them out of the water at the end of the Glenbrook pier. Figured you'd all find out sooner or later."

"Jesus," Ronin said. He wondered how a couple of Indians would find their way to what had to be one of the more exclusive spots on the lake. "Where they drinking?" he asked, remembering

that Glenbrook had been dry, despite some of the larger boat owners on the lake attempting to establish a creative alternative by
mooring up to the pier and offering a variety of alcoholic libations
onboard. "I thought Glenbrook didn't allow alcohol."

"Yup, me too. Seems that Captain Pray is getting up there
in years. He's the oldest guy at the lake, I think. Anyway, the
town is due to have a saloon or two by the end of next year. So it
goes, I figure."

"Guess so," Ronin said, spotting Dustsucker and Spinnaker
heading their way. Crum was in hand and leg irons and was situated between them.

"You've got apples?" Dustsucker hollered from across the
street.

"No. Did have, don't any longer," Ronin hollered back as
his friend came closer. "Apologies though, I should have thought
ahead."

"It's no problem," he said, holding onto his prisoner by suck-
ing up his arm close to his chest. Spinnaker was doing the same,
but was having trouble because of a large canvas bag trailing over
his left shoulder. "We brought some food, probably enough for all
of us. The trip is four hours long, if I remember correctly."

"Yup," Ash said. Suddenly, without warning, Ash grabbed
Crum by the front of his shirt and swung him onto the boards.
Crum crumpled to the boardwalk cursing, whereupon Ash imme-
diately stepped onto his right shin, causing him to scream in pain.

"Jesus, marshal!" Ronin grabbed Ash's arms and pulled
him away. Dustsucker stepped in between the two of them.

"Ash, knock it off!"

The U.S. district marshal put his hands up and stepped
back. "I'm just trying to get this man to tell me what the hell
is going on! If he's going to waste my time, he's going to feel a
little bit of what I'm feeling, having to go to Lake Tahoe and not
knowing shit."

"Fine, Augustus. But I'll not have my prisoner abused!"

"Hell you won't!" Ash yelled, breaking free of Ronin's grasp and pushing Slade out of the way. He raised his foot to stomp on Crum's private areas as Ronin slammed into him, knocking him into the wall. Ash looked at Ronin and winked.

"Okay, okay!" Larry Crum pleaded, hiding his face with his hands. "Just keep this crazy man away from me!" he yelled. He looked over at Ronin, who was smiling. "Help me up, and get me a cup of coffee. I'll tell you what I know."

"Fine," Ash replied, pulling his coat around him, hiding his firearms. "It's about time you said something worth listening to."

Chapter 34

CONVERSATION

"Tell me again why you've got a person screaming outside my place of business!" Benton hollered, running through his doors onto Carson Street. "I mean really, marsha! Is there any reason you've decided my boardwalk should be the site for your carnival show instead of some other?"

"My apologies, Doc," Ash muttered, picking Crum up and sitting him down on the bench. "My enthusiasm got the best of me. Since you're here, four or five of us are going to want passage on the lake stage this morning, if you've got room."

"Well, which is it? Four or five, marshal? The last thing I need to be doing this morning is trying to figure out your comings and goings," Benton said, handing a raft of papers to two of his drivers. "Don't make me stand here with my mouth open, marshal. I've got a business to run." Benton stood there, tapping his feet.

"Well," Ash replied, a little chagrinned. "How about you give us a couple of moments to confer together and we'll be in?"

"Good enough, just keep it down." Benton shut the doors after shoving his two drivers back inside.

"Doc used to be a surgeon, Augustus. It's either cut or no cut, you know what I mean? And I'm sure he's a little sensitive to the screaming," Slade explained, having become acquainted with James Woodward Benton in 1864, when he'd arrived in Dayton, Nevada a few miles east of town. He'd owned a mill in Silver City and done some prospecting. Slade had heard about him selling liniment oil and mineral water prior to opening his livery, stage and ice business in 1867. "He's probably afraid he's not going to make any money with us sitting here."

"Yeah, well I guess he won't if he keeps yelling at us," Ash responded before turning his attention to Crum, who was blowing his nose on his sleeve. "Good God, guy! Can you be more disgusting?"

"I don't need to impress you," Crum sneered. Ash raised his hand as if to strike him. Crum winced.

"How about you tell me what you know about the dead Indians at Tahoe," Ash demanded.

"How about you tell me what you already know," Crum answered, spying Happy Hands running north on Carson Street. "No, how about you tell me what he already knows?" He gestured toward their Indian friend, who was still a few hundred feet away.

"Look, Larry," Ronin said. "The Indian has already told us you live in the valley, and while I don't get why none of us have met you before, you obviously know something about the dead Washoe men. Spill the beans, we let you go back to jail to wait for your trial. It will be the most pleasant time you spent in Carson City. Don't, and I'll beat the shit out of you all the way up the mountain until you do."

"Ronin ..." Dustsucker cautioned.

"What?" Ronin exclaimed. "Ash pummels your prisoner on Carson Street in broad daylight and you're worried about me doing the same in the confines of a stagecoach? You're kidding, right?"

"I'm not afraid of you, Mister Ronin."

"Then be afraid of me, Mister Crum," Ash interjected. "Because I'm not going to be so nice once I see you lodged in prison. The physical examination alone should be worth your attention. And the gallows they've got?" Ash began shaking his head, "Well, that's just sugar on your strawberries, friend."

"They wouldn't hang a Mexican," Crum said.

"You're not Mexican, Larry," Ronin said, stepping in. Dustsucker grabbed his sleeve.

"Listen, I'm willing to talk, marshal. You don't need to threaten me. I just don't need my neck broken, by this *loco* or by any prison gallows. So have we got a deal?" Crum asked.

"I'll do my best," Ash responded.

"Good enough. How 'bout I start with the fact that your dead Indians didn't drown, marshal. They were beaten to death."

"Who said anything about drowning?"

"I'm just saying. You might have fished them out of the water, but that doesn't mean that's where they died. I suggest you figure out what happened to them before they got put into the water."

"Put into the water?" Ash asked.

"That's all I know," Crum responded, as Happy Hands came up to the walk way and stood under the roof next door. "I'm not involved in the slaying of a couple of Indians, marshal. I might have taken a wallet or two. I might have melted down a few silver candlesticks or coins. And my trigger finger isn't exactly asleep for folks who need shootin', but I never shot me any Indians."

"And we're to believe you when you say that?"

"Doesn't matter to me what you believe. Looks like you've got me good on trying to put a few holes in your deputy friend here and his mental patient partner." Ronin's eyes narrowed. He'd never been called a mental patient before and didn't particularly like that it was coming from a man in chains. "I don't need to deny anything. I'm just saying, whatever you think you know about these men at Lake Tahoe, you might want to think again."

"He's telling the truth, marshal," Happy Hands interjected, "and good morning."

"Good morning, Happy Hands. I'll be finished in a few minutes," Ash said, without taking his eyes away from the prisoner.

Crum looked at Happy Hands and then looked back to Ash, who didn't seem satisfied. "Look, it's like my brother says," he continued, "Indians don't have a lot of money. And you generally don't need to keep your eyes on an Indian like you do a white man."

"So, you're saying what happened to the Washoe men wasn't accidental, is that right?" Ash summarized.

"What happens to Indians in these parts is rarely accidental. The Indians simply were in the wrong place at the wrong time."

"All of us have been caught that way," Happy Hands interrupted.

"Happy Hands, I don't need your crap right now," Ash said, turning to his left. "How about you let me finish?" Ash pulled his duster back and put his hands on his hips. Two strong-side handguns hung by his side, a bone-handled knife behind the gun on his right. The meaning was clear. "Crum, I'm going to ask you how you came to this knowledge?"

"My brother told me, marshal, my brother Leonard."

"Where is this brother, Larry? I'd like to talk to him."

"Oh, you'll meet him, marshal. You too, Mister Ronin." Larry Crum turned toward Happy Hands, who had taken to looking in the window at Benton's Livery, past the toothpick that hung precariously underneath the name Benton's. "He'll be waiting for you at Lake Tahoe. He'll be waiting for all of you."

Chapter 35
LAKE TAHOE

"You boys got lucky," "Big John" Littlefield said as the four of them crowded into a coach headed for Lake Tahoe: three bench seats, six horses and a carriage capable of carrying twice as many people, without counting any extras who might sit or hang on up top. Littlefield and an unnamed youth were putting the final straps across a rectangular trunk that Ash had brought "in the event we run into something," when Littlefield asked, "What the hell is in this?" He didn't wait for an answer, but jumped to the ground so as to lift a woman's luggage into the coach's rear boot.

"You ask all of your passengers what they're carrying?" Ash replied. Littlefield was a large man in his thirties, with a significant and well-groomed go-to-meeting beard if he knew ladies would be riding on his run. An otherwise pleasant fellow, Littlefield was the captain of his coach and knew it. He looked at the marshal sternly and replied, "If I want to."

"Just asking," Ash said smiling, as he climbed into a forward-facing middle seat and made room for his knees. Ronin and Dustsucker sat facing him, with their backs to the driver and a large bag between them.

"It being a Thursday and all, the boss only has a couple of stages heading to the lake and pretty much everybody else who was going has already gone, I guess," Littlefield continued.

"Happy for the extra room," Ash responded, wondering how they would have fit anyone additional without strapping them to the top rack. Sitting three abreast, the marshal and two businessmen faced Ronin and Dustsucker, their knees interlaced so as to allow adequate space for seating. Two ladies sat in the rear, with Happy Hands sitting in-between them. He was smiling; they were not.

"Everybody ready to go?" the boy asked, looking down from the driver's box a couple of feet away. Ronin pulled the curtain. "I guess that means 'yes,'" he said.

Littlefield climbed up to his seat after inspecting the running gear and harnesses. "Let 'er go, Doc!" Benton dropped his hands and stepped aside as "Big John" gently pulled the reins up until he could feel the horses' mouths. Loosening them, he simultaneously released the brake and shouted, "Let's go!" And with that, they were off. Six chestnut-colored horses pulled against their collars in unison until the coach began rolling south on Carson Street toward Clear Creek.

It had been a while since Ronin had been in a coach. Glancing about a well-appointed cabin, he noted an engraved wooden sign affixed to an attractive leather wall. A fancy piece of red upholstery was fashioned as a mat, so that the coach's rules would be hard to miss. Leaning forward, he read it aloud.

Abstinence from liquor is requested, but if you must drink, share the bottle.

If ladies are present, gentlemen are urged to forego smoking. Chewing tobacco is allowed, but participants must spit with the wind.

No rough language. No fucking exceptions.

Don't snore while sleeping. Do not use your neighbor's shoulder as a pillow.

Firearms may be kept on your person, but those firing them will answer to the horses and to the driver.

In the event of a runaway team of horses, stay calm. Leaping from the coach may get you injured. It is a rare event that this stagecoach contains a doctor.

Gentlemen guilty of un-chivalrous conduct will be put off the stage. It's a long walk back.

He smiled. Looking around, it was apparent everyone else had already read it, or didn't care. He remembered similar signs when he rode shotgun on Pinkerton coaches throughout the southwest. Ronin was glad, for Happy Hands' sake, that the usual words to "refrain from talking about stagecoach robberies or Indian uprisings" were absent. He looked over at Ash, who was already beginning to nod, and then to his friend. "At least, we're not riding with Hank Monk, right Dusty?"

The deputy raised his head long enough to say, "I guess so, why?" before drifting off to sleep. Ronin had read Mark Twain's account of Hank Monk taking Horace Greeley, a New York newspaper owner and one-time presidential candidate, to Placerville, California. A well-known journalist, Greeley had expressed anxiety throughout the trip about arriving on time. Monk, the best known of Benton's stagecoach drivers, didn't care for Greeley's worrying and made the trip in record time, albeit somewhat recklessly, Greeley later argued. "Hold on, Horace!" had become a rallying cry during Greeley's presidential bid some years later. Greeley lost, Union General Ulysses S. Grant won. Greeley died shortly thereafter.

It wasn't Greeley's only harrowing experience while traveling. Once, when heading to Denver, Colorado, the coach's mules were startled by the sudden appearance of Indians. The mules bolted down a steep grade, dragging the stagecoach on its side. Though Greeley was badly bruised in the experience, he arrived on time.

"Either of you boys ever hear the story of Horace Greeley riding on this stage line?" Ronin asked of the businessmen, whose names he had yet to catch. The men groaned, and turned to face the window, pulling their hats down over their eyes.

"What? I'm just makin' conversation," he said.

"I don't believe anyone wants to hear that story again, Mister Ronin," Happy Hands responded from the back seat. The two women, sitting on either side of him, had apparently begun to find the Indian charming, as Ronin watched them touching and pulling at the beads and fringe of Happy Hands' hair and jacket. "Benton has instructed his drivers to refrain from telling it, Mister Ronin. I expect that rule probably extends to his passengers as well."

Ronin smiled and raised his curtain so as to look out the window. Monk had at one point been offered the sum of $250 a month — a tidy sum, Ronin thought — to join an east coast traveling show. Monk had refused. "Don't want to be hauled around the country in a dry goods box and exhibited between a fat woman and a big snake," he'd responded. Rumor was the fat lady was offended at the comment, though the snake confessed to no particular disappointment.

Heading past the Carson and Tahoe Lumber and Fluming Company lumber yard south of Carson City, Ronin closed his eyes and drifted off to sleep.

Chapter 36
DREAMS

W. W. Ronin was of the opinion that a man's dreams were simply that, nighttime visitations, ruminations if you will, of the day's business and aspirations. When they were filled with hope — a larger home, a longer journey, a peace-filled room full of happy family and friends — they suggested a hoped-for future, or reality not yet enjoyed or accomplished. In that sense they had content or meaning, but most of the time — despite the protestations of soothsayers and holy men — in Ronin's mind anyway, dreams were simply the continuance of whatever a man or woman was doing prior to falling asleep.

How Emma had appeared in his mid-morning's rest along the Clear Creek grade heading to Lake Tahoe was a puzzle to him. Facing him, as she did, to announce that the lake been discovered by people "just like him on February 14, 1844, Valentine's Day" was enough to jolt him awake him a few miles out from Captain Pray's newest project at Tahoe, the Lake Shore House. "I don't know that there's a necessary connection, Emma," he responded in the dream.

He woke when she replied, "There might be, or could be, Ronin." It was actually her smile that provoked him to wake.

Pray was a native of Maine, a maritime state whose rocky coastline produced men equally as strong and sturdy. A real-life sea captain who sailed both American oceans before building his home on the south meadow at Glenbrook, Pray had arrived a couple of years after Murdock, Warren and Walton began squatting at the lake, which of course is what they were doing because the

Washoe Tribe, or tribes to be more accurate, had been there for thousands of years before Freemont and his cartographer had first spied it.

Pray bought out the squatters' interests and began to farm and harvest the lake's mature stands of timber. In 1861, Pray he was harvesting 20,000 board feet of timber a day. Twenty years later, most of the trees the Captain had originally set eyes on were gone.

Ronin looked up at the hotel as they pulled to a stop. Painted white with ship-lap walls and a dark beige trim, the three-story structure was fronted by a large porch on its first level and a building-length balcony on its second. Under the window on the third story hung a seventeen-foot sign that prominently announced, "Lake Shore House." A long, wooden staircase ran to the second floor balcony, where a half-dozen residents were having an afternoon repast. Four large doors on the bottom level opened to what Ronin assumed was a dining room or offices.

"Amazing, right?" Dustsucker asked, waking as the carriage creaked to a stop. A Benton's employee grabbed the reins and began to direct people to disembark.

"It is that," Ronin replied. Never having been to the lake, Ronin had assumed Glenbrook to be something less than it clearly was. A lumber town, perhaps, dominated by churches and women's groups, given Pray's embrace of an abstinence lifestyle. But the Lake House was a first-class hotel accommodation. A sign proclaimed a dancing hall, billiard and bowling parlors, fishing boats to rent, and a saloon. Ronin pulled his coat shut, so that it covered his sidearms and stepped down into the street. He was hungry. He couldn't wait.

"You've been here before, Dusty?"

"I've been everywhere, Ronin. I've been around these parts much longer than you have, my friend."

"That you have," Ronin acknowledged. "Does Pray still own this?" Ronin asked, as he helped one of the women off of the stage. Happy Hands was busy with the other woman, who seemed equally transfixed by his attention.

"Nah," Dustsucker replied, "the Carson-Tahoe Lumber and Fluming Company owns it, I think. They're the largest wood and timber company up here. And while things seem to be slowing down a bit, they still seem to do a good business."

"How often you get up here, Slade?" Ash asked, taking one side of the rectangular crate from the driver and motioning with his head that Slade should take the other.

"Maybe twice a year. Glenbrook is still part of Nevada, though I wonder what California is thinking, given its occasional plans for the lake. And it's in my county."

"Plans?" Ash asked.

"Well, sure. From time to time, someone says it would be a good pond to drain, so as to supply water to San Francisco," Slade replied. "And as I've told both of you before, the boundary line keeps moving. Not by much, but with the railroad, the barge and boat traffic, I wouldn't be surprised if California wanted, or intended on taking, it all."

"Whatever," Ronin replied, tapping Happy Hands on the back. "Wanna get off, partner?" he asked.

"Sure," Happy Hands replied, missing Ronin's point that he was preventing passengers from moving by remaining where he was.

"I imagine they'll run out of wood at some point," Slade continued, hefting the other side of the box and raising his eyebrows at Ash, as if to ask where they should put the box. "Maybe the mines won't need so much wood anymore. I mean, how much timber can you put underground and still have room to climb around?" They set the box down so that Ash could grab a leather saddlebag and rifle from the coach. "You ever see the flume, Ronin?"

"Not up here. Never been up here before, Dusty, not to speak of anyway. But I've seen the Carson City end, at the timber yards down by Clear Creek."

"Well, there are three of them at the lake. And you'll want to take a look at the Clear Creek one, Ronin. It's pretty magnificent. A train runs from the meadow up to Spooner, where it dumps timber out into the flume. Before you know it, stuff's floating into Carson City."

"Stuff?" Ronin asked.

"Excuse me," one of the businessmen said, grabbing a valise from the rear boot of the coach. Ronin stepped aside, but wondered if he recognized the man.

"Sure thing, partner," he said, turning back to face his friend. "What stuff are you talking about?"

"Well, square set timber, of course. The flumes were built for that. But on a Friday, I'm told, you might catch a timber man trying his luck in a wooden canoe. It'd be crazy, but I hear there have been a few folks who have done it!"

"Jesus," Ronin replied, grabbing his rifle and beginning to walk up the steps onto the Lake Shore House porch. "I can't imagine that would be a good thing."

"No, me either."

"Everything used to run down the Toll Road on King Street, of course. But now it slides! Wanna watch a fat man slide, Ronin?"

"What?"

"Just kidding, my friend. Let's get something to eat."

Chapter 37

SMITH AND JONES

Marshal Ash and W. W. Ronin stood at the desk, waiting for the two businessmen to finish registering, while Dustsucker and Happy Hands looked around the Lake House lobby. Not wanting to appear as if he was eavesdropping, but still remaining curious about one of the two men, Ronin picked up a newspaper and stood next to the counter, pretending to read its headlines.

"Mister Cobb?" the taller of the two men asked of the man standing behind the counter.

"Yes sir. How may I help you, sir?"

"My associate and I are hoping to meet some friends while we're here. Is it possible for me to leave a message for one of them?"

"Of course, sir. Do you wish to tell me the message? I'll be here until midnight, or should I secure a piece of paper and an envelope? I could leave it in your box should your friends call later than that."

The men looked at each other before the shorter man replied, "You can get me a piece of paper. I'll not have our business spread all over the hotel."

Ronin raised the newspaper so as to cover his eyes and glanced at Ash, who didn't appear to be paying attention.

"My apologies, gentlemen," Cobb responded, "I didn't mean to suggest that your message would be treated with anything other than the utmost privacy."

"Can't see how my telling you something in front of a half-dozen people could be considered private, mister. Maybe I should teach you something about keeping a man's business to yourself?"

Ronin peered around the side of the newspaper, catching the taller businessman's glance. The businessman then looked at his partner. "I can't imagine Mister Cobb wanting to be anything other than helpful, Henry." He looked back at Ronin and smiled. Ronin returned the smile and raised the paper.

"Again, my apologies gentlemen," Cobb offered. "If you will give me just one moment, I'll fetch a piece of paper and an envelope. Perhaps you would sign the register in the meantime?"

"Mister Ronin!" Happy Hands exclaimed from across the lobby. "Have you seen this? The hotel will rent us boats so that we can fish on the lake. Why wouldn't one just fish from the edge of the lake, or in one of the rivers leading up to the lake?"

The two businessmen looked at each other anxiously. Ash looked over at Ronin, who had decided to fold the paper in half so as to afford a peripheral view of the men at the counter. Ronin noted their excitement and resisted the urge to look at Happy Hands.

"Ronin, did you hear me?" he called again. "And there's a bowling alley! Your deputy friend is heading there now to look things over. Should I go with him or stay with you and the marshal?"

Ash looked up from a train schedule he was pretending to read and saw the shorter of the two businessmen reach under his jacket. *Was he reaching for a gun?* "Excuse me, gentlemen," Ash said, stepping up to the desk and placing his hand on the man's forearm. "Have we met before?"

"No sir, I don't believe we have," the taller man said. The shorter man remained silent, his right hand still under his coat, Ash's left hand still resting on his arm.

"I didn't think so," he said. "I'm the U.S. Marshal for the Nevada district. We rode up together from Carson City, of course. I'm wondering what kind of business you're in."

"Buying and selling," the shorter one sneered, clearly irritated. With dark hair and a ruddy complexion, the man could have passed for a Mexican had he spoken differently. Ronin thought the taller man to be European, perhaps, or Canadian.

"I'm sorry. My friend is new to the trade, sheriff. My name's Smith. His name is Jones. We've opened a catalog business and are doing some research at the lake for what we hope will be a very profitable territory."

"Well Mister Smith," Ash said, "it's marshal, not sheriff. And your friend," he said slowly, looking the shorter man in the eyes, "might want to take his hand out of his pocket and put it where I can see it. I've not met a businessman in some time with such an irascible temper."

Ash waited. Ronin unbuttoned his jacket and put his hand on his gun. Happy Hands stood silently, across the lobby, with his head down.

"My apologies, marshal," the shorter man said, offering his hand in greeting. "I've not met a real U.S. marshal before," he smiled. Ronin judged the man's tone as sarcastic. He wondered if it would pass Ash's smell test.

"I have a hard time believing that, Mister Jones. And I appreciate your taking your hands out of your pockets," shaking the man's hand. It was cold and moist. "A marshal can't be too careful, you know."

"No, I don't imagine he can," Jones replied, wiping his hand on his suit trousers while looking at his friend who was beginning to inscribe his name on the register. "I apologize marshal, really. I got a little riled up." Despite the friendliness, Ash noticed that his face had yet to change. It sent a conflicting message.

"Well, perhaps we can all make Mister Cobb's job easier today by keeping our tempers in check." Ash glanced at Ronin, who still had a hand on his gun, and then took a step away. "Perhaps we can visit at supper, Mister Smith, Mister Jones? I wouldn't want you to leave the lake without getting to know your friendly Nevada marshal," he said, smiling.

"That'd be nice, Marshal," Smith said. He pulled his friend's hand to the counter and handed him the pen. "We'll be out of the hotel for a while this afternoon. If we're back here for supper, we'll stop by your table. Mister Jones, please put your name in the register. We need to head to our room."

Cobb opened the office door and walked to the desk, carrying a couple of pieces of paper, a pen and an envelope. "I believe I have what you need, gentlemen."

"I hope so," Jones said, "I'm hoping to leave Glenbrook as soon as I can."

"I'm sure you are, sir." Cobb replied, glancing at the marshal.

Chapter 38

LAKE HOUSE HOTEL

"My apologies marshal. It's been some time," Cobb remarked, regaining his composure.

"It has, sir. And your apologies are not necessary. This is Mister Ronin's first time here, I believe. And likely Deputy Slade's and our Indian friend's as well. If you have four rooms, Mister Cobb, we'll take them."

Happy Hands walked across the lobby. "Ronin, I'm sorry," he whispered.

Ronin held his hand up to stop Happy Hands from speaking further. "We'll talk about it later," he said, taking the pen from Ash and signing his name.

"William Washington Ronin, what a delightful name," the hotel's proprietor said, is it a family name?"

"Thank you, Mister Cobb. It is a family name, my grandfather's name, to be exact."

"Well, I'm sure he'd be proud to know you were using it, sir," Cobb said, taking the pen back from Ronin and offering it to the marshal. "Does the Indian write?" he asked.

"Well, I don't know. Happy Hands, do you write?"

"In what language, marshal?" He came over to the desk and made an "x" where the signature line appeared. "I don't write American if that's what you're asking."

"I'm sorry, and Mister Cobb?" Ash said, looking back to the hotel's manager, "It appears that we've lost Deputy Slade to your bowling alley. Can we send him down later?"

"You may, marshal. I show three rooms available. I can have an extra bed sent up to one of them, if you like?"

"That'll be fine sir. Put it in Slade's room. Given what good friends Happy Hands and he are, I'm sure they'll appreciate each other's company," he said, looking at Ronin. Ronin nodded. "If we can bother you for a few moments, we'd like to talk to you in your office, if that's possible."

"Of course, sir. Why don't the three of you go back to the office, help yourself to some coffee and I'll be there momentarily. I want to get someone to watch the front desk," Cobb replied.

Ronin, Ash and Happy Hands entered the office and pulled the door shut. It didn't take long for them to check in with each other. "What the hell was that?" Ronin asked Happy Hands, before Ash could open his mouth. "Identifying me like that, in front of those men? And the marshal? You might have got us both killed!"

"I'm sorry," Happy Hands responded, wringing his hands. "I had no idea it was careless to call out your name until the businessmen began to react. Marshal, I won't do that again. I promise you."

"No, you won't, Happy Hands. I assume you have business here at the lake, else these men wouldn't have brought you along. But I'll not have you interfering like that in my affairs. Perhaps you can take care of your business while we are conducting ours?"

Happy Hands lowered his head. "I meant neither of you any harm. It was a mistake I will not repeat. And I will be happy to separate myself from you, if that's your desire. However," he said, looking at Ronin, "Ronin and I have some things to do while we are here that are just as sensitive and private. Perhaps William, we can attend to those tomorrow?"

"If we need to," Ronin shook his head. "How about we meet you at dinner, Happy Hands? We can nail everything down then."

Happy Hands smiled, shook hands with both Ash and Ronin, and left the room.

"I don't believe I've ever seen him shake hands before," Ash said, pulling a chair away from the front of the desk. A nameplate with "W. A. B. Cobb, Proprietor" sat on the desk facing two chairs. Fresh flowers were gathered into a vase, next to a dust-covered Bible and dictionary. A picture of Captain Augustus Pray sat behind the desk. The room was paneled with cedar and was attractively done with woods native to the area. It had a nautical feel to it.

"No, me either. I think he's just trying to fit in, what with being Indian and all," Ronin replied.

"He doesn't need to. Simply said, he doesn't belong."

"I'm just saying, Augustus, he's trying, and from where I'm sitting, he's got something to contribute."

"How do you figure?"

"Well, for one, he recognized Crum. And Crum, so it turns out, knows something about the murders. Hell, Happy Hands knows something about them as well, and it wouldn't surprise me if he hasn't told us everything yet."

"Okay ..." the marshal responded, waiting for more.

"So I'm saying," Ronin argued, "that we keep him here until we know a little bit more about what's going on."

"Tell you what, Ronin. You seem like a patient fella, how about you keep him? You and Slade keep him, I don't care. I've got my own way with these things and I'll not have an Indian breathing down my neck, let alone putting my neck in jeopardy," Ash said, looking for a match. "I don't like people getting in my way."

"Marshal, if it wasn't for us 'getting in your way,' as you put it, you wouldn't be up here," Ronin responded.

"Don't remind me."

"Sorry to have kept you, marshal!" Cobb said, as he entered the room. "And Mister Ronin, what a distinct pleasure it is to finally meet you!"

"Meet me?" Ronin asked. The former pastor was always uncomfortable with folks greeting him in a friendlier-than-thou manner. It made for poor bedfellows, he often remarked, and rarely led to anything comfortable. "Why were you looking forward to meeting me?" he asked.

"Well sure, Mister Ronin," Cobb continued, "may I call you William?"

"I'd prefer you didn't, Mister Cobb, but go on …"

"Well, we get just about every newspaper there is here at the Lake Shore House. The Morning Appeal, the Nevada State Journal, the Reno Evening Gazette, the Territorial Enterprise, the Sacramento Bee. Hell, we even get the New York Tribune. We get 'em all."

"I'm sorry, Mister Cobb, I'm not following …"

"What I'm saying, Mister Ronin, is that I've got a stack of papers behind my desk with your name in them. The Morning Appeal, the Gazette, we get them all here at Glenbrook …"

"You said that, Mister Cobb," Ronin interrupted, growing impatient. "You've got a stack of papers with my name in them."

"Well, yes sir I do! Why, there were the shootings in Virginia City, for instance, and then the killings of that gang in Reno, what was their name?

"The Crestwells?"

"Yes, of course. Then there was the rescue of the mission children. My God! Hidden in the basement of that mansion, the entire time, is that right, William?"

"Call me Ronin. I prefer my last name."

"Of course, Mister Ronin. They're going to write a book about you, I swear, all the killing and making right that you're doing! I mean, it's just a blessing having a man like you clean up what's left of the wild, wild west! I'm just flabbergasted that we haven't seen you up this way before..."

"He doesn't like horses," Ash interrupted, trying not to laugh.

"Or criminals either, I'd say, Augustus!" he continued. "Of course all the papers mentioned you too, marshal. Hell, they led with you, I guess. But it didn't take long for some of us here to see that there was a pattern," Cobb said, making his way over to his desk chair. He put his feet up on his desk, pushed back and placed his hands behind his neck.

"Us?" Ronin asked.

"I'm sorry, gentlemen, I'm speaking of the vigilance committee, of course."

"Of course," Ash echoed.

"I assumed it was why you were here, I mean the murders and all."

Cobb put his feet down suddenly and straightened his tie. There was a knock at the door. "I thought I heard someone there," he said, getting up. "A person can't be too careful, you know."

"Of course not," Ash said.

"Alright if I join you guys?" Dustsucker asked.

"Yes, deputy, we were just talking with Mister Cobb about his vigilance committee. You'd be most welcome," Ash said, standing with his hand on his gun and then relaxing.

"Cobb, I thought we talked about this last time I was up here," Dustsucker said. "No vigilance committees. No pioneer justice. It's a different time, you know? You can't be hacking Chinamen and Canadians over the head every time someone insults one of your women!"

"I know, I know. You've got nothing to worry about," Cobb continued, sitting back down at his desk. "Everybody is behaving up here, it's not like the old days, Marcus. We're just nervous."

"I'm not following, Cobb. Who's nervous?" Ash interjected.

"The committee, marshal. What do you think I'm talking about? A couple of guys from the Glenbrook Hotel — God bless 'em, like they don't have their hands full with us opening — one of the steamer captains, myself and a few businessmen from town."

"Nervous about what, Cobb?" Ash asked, a second time.

"About the murders and robberies up and down the Bigler Toll Road, of course. And a couple of weeks ago, well Mister Ronin here shot six of them, right? Or was it eight? I don't remember. But that's not like it's the end to it, of course. I got a couple of dead Indians floating off my pier a couple of weeks ago to prove that."

"What are you talking about? There are more?" Ronin asked, standing up to part the curtains on Cobb's nearly six-foot window. Smith and Jones were stepping off the porch into the street, heading toward the water and seemed to be talking to a small, uni-browed Mexican man.

"There are if you count two dead Indians, Mister Ronin. Someone is killing people here at the lake. And it certainly isn't our food that's doing it."

"That reminds me," Dustsucker interrupted, "that was an amazing display of tropical fruit down near the saloon and bowling alley."

"Yes?" the three of them said.

"Well, I was just wondering, weren't we going to sit down for a beer?"

Chapter 39

GLENBROOK

"Marshal, I think you want to see this," Ronin said, standing by the window in W. A. B. Cobb's office at the Lake Shore House.

Ash got up and walked to the room's western wall, where a six-foot tall window looked out onto the Glenbrook street, and just past that, to the Glenbrook pier. "Is that who I think it is?" he asked.

"It is," Ronin replied.

"And the man with them?"

"Well, I don't know, marshal. But if I had to guess, I'd venture to say that's Larry Banderas' brother, Leonard."

"Crum," Ash corrected. "There are no Banderas brothers."

"I'm looking at a Mexican, marshal. If he wants to call himself Crum when he's not dressed as a Mexican, that's great. But this uni-browed, stooped over, dull-witted Mexican man looks like a partner to the other scoundrels I killed a week ago. The bling gives it away, brother. That makes them family."

"Okay," Ash said. "What do you want to do?"

"You should kill them!" Cobb said, jumping out of his chair. Both men turned with a start. "Seriously, if they're the ones causing all the trouble up this way, marshal, you should kill them. Do it now!"

"Cobb, you can't be killing people in Glenbrook just because they're dandied up like Mexican bandits! Dusty, I thought you talked to this guy?" Ronin said, taking his eyes off the window to look at the Lake House Hotel's proprietor, an otherwise "genial, accommodating and attentive host," someone had said in a Nevada guidebook Emma had given him a week or so before, hoping he'd take her along.

No person was as he or she seemed, Ronin had concluded early in his career as an Episcopal priest. His years as a detective confirmed the observation. Once a door was shut and the neighbors were out of hearing range, a man or woman's true self typically emerged.

Dustsucker had already pushed Cobb back into his chair and whispered, "Stay right here, Cobb. So help me ..." before joining Ash and Ronin at the window. "I say we follow them," he offered. "We see if we can't get a little closer, maybe hear what they're saying and find out who they're consorting with. Just a little detective work, if you ask me."

"Your friend is going to stay calm, Dusty?" Ronin asked.

"He will, with a little help," Dusty replied, looking over at Cobb.

"Listen Slade, you might not be aware, but they've already made us. Your Indian friend blurted out our names at the registration desk and we had a testy little confrontation that led nowhere. I don't think the two of us would get within 12 feet of Smith and Jones, or whatever their names are, let alone their Mexican friend. How about another idea?"

"Okay, here's one Augustus," Ronin offered. "Let's find Happy Hands and let him try to rattle up to them. They know we're angry at him and it might not be as dangerous, him being an Indian and all. Worse they'd probably do is say 'skedaddle.'"

"Or drop him into the lake," Cobb yelled.

"Dusty, keep your friend's mouth shut, would you? It's not like these walls are made of cement," Ronin chirped.

"Skedaddle?" Ash asked.

"It's a word," Ronin replied.

"Yeah, I'm sure it is, in some other half of the world. But it's a decent plan. Where is your Indian friend, anyone know?"

"He's sitting right outside, marshal," Slade said. "On the porch, I think." Slade bent forward to take a better look. "In fact, that's him already beginning to talk to them."

And sure enough, the Indian that no one wanted around while they were discussing important matters had already begun to talk to the three men in the street. Staggering up to them like he had been drinking, Happy Hands tossed a bottle into the lake — a decent throw for a man, especially a drunken man — and asked if he could stay with them. Right there in the street, he wandered up to them. If you ask me, that was taking chances.

"...'scuse me, fellas," Happy Hands hiccupped. "I saw you in the hotel there with my friends, or those I thought were my friends. They told me to get lost. They promised me a night in the hotel to get cleaned up and now I've got nowhere to stay. Can you help me out?" Happy Hands asked, stumbling toward the tallest one, whose name he hadn't heard or didn't remember.

"Sorry, friend. I don't know what you're talking about," he replied.

"I was across the lobby when you and your friend were checking in!" he hiccupped. "I called out to those men next to you, the lawmen, remember? They seemed curious about you, you know. Did you find out who they are?"

"Lawmen?" the Mexican-looking man asked, suddenly agitated. "You brought lawmen to the lake?"

"I remember this guy," the shorter one said. "He identified Ronin and the U.S. Marshal for us."

"You brought a U.S. Marshal to the lake, you morons?"

"I remember," the taller man said, slapping the smaller man with his hat. "I was just getting to that with Leonard here before he interrupted."

"Leonard, is it?" Happy Hands said, "I have a brother named Leonard. He's a very nice man. Can you help an Indian out, gentlemen? I haven't had anything to eat in a couple of days."

"Get the fuck away from us," the Mexican said, lunging toward Happy Hands and pushing him down into the street. "What the hell are you guys doing bringing Ronin and Ash to Glenbrook? Are you nuts?"

"Come on Leonard, they just happened to check in when we were checking in. They don't know who we are. And they don't know who you are either."

"Hell, they don't," Leonard said. "They were in Washoe Valley where those Indian kids were. Larry and I were the last men to leave Bowers Mansion, if you don't remember. You guys left with the boys I buried a week ago, you jackasses. If they're here, it may be because they know the rest of the story."

"Jesus," the taller one said. "I didn't know. What are we going to do?"

"We're going to kill them," Leonard said, "and then we're going to kill their friends. Hey injun," the Mexican yelled to Happy Hands, who was picking himself up in the middle of the street. "I'm going to come back for you when it gets dark. I've got a quiet place you can sleep, my friend."

Happy Hands nodded, because he knew exactly what they meant and what they were planning to do.

Chapter 40
THE REVEREND

The Reverend George R. Davis sat in the front room of the church's rectory thinking of a church picnic at Bowers Mansion, held six years prior to his coming to Saint Peter's. One of his predecessors, the Reverend George B. Allen, had arranged for the Sunday schools at Saint Paul's in Virginia City, Saint John's in Gold Hill and two other churches to join Saint Peter's in using the mansion's considerable facilities. Twelve-hundred people picnicking was the result, 700 of them were children.

Though Davis couldn't be sure, he figured there had never been a larger gathering of Episcopal parishioners anywhere in the Silver State. Per the church's progressive leanings, a band played. There was dancing — Episcopalians didn't have any issues with people feeling good about themselves, good enough anyway to swing and sway to music and contemporary rhythms — and the food, well the people at Saint Peter's were still talking about the variety of heavenly concoctions that were available.

Davis wouldn't normally be thinking about the church on his day off, but a certain woman in his parish had remarked the day before "what a wonderful idea it was then," and "couldn't they do it again," particularly since the church and town around it "had suffered such a considerable depression," she said. Davis pulled a piece of paper off of one of the shelves in his study at the west end of the church — the building was shaped like a Latin cross, after the additions in 1873 and 1874, his office sitting at the top of the cross directly behind the church's front or chancel — and he wrote down some of his pastoral statistics. Wetting the pencil with his tongue so that the figures would be dark enough to show any-one who might be interested, he scribbled the number of persons baptized, the number of people he had prepared for confirmation, the number of marriages and burial services over which he had presided and the considerable debt of $3,000 he been able to pay off in the 18 months since his arrival as pastor. The woman he had spoken to saw Saint Peter's as having become something less over the time he had served — only two, he pointed out to her, again, it wasn't their first conversation — rather than the parish becom-ing something more.

The conversation had been particularly painful, so much so that Davis had mentioned the incident to Ronin last time he had seen him. Ronin said simply, "Hardly an incident, rev-erend," without any discernible care or compassion he thought, adding the words "more like a conversation," before he could hide his surprise or regain his priestly composure. They were harsh words from a fellow cleric he said only to hear Ronin point out that he was hardly a cleric anymore given all of the incidents that had happened in his life since leaving the priesthood seven years before.

Ronin also said that the mansion was closed anyway, and that Sandy Bowers, the owner of the mansion, had moved on though he wasn't sure where, even though the thought or pos-sibility of reinstituting the Episcopal Mission District's summer picnic was hardly his chief concern or point.

In the back of Davis' head, he had hoped that involving Ronin in a larger event might encourage him to attend some of the smaller gatherings in the parish. He had noticed that most days, when Ronin visited the church, the ex-priest would simply sit alone in the sanctuary feeling whatever it was ex-priests felt simply by sitting there. "You know," he said, "you've never actu-ally been to church." It was passively-aggressive, though he hadn't intended it to sound so at the time.

Ronin argued, "Sunday mornings hardly constitute 'being to church, reverend."

Initially missing the ex-priest's point, he subsequently asked when the last time was that he'd been to church, accidently inviting Ronin's retort that being the priest of a congregation hardly meant that he was participating in the life of a congregation, either.

Davis sat in his easiest chair thinking.

While his ministry had not been nearly as interesting as Mister Allen's had been previous to him — Allen had been the first pastor to congratulate the congregation after having built its sanctuary, paying off its debt and, three years later, beginning a significant addition to the church adding Sunday school wings north and south. Allen's legacy included packed classrooms, the building of a Chinese chapel on the other side of Carson Street and being the only pastor in the capital city to preach to both houses of the Nevada legislature — it wasn't as if he wasn't trying.

Davis' only relief was that his predecessor had built a church without a center aisle, a unique faux pas, as far as Davis was concerned, west of the Mississippi. On that, Ronin and he agreed. "Put one in and I might attend church," Ronin had often said, laughing. God, he found the man aggravating.

He blew across his morning tea, an imported cup of Earl Grey, and thought about Saint Peter's sanctuary — tall stained glass windows throughout, one of which, when illumined just right, gave the preacher of the morning a faint, but distinct, heaven-like glow. Ronin typically sat in one of the five pews reserved for the Nevada Orphan Home's children. "I'm simply making a point," Ronin admitted one morning, when Davis had found him sitting there in the dark, alone and quiet. "'The eyes of the wise man are in his head,'reverend, 'but the fool walks in darkness,'" he'd said, quoting the book of Ecclesiastes. "Good text for a bunch of politicians, don't you think?" Ronin said laughing, as if he knew that quoting the exact biblical text that Allen had chosen it to speak about when in front of the Nevada's legislature would bother Davis the rest of the week.

"Listen, you're not a bad pastor," he'd said more recently. "You had a couple of dead vestry members when you started, but you fixed that. You paid off the debt, when neither the church or the community could afford to do so. Nice job. And you obviously care about folks like me," he'd said. "Is there anything more Christian?"

The ex-priest — what was it he said he did? — would typically visit the church after breakfast, a little before Davis would arrive, given that there was no need for a priest to rise that early, Davis figured, save for a few moments in prayer or Bible study, practices that were of intermittent interest to him except during the more saintly times of the year like Easter or Christmas. "Ronin, you dress like an Idaho lawyer," he told him at one point, echoing an article he had seen in the Daily Appeal, suggesting a shirt collar and a pistol belt, two generally discordant pieces of clothing, were something to note.

Ronin had simply responded, "Whatever," a word he'd heard from Ronin's mouth rather frequently over the last two years, initially thinking it rude, but later discovering it was Ronin's way of staying sane and sober.

"Listen, you're not a slacker," Ronin had said the other day. He told him he didn't know the word. "It's obscure," Ronin had replied. The man's vocabulary amazed him. "It suggests someone who is shirking his duty. You're not like that." Ronin was all about duty. "There will always be people who will think you're favoring one aspect of ministry or over another. Don't pay any attention to them. Whatever the hell they mean by saying that — and it's generally always nasty — that person probably does a lot less than you do." The encouragement meant a lot to him.

"Last Easter," Davis pointed out, "we had the Orphans Home and Scottish Rite Masons over to attend services. A couple of months later we had a service where the Grand Army of the Republic and the Mexican War veterans attended."

But Ronin's good-natured encouragement had given way to plain speech. "Look George," he'd said, "Masons and war veterans don't suggest you're making more Episcopalians." He'd visibly winced at the mention of the G. A. R., a Union soldier veteran's group. Had he thought of it, he'd have remembered that Ronin was a Confederate veteran. "I'm not sure you get it," he'd said. "It's not about what we accumulate, George — and pastors are at risk here the same as other people — it's what we become, my friend."

Given the frankness of the conversation, he'd taken the opportunity to ask the state of Ronin's soul. "Tell me about how you're doing?" he'd asked after the mission kids had been returned to Emma Nauman's group south of town.

"I'm fine," he'd replied, rebuffing his attempts to be helpful. An ex-priest had to entertain a certain amount of confusion or pain, he figured.

"Doing what you did, Ronin ..." he'd never finished the sentence because Ronin turned away, unwilling or perhaps unable to talk.

He wondered what Ronin was doing with his innermost questions, and while he didn't exactly know what to do with his own, he was concerned. It couldn't be easy to be a gunslinger — he guessed that's what Ronin meant by "detective" — still, he wasn't sure. Even if the man was working to right people's wrongs, it couldn't be easy to live that way.

Davis heard a knock and the door and rose to meet it. He'd have to talk to Ronin again, soon, he thought as he looked out the rectory's window. Emma Nauman was calling. How odd. He couldn't remember when Mrs. Nauman had come to his door before.

Chapter 41

MAY I CALL YOU EMMA?

"Miss Emma," Davis said, speaking through the screen door of his church-owned home. "What a surprise to see you here, ma'am. I was just about to walk over to my study at Saint Peter's. Would you like to join me for a stroll?"

The Reverend Davis was not just about to walk over to his office at the church, nor anywhere else for that matter. But meeting a woman, particularly a woman of Emma Nauman's stature and status in the community — she was unmarried, or at least pretended to be after her husband's disappearance the year before — would have been inappropriate at best.

When Davis was in training to be a priest, he was told the story of a minister who lost his reputation in the church and community when a woman's carriage was found parked out front his house overnight. As it turned out, it was all a mistake. The woman in question had not spent the night at the clergyman's home, but had left her carriage there simply to make the point that the pastor's chatter about her was dangerous and undeserved. Davis didn't know if the story was true, but had made it a point early in his calling never to leave his carriage anywhere he wasn't comfortable visiting overnight, nor to be found alone with a woman unless it was his wife. Visiting with Mrs. Nauman at the church would be difficult enough. Talking with her in his home, without his wife present — well, that could court disaster.

"I'd be happy to," Emma said, surprised to find the priest at home. "I was hoping to catch your wife so as to leave a message that I'd like to speak with you. This is even better," she said, thinking that the walk and talk would do her good.

"My wife is at the church," Davis said, "with some of the other woman working on the Sunday school fair. Have you bought your ticket yet?" he asked. "You know they're only thirty cents. There's hope we'll raise enough money to repair that bell!"

The Episcopal church's bell was supported by an old wood and cast-iron yoke, so as to facilitate the bell's swinging by parishioners on Sunday mornings. It had been a constant headache to many in the congregation, not just the men ringing it. After a crack was found in the bell, the church vestry had rejected Davis' advice that the bell should be relocated to a separate tower to lessen the dreadful thumping and banging, a suggestion he was sure would have been accepted had his predecessor offered it. Some men in the church believed that recasting the bell with a copper and tin alloy was likely necessary. Davis hoped it could be done at the Virginia and Truckee Railroad foundry in town rather than to ship it west or east.

"It preaches a sermon to us all," Emma replied, though she was actually unacquainted with the bell's sound, living so far out of town. She was undecided about its importance.

"It does that, Mrs. Nauman. "I'm hoping after its re-hanging and clanging, there will be new worshippers bending their knees at Saint Peter's every Sunday," he replied, happy with the rhythm and rhyme of what he had said. "What brings you to town, ma'am?"

"Well, Mister Davis, I believe you are Mister Ronin's friend, spiritually speaking. I don't know that he confides in any of the other clergy in town. If it's not too presumptuous to inquire, I'm wondering if you've heard anything from him regarding his recent trip to the lake?"

"It's not presumptuous at all, Mrs. Nauman, though I can't say that I hold any of Mister Ronin's confidences. He's very much his own man, as you probably know. Why don't you simply ask him?" he asked, thinking that there must be something to the gossip he had heard in church, not that it was any of his business, that Ronin and Nauman were courting.

"We don't see each other that often," she responded, "not since his leg has healed and the children returned, praise God. And to be frank, if I may, Reverend Davis ..."

"Of course, you may, Mrs. Nauman. Whatever you say I will hold as a pastoral confidence."

"... well, as I was saying, I'm concerned about Mister Ronin, reverend. Not that he's done anything wrong. I'm speaking simply of his safety. Whatever is going on up the lake has already cost a couple of men their lives and I'd hate to see Mister Ronin caught up in it. I believe God has a plan for him. I don't believe it involves his being hurt at Lake Tahoe," Emma blushed.

Davis was silent for a moment. Clearly, Emma Nauman was a spiritually-minded woman, given the work she and her former husband had dedicated themselves to doing at the American Gospel Mission. Inviting children from the Washoe, Paiute, Shoshone and other western tribes to stay and learn at their ranch overlooking the Eagle Valley was a noble work, to be sure. But her interest in Ronin sounded more personal than spiritual. But it was beyond their relationship for him to question further. He considered the fifty-some communicants in his church and the one-hundred and twenty-five scholars in his Sunday school. She was not a parishioner nor was she related to any of the people in his church. If he mis-spoke, he hated the thought that he'd get caught in-between some-one's feelings or financial subscriptions, there'd probably be hell to pay. "Mrs. Nauman," he ventured anyway, "may I ask why you're concerned about his safety? I don't mean to pry into your personal business." He was helping, he figured, and a priest needs to know a certain amount of information to be helpful.

Emma's color reddened. "I might as well tell a priest, I guess. I have no one else to confide in." She paused at the corner of Musser and Division Street, by the white picket fence outside the Methodist Church. She noticed the Methodist minister gardening a hundred or more feet away. "You probably know that my husband abandoned me, Mister Davis," she whispered. "And you may be aware that his prior behavior in this city was, how shall I put it, inappropriate and humiliating to me?"

"I had no idea," he said, though he had heard the rumors. The Methodist pastor looked up and waved.

"To state it simply, I believe I have certain feelings for Mister Ronin," Emma continued. "I'd hate for anything to happen to him." She hesitated before continuing. "I'm hoping something comes of our relationship that will make Christ proud."

"And you happy?" Davis asked, placing his hand on her shoulder and waving back.

Her eyes filled with tears, but she did not cry. "I'm worried, reverend. I'd hate for something to happen to him. He means so much to me."

"He means so much to us all, Mrs. Nauman. We'll go to the church and pray, if you like."

"I'd like that, Mister Davis," she responded, surprised that she had finally trusted another man, since her Henry had left her high and dry in the northern Nevada desert. If she could trust a minister, maybe she could learn to others. Maybe she could trust God again, too.

"Mrs. Nauman, may I call you Emma?"

"Of course you may, Mister Davis."

"Then let me speak frankly, and faithfully I hope. What happens to Mister Ronin at Lake Tahoe is beyond our control. We can pray. We *will* pray, but the outcome of our prayers is with the One who looks over us all."

"I'm counting on that, reverend. I really am."

Chapter 42
STREET SCRAPE

The last thing two women expected to see while registering at the Lake Shore House hotel was a man sliding across the counter on his buttocks with his gun drawn. But that's exactly what occurred when Ronin broke from the office window where he was gazing so as to grapple with what he judged to be a dangerous and developing situation outside. Happy Hands was laying in the street, with Smith and Jones looking on as Leonard Crum, or the man he guessed to be Leonard Crum, was shouting angry epitaphs Happy Hands' way.

Never one to tolerate disrespect — whether it was happening to him or to a friend — Ronin believed the shorter man to be the brother of Larry Crum, the prisoner he'd recently housed in the Ormsby County Jail. A squat, slope-headed man with a single bushy eyebrow and large hands, Leonard Crum appeared to be angry, shouting loudly enough to be understood inside the hotel office. Ronin believed that a bird in hand was better than three to be looked for later, so he ran to provoke a situation that might flush the true nature and business of the suspicious men out in the open. There was Happy Hands' immediate safety to be considered as well.

Ronin was not disappointed as he crashed through the hotel's front doors, stumbling across the porch and onto the Glenbrook street. "Can I help you men?" he shouted, only to watch the man identified earlier as Jones drop to both knees and draw a small, nickel-plated double-action revolver from underneath his jacket.

Ronin banked left as multiple shots pinged off a cast iron planter to the right of two men in rocking chairs. The gray-haired vacationers fell to the porch boards, grasping what they could for safety. Ronin counted three small caliber ricochets before being able to cock and fire his own gun two times, continuing to move. His first shot threw a 230 grain bullet into Jones' torso, twisting him sideways. His second blew a hole through the back of Jones' hat. The man crumpled to the ground as his taller friend, Smith, took off running toward the tree line. In the excitement, Ronin lost track of Crum.

"To your right!" shouted someone behind him. He turned to see and found the marshal with his rifle firmly fitted to his shoulder, waiting to shoot.

"What are you waiting for?" he yelled, as he watched Leonard Crum jump onto a horse and gallop north toward Incline.

"I'm waiting for a reason to shoot, Ronin, not that that would occur to you. Jesus, man! You make dead people faster than they fell trees up this way."

"I should hope so, marshal, or didn't you see him roll his gun my way?" Ronin walked over to Jones, who was still breathing, and turned him over. Kicking off his hat, he couldn't find an exit wound. Jones looked up at him, blankly. He pulled a nickel-plated double action revolver from Jones' right hand and checked his left to see if he had another. He then looked over at Happy Hands, who was just beginning to stand and dust himself off.

"You okay, my friend?"

Happy Hands smiled, and then watched as the hotel's front door opened and the two women came running toward him. "Happy Hands! Are you hurt? Let us look!" the woman from the stagecoach cooed. Ronin blushed and turned toward the porch where Ash and his friend Dustsucker stood, talking to some men on the porch floor.

"Augustus, take this," he said, offering Jones' gun with his left hand as he holstered his own and walked toward the Lake Shore House hotel.

"I don't understand," the marshal said, holding out his left hand.

"I think you will if you look at it," Ronin replied. He pulled his coat shut so that his firearms were no longer visible to people gathering on the porch and street. Two men hurried up from the Glenbrook pier.

"Well, I'll be," Ash said. "A .45 caliber Webley. This is Tom Kelly's gun."

"It is," Ronin replied, "a Webley Royal Irish Constabulary Model, I believe. Not rare, but rare in these parts, marshal."

"Well, he hasn't seen this since, well I don't know when," Ash continued.

"I'll tell you exactly when," Ronin said. "He lost it when the two of you attempted to arrest that Crestwell kid in Virginia City, that's when. Remy, wasn't it?"

"You're absolutely right," he said, reading the engraving on the firearm aloud, "1868 L. P. Webley & Sons. Lordy! Thomas is going to be happy to see this. He's carried this as long as he's been a lawman, as a police chief, sheriff and my occasional deputy."

"Marshal, I think you're missing the point."

"The point?" Ash asked, tucking it in his pocket.

"Yeah," Ronin replied. "If this piece of slime was carrying Tom Kelly's gun, it means he had something to do with the folks we shot up in Washoe and Reno. I've never seen another one of these. It's hard for me to assume that the Crestwells or the Clancys ..."

"... or the men who fled the Bowers Mansion before we arrived," the marshal interrupted. "You're totally right, Ronin. This places this man, and maybe those men, in the middle of a crime wave, my friend."

"Exactly," Ronin replied, "and it's not exactly where we want them, if you ask me."

"Mister Ronin?"

"Yes, Happy Hands," Ronin said, turning toward a man who, he now believed, because of his actions, to be his friend.

"The man who fled on a horse? His name is Leonard. Isn't that the man your prisoner would meet us here?"

"It is."

"Then it is time for us to go."

"Go, Happy Hands? I don't follow," Ronin replied.

"It is time for us to climb Cave Rock."

Chapter 43

BED MATES

With eighteen rooms, the Lake Shore House was Captain Augustus Pray's answer to what the Glenbrook House might have been had his two sawmill partners, Joe Winters and Lou Colbath, known what they were doing. A reputable hotel for the first dozen years of Glenbrook history, the two and one-half story wayside inn called the Glenbrook House fronted the new road to Carson City and was built a half mile from the lake in the Glenbrook meadow. But a series of proprietors and a change in owners couldn't prevent the town's activities moving closer to the lake.

Despite the Glenbrook House having a notable hotel registry that included past presidents, generals, artists and titans of American industry, there was little comparison in Dustsucker's mind. It was the difference between riding a new horse or a tired-out donkey. Or hiking uphill to sit in a meadow on a hot summer day, or hanging your feet off a pier and having an afternoon beer. As far as Dustsucker was concerned, the Lake House was the place to stay. "So, how is it, with so many rooms in this place, you and I find ourselves bunking in together?" the Carson City deputy said, shaking the Washoe man who had ignored the bed and laid down beside it instead.

Happy Hands awoke and turned onto his side so as to sit up. "Deputy Slade, I don't understand why you are waking me in the middle of the night. Why are you doing this?"

"First off, my Washoe Indian friend, it's not the middle of the night. It's like … well, maybe nine o'clock or something. A white man would know such a thing," Dustsucker challenged.

"Only a white man would think it important to know such a thing."

Dustsucker shook his head angrily. "I'm just saying, how is it that I've got a roommate and our other two friends do not?"

"I believe the hotel is full, Mister Slade. Is this important enough that I remain awake with you?"

"You're sleeping on the floor?"

"I was."

"I mean, not on the bed?"

"I am."

"Then tell me again how it's important that you sleep here with me. You snore, my friend," Dustsucker said.

Happy Hands sat silently on the floor, curling his legs up underneath him. He reached for his jacket, pushing it in between his legs to keep warm. "There are many places I can sleep, deputy."

"Oh, now we're talking about your women friends, are we?"

Happy Hands smiled. "Deputy Slade, what is it that bothers you so much that you've wakened me from my sleep?"

Dustsucker stood and walked over to a table by the door. He picked up his sleeping shirt, a cavernous piece of red cloth that two normal-sized men could fit into, and held it up for Happy Hands to see. "I need a certain amount of privacy, my friend. A man can't sleep with an Indian rolling around on his floor."

Happy Hands looked down into his lap, and pulled the jacket over his legs. He prided himself on understanding white men, but there were times when their behavior challenged him. "Marcus," he said, "my wife is a big woman. My new wife is a big woman, too."

"You're married? I didn't know that. I'm sorry."

"You're sorry for what, deputy? That I'm married to two women? Lots of Washoe men are, or were anyway. It takes a rich man to keep two women happy, and I'm afraid I don't do very well at that."

"No, I'm sorry that I didn't know. I mean, I've known you for a couple of years now. I should have taken a more personal interest," Dustsucker said, putting his night shirt on his bed, a single sized coil-spring and hair mattress, set on top of a captain's trunk. He appreciated the nautical theme to some of the rooms at the Lake Shore House and wondered how much of it was Captain Pray's continuing influence.

"I'm merely saying that a fat woman is no embarrassment deputy, nor is a fat man. There are very few Washoe who are thin like your friend Ronin, deputy. There are many different tribes in the world, my friend, and many different sizes as well."

"How come I haven't met either of your wives, Happy Hands?"

"You haven't met them because I no longer live with them," he responded. "A holy man's path is a difficult one. His dreams are oftentimes his reality."

"I don't understand."

"It makes for difficult sleeping, deputy."

"Oh," Dustsucker replied, thinking their having been assigned to the same room was maybe a good thing. He was coming to know the Washoe man in a new and deeper way.

"Happy Hands?"

"Yes, deputy," Happy Hands said as he pulled his coat over himself and turned to face the wall.

"I was just wondering. What's it like to be with a fat woman?" he asked.

"Every woman is different," he smiled. "They are each a different bowl of joy."

Dustsucker took off his gun belt and set it on the floor beside him. He lowered the light and began to get undressed. He'd felt fat and ugly his entire life. *Maybe that's why I smile so much. I want to be a smaller person.* He pulled the shirt over his three-hundred and some pound frame. *I want to be like everyone else.*

"Deputy," Happy Hands said, barely moving and still facing the wall.

"Yes?"

"We are all different. Every one of the Creator's breaths are different," he said. "Yours is most special."

"I don't follow."

"It is a beautiful shirt you sleep in, deputy. It would not be nearly as striking if it were half full."

Deputy Marcus T. Slade smiled to himself as he lay down. "Call me Dustsucker," he said. "All of my friends do," he added, drifting off to sleep.

Chapter 44
MEANWHILE

It took six hours for Smith to stumble into Leonard Crum's camp in the woods just south of the north shore timber village of Incline. The Crums liked to keep things private, having stolen what they could from the eastern slope towns of Franktown, Galena and the former county seat of Washoe City, now a near-ghost town. While Incline positioned them close to the constant stream of travelers up and down Kings Canyon — providing Leonard, Larry and an always changing group of other outlaws with an easy income given that Glenbrook was closer to the old Bigler Toll Road than Incline — it kept investigations into their banditry at least a town away.

A California marshal had at one point stumbled on their scam to rob Sierra travelers of their cash and other valuables, but hadn't stayed in camp long enough for either Leonard or Larry to catch his name. The man was buried a good ways away from the log house Crum was using for shelter. Neither the marshal's family nor his agency knew what had happened, which was exactly how the Crums preferred to handle things when folks began prying into their business.

Leonard touched his beard as he squatted to make a fire outside the one-room cabin, erected sometime in the mid-sixties. Larry had told him the cabin belonged to an early settler, though Leonard hadn't seen any signs of someone farming nearby. Given the cabin's condition — pretty raw, compared to the houses they'd stayed in while preying on Washoe Valley folk — fine oak flooring had given way to mud and dirt. The purloined furnishings of a hundred abandoned homes in the Washoe Valley were just a memory now, though Larry made occasional trips there to attend his Masonic Lodge in Washoe. Leonard found it as comfortable outside as he did inside, and generally if the weather was nice, more so.

He struck a match and ignited some tinder, moving his favorite rock closer to the fire pit. He would have stayed in Washoe Valley if they hadn't been stalked by the U.S. Marshal and his steely-eyed accomplice, W. W. Ronin. A former reverend, Leonard remembered shaking his head. "Not shooting like that!" he'd said aloud to no one in particular.

Smith staggered into camp around sundown. Cut-up and badly bruised, it appeared to Leonard that the man had wrestled a mountain lion. "What the hell?" he exclaimed as Smith collapsed onto a stump by the fire.

"Indeed."

"No, I'm asking," Crum said. "Jones is dead, I figure, but what happened to you?"

"I hit the tree line running, you narrowed-eyed fool. You took the only horse!" he said in an unguarded moment. When the younger Crum brother stopped kicking and stomping on him, Smith could only lay in the sandy dirt and pine needles, groaning. "I'm going to see what we've got to eat," Crum grumbled. "When I get back, I'm hoping you'll have a different attitude about being here. Your pal was a shifty piece of shit, if you ask me. It wasn't the first time he got himself into trouble. You're a lucky man that he didn't drag you down with him."

Smith managed a moan to show that he was listening. The brothers were tough hombres to live with, for sure, but the pay had been good. A beating now and then would teach him to keep his mouth shut, and with one less mouth to feed on the permanent crew, there might be a larger share.

Leonard walked back inside the cabin to a metal-lined box set on top of a tree stump. He pulled flour, salt and dried beef from a bag inside it before closing the lid and looking for the cabin's water. "I thought I told you to fill the bags! Where are they?"

Smith propped himself up on one elbow. "Right rear," he squeezed out between swollen lips and a jaw that didn't seem to want to move like it used to.

"What?" Crum yelled, coming to the door, snarling his disgust. "Speak up, boy!" The taller man gestured to the corner of the log house, where two canvas bags hung on a stick punched haphazardly into the houses' mud and newspaper chinking. "Why didn't you just say 'right here'?" he asked. He raised his right boot to kick at Smith's ribs, laughing. "Just kidding," he snarled, pulling a bag from off the side of the house.

Smith groaned. Laying out front of a deteriorating piece of shit log cabin was a far cry from being a company accountant in Sacramento. He pushed himself up so as to manage a smile. "My face is swollen," he mumbled. "It makes it kind of hard to talk," he said, without moving his lips.

"Imagine that's true," Crum laughed, tossing the water and a pan his way. "What do you say about biscuits and gravy for supper?"

"That sounds nice," he forced himself to say.

"Well, get busy then. Supper isn't going to fix itself." Crum pulled a folded piece of paper out of his vest. "I've got work to do," he said, heading back inside. "We'll talk when everything's ready."

Chapter 45
IN THE SALOON

"Here's how I see it," the ex-priest said to the marshal, both of whom had crept downstairs to grab a drink when the lake's gentle but constant lapping had kept them awake. "Crum is going to have to find some more men. He's not going to find them here," he concluded, arguing that the late Mister Jones and his still-at-large partner didn't seem much acquainted with Glenbrook. "They're going to have to come from somewhere else. And given that I've killed a half-dozen of them so far ..."

Ash interrupted. "I think the count is nine, Ronin, unless you've got stories you've yet to tell."

"... okay, nine of them, I'm not counting. But my point is this. They've got to have a connection, or have had at least, to some timber or lumber company at the lake. There are not enough idle mine or timber workers in the mountains for these men to pull together a new gang."

Ash thought for a minute, sipping on his whiskey. "Seems to me," he said, pausing to consider the options, "that the possibility also exists that this gang is now down to a few men and isn't looking for any others."

Happy Hands was surprised to see anybody up, pushing the saloon's doors open a crack and begging a barmaid to let him in. "We're closed, Indian."

"What about these men?" he asked, "they are my friends." A tall, squeaky woman, with a derringer shoved between her breasts, the woman glanced toward Ash for his approval. He shrugged his okay.

"Fine," she said, dropping the latch. "Just don't be lightin' any fires, honey. This isn't no Washoe hunting camp." Happy Hands frowned and looked past her as Ronin broke into laughter. "Not every woman finds you irresistible, Happy Hands," he said, gesturing that the Washoe man sit down.

"Apparently."

"Where's the deputy?" Ash asked.

"He's upstairs, wearing a very attractive shirt," Happy Hands answered. Ronin and Ash looked at each other. "I'm just saying."

"Okay ..." Ronin replied.

"What are the two of you talking about?" Happy Hands asked.

"Well, injun. Your friend here is telling me that the Crum brothers have some magical source for recruiting murderers, thieves and the like, and that they're about to round up another bunch."

"I said, 'might,' marshal, or 'have.'" Ronin signaled to the server to see if she'd pour him another beer before shooing them out of the place. "I'm simply trying to get some flesh on this thing. Happy Hands, you said you knew these guys from Washoe Valley?"

"I did." He borrowed the marshal's glass and raised it, imitating Ronin. Perhaps the pretty maiden with the piece sticking out of her brassiere would bring him something to drink as well. "They used live in some of the houses in Washoe City," he replied, putting the glass back down. The marshal looked irritated.

"You said 'houses,'" Ash interrupted. "Should I take that to mean they didn't *own* a house, but squatted in *many* houses?"

"Call it what you want, marshal. I'm just saying that I've seen them before. But they were dressed as Mexicans."

"Well, I'll be damned Ronin, you might be on to something," Ash said, pulling the half-full glass back his way. If they're posing as Spaniards, businessmen or whatever, we might want to investigate their known associates. Or ask around, anyway. I don't know how I missed that."

"You're a busy man, marshal. I don't imagine you spent too much time in any one place. This is something I've been thinking about for three months. Peter Clancy said it would have been a different fight had his friends remained."

"I remember."

"And the Mexicans he spoke about, horse handlers, kidnappers — hell, whatever skedaddled into the hills before you and I found the children and killed the brother."

"Right ..."

"So these men, let's just say the ones I killed in Kings Canyon or the short, irritable fellow out front, are down to just a few men. Count 'em with me — Larry Crum, who's in the Ormsby County jail, Leonard Crum, who just rode toward the Incline timber mills on a stolen horse, and what's-his-name Smith, whom I'm guessing is heading toward, or has already reached, a predetermined meeting place. It's not like these guys are going to pack up and go. They've got quite an investment here in the Sierra."

Happy Hands smiled as the tall, brown-haired girl who originally barred his way into the saloon, handed him a glass. He raised it to her, smiling. "The men you are seeking are the men who killed my friends," he said, hoping to contribute to the discussion without looking their way.

"Well, duh, my friend. That's what we've been talking about."

"So you're saying the men who fished them out of the lake, and dragged them to the hotel's front door, may not have discovered them, as Cobb said, but might have actually killed them?"

"Exactly," Ronin responded, watching the saloon girl walk away, "and caused and contributed to whatever list of crimes you've got happening in Washoe Valley, Kings Canyon, Glenbrook, God only knows. Have we talked to Hangtown and the points in between?"

"We have not," Ash said, finishing his drink. "I should have brought Tom Kelly up here with me. He's good at following up this kind of stuff."

"Well, you've got his gun — you might think of telegraphing him," Ronin reminded the marshal, who was rocking backward on his chair and exhibiting a fresh sense of confidence.

"Mister Ash," Happy Hands interjected, "may I ask you a question?"

"Sure, injun. What?"

Hands grimaced. "Did the men have water in their mouths when they were discovered by Cobb or his people?"

"I'm not following," the marshal said, tapping his glass on the table. "What's your point?"

"A drowned man swallows water, my friends, he does not swallow rocks."

"Swallow rocks? What are you talking about, Happy Hands?" Ronin interrupted, leaning forward. He hadn't heard anything about rocks before.

Ash looked at Ronin and then back to Happy Hands. "Who said anything about rocks?" surprised a second time by Happy Hands' knowledge of the murders. "You been talking to people?" he asked, suspiciously.

"A Water Baby came to me in a dream, my friend. His long, brown hair streamed behind him as he floated over to me on the big water. He opened his ugly, grey mouth and showed his teeth. I did not want to look, but he insisted. His mouth was filled with small rocks."

"Oh God, make it stop ..." Ronin interjected, putting his hands to his head.

"Ronin, knock it off. I'm listening, Happy Hands. Go on."

"The Water Babies are dangerous, and I would, if I could, live my life without them. But I cannot. One visited me and told me this thing. Others are waiting to tell me more things." Happy Hands was clearly shaken by the dream. "Did they have rocks in their mouths, marshal? Or will one of us have them in our mouths, before this thing is over?"

"Whoa, Happy Hands," Ronin interrupted, "it's late. And while I'm not a superstitious man, I don't cotton to people talking about all the bad things that might happen to me before morning."

"There were small pebbles in their mouths, Happy Hands. I don't know how you knew that. I have no knowledge whether their mouths contained water," Ash replied.

"A drowning man swallows water, my friends. He does not swallow rocks."

"So he does," Ash said, thoughtfully. The U.S. Marshal for the state of Nevada stood up. "Gentlemen, I think I've had enough for this evening. It's time to get some sleep."

"Before you go, Mister Ronin," Happy Hands said, "may I ask if you have plans for tomorrow morning?"

"I've got a date with some eggs, maybe a big fat biscuit and some jelly, why?"

"I'm thinking we might visit the Standing Grey Stone."

"Lady of the Lake, I heard it called today," Ronin grinned. "Seems that the lower half of the rock looks like a woman. Always has, probably always will."

"It does, Ronin." Happy Hands smiled approvingly. He lifted his glass to salute. Both men nodded, picking up their hats. "It appears to me, gentlemen, that the Lady of the Lake has something to say. Trust me when I say, we should not miss it."

Chapter 46
MAKING A LIST

Keeping out of Incline was a good choice. A former lumber camp that exploded when the Sierra Nevada Wood and Lumber Company employed 150 French Canadians as lumberjacks and an additional 200 or so Chinese as woodcutters, the camp provided a constant source of hold-up men, willing to better themselves without assuming much risk. Locating too close to the north-side timber camp could lead to familiarity or worse.

The Crums were happy confidants to many in the camp, providing liquor and buying an occasional supper for a hungry mountain man. When the need presented itself — a half-dozen men to hole-up with a bunch of Indian children, three or four others to assist with a mountain heist on the road to Marlette Lake or the old Bigler Toll Road heading down to Carson City — it was a simple matter. Civilized folks generally left their squirrel guns and other firearms at home when traveling short differences. Working for the Crum brothers meant wages equal to a man's effort — generally safe surroundings, spiffy new clothes to wear at work or, with some care, the opportunity to visit sexually as one might wish with cultured women in the surrounding towns.

Larry Crum stood up and rattled on the bars so as to use the jail's latrine. It was no surprise to him that the men employed at Incline might desire something more. Lake living was hard, and timber camps were even more so. Noisy, often dirty affairs, a man's only way to better himself was to stop drinking away his wages. If he was whoring with some of his money — many of the camps provided women who were inclined to show a man a good time — he might find himself too short at the end of a week to afford a game of cards or even a warm beer.

Crum brushed the dirt from his favorite jacket, a mid-length Union army frock coat with silver buttons on both sleeves. (He'd had the brass buttons replaced.) Crum hated what being in jail was doing to his clothing. Funny that he should care, as he only wore the jacket when his intention was to rob or rape, the latter option always left up to the individual man. Sitting in the Ormsby County jail waiting a jury trial hadn't been a picnic. Still, the silver should shine, and wouldn't, if he wasn't able to give it some effort. His yellow kerchief, lent to him by his mother, was soiled. He had no way of washing it. And his hat, a nice Mexican number, was beginning to unravel around the sombrero's brim. He preferred that the laces stay intact. It would be some time before he could repair or launder any of it, including his blanket.

He took his poncho off and laid it on a chair, then began to pull at one of his spurs. Looking at the deputy who was asleep by the door, he began to wonder if he could scrape his way out of the cell, as its outside wall seemed to be made of simple adobe.

"Guard," he called, waking the older man up. "You must be old enough to have fought in *La intervención norteamericana*"?

"Cut the crap, Larry," Ormsby Sheriff Lloyd Hill responded, looking up. "We know you're not Mexican, remember?"

"I didn't see that it was you, Lloyd. Your boys are not nearly as quick-witted. What are you doing back here, anyway? I figure a man of your position should be out in the street meeting folks."

"I was trying to grab a few winks, if you don't mind. What do you need?"

"I was simply curious. You look like you're old enough to have fought in Mexico."

"I'm only thirty-five, moron, thirty-six maybe. So I wasn't there." The sheriff's tone and look turned stern. How old he was, who he was, where he lived, how many children he had to feed, whether his wife was comely or not, was none of his prisoner's damn business. He didn't know why he always gave up personal information so easily. "Listen, Larry," the sheriff said, "I don't give a shit about the Mexican-American War. I don't give a shit about you, either. The war was a long time ago, and you all probably deserved it."

"Yeah," Larry smiled. It didn't take much of a brain to know that Hill was likely a one-term sheriff, given that he was sitting in the jail instead of politicking on the street. He mumbled a few bad Spanish words to reinforce the misdirection. "Look," he said, "I was just looking for some paper. Would you mind giving me an envelope or something?"

"Yeah, like we're going to let you write your mother, you stupid son of a bitch." Hill settled back against the wall, propping his legs up on a nearby chair. "I'm not going to be back here long, anyway. You can talk to Spinnaker. You need paper, you can ask him."

"Stupid gringo," Larry muttered, removing his right spur so as to write on the wall. "I just wanted to make a list, *amigo.*"

Hill dropped his feet to the floor and stood up suddenly. He grabbed the cell door. "What the hell kind of list do you need to make, Larry? You want a list of your chores? You want to make a list of your half-witted children? Maybe a list of your groceries? God, you people are so dumb!"

"'Us people,' sheriff?"

"You people, son, the derelicts and the deranged, my friend; the stupid people who find their way into my stupid jail and clutter up my life. I've had it up to here with your kind!" he said, snapping his right hand to his hat. Sheriff Lloyd Hill sat back, rubbing his chest and obviously annoyed.

"Then you'll want to know something, sheriff."

"Know what?" He stood up again, his face red as he walked over to the cell door.

"Santa Anna is coming."

"General Santa Anna?" the sheriff asked, "the lame son of a bitch who found his way back to Mexico so as to take on the whole an American army? Hell son, I wasn't there, but I know my history. Winfield Scott was no Jim Bowie. Second time around, we put our foot up your ass. What the hell's the matter with you, anyway, talking about Santa Anna? He your hero, son?"

Larry Crum looked the sheriff in the eyes. "Believe me when I say, Santa Anna is coming."

"You're so full of shit, Larry. Here's one for you. My brother knew the former Mexican general." His head swaggered left and right. "The stupid fuck lived on Staten Island in New York City. New York City, you dumb shit! Your esteemed folk hero was trying to raise money to go back to Mexico and build an army. The boy liked roosters, son. He was at least good at that, but he's long gone. He's an old man now, lame, blind and someone else who doesn't give a shit about you. Or maybe he's dead, rotting in a boy-sized grave. I don't care." The sheriff spit in a brass spittoon outside the cell. The inference was clear.

"He's coming," Crum reiterated, staring the sheriff in the eyes. "I tell you, Santa Anna or not, the army's coming, my friend. And you will be here to see it."

Chapter 47

LEONARD'S LIST

Leonard's list began with the words, "Make a list." He was careful to capitalize the first letter of the first word and debated whether or not he should use a period. When he was done, Leonard Crum was confident he had put together a plan that his brother Larry would be proud of.

Leonard pulled the chair away from the table, where he looked out on a forest of stumps and discards. He set the simple wooden chair — Larry's chair, as Leonard didn't have one — closer to the metal stove. Taken from a sheep herder a couple of years before, the small iron box set in the middle of the cabin's back wall allowed a half-dozen fellows to gather round, warm their hands and cook a meal. When they had first discovered the dilapidated log shelter, Larry had said that it wouldn't be of much use during the wintertime. But Leonard had re-chinked the cabin, mixing mud and newspaper, so that it was more weather tight. Timber discards from an Incline mill were hammered together for a simple door. With the stove's addition, Leonard had found that he could stay there during the winter months, some of them anyway, as Larry always insisted on living elsewhere once the snows began.

"It's not the cold that bothers me," Larry had stressed, though Leonard wasn't sure he believed his older brother, who had a penchant for wearing fancy jackets, even in July. "It's being wet," he said. Neither of the Crums liked water, and for good reason.

Growing up in Logan, Utah, the Crum family (then spelled with a "b") enjoyed the Great Salt Lake during their summer vacation. Bill and Diane Crum would close the bakery and take their children to the dark sands for an entire week. "It's just like the ocean," Diane would tell her sons, only to discover many years later that the ocean — the Pacific Ocean anyway, the Crum brothers had never been to the Atlantic Ocean — was much nicer. The brothers never learned to fish, as the high salinity of the lake limited fish to only a few areas, and then only after a hard rain. Summer after summer, for a week at a time, the boys played in and about the sand, shrimp larvae and flies wondering why other families didn't enjoy their summers there as well.

Coming to Lake Tahoe had helped heal those memories, though not completely. While they had yet to bath in the lake, they believed it to be beautiful. The clarity of the water, the broad expanse of mountains, the lake's always-changing colors, the slow ride of a tourist steamer from one end of the lake to the other — all of it called to them emotionally. But they never swam in the lake, because the water was too cold.

When Larry said that they were moving from their Washoe Valley home to Lake Tahoe, Leonard hoped they could establish something more permanent, something closer to the shoreline, a house with a view, on the road to Marlette, for instance, or from a much higher point like Cave Rock. But Larry's opinion was fixed. An old settler's cabin, situated amidst the felled and fallen timber but near a good spring, in an area already logged over so that it wouldn't be looked at again, would provide them the privacy they'd need to conduct their business.

He folded the paper up and put it back into his vest pocket before placing his pencil in his hat brim and heading outside. "How's supper coming?" he asked. Smith was bent over a small cook fire, the wood banked on one side to reflect the heat. An iron skillet sat on top of hot, red coals as Leonard's sole remaining *compadre* blew at its base. "Jesus, man!" Leonard shouted, "you're blowing cinders onto the biscuits!"

Smith stood up immediately and cringed. He held his jaw with his right hand and waited a moment, then motioned for Leonard to sit on a rock nearby. "I'm trying to heat up the fire, Leonard. I'm sorry about your biscuits, but they'll be alright."

"Sorry about your face, man. I shouldn't have kicked it," Leonard said.

Smith nodded and, looking up once more before sitting down, went back to stirring the coals of the fire with a fork.

"It looks like your swelling has gone down," the younger Crum brother said, hoping to repair things between them.

"It will be fine by morning," Smith replied quietly, handing him a tin of biscuits and spooning out some gravy. "Know what we're doing yet?"

"I do," Leonard replied. "I've made a list and I'm already crossing things off. 'We need to go get Larry out of jail' is number two. Number three is 'we need to kill Ronin and the marshal.' There is no number four, not as much as I can see anyway."

"What about number one?" Smith asked, feigning interest as the younger Crum brother was a moron. Being concerned at times for his own safety when he was alone with either of the brothers, he was afraid Leonard's unspoken item might include another beating.

"Number one was 'make a list,'" Leonard replied, smiling, "but I've already done that."

"Oh," Smith responded, thinking it was perhaps the dumbest list he had ever heard. Hoping not to give Leonard any clues to his thinking, he struggled to keep a straight face. "Then I guess we ought to get going," he sputtered.

"Oh no," Leonard replied. "We'll wait for morning, or maybe the morning after that. This will be a big deal. We're going to have to do some thinking, and maybe rest up a bit, and maybe make some more bullets."

Leonard took a pile of small stones out of his pants pocket and placed them on his tin, swooshing them around to clean his plate. "Know what bothers me most about living in these woods?"

Smith surveyed the chaotic jungle of stumps and trees that the Crum brothers called their home. "No, what?" he replied.

Leonard pulled the pebbles from his plate and rubbed them on his pants so as to make them clean again. "That nobody comes to visit."

Chapter 48

BEARS

Ronin woke up with a start, realizing that the bear had come to him in his dreams again and asked him the same question. He was sitting in a meadow, with a few friends, he remembered, when the bear had suddenly appeared. Rearing up on his hind legs, the bear asked him, "Where are my babies?" The whole thing seemed bizarre, given that the ex-priest didn't usually dream, or "recall his dreams," Dustsucker had suggested. Now in the course of a couple of weeks, he'd had a few that featured a large, apparently friendly, Tahoe-sized black bear either staring at him or asking him questions.

He pulled the blanket up around his shoulders and tried to close his eyes. A crisp breeze blew through the hotel's second story windows. If he was going to sleep inside, he typically did so with the windows wide open, though it often meant his receiving unexpected visitors. A wind-up clock beside Ronin's bed ticked quietly, its night song ending in a couple of hours.

He hadn't realized he had fallen back asleep until he heard Happy Hands knocking at his door. "Mister Ronin, you wanted me to wake you. Are you up?" He threw his feet to the floor and took a moment to rub the heat back into his legs. He then pulled on socks, rose to shut the window and moved to answer.

"Come in, Happy Hands," he said, yanking a pair of dusty brown pants to his waist and fastening the front of his braces. "Grab me that shirt there, would you?" He pointed to a chair by the door, which only a few minutes before had been leaning up against the door's knob and lock to prevent anyone from entering while he was sleeping.

"This is a good day, Mister Ronin. I will talk to the bear and we will know where we should go."

Ronin stopped buttoning his shirt, his braces down again, hanging from his waist. He wore a grey undershirt, though it wasn't clear to Happy Hands if the color had always been grey or if it had ever been white, not that it made any difference. White people had so many clothes. "Talking to a bear?" Ronin said, alarmed and thinking of his dream.

"Yes, my friend. The bear is my ..." Happy Hands hesitated, as if to consider his words, "... my friend, or my familiar, I guess you'd say." He didn't seem quite pleased by his description.

"Your totem?" Ronin responded.

"What is a totem, Ronin?" he asked.

"I think the word is Indian, Happy Hands. You don't know what it means?"

"Not all Indians are the same, Ronin. We are like you."

"Of course," Ronin replied, embarrassed. "A totem is an animal or object in your life, or your tribe's life, that identifies you as kin or family."

"So ..."

"So, more often than not, it's thought to give you power, to remind you of things, to tell you what you're doing or ought to be doing."

"Like a gun is for you and the marshal," Happy Hands ventured, "or your Confederate uniform before that?"

"Well, I'd hate to think those are things that define me, but yes, or sort of." Ronin had never thought of them that way. "It's more like the gold or silver cross you see some people wear. It suggests that they are Christians."

"Not everyone who wears the cross acts like a good Christian, wouldn't you agree?"

"Of course, but that's not my point," Ronin growled, still thinking about the bear.

The fact that members of the Christian church didn't act like church members should had bothered the ex-priest for a long time. He'd recently given up that expectation, finding it easier to accept that people were people, some aspiring to do good and others not so much. Still, when he left parish work in 1873, it was in large part over the question of whether his parish work was doing any good at all. Had he been more relaxed about it, he might still be working as a priest. "I'm just saying that ..."

"I know," Happy Hands interrupted, smiling. "I was simply curious about what you thought."

"It's a little early for those kinds of discussions," Ronin responded, looking at the clock, which read a quarter after six o'clock. "If you want to talk religion ..."

"I do not, not right now, anyway. But yes, the bear is my totem as you say, and my son's as well. He comes to us in our dreams. The first time he visited me, he just sat down and stared."

Ronin looked up. He stopped pulling at his boots, boots that would have slid on more easily if he had remembered to remove his spurs before leaving the capitol city. "A bear comes to you in your dreams?"

"Often, my friend."

"Wow," Ronin said, standing there.

"Why?"

"Give me a few moments to think," Ronin said, standing with one foot up on a wood and rattan chair. "Maybe we can talk about this while we walk to the mountain. How far is it, anyway?"

Ronin had failed to notice Cave Rock, despite the stagecoach allowing views of it as it approached Lake Tahoe, and having spent a couple of days lakeside without apparently gazing south. Happy Hands smiled. "It is as far away as we want it to be, Ronin, and as close as we need it be. Powerful places are all around us."

"Well good," the ex-priest said, switching feet on the chair. "I don't have all day. I want to check in with Deputy Slade and Marshal Ash before nightfall. They're going to be looking for some witnesses."

"You might want to spend all day, Ronin. Why don't we bring some food and some of the beer you were talking about drinking with the deputy, and perhaps your coat? And then we'll see."

Ronin didn't remember relating the original invitation he had made to Dustsucker. He was pretty certain that the two of them were alone when he suggested they watch the sun go down and drink a couple of beers lakeside. Maybe Dustsucker had told him about the beers, he thought as he buckled his gun belt, pushing it lower so as to sit farther down on his waist. He removed his guns and placed them on the bed, picking the short one up first. Opening the loading gate, he inserted a sixth cartridge, not the perfect way to travel but important if there was a chance of trouble. He wiped the handgun off and returned it to his holster, with the hammer thong down. He did the same with the longer gun, spinning its cylinder to make sure it was operational.

Ronin was getting the impression there were a lot of things he wasn't remembering. Or was it possible that Happy Hands knew things about the murders that he or anyone else had not yet revealed?

"The Indian is talking to bears in his dreams," he mumbled while lumbering down the Lake Shore House's outside steps. "Hell, I'm talking to bears in my dreams." It was all beginning to feel a little spooky.

Chapter 49

WALKING

Ronin took a few steps away from the porch before turning and heading back into the hotel to see if there was any bread or fruit they could take with them. He noticed the proprietor's office door ajar. A kerosene light or two began flickering in the darkness. "Cobb, it's what, 6:30? And you're up?"

"Is that you Ronin?" he said, coming out of his office to meet his guest. "Oh, and you too, Happy Hands!" Cobb wiped the kerosene off of his hands and onto his pants.

"It is I," Happy Hands replied. "Can we borrow a loaf of bread, sir, and perhaps something to go with it?"

"Well, I don't believe they're cooking breakfast yet, gentlemen, but go ahead back to the kitchen. Tell them what you're up to and they'll set you up for the day. Speaking of that," Cobb continued, "what are you doing?"

"We're hiking," said Happy Hands. Ronin's mouth was agape as he hadn't yet thought of a word to describe the craziness Happy Hands had gotten him into.

"We're heading over to Cave Rock, Cobb," Ronin replied. "Hands says there's a great view I need to see and some bears that might want to talk to us."

Cobb and Happy Hands spoke simultaneously, Happy Hands asking what Ronin meant by the word "us" just as the hotel proprietor inquired if they needed to borrow a bear rifle or gun. Ronin pulled his duster back to show Cobb that he was armed, while looking at Happy Hands, who was looking at him. The Washoe man smiled.

"If you take your time, it might take you a couple of hours," Cobb said, indicating that a lakeside trail could make the trip more enjoyable, ultimately placing them at the same place as the road their stagecoach came in on. "It's not too bad a hike from there uphill. Just remember that you're a couple of thousand feet higher than what you are at home. You're both from Carson City, right?"

"Yeah," Ronin said, typically not given to small talk and wondering where the proprietor was headed.

"Well, you're probably not aware that Cave Rock is actually the distant remains of a volcano. The rock was cut by wave and wind action, mostly waves I suspect. Look around, you'll see a lot of glacial debris as well. You know this lake used to be a lot bigger," Cobb commented.

"No," Ronin stuttered, wanting to look interested. "But, we're just taking a walk ..."

"I don't mean to push," he said, "it's just an absolute privilege to work here at the lake and an even more distinct one to have you visit the lake."

Ronin looked over to find Happy Hands smiling even more broadly. "Well, listen Cobb, deputy Slade and Marshal Ash are going to head your way after breakfast to get some names. They want to interview a few people who maybe saw those murdered Washoe fellows. Did we ever get names on those guys?"

"They're Indians, Mister Ronin, they don't have names."

"We have names," Happy Hands responded.

"I apologize sir. Of course, some of you do," Cobb said, looking sheepish.

"All of us have names, Mister Cobb. And none of our names sound like 'Happy Hands' or 'Little Wolf,' or any other name you've given us."

Cobb walked over to where Ronin was standing and offered his hand. "Gentlemen," he said, shaking Ronin's hand first and then extending his hand toward the Indian, "take whatever food you find back there. The staff will help you, and I'll be interested to hear how your day went when you get back."

Happy Hands just looked at him. He didn't raise his hand, as a Washoe man typically did not greet another man in that way. He looked at him and waited. It took a moment, but finally Cobb spoke.

"I'm truly sorry, Happy Hands. I'm glad you're here too, and want to see you also when you get back," Cobb smiled, with his hand still outstretched.

Happy Hands looked down at Cobb's hand, took it in his own and shook it, firmly. "I'll look forward to sitting with you as well, W. Perhaps we can tell each other stories."

"Yes, yes, that'll be a fine thing," W. A. B. Cobb said, as he turned to walk back behind the desk. He sat down in the Lake Shore House's office, a comfortable well-paneled room with built-in book cases, well-crafted windows and blinds, and a large hardwood desk that said, this man is important. This man is in charge. And he smiled. No one had ever called him "W" before.

Chapter 50
STEAMER PIER

Stepping back into the street from the hotel, Ronin and his Washoe friend crossed carefully, cautious to avoid the ruts made by Benton Livery's daily stagecoach service. In the middle of the street, they stopped to observe the place where Happy Hands, a couple of days before, had laid beaten by one of Leonard Crum's men. It was also the final resting place of the man named Jones, until he was picked up by a Lake Tahoe mortuary service for a quieter and greener piece of earth.

"Tahoe has become a confusing place, my friend," Happy Hands offered as he gestured to the Glenbrook pier just ahead of them.

"How so?" Ronin asked, stretching his gait so as to keep up. The Indian seemed to be in some hurry, though they'd have hours to hike before they arrived at Cave Rock.

"Well, for one, there didn't used to be an iron beast here. Now it runs from the lake to the top of the hill to accomplish the white man's harvest of trees. When they have taken all of the trees and slid them down to Carson City, what will they do with the beast then?" Happy Hands shook his head.

"Probably turn it into a tourist attraction, I guess," Ronin mused. He had seen the railroads come, but in his thirty-some years of living, he'd never seen a railroad go. It seemed that the iron tracks and creosote beds, scarring mountains and prairie from one coast to the other, would always be there. The trains on them would always run, whether they were profitable or not. "There seems to be some hurry for folks to get to Reno," Ronin said, "not that I understand it, Happy Hands. I much prefer the places that lead nowhere, my friend. How about you?"

They stood at the end of the steamer pier at Glenbrook, gazing at the lake as the sun came up behind them. Happy Hands pointed to a bald eagle, drifting over the lake toward the mills at Incline. "The eagle is early," he said, "Eagles are rarely seen prior to the snows."

"You sure it's an eagle?" Ronin asked, squinting his eyes. His distance vision, since leaving the Pinkertons, had turned increasingly more difficult. Emma had once said she'd like to see the summer ospreys at the lake. It was an invitation he figured, maybe one he shouldn't have passed up. In any case, he didn't think he could tell the difference between an osprey or an eagle unless he saw the birds close up.

Happy Hands smiled and didn't answer. "Look at its wingspan, Ronin, maybe six, maybe seven feet! What a magnificent bird, isn't it?"

"It is that," Ronin replied. He was hard pressed to remember seeing anything as beautiful as Lake Tahoe. The waters lapped up against the pier's pilings, as steam ships tethered there rested deeply nearby. He'd seen Reelfoot Lake, in northwestern Tennessee. That was big. But its murky, shallow brown waters weren't anything like this. There had been others, of course, as he made his way west. He looked off the cedar boardwalk and gazed into the water as a mountain chickadee sang its distinctive three-note song. He'd never seen anything so clean, so pure or so wonderful. Tahoe was healing. It was exactly what he needed.

"This is where they found them, Ronin, the two men, just off to the left."

"Right here?" Ronin said. The lake was so beautiful, how could anyone do violence in so pristine a place?

"That's what I was told. There used to be store here on the pier, but it burned down."

"I can see that," Ronin said, looking at the scarring along one section of pilings to his left.

"The owner, Mister Childs, was a kind man to our people in the summer months when we fished and hunted these parts. Even then the lake was changing. My friends weren't the first men to die on the pier," Happy Hands said, frowning.

"I didn't understand that they were your friends, Happy Hands. I'm sorry."

"I did not know them," Happy Hands commented, "but they were my people. There are so few of us Washoe, it's helpful to think of all Washoe as friends. Mister Childs is thought to have drowned here as well, though it's hard to say."

"How so?"

"No one ever found him. A couple of years later the store burned. By that time, our people were less tolerated. The white man had built so many houses, logged so many trees, built so many boats, that it became impossible for our people to gather, to fish or to camp without offending someone. So much has changed." Happy Hands moaned briefly while looking out toward the lake's west side. "What used to be an easy journey toward our holy place is now a little more difficult."

"I thought Cobb said that we should follow the road out of town and then head southeast on the wagon road, toward Placerville."

"He did, my friend. I'm only saying, it used to be that a man could walk along the shoreline until he came to the rocks. It was a pleasant journey. One could see the Lady of the Lake in the rock formation just below the white man's road. She watched, as the Creator watches, over all of us, though not so much anymore."

Ronin nodded.

"Now it will just be a walk."

"You used to come here a lot?" Ronin asked.

Happy Hands nodded. "It's the center of our civilization, Ronin, what there is left of it."

"Ah," he said, looking off the pier for pebbles similar to the ones that Ash had described finding in the dead Indian's mouths. He saw none.

"The lake is, in every real sense, our provider. The food that we harvest here during the summer months becomes the food stores we eat from during the winter months — the fish, the deer, the bear and berries, all of it. It is our Mother, in every sense of the word."

"Some places are more sacred than others, Happy Hands. At least, that's how it always appeared to me."

Ronin remembered back to the hills of western Tennessee, where he had gone to fight alongside his father during the war, and to the gentle mountains of Pennsylvania, where he had played as a child and later worked and studied as a man. Special places were made so by special memories, he figured. He couldn't imagine they were sacred just because.

"There is a story or two that I must tell you as we walk to the Standing Grey Stone, my friend. Are you ready to leave?"

"I am," the ex-priest said, placing his hand on Happy Hands' shoulder and looking up from the water. "I'm sorry for your pain, my friend. I know I can't take it away, not all of it anyway. But I'm hoping I can lessen it by getting to the bottom of these murders."

Happy Hands smiled as they turned to leave the pier. "You're feeling better, then?" he asked.

"Better?"

"Better than what you were feeling in Carson City?" he clarified. "You were enduring aches in your stomach and dizziness in your head."

"Oh, yes," Ronin replied. "I wonder what's up with that?"

"Me too," Happy Hands said grinning. "It's as if you've said 'yes' to something that was bothering you and a great weight has lifted."

Ronin looked at his Washoe friend, a tall and lanky man by Indian standards, at least among the Washoe men he'd seen. Keeping up with him was difficult. Happy Hands appeared as if he was waiting for an answer. He took a few moments to ponder the possibilities.

"Perhaps I have, Hands. Some things anyway," Ronin replied, thinking of Emma, and the growing awareness he had of his feelings toward her. And there was also his decision to find the outlaws behind the killing of the two Washoe men, despite the lack of a financial reward, and the necessity in Happy Hands' mind, of spending time in a Washoe holy place. "To be honest, I'm not at all certain all of what I've said yes to," he added.

"None of us ever are, Ronin. The universe simply asks and then waits patiently for us to listen."

Chapter 51

THE FIRST ROADS

The first roads in and around Lake Tahoe were Indian paths, worn over thousands of years as the Washoe people traveled to their summer homes at the lake. Geography divided the tribe into three main groups, northern Washoe generally camped on the north shore, eastern Washoe at the east shore and so on. During the summer months, as well as for war and other special occasions, the Washoe people would gather as one.

"It wasn't unusual for us to fish together," Happy Hands said as they began to walk toward the wagon road, a couple of hundred feet above Glenbrook. "There was some mixing, of course, between our people and others. My first marriage, for instance, was the product of a warm summer memory. But it turned out that the woman I thought was Washoe was actually Northern Paiute. Generally, we got along with everyone," Happy Hands said, looking at Ronin to see if he was keeping up. "This is where our people come and summer."

Happy Hands looked happy with his use of the word "summer," as only the white people spoke of their mountain homes in such a way. Ronin seemed to appreciate that the two of them were spending time together. It pleased Happy Hands to find him so at peace.

"Only the Washoe camped here?" Ronin asked.

"Pretty much so. A Washoe man keeps to his own, my friend. Knowing a particular area is helpful. If a man moves his family, he soon forgets where the plants are that make medicines, and the animals are that lend their meat and hide. As for the Paiute, we have quite a history with the Paiute tribes. It's not easy for us to be together, but where others are concerned, we do our best."

"I remember," Ronin said, as they cleared the road to Glenbrook and began hiking toward the large gray rock that jutted above the trees. "So the Washoe generally get along with each other, but the Washoe and the Paiutes do not?"

"That's correct," Happy Hands said, looking confused. "Certainly, you've noticed one or the other in Carson City or in Virginia City? You'll rarely see us together. It may change someday, but it is not that way now."

"Did you ever meet Sarah Winnemucca?" Ronin asked, trying to keep up. "She was a Paiute, right?"

"I have." Happy Hands slowed down, so as to allow Ronin to catch his breath. "Did you ever hear Sarah Winnemucca speak of the Washoe?" Happy Hands asked, smiling.

"No. I heard her speak in San Francisco once. And Emma has shared some of her pamphlets with me. Emma's a big fan, you know."

"No doubt they are helpful to her," he said, remembering that for an Indian missionary, Miss Emma seemed unacquainted with Indian ways. "Sarah Winnemucca doesn't speak of us," he continued, "except to tell a very sad story of when the Washoe were first falsely accused and killed by white men." Happy Hands shrugged. "Your Mister Ormsby was part of that, before he met his fate with the Paiutes. You have heard that story?" he asked.

"I don't think so," Ronin replied, picking up a stick with which to hike, as the road appeared steeper than he remembered when he had arrived on the stage, and the soil at times was sandy. Happy Hands seemed to glide over the rocks and cinders as if his feet were wheels.

"Most people have not," Happy Hands said. "Winnemucca's family is a good example of what I was telling you. Sarah's grandfather, 'Captain Truckee' the whites call him, was first a Shoshone before he was a Paiute. He was loved by many people."

"It takes a special person to get along with others," Ronin offered, thinking of his time in the church, and Emma, who didn't seem to get on the bad side of anyone.

"Sometimes it takes more than that, Ronin."

Happy Hands slowed down and pointed to a spot on the mountain. "I used to watch the men who built this road, maybe thirty years ago. I used to sit as a child as the men shoveled this path with explosives." Happy Hands pointed to a large rock, still towering above the highway. "Over the years, I watched the road bring horses and then wagons. The people were hungry for silver and gold. There was no end to their numbers for a very long time."

"It seems that time is over, Happy Hands," Ronin said, thinking of the downturn in the capitol's economy. Fewer miners meant fewer farmers. Whole groups of people had been seen leaving Carson City for more promising places. Even a few restaurants had closed. Difficult times, however, meant that he was more plentifully employed.

"That is true, my friend. And the Washoe's day is over as well, I'm afraid. Witness the fire-eating beast at Glenbrook or the large house in Carson City that tells trains to go to Virginia City and Reno. Soon a man won't walk in these hills, like you and I do today. They will ride beasts that they've built, iron monsters they've made, to take them far away from where they live. They will forget who they are, Ronin. I've seen this already with my own eyes."

"Are you talking about the whites or the Washoe, Happy Hands?" Ronin asked, remembering what Dustsucker had said about their being too few Washoe for the federal government to bother finding reservation land. Their numbers were so rapidly diminishing.

"I'm talking about your people," Happy Hands said, laughing. "They've built roads, like the stagecoach road we took south of Carson City and the one you and the deputy had trouble on in Carson City. Your people lay track and build roads wherever they go. And now, you're sliding logs down the mountains! I've never seen people so crazy," Happy Hands exclaimed, waving his hands and pausing on the road so as to make his point.

"I imagine that's true," Ronin said, catching up to his friend. "Mind resting a spell?" he gasped. "I'm a bit winded."

"Of course," Happy Hands smiled.

They sat alongside the road in silence for a few minutes, and watched a Wells Fargo coach fly by. Three teams of horses struggled to keep its eight-mile an hour pace. They covered their mouths and eyes because of the dust, but waved in the event that someone they knew was on board. Passengers waved back.

"Let's sit for a while, my friend. I should probably tell you this story now. It will become increasingly more important for you to understand where you are going, as we come close to the Standing Grey Stone. This is our holy place, Ronin. And you have every reason to be afraid."

Chapter 52

INDIANS, NEGROES, MEXICANS AND WHITES

Dustsucker was finishing breakfast as Marshal Ash entered the dining room. "Augustus!" he shouted, "over here!" as if the hotel's dining room was cavernous, which it was not. A modest parlor-sized room, the Lake Shore House's dining area was an accommodation to its seasonal guests and travelers, and an attempt to keep the hotel's customers hotel-bound when a brief stroll could take folks to the Exchange Billiard and Bowling Parlor, the Glenbrook store or a nearby saloon.

Pray had intended the hotel to be first class in every way, and Cobb was charged with keeping it so. "Marshal, can I get you coffee?" the hotel's proprietor asked as Ash tipped his hat Slade's way.

"You may, Mister Cobb," the marshal replied, "and perhaps a Virginia City paper as well."

"Do you have a preference, sir?" Cobb asked.

"I do not," he replied, "whichever is freshest." He smiled, wondering if he had ever referred to a newspaper in that way. The day's events didn't matter much to Nevada's district marshal, except as they pertained to marshaling and mining interests, though he had to admit, it was occasionally nice to see his name in print. Sorry would be the day if the paper ever carried the intimate details of his business or personal life, as he'd seen a number of men's lives ruined by such writing.

Cobb called from the front desk. "I have the Evening Chronicle sir. I seem to be out of the Territorial Enterprise. I'm sorry. I could go next door, if you'd like."

"The Chronicle will do fine," Ash said, pulling a chair out from underneath Slade's table. A couple of pieces of toast and an open but near-empty jar of strawberry jam was all that remained of Slade's breakfast. Ash fingered a piece toward his lips, parting his mustache with the index finger and thumb of his left hand. "How were your eggs?" he asked, his eyes narrowing.

"They were fine, Augustus. Something going on I need to know about?" Slade asked, thinking the marshal unusually tense. Others in the room were more relaxed and the crisp September lake air seemed uncommonly inviting. "I'm wondering if you'd like to get some fishing in?" Slade asked. "Ronin and Happy Hands walked over to Cave Rock earlier this morning. I'm sure we'd have time before they got back."

"Nah," Ash replied, picking up a butter knife and reaching for the preserves. He looked around for a server and, not seeing one, placed the knife on the table and stood to get some coffee. Cobb entered the dining room with hot coffee in one hand and a paper in the other, just as Ash was getting up.

"No need to rise, Marshal Ash. I'll send a waitress your way in just a moment. Will you need a creamer and some sugar?"

"I will not," he said, waving Cobb away. "Slade, let me ask you a question," he continued. "What do you make of this Indian? You're rooming with him."

"I'm not following, marshal."

"I'm simply saying, how is it he knows so much about these murders?"

"The man gets around, marshal. I mean, Happy Hands has been living in the Washoe Valley for as long as I've been in Carson

City. His living along the road to Reno is pretty new, but I've known Happy Hands, or known about him anyway, for a dozen years or more. I remember when he used to live with his wife, son and others alongside Washoe Lake."

"That's what I'm saying," Ash said. "What's the deal with his living separately from everyone else?" Ash picked up the knife and began spearing at a single strawberry in the preserve jar. Slade watched, perplexed as to how he had left a piece of fruit in the jar. He enjoyed the Placerville berries so much.

"Listen, Augustus, you know him as well as I do. I don't know why you're asking me these questions. He lives alone, I think, so as to mentor his son in the spiritual ways of the tribe, at least that's what I'm assuming. They're back and forth to the lake enough, so I'm guessing it's to do whatever Washoe holy men do on the rock. Nobody's ever seen a Washoe on the rock, so nobody knows."

"And you think these things that they do," Ash's head shook back and forth, "help them to know things that other people don't?"

"Hell if I know about that!" Slade bellowed, picking up a spoon and pulling the jam jar his way. He spotted a second berry at the bottom of the glass and began clawing at it. "That's more Ronin's place, isn't it? I mean, his being a minister and all?"

"Yeah, I think he's pretty sensitive to that, Marcus. Ex-minister is the term he prefers, or ex-priest anyway." Slade sat smiling. If there was food to be had, Slade was going to find it.

"I'm asking," Ash continued, "because we ought to be out talking to people at the lake today and the only person in my head I want to talk to is that damn Indian."

"Can I take your order?" asked a young brown man standing next to the table. Ash looked up at a teenage boy wearing a white shirt and black apron.

"I'm sorry, son. I wasn't talking about you."

"I figured, sir, since we haven't met." The boy appeared to be Washoe, or Paiute, not that Ash could tell the difference, about 15 years old and clearly Indian.

Slade looked up, laughing. "Son, this is the U.S. Marshal for these parts," he said. "We're here investigating the death of two men drowned at the lake a couple of weeks ago. Do you know anything about it?" Ash sat there red-faced.

"Sure, Mister Slade, everyone knows about it. But they were not drowned, Mister Slade. They were beaten first and thrown in the lake. That's my best guess."

"How so?" Ash growled. The Indian boy winced, as he was facing the deputy when the marshal interrupted. Ash's angry tone took him by surprise.

"Everyone knows, marshal. Only their clothes and hair were wet. Their mouths were dry. In fact, their mouths were filled with dirt and stones. A drowning man doesn't swallow dirt and stones, you know."

"Yeah, so I hear." Ash looked over at Slade, who was still smiling. He nodded. "How do you know they were beaten, boy?"

"They were bleeding sir, or looked as if they were bleeding before they died, that is."

"Before they died?" Ash asked.

"Yeah, it looked as if someone had stomped them pretty good and then dragged them up to the hotel door."

"But they were wet, you said?" Slade interjected.

"They were, Mister Slade. The drag marks led from the pier. But by the time they got to the door, they were pretty dirty, muddy in fact. A few of the men, Mister Cobb included, thought since they were wet they had drowned. And a drunken Indian is ..." The boy looked at the Ash. "Well, you know marshal, a pretty common sight up this way."

Slade noticed that the boy was smirking. "Son, are you serious? Or are you joking around?"

The boy was silent for a moment and appeared to be considering his response. "It's not so common, Mister Slade. I'm sorry Marshal Ash. Generally Washoe don't drink during the summer months we're at the lake. I was just ..." he hesitated.

"Making a point?" Slade asked.

"Exactly, sir."

Augustus Ash looked down at his menu. *Maybe a couple of eggs and some sausage, or perhaps some bacon.* "How are the flapjacks, son?"

"Made as they always are, sir. Healthy and true."

"You cooking?" Ash asked.

"No sir. No Indians, no Negroes, no Mexicans. Only white people in the kitchen, sir."

"Then I'll have two."

Chapter 53
THE ONG

"When I was young, I was taught to leave an offering when I passed by the Standing Grey Stone. My family was not permitted to visit as we are today. We were told to avoid it, as only holy men were welcome here." Happy Hands stood beneath the tree line, a few feet from the roadway. A pebbly ledge afforded them a place to sit and view the pristine waters of Lake Tahoe below. A soft breeze raised ripples on the lake, as wispy white clouds in an otherwise bright blue sky led to mountains a few miles away.

"How far are we?" Ronin asked, pointing to the other side of the lake.

"A half a day's walk," Happy Hands replied, "if we could walk on water. But very few can," he said, smiling.

Ronin looked up. "Don't believe I've ever heard of an Indian walking on water before."

"Only in winter, my friend, and ice never forms at Lake Tahoe." The two men laughed, Happy Hands, clearly anxious to get moving again and Ronin, who was satisfied to sit there, even though he had been told he wasn't permitted to come any further. "Thank you for understanding that this place is for holy men only," Happy Hands continued. He crouched lower, so as to not hit his head on the timbers supporting the road along the edge of the rock. The construction provided some shade.

"I completely understand," Ronin replied, thinking of the rules about handling the sacraments in his own religion, a faith he now barely embraced but still remembered. "I want to be respectful, Happy Hands, though I'm sure I don't always act that way." Being an Episcopal priest had been hard for Ronin. Being an ex-Episcopal priest had been harder. Seven years had elapsed since he had left the priesthood and he was still trying to act like he was a good man. "I apologize, Happy Hands. I haven't always been the most caring of persons." Coming on the walk had been helpful. He could see that despite being an Indian, Happy Hands was a man just like himself: trying to do what was right, not always knowing, distracted at times by his emotions, by people and the tasks at hand. He began to say something more when Happy Hands stood up.

"There are stories, Ronin, of men and women who didn't belong on the Standing Grey Stone, who were grasped by the large bird that lives in the center of the lake. They were taken up into the sky and eaten." Ronin smiled. Not hearing a response, Happy Hands continued, "The lake is where the Ong lives, and also the Water Babies. Despite their being important to my religion, my friend, I do not enjoy seeing them."

Ronin laughed. He felt the same way about church ladies.

"Look Happy Hands, I'm fine sitting here. If I push back underneath the trestles a bit, and up against the retaining wall, I can probably stay out of the sun. And assuming no one comes along to startle me, I can probably keep from falling into the lake. I may even snooze a bit. But Water Babies and big birds with wings as tall as a pine tree? I'm not much of a believer in either."

"So you've heard of the Ong, then?" Happy Hands asked, surprised.

"Never heard it called that before, but I've heard of the scaly thing with the big webbed feet. I heard that he used to live in the middle of the lake, not that any of that concerns me." Ronin grinned. "I do like the fact that he grabs folks who don't do their duty however, and eats them!" Ronin laughed heartily, but stopped when he noticed that Happy Hands wasn't laughing at all.

Happy Hands winced. How could someone enjoy hearing that a human being had been eaten? He shuddered, thinking of the stories he'd heard about the Donner party thirty-some years prior. The Washoe had been witness to their sufferings, and had tried to keep the white men from eating each other. Perhaps Ronin was simply teasing.

"My father told me there was a time when we could communicate with the bear, the coyote and the birds. Now, it is a gift that only a few can entertain, and only sometimes. But this bird is not dead, my friend. The Ong still lives, and he does not communicate with anyone."

Ronin smiled, as he sat back and pulled his hat over his eyes. "A watched pot never boils, my friend. You ought to get going."

"You've heard the story then?"

"I have," Ronin responded by tipping his hat further downward, until it touched his nose. "But I won't keep you from telling it again, if that's what you're intent on doing."

Happy Hands squatted again, alongside the roadway, holding onto a shrub. He looked over at the rocky ledge where Ronin sat, fifty or more feet above the lake's surface. "Since you've heard it, I won't tell it again. But I will say that the Ong is nothing to be trifled with. No rivers feed this lake, Ronin, only the waters from his nest. As the nest is at the center of the lake at its deepest part, all of the waters of this lake rush into the nest, and then rush out again. The Ong's power exceeds its grasp, my friend. Even the fish get caught in these currents and he eats them all. Do not fall in."

Ronin pushed his hat back up. "Happy Hands, there are plenty of rivers and streams that feed Lake Tahoe. Just look around you. The water doesn't come from a big nest in the lake's center any more than ..." Ronin stuttered ... "the stars are thrown out into the sky by a white bearded old man."

"I'm not talking about the stars, Ronin, or the white man's god. I'm talking about you, and the men who are responsible for these murders. I'm talking about people everywhere for that matter. Those who know what to do but don't do it will find themselves in the Ong's nest, sooner or later. Whether he is a giant beast or not is unimportant, bad catches up to all of us. And the good, sometimes, cannot keep us from it."

"We agree about that, my friend," Ronin offered, touching his hat. "There's not a good person who's been born that doesn't experience a little bit of shit in this life." Ronin looked up and noticed Happy Hands appeared frustrated. He hadn't intended for his comment to leave him that way. "What?"

"I don't think you're taking me seriously, Ronin. I'm talking about you, your dreams, the larger call of your life, my friend. You can't run from it all forever."

"I don't know what you're talking about, Happy Hands, 'the larger call of my life?' Jesus, man! You sound like my bishop."

"You've been dreaming about bears?" he asked.

"Yeah, how did you know?" Ronin sat up, annoyed. Walking with an Indian was one thing. Sharing his dreams with one was another.

Happy Hands shook his head, incredulously. Could Ronin be this dense? How could the bear pick such a stupid man for such an important task? He didn't understand. "And he's asked you something, hasn't he?"

The Indian needed to climb the damn rock. He didn't need to be standing above him on the roadway, shouting.

"I'm not trying to get you angry, Ronin. I'm trying to help you."

"Yeah, the bear asked me a question," he shouted back. He couldn't believe he was discussing his nightmares with a man who, however human, was still a heathen.

"And?"

"And he asked me, 'Where are my babies?' Ronin growled. "How the hell is that important?"

It was supremely important, Happy Hands thought. How could he have missed it? No one had considered where and how the men were buried.

Chapter 54
LITTLE WOLF

Cobb joined the two of them as soon as the marshal's eggs were served. The young man set the plate directly in front of the marshal and turned it slightly, so that his eggs were at one side, faced by two sausages and a biscuit at the top. He then positioned an additional plate at 10 o'clock, with pancakes, a pat of fresh-churned butter and a tiny syrup pitcher on the plate's edge.

"Little Wolf?" Slade asked, "Is that you?"

"Deputy. It is good to see you."

"Well, isn't this a surprise! I didn't recognize you with your white shirt and your hair all slicked back. How long have you worked here?"

"This is my first summer, Mister Slade." Little Wolf looked at the hotel's proprietor to see if he was lingering too long at the table. Cobb nodded. "My father is not aware that I'm working here, deputy. I don't know that he would approve. My mother and some of her family are camping nearby and it seemed like ..."

"Well, it's a wonderful thing to do, Little Wolf! I mean, getting a taste of Christian culture and all that, and earning a little bit of money to boot." Dustsucker laughed. He had always enjoyed the boy. It was nice to see him making something of himself. "Ronin said he'd seen you up here a couple of weeks ago. I figured you were with your family — fishing, hunting, that kind of thing."

"I am, Mister Slade." He looked over at his employer again and, not seeing a nod, concluded his time had run out. "I'm here a couple of days and off a couple of days. All in all, it works very well. Mister Ash, is there anything else you would like?"

Augustus Ash shook his head and smiled. "It does a man's heart good to see an Indian work, son."

"Yes sir. And Deputy Slade, can I get you anything?"

"I'm fine," Dustsucker said, picking up his napkin from his chest and laying it on the table. "Ash, I assume breakfast is yours, since Ormsby County picked up the bill last night. I'll be up in my room when you're ready." He stood up. "Ronin was hoping we'd get a couple of names this morning and then maybe spend the rest of the day talking to folks."

"I'm aware of that. I don't need a county deputy to tell me what to do, let alone a private detective. Mister Cobb, can you remain a few moments?"

"I can."

"Then I'll see you in your room in about half an hour, Slade. Little Wolf, is it? Would you mind bringing me some coffee in about ten minutes? I like my food and coffee hot."

"Certainly, sir."

"Cobb, you run a real nice place here."

"Thanks, marshal. Why do you say so?"

"Well, employing Indians and the like. It keeps them off the street and off the war path." Ash laughed as he stabbed a fork into his pancake and touched it to his lips. Looking at his plate, he began to wonder if his food had been contaminated or played with. "Mister Cobb, this pancake is cold."

"I'm sorry, marshal. Shall I have the boy bring you another?"

"No, I'll be fine with what I have." He put his fork down and, picking up a dark blue napkin from the table, folded his biscuit into it. "Cobb, let's you and I make a list of the people who saw these two dead Indians the night they turned up at your door."

"You bet," Cobb said. The Lake Shore House proprietor took a short pencil from his vest and began scribbling in a notebook.

"It's hard to remember who was working that night. We'd closed the restaurant already, but there were folks at the bar. I believe the boy was the first one to notice the corpses."

"The corpses?"

"Well, sure. There were two of them, of course, laying up against the stoop, as if they had been dragged there. Everything was pretty wet, I mean their boots, their clothing and so on. And the boy came running in, asking that we find some blankets. I yelled, 'What the hell for?' thinking that the housekeeping staff had forgotten something, and that's when a half-dozen men from the bar piled out onto the street."

"Half a dozen men, you say?"

"That's right."

"So, you figure that Little Wolf saw the dead Indians first, and then these others came out of the hotel as well."

"Yes, that's right."

"You were with them?"

"I was. I think I was the first one to figure out that they were dead."

"I'm not following. You all didn't know that they were dead?"

Cobb shook his head, "Well, no marshal, what with the way Indians drink and all."

"Right."

"Apparently, Little Wolf was wanting the blankets so as to warm the men. When we knelt down to rouse them, we could see all the blood."

"Tell me about the blood," Ash asked, squinting.

"There was swelling and blood around the eyes, that's all. Like the men had taken a beating. And their lips, too."

"Their lips?"

"They were split, pretty mangled up if you ask me. That's when we noticed the rocks."

"The rocks?"

"Right, the rocks in their mouths."

"Wow," Ash said, taking Cobb's pencil and notebook and beginning to write. "I really don't think I've ever seen that before. You saw this, for sure?"

"I certainly did, marshal. Tiny pebbles. It was the damnedest thing."

"Where are the bodies now?" Ash asked, pencil poised so as to write down their location.

"Well, I don't rightly know, marshal, them being Indians and all. But I believe they were taken up over Kings Canyon and planted up there. Little Wolf might know. Do you want me to check with him, sir?"

"More, coffee marshal?" Ash flinched. The boy seemed to appear out of nowhere.

"I don't think so."

"You haven't touched your food." Little Wolf smiled.

"Wasn't hungry, son." Ash looked at the boy like a man looking at his dog, wondering if the dog had done something bad. "Since you're standing here, son, do you happen to know where those Indian men are buried?"

"Of course, sir. Everyone knows that." Cobb winced. "They're buried up Kings Canyon way. A couple of freighters took them there. Imagine you can find the graves quite easily, marshal. It's this side of the divide. They've got a cross on them, I think. Don't believe there are that many crosses up there, marshal. It should be easy to find."

"Oh, there are son, a lot more than you might imagine."

Chapter 55
ALLY

Ally pushed past the men who were chatting up the Indian boy and wondered what the United States Marshal would be doing up at the lake in September. She nodded to Cobb as she headed toward the hotel's front door, after setting her apron on a chair by the kitchen.

The last week or two at the lake had felt like an "Indian summer," one of the French wood cutters had remarked last night as she had poured him a glass of red wine. When she confessed some confusion over the words, he explained they announced "a sudden and appealing mildness to weather that was expected to be much brisker," a speech she hadn't expected out of a French Canadian tree cutter, even if he was trying to impress her.

Stepping off the hotel's steps and into the street, she turned right toward the cabins, where she hoped she'd be able to get a good day's sleep before her restaurant shift began again. The dinner bunch wasn't all that bad, though the evenings could sometimes wear on. But the late night bar room rabble was unpredictable. She'd seen the marshal and two other men after midnight, one of them an Indian, at whom she had smiled while hoping she'd be able to shut down early. An oddly entertaining man, she wouldn't mind meeting him again, though nothing permanent could come of it, she thought, so why bother?

"I don't believe the thought is all that kind," she had told the Frenchman who, while attractive, appeared surprised that she had any wits at all. Most men simply stared at her breasts, ample as they seemed because she needed them that way. "Look," she said, "it's a little like calling someone an 'Indian giver,' that's all I'm saying. Or rubbing someone's arm and calling it an 'Indian burn,'" though she didn't really know what she was talking about. That didn't stop the men she knew — why should it stop her?

When she had lived in Carson City, she really appreciated the autumn months. A couple of streets west of the capital, her second story apartment on Ormsby Street allowed a view of the Carson hills. When the autumn rains came, the smell of the west side trees and sage was over-powering, particularly in Ash Canyon where she sometimes went to walk or muse. She smiled every morning when first rising and, looking out her west-facing windows, would briefly imagine the direction her life was going. "California is just over that hill," she used to tell her customers, who seemed amused by her simple observation.

"Everybody knows where California is," the less sensitive men would remark. Some knew what she meant and wanted. Henry knew for instance, though in the end it didn't seem to make any difference. Jack knew as well, the son of a bitch. It took her a while, but she finally figured out that neither of them would take her there.

Some of the maple trees in front of the capital building turned bright red when the weather was just right. "Just like a woman's lipstick," her friend Henry used to say, not that she had seen him after moving to the lake, and not that she ever expected to see him again. She hadn't even told him she was moving. She had simply taken her hand off his jimmy, stood up from the table where they were sitting and remarked that she was done for the day. She moved to the lake shortly after that, and that was that.

She paused for a moment, turning left to appreciate the quiet magnificence of what someone had said was one of the world's largest lakes. She would never get used to the grandeur, she thought to herself as a white and black robin-sized woodpecker began to tap-tap-tap into a tree. San Francisco was the place to be, she had figured all those years catting around with Henry Nauman, the director of the gospel mission south of the city, while still having to please another man, the owner of the Ormsby Street bar, every night. Jack's happiness meant that she stayed employed. It was a no brainer. Henry's bliss, however, had amounted to shit. But she was better off this way, having nothing, sharing a room with someone she hardly knew while working alongside and for men she figured she'd never get to know because she was so bruised, so beaten, so battered inside.

She tugged at the gun between her breasts. When it pulled free, she placed it in her right coat pocket. The four-barreled pepperbox revolver wasn't even loaded. She didn't even know if it worked. It simply let men know that they might want to look at her face for a change, or consider her heart or wonder in what ways she was hopeful and human.

When the two men were dragged up from the pier a couple weeks prior, it seemed like they were still struggling, at least to her point of view, from one of the tall windows at the front of the hotel. Occluded in part by the hotel's fancy porch furniture, she'd gone over to see if someone needed help, but there were three men already there doing the helping, or so it seemed. The next morning, of course, she heard that the men struggling were Indians — it was hard to tell in the dark, and the Washoe dressed just like white men, for the most part. She heard too that they were dead Indians, which meant that the marshal might want to talk to her, though given her previous employment she wasn't sure she wanted to talk to him.

She quickened her steps as the morning air wasn't nearly as warm as it had been the previous mornings when she had walked to the cabin she shared with a daytime employee, which worked out okay, though only one of them could sleep at a time, which was fine. Though getting to San Francisco was no longer important to her — she enjoyed Lake Tahoe that much — it would be nice, she imagined, to have her own place. Ally stuck her hand in her left pocket to weigh how much money she had made last night in tips and wages. It might take a very long time to earn the amount necessary.

Her dream had died in Carson City. Jack the saloon owner had turned out to be a dud, and she had discovered the enterprising weasel of a man who ran the gospel mission to be an insensitive, self-absorbed, two-timing prick. But life had its way, she mused as she pushed opened the heavy cabin door and settled into a dark colored wooden chair to take off her shoes. She had learned the hard way that life's expectations were sometimes meaningless. Looking back, she hadn't become or achieved anything she'd wanted to. And yet, she had gained so much more.

Ally pulled her dress over her head and stood naked in front of the window, which had a partial view of the lake, if she stood with her left side up against the pine paneling and looked just beyond the aspen trees, still mostly green. Embracing her body — still beautiful, despite the wear and abuse by men who should have been kinder, and moments she had spent with them when she might have been more thoughtful — she ran her hands down her sides, warming her chest and legs. She slipped between the covers of the bed. Before pulling the shade down on the window beside her bed she considered: if tomorrow wasn't any better or worse than last night, or even the night before that, it would be still be a wonderful day.

Chapter 56
WE GOT NOTHING

On a couple of rental horses just after lunch, Slade and Ash began to make their way up to the Spooner Meadow. By the late 1860s, timber ranches had sprouted east of the lake, toward Carson City and the Comstock. Twenty years later, the mountains were nearly bare. Timber cutting had to move north and south of Glenbrook. A complex system of barges, timber carts and railroads moved lumber to Spooner, where it was pushed downhill by a series of flumes and the downward pressure of millions of gallons of water.

"It's unbelievable, isn't it?" Slade asked as he walked his horse through the moonscape Lake Tahoe had become. "I was here pretty early on, Augustus. It was amazing, the trees, the standing waves of grain and all that. That Augustus Pray sure had it together, didn't he?"

"I imagine so," the marshal replied, not one for small talk even when small talk was big talk in someone else's mind. Ash was focused on the task at hand, thinking of the murder investigation rather than the geography of the Bank of California's timber industry.

"Ronin hates it here," the deputy continued, noticing Ash's lack of attention. "I mean, it's the first time he's been up this way, and all. Emma has asked him to go, take a boat ride and all that. He's not enjoyed this at all ... all this emptiness and machinery grinding up the landscape. He says it reminds him of the railroads in Wichita ..."

"Right," Ash replied, undeterred from the task at hand.

"... and I guess that makes him uncomfortable. Modernity and such," Dustsucker said, nodding his head up and down, as if he understood the word.

Ash looked over. "I guess Ellen and I see the other side of it. Mining has kept food on the table for us, and a lot of other people as well."

"Ellen?"

"My wife."

"I didn't know you were married, Augustus. I mean you've been marshal since what, 1876? That's four years we've known each other and I don't even know you're married?"

"Slade, we hardly know each other. We hardly see each other. That's probably why you don't know I'm married."

"Jesus."

"Your point?" the marshal's eyes squinted as he pulled up on the reins. While he was proud of his family, and happy to be making a living in what had to be one of the most exciting places on the planet, talking about his family with someone he hardly knew was not something he was used to doing. Nor did he care a whole hell of a lot about Tahoe's trees. "Well?"

"Well, nothing," Slade replied. "I just didn't know."

Ash kicked his mare with his boot and the two began to climb toward Spooner Meadow. "I'm saying, Slade, that I get the need for timber. I've got some interest in the mines. Who doesn't? And you can't build mines on the Comstock without timber. Listen," he said, doubling down on his effort to crest the hill by leaning over the horse's front legs, "I'm sure it was all very pretty up here, before Bliss and Yerrington started their little timber and fluming company."

"It's a pretty big company," Slade interrupted, "especially after buying Pray out."

"You're missing my point, Slade. I'm sure it was real nice, the Indians fishing at the lake and wagon loads of white people coming up to spend the summer. But it was a giant waste of resources, if you ask me. These men, and a whole bunch of others, made this country what it is, which is one of the greatest places on earth."

Slade hadn't seen the marshal so enthusiastic before.

"Look, it will come back. It always does. And as for Ronin, I don't have to tell you this, you're his buddy, but that man's got some issues."

"Guess so," Dustsucker nodded, thinking of his friend and wondering when he'd get back from Cave Rock, as Ash wasn't much of a conversationalist unless he got wound up — and then it was hell to pay. "Mind telling me where you think we are in this investigation?" he asked. "I'm not clear why we're heading to Spooner."

Augustus Ash was a wizened and moody man. The glaring Nevada sun did that to just about everyone who spent enough time out in it. Slade watched as he took an uncharacteristically somber mood. "I wish I knew," he said, dropping one hand to his side, checking to see if his rifle and saddle bags were still there.

"You wish you knew?" Slade asked, surprised.

"I don't know that we've got anything at this point, deputy, except to say that someone dumped a couple of dead Indians on the front stoop of the Lake Shore House a couple of weeks ago. And though they might have been wet — the kid had a good point, dead guys don't eat dirt — there's a good possibility that they may have been beaten to death. Why, I don't know. And as for suspects, the mountains are probably full of people who'd want to roll an Indian at the right time of night who's lingering where he doesn't belong. We got nothing."

"You thinking the Crum brothers might have had something to do with it?" Dustsucker asked, happy that they were nearing the end of the short gauge that hauled timber to the top of the hill. The horses didn't seem to care for the grade or the gravel.

"Maybe, maybe even probably, if there's a connection between the boys we met and the gang that Ronin and you put away. That would at least suggest a motive." They were coming to the summit, which looked remarkably similar to the lumber yards in Carson City, except for a giant wooden flume and a few more trees.

"How so?"

"If these men are the same men you all shot up the other day, Slade, they're either out of business or they doing business, recruiting."

"And the Indians were among their recruits?" Dustsucker didn't think that was likely, as the men they had killed were dress as Mexicans. It would be hard to get a Washoe man to look like a Mexican, at least in his experience.

"Nah," Ash replied, pulling the reins to one side so as to tie his horse to a large stump. "But there's every chance that the Indians saw something they shouldn't have, or stumbled onto something or someone that cost them their lives."

Chapter 57

TIME TO GO

"It's time to go," Leonard said, pushing the sleep crud from his eyes with the knob on the end of his knife. Leonard had learned a long time ago to be careful when touching his eyes. His brother had noticed that dirty hands made for itchy eyes, bloody hands even more so. So Larry had given Leonard a Masonic ceremonial dagger made in Columbus, Ohio. The dagger had a bone handle, which was easy to clean, and a nice silver button on the end, in the shape of a tiny helmet. The helmet's plume had an edge on it. While it wasn't suitable for shaving — he kept a smaller razor in his saddle bag for that — it did make it easy to scrape the itchier places on the back of his neck when he wasn't able to wash, which wasn't all that often when they were camping above the tree line near Incline.

Larry had told him to always be careful using the dagger on his eyes, because he'd seen a man slip one time scratching his face with the edge of his blade in a Washoe City saloon and nearly lose his eyesight. As it turned out, the fine fillet the man's knife made of his face wasn't much appreciated by folks at the poker table, who upon seeing the hapless slice of meat laying on their discard pile, gut-shot the man, which seemed appropriate to everyone, especially those who were enthusiastic about dragging the bleeding bastard outside.

"It's time to head to Carson City and get my brother," Leonard barked as he rolled out of his rope bed, pulling his cotton mattress off of the bed with him. The noise woke his companion, who immediately grabbed his still-swollen jaw hoping he wasn't about to be beaten again. But Leonard just sat there, staring at him from the bed's creaking wooden frame.

"I thought you said that we needed some Indians first," he said, lowering his blanket. Smith remembered something about how risky it was to be seen in the Glenbrook or Incline timber camps right now to recruit, and that a couple of Indians would have to do, if they could find some.

"That was before those two brown-skins started complaining about it being the wrong time of year to be working for a white man," the unibrow said. "All that hunting and fishing shit, I can't stand it."

"You can't stand what, Leonard?" he said pulling himself up off the floor, so that he sat in one corner of the shed, a crumpled wool blanket laying by his side.

"I can't stand that you can't buy a goddamned Indian or Mexican when you need one, you jackass."

"Well, that's 'cause they're working the flumes and donkey engines, pushing logs, Leonard," Smith said, immediately regretting his tone. The Crum brothers were sensitive to being called stupid, and while one was a bit slower than the other, neither liked to be thought of as feeble-minded. He watched Leonard pull on his boots and figured the tone had escaped him. "What do we want with grease monkeys and donkey punchers anyway, Leonard? It's not like they're fun to be with."

Leonard looked up and then stood, pulling up the copper-riveted pants he had removed from a wagon-driver a couple of weeks prior to his brother's arrest. "That is a good point, my man ..." Smith relaxed, turning his back to find his socks and shoes. He'd yet to find a sturdy pair of boots that would fit him. In time, the Crum brothers had said, they'd roll somebody whose boots would make a good fit. "... and thinking on it a bit this morning, I remembered 'finding more people' wasn't on our list. Rescuing Larry was. So let's go. Get the fuck up and get ready."

"I'm moving," he replied, cringing. That was two, he'd likely not get another before Leonard hit him again. "I meant I'll be just a minute, Leonard. I'm untying my socks and shoes now." Smith had learned that sleeping with his shoes on made for warmer feet, and while he understood why the Crum brothers never slept with their boots on, he didn't get why anyone would want to rest their head on them at night, given where their boots had been. He preferred to keep his shoes between his legs, with the laces tied. In the event someone was thinking of stealing them — a common crime, his brother had said, but no big deal — the short tug on his scrotum would wake him, though the blister the shoes had made rubbing up against his private parts was beginning to be painful.

"Leonard, shouldn't we make something to eat first? I could make you some biscuits again," he said, looking for a way to redeem himself from the previous night's episode. "I'll be very careful this time."

"We'll get something to eat as soon as we get to Summit Camp. Then it's only twenty or so miles downhill from there. We can be in Carson City by supper."

Leonard gathered up his stuff. It would be a while before they headed into the mountains again. Larry typically spent his days in jail thinking up good adventures they could take. Maybe they'd head to Bodie for a while, or to Enterprise or Silver City. He picked up his Masonic dagger from the floor and put it back into its carved wooden sheath. A silver chain attached the knife to his belt, 17 inches from end to end, his brother had said, though Leonard had never stopped to measure it. The blade was long enough to have been a sword at one time. "It might have been used in a ceremony, Leonard," his brother had told him when he handed it to him. One side had a silver crucifix on it. Leonard ran his thumb over the raised part, which portrayed Jesus Christ shedding his blood for the sins of mankind. The other side read, "Knights Templar."

Leonard smiled, missing much of what his companion was saying about biscuits and honey, ham and beans, though he knew they'd be able to get any and all of that at Summit Camp if that's what they wanted. "It's the symbolism," Larry had said. "It's part of our calling." And while he didn't understand the words at the time, he understood them better now, after the Indians were dead. They were fellow soldiers with Christ. Like the Templars of old, Larry had said, the two brothers were exempt from all authority, except for a man named Pope. And to date, he hadn't met anyone named that.

Chapter 58

SUMMIT CAMP

"What we need are some bodies," the marshal pronounced as he got off of his horse. "Anything else is going to be circumstantial, my friend. No bodies, no murders. That's the rule, particularly given that they're Indians."

"I guess we should have got here sooner then," Slade said, looking for something to tie his horse to. He spied a beetle-ridden log a few feet away and, figuring it would provide ample entertainment for his horse, pulled up on the reins.

"We got to the lake as soon as we could," Ash replied, looking over at a steam engine on the short line and wondering why they hadn't taken Cobb up on his offer to run them to the summit rather than have them climb a series of hills and zigzags to get to the same place. "I don't believe I've been here before, Slade. How about you?"

"Nope. I generally stay away from the business side of things, Ash. Don't mind hitting the camps and towns along the way, but I don't like bumping into the businessmen. And folks up here tend to take care of their own business pretty much, without me wandering around sticking my nose into things. Wanna get something to eat?"

"We just ate, Slade. You hungry again?"

"I wouldn't mind a cup of coffee, if one was offered to me, Augustus. Maybe someone will know where the graves are on the toll road. Save us a lot of time looking up and down Kings Canyon, if you ask me."

"Sure 'nuff," Ash said, looking for a mess tent among the flume trestles and stacks of lumber. A few buildings sat alongside the railroad tracks uphill from the flumes. Ash and Slade grabbed their rifles from their saddles and walked over to a Negro flume-tender, sitting next to a 4-foot-high V-flume. Feeder flumes caught water from a nearby mountain stream or reservoir, filling it with water ten or so inches high so as to push timber to Carson City. Ash spoke first. "Cup of coffee?"

"Love one," the man said.

"No, I mean where can we get one?"

"Over by the tool shed, marshal," the man replied, looking at Ash's badge, laughing. "Don't know that we've seen a sheriff up this way in some time," he drawled. "You lookin' for somebody?"

"It's marshal, son, I'm not a sheriff. You afraid of a U.S. marshal, boy?"

"No sir, I'm a long way from home," he drawled, "but never did have much use for a badge, sir."

"Me either," Ash said, "until I became one." Ash smiled. "Over there?" he asked, gesturing toward a white tent parked next to a pile of railroad wood. The man nodded. It made a marshal feel good to see another man work, who might otherwise feel angry about the way he had been treated a long time ago. "You want one?" he asked, his head turning over his left shoulder as they headed to the cook tent.

"Nah," the man said, looking back toward his work. "Never much liked coffee either."

Chapter 59
BY THE EARS

"Summit Camp on a Sunday won't be nearly as busy as it would be on a Monday," Cobb said before the two lawmen left the hotel. "It's a small crew most weekends," he added, sitting down at his desk in the cedar paneled office he enjoyed at the Lake House. "The last couple of years have been tough on everybody. There's talk of mills shutting down. Less fallers, sawyers, buckers, teamsters, river hogs, grease monkeys, donkey punchers and whistle punks."

Slade grinned, because he didn't understand a damned word Ash was saying — he was relating what Cobb had said — except that folks weren't working as hard as they used to at the lake, the jobs being so few.

"The guy says to me," Ash took a sip from his coffee, "that Bliss actually told him that 'the lake is becoming a tourist destination. Imagine that!' he says. 'I've got people every day now asking if our "tourist cabins" are available!'" Ash sat laughing. It was evident that he didn't like W. A. B. Cobb that much, or at least didn't like him talking so much so early in the morning.

"'For every three French tree-fallers who move out, I've got an adventurous young couple and a baby who want to move in. Hell, it wouldn't surprise me if Bliss yanked his short-line someday,' he says, 'and ran it to Reno to entertain fat ladies and dopes in derby hats.'" Ash laughed again, blowing at the steam lifting from his coffee and savoring its smell. Hot coffee was the key to Ash's heart. It was a shame Slade hadn't found out sooner.

"Sounds like he was pretty animated, Augustus. What do you suppose he was getting at?" Slade noticed that the cook had taken a sauce pan from a rack above the stove and begun pounding along the bottom of the tent, about every six inches or so, until he had covered a space of twelve to fifteen feet.

"So he says," Ash continued, unaware that anything odd was going on, "'the teamsters used to haul trees from the east and north shores. Now, they're cutting trees further south and west. If money wasn't a problem, which it is of course, they'd be pulling trees all the way back to Strawberry.' Can you imagine that? Cutting trees back to Hangtown and Sacramento? Yeah, I doubt it."

"So I say, 'Your point, Mister Cobb? We're not interested in mining,'" and he says, 'I'm sorry, marshal, I was just making conversation. I thought you had a few shares in Gold Hill and had done some mining yourself.'"

"I say, 'I do, and have. What we want to do is talk to a few boys at Summit Camp and then head down Kings Canyon a ways. I've got to find some bodies, Mister Cobb,' I tell him. 'Yup — no corpses, no criminals.'"

Ash suddenly stopped talking when he heard the cook hit something, or someone, just a few feet from him down around his legs and through the canvas. "What the hell are you doing?" he yelled, jumping out of the way.

The heavy-set Washoe Indian woman, about 4-feet-tall, who had poured them their coffee a few moments before, jumped as well. "I'm hitting him! The stupid boy who comes here on the weekends and steals my supplies, look at him!" she hollered, picking the canvas up, but seeing no one. "I know I hit him!" she shouted.

"Keep it down, woman, can't you see I'm telling a story?" Ash turned back toward the deputy to continue, when the boy they knew as Little Wolf came barreling in the front of the tent on his tiptoes and holding his head. A large German man had him by the ears.

"Is dis da boy you were chasing?" the man asked, every word sounding like the beginning of a folk song. Over 6-feet-tall and easily Slade's equal in girth and weight, the man was all smiles and muscles. The Washoe woman nodded. "Vat do you vant da do wit him?" he asked, still singing.

"Now, hold on young man," Ash said, standing. "What's going on here?"

The German looked his way and then back toward the Washoe woman, who had placed the saucepan back above the stove and was drying her hands on her apron. "He takes my food, sir. And what business is it of yours, if I may ask?"

Ash folded his lapel back to expose his badge, "U.S. Marshal, District of Nevada" it said.

"See. Vat business *is* it of yours?" the German asked. Ash pirouetted toward the man to show him his badge, only to see him drop the boy and begin to charge.

"Holy mother of God!" he barely exclaimed before being picked up at the waist and folded over the man's right shoulder. The German spun and collapsed onto a table to his right, the marshal beneath him, as Slade began to stand.

"Now, hold on there, young fella!" Slade shouted, grabbing hold of the man's shirt and vest and pulling. The red and black woolen vest ripped from his back as the German turned to see who was yanking on him. Seeing it was a man similarly sized, he pushed a ham-sized fist at Ash, hitting the table instead, before rolling off of the marshal to face the larger man.

Slade felt a wild anger well within him. Gritting his teeth, his eyes flashing, he pulled his Winchester into the air, swinging the 24-inch barrel so that the walnut butt of rifle hit the German square in the forehead. It fractured on impact, leaving Dustsucker with a decent rifle — capable of driving a 200-grain bullet 1,200 feet per second into an unfortunate animal or man — without a stock, not that it mattered. It could be fixed. The German spun around once and sank to the ground, out cold.

"Force multiplier," Slade said, hitching his pants up.

"Jesus, guys! I didn't mean to get either of you into any trouble," Little Wolf said, sitting up, still rubbing his ears and his head. He looked over at the Washoe woman, who had backed as far away as she could toward the stove without setting her skirt on fire. "I'm sorry, Mary. I was just looking for some bread," the kid said. The shocked woman nodded.

Ash got up off the table and shook his head to see if everything was still attached. He bent over the German man and placed his hand in front of his mouth to see if he was still breathing. "Yup," he said, satisfied. "Jesus yourself, Little Wolf! What are you doing up here? Why the hell are you mixing yourself up in our business?"

"My father was busy today, with Mister Ronin, Marshal Ash. I thought perhaps you'd want to see where the bodies lay?"

Ash and Slade looked at each other, their mouths open. Ash tugged at his ear. "You know where they are?"

"I do."

"Well, I'll be damned how you knew where we were, son. But we'd love for you to show us where the men are buried. You got a horse?"

"Washoes walk, marshal."

"So you do, son. Slade, what do you say? Time to go?"

Slade nodded, pushing the German man's arm off his chair and sitting down. "Just as soon as I finish my cup of coffee."

Chapter 60

RENT A HORSE

Ronin got back to the Lake Shore House around noon, having fallen asleep at the base of Cave Rock, "the Washoe people's traditional holy place," Cobb said as he walked in. "You didn't spend much time there, I notice, though you probably absorbed something," he said, laughing.

"I don't have much use for holy places anymore, Cobb. And Happy Hands wasn't at all sure when he'd be coming back down. I imagine he might he'll stay all night, despite how cold and windy it is up there."

Cobb looked surprised by the thought that an Indian would choose to sleep outside instead of inside, given that the hotel had provided him a room. He shrugged at the news. "I guess you'll want a horse at this point."

"And why is that?" Ronin said, pulling off his gloves and setting them in his gun belt. He reached for an apple on the corner of Cobb's desk and took a bite out of it. "Is this a Pippin?" he asked.

"Uh, I don't know sir, all I know is that it's a Georgia apple. The cook was pretty happy about getting them this week. What I was about to say is that your friends have ridden up to Summit Camp for the day."

Ronin looked at him blankly. Geography wasn't his best subject in school and held little interest for him as an adult. Even Holy Land geography — the supposed key to who did what, when, where and why in biblical times — left him disengaged. Once he figured out that the ancient area wasn't much bigger than the state of New Jersey, he found the biblical story less interesting. The rest of the world seemed so much larger.

"Summit Camp is at Spooner, Mister Ronin. You passed Spooner meadow on your way into Glenbrook a couple of days ago. We have a narrow gauge railroad that runs from Glenbrook to the summit — you must have noticed — pulling logs out of the lake and timber from the mills. The flume takes it all downhill from there. There's a similar flume over in Incline and one further north, I believe.

"Oh," Ronin said, looking at the apple. "I'm telling you Cobb, this is a Pippin. I remember them from the campaign through Georgia. It's a hell of a baking apple, Cobb, though most people think of Pippins as a good apple for jam or cider. My, what we could do with them when there was nothing else to eat!" Ronin mused quietly for a moment, turning the yellow-green apple over in his hand, tracing the red blush with his fingers. "Thank you!"

"No ... thank you, sir," Cobb said, startled by Ronin's sudden burst of enthusiasm. "As I was saying, your friends Marshal Ash and Deputy Slade are headed to Summit Camp, where they are hoping to find out where the Washoe gentlemen are buried. They said they might head on back to Carson City if the results of their investigation in Kings Canyon were close by."

"I don't recall anything being said about Kings Canyon, Mister Cobb." Ronin took the apple from his mouth and waited. "Did I miss something?"

"At breakfast sir, after you left. Little Wolf said something about it."

"Little Wolf?"

"Yes, he's one of our waiters, Mister Ronin. I assume you know the boy?"

Ronin looked perplexed. The boy didn't at all look like the kind of young man the Lake Shore House would be interested in, many of the lake's resorts hiring only white men and women to do their public labor. Nor had Happy Hands said anything about his son being employed at the hotel. But that would explain the boy's sudden appearance at the lake a month ago, when he first reconnoitered the area prior to the three of them coming up on the stage. "I had no idea he was here, Mister Cobb. You have the most interesting information at times."

"Well, thank you sir. As you know, I think a great deal of you as well. I'd be happy to get you a horse so that you could join them, but I don't believe the livery has any more horses."

"Hmmm ..." he said, picking up one of the menu cards on Cobb's desk. "Today's menu in the restaurant, Mister Cobb?"

"That was breakfast and lunch sir, but I'm sure they'd be happy to fix you something should you be hungry. I know they're making a nice stew for supper." He paused. "If you can wait a few minutes, Mister Ronin, I'd be happy to drive you to Summit Camp myself in my carriage. The flumes are silent on Sundays. The company holds occasional picnics there on Sundays. I often go up just to see what's happening and to catch my breath."

"I'd much appreciate that, Mister Cobb. I believe I'll head to my room to freshen up and then to the restaurant. I've got a lot to think about. Did you know that if you sit at the base of a mountain long enough, you absorb some of its magic?"

"I'd heard that, sir."

Chapter 61
DREAMS

It's not that Ronin didn't notice the change, he just didn't know what to make of it. He could tell that his mood was lighter that he felt happier than he usually did. There was an unusual color to the world around him. Everything seemed simpler, more vivid, brighter. And while he never thought of himself as sullen or moody — sure, he could be tense or temperamental, but he figured those qualities kept some edge to what he was doing and helped him stay safe — he had a sense that his life had suddenly deepened.

How his brief retreat at the base of the Standing Grey Stone, as Happy Hands called it, could be so refreshing was perplexing. As a priest, he'd spent hours in prayer and not found his mood so lifted. Emma had said many times in the months he had lived at the mission that he wasn't spending enough time simply sitting and reflecting. "You're a good man, Ronin. But I bet you were a better man before you took all this anger upon yourself," she'd said on one occasion as they sat by the Carson River. When he had taken exception to the word, pointing out that he felt a profound compassion for the people he worked with, even "the stupid ones," she pointed to his choice of words. "But some people aren't very bright," he'd said in return, thinking of not so much of folks who seemed less gifted than him, but of felons who had done again and again what they had done so many times previously.

"These are the stupid people of the earth," he'd said, words that sounded even too harsh or spiteful to him, and she had simply smiled. There was a kindness to Emma's response that he couldn't understand or fathom until a couple hours before at Cave Rock.

He had never held an apple in his hand and looked at it in quite the same way. Nor had he made it a habit to compliment people, as he had Cobb on his "most interesting information." And he couldn't remember the last time he had taken a person up on an offer to help him, save perhaps Emma's proposition that he move into the mission while his leg healed. It took an unfamiliar and unpracticed humility to accept so much from Emma and her staff over the three months he stayed there. He'd thought it had left him a better person — quieter, more patient and reflective — until he sat at the base of the mountain and realized he had so much more man to grow into.

He turned the knob on the door to his second story room at the Lake House and, pushing it open, stood in the doorway wondering if his life was about to transition again. So much had happened over the last seven years: closing the door on his priesthood and the subsequent changes he had experienced in his faith and practice as a human being. Simply moving from the east coast to the west coast — leaving family and friends behind — had taken its toll. Perhaps he had become angry. There was so much hurt in the world and, while he couldn't stop it all, the effort he was making to stop what he could had oftentimes left him exhausted. Maybe there *was* a better way, as Emma had encouraged him to consider — something less violent, something less exhausting, something less lethal.

He closed the door behind him, crossed the room and unlatched the doors that led to the second story porch. Taking a deep breath of mountain air, he pulled a chair from the room and lifted it onto the roof so that he could get a good view of the lake. He looked around the room for a pencil and finding one, he licked it and put to his journal. He sat there for a few minutes considering.

A striking, young woman appeared in a window across the way and, before pulling her curtains closed, she paused to notice the man sitting on the roof at the Lake House Hotel. She had seen him a couple nights ago with the marshal. He had acted rudely that evening, she remembered, to an Indian he was sitting with. He had remarked that not everyone found the Washoe man attractive. Similar comments had been hurled her way over the years; none of them had been received kindly. All of them had hurt in some way or another.

She sat in her bed naked, with the covers tightly gathered up around her. She was surprised to see the man sitting so peaceably on the hotel balcony. He was much more attractive than she remembered. Of course, a man with a hat on his head always seems more dapper. She watched him put a pencil to paper and sit quietly. Perhaps he was a poet, she thought, but what would a poet have to do with a marshal? Or maybe a newspaper man, she mused, though she thought he might have been carrying a gun. Funny. The handsome, sandy-haired man could just as easily be a priest or a railroad engineer — it wasn't as if she knew him.

Ally restacked her pillows and then laid back in the bed, shielding her eyes from the sun. She had a few more hours to rest until she needed to get up. Perhaps she would see the man again. There was so much about men she didn't understand, and it wasn't as if all men were the same. Her mother had told her that some men were good men and some men were bad men. The trick, her mother had said, was being able to tell the difference. Her own experience was different. Some men were both good and bad, but others were all simply all bad. As she relaxed, she remembered there was still the matter of those men who had been murdered … some men, she figured, never had enough time or experience to decide.

Ronin licked his pencil again and began writing. "Things I need to do differently in the New Year," he wrote across the top of the page. "Number 1: take time to recreate." *There's so much more living I need to do. And so much crap that I can leave behind.* He paused for a moment, resting the pencil between his lips before crossing out the word "crap" and substituting the word "stuff." "Number 2," he wrote, "stop should-ing on yourself." He shook his head. Having lived on a steady diet of "oughts" and "shoulds" while working in the church, he hadn't yet found freedom. He paused again, and then licked the tip of the pencil to make sure the next line was dark enough. "Number 3: be kinder to others." He laughed quietly to himself. *Big chance there.* W. W. Ronin's business, simply put, was helping some people meet the LORD sooner than others. Being kind wasn't always helpful.

Changed or not, he had business to attend to near Carson City. If he could catch up to his friends, he'd be able to tell them what he'd found out. A Water Baby, of all things, had appeared to him in a dream while sitting at the lake, and recited the following: "Rocks will show you, this I know; their open mouths will tell you so." He had no idea what it meant, but the rhyme of the words seemed almost like Sunday school.

Chapter 62
OFF THE BEATEN PATH

Timothy Edwards Smith stuck his head up so that it sat amidst the sandy, wind-blown boulders a half mile or so south of Spooner Summit. A small, granite outcropping hung above the mountain path, punctuated by small stands of white and yellow pine trees, too thin to be of much value to the mills below. What the Manzanita bushes didn't obscure sprinkled among the stones, similarly-sized gray rocks did, making it seem that Smith's vigilance on the trail from Marlette Lake was no more notable or invasive than that accomplished by the boulders themselves. Two mustangs were tied a hundred feet back and were quietly munching on some cheat grass as Leonard Crum looked on.

"I don't get what we're looking for," the taller man shouted down to the stooped, bushy- eye-browed man below. "I thought we were getting something to eat," Smith continued, looking up the road a ways toward Summit Camp, where he knew the morning's flapjacks were beginning to get thicker and drier, given how the number of hours the batter had likely been sitting above the cast iron stove. His late partner and he, the former Mister Jones, now diseased due to the bullets of a certain ex-reverend named Ronin, preferred their pancakes thinner instead of thicker. They better absorbed the butter that way, Jones had pointed out. And given the price of maple syrup in Nevada — neither Smith nor

Jones had contacts back east — thinner was always better than thicker, particularly as it pertained to pancakes.

"We're getting there," the bushy-browed man said, looking up from a nearby rock as he stroked the edges of his Masonic dagger with a flat stone, hoping to sharpen its largely ceremonial blade. "It's good thinking to reconnoiter a situation before you commit to it, you know. At least that's what my brother says."

"Well, that doesn't explain his being in jail right now, I don't guess," Smith shouted back, only to immediately wish he hadn't spoken so quickly. Eating a healthy breakfast first thing every morning typically kept him from getting too crabby. And there was no telling how Leonard would take crabby this early in the morning.

"How about I come up there and kick your ass," Leonard yelled back, a much better response, Smith figured, than skipping up the mountain and placing his foot halfway *up* his ass, which he had done before — or so it seemed — which wasn't fun. "What the fuck do you think we're doing?" Leonard shouted. "We need to know what's going on before we head in there, you moron. Breakfast will come shortly."

Smith swallowed hard. His jaw still ached from the beating he'd been given the day before above Incline, when he'd complained about having to walk to camp rather than ride, Leonard having taken the only horse.

Truth be told, he wasn't looking for any more difficulties with the Crum brothers. As soon as Larry was out of jail, he'd be heading to greener pastures, as the saying went, or at least safer ones, not that he had any aversion to finding trouble. A good fist fight was a welcome thing, as long as it wasn't standing in between him and a meal, which sitting up on the mountain trying to stay out of one certainly was.

"I don't see nothing, Leonard. Can't we just head in?" He took a long, hard look in the direction of Glenbrook, and while he couldn't see into town — the right lens of his glasses was cracked but the other lens was still quite clear — he could keep an eye on the railroad out of town and any traffic that appeared alongside. A carriage was headed up toward the summit, for instance. From where he was situated, he could also see some of the buildings at Summit Camp, including the mess tent where he was sure the Indian lady was ladling out steaming portions of mountain porridge and morning pie. She sure made a hell of an apple pie! Why she didn't make more of them he didn't understand, as they rarely lasted beyond 11 o'clock, the Summit men preferring a freshly baked apple pie to sandwiches or eggs, not that anything was wrong with either. It was just that her pie was better.

"I don't see nothing, Leonard," he repeated, "Maybe the Negro at Summit Camp and a horse or two outside the mess tent." He paused to take a better look at the carriage coming up out of Glenbrook. "It looks like your friend Cobb might be headed up this way; it's his carriage from what I can see. But that's it. What do you say we just head in?"

"We'll head in as soon as I get an edge on this dagger," Leonard barked. "It will only take a minute or two." Leonard pulled a piece of rock across the cast metal blade. "Love it a long time," his brother had said, speaking of how to sharpen the blade, when he presented him with the knife. "It's not like a regular knife," he said, pointing out that it hadn't been forged, as far as he could tell. "But if you take your time, with a rock, say a river rock or other smooth stone, it might sharpen some."

Larry hadn't intended for the knife to be a part of Leonard's wardrobe, or to be used in a defensive or offensive way. He'd wanted simply to impress upon his brother that the Masonic traditions were deep and precious. "Maybe someday you will be a Mason, Leonard." Larry had waited for Leonard to ask about membership, not being allowed to ask himself if his brother was interested.

Maybe he didn't know that he was supposed to, Larry figured, when his months at Lodge *2 in Washoe City turned into years, and his merely attending meetings took the shape of his leading them as a Master Mason.

Leonard was counting the strokes he'd made on one side when he put two and two together, or maybe it was the influence of his brother's higher-level Masonic training. But the coach coming up the mountain didn't look like Cobb, as his granite-headed friend had suggested. It could just as easily be someone they didn't know, someone with money to spare, someone he might try his newly sharpened knife on if cordial efforts turned crusty. "Damn it," he shouted, "You made me lose my count, Smith. And it's not nearly time to turn the blade over and start sharpening that side! How close is that carriage?"

Smith winced, so much so that he hit the side of his face on the rock next to him. But he looked anyway, his left lens now scratched. "Maybe a hundred yards, Leonard. Why?" He took off his glasses and tried to rub the scratch out by touching it to his canvas coat. It only seemed to make matters worse.

"Because I think we've found someone to buy us breakfast, someone who might want to see my nice knife."

Chapter 63

THE SHACK

When the bushy-browed, stump-sized man jumped in front of the horses, Ronin pulled up sharply on the reins. But the horses were startled and there was nothing he could do to keep them from running up the side of the rail bed. Their hooves hit the crushed rock and all hell broke loose as the carriage tumbled, wedging itself in between a switch tender's shack and a large tree. Cobb was screaming for his life and Ronin — not a fan of horses anyway, but tolerant of an easy ride if it was on wheels except for the railroad — reached for his strong-side sidearm only to see it laying a couple of dozen feet back in the weeds. He attempted to draw his 7.5-inch Colt when the hump-backed man bore down on him with both his fists.

Crum hadn't expected there to be a second man, but when he recognized the Lake House Hotel proprietor *and* the ex-priest there was little he could do to back down. The one would carry little money as he didn't need it on company property, but the other would be a handful.

"Smith!" he screamed, before Ronin had taken hold of his neck and slammed him up against a stove pipe on the entry side of the building. Ronin's right fist hit pay dirt when he drove it up into Crum's side, breaking a rib. A second right hooked into the side of Leonard Crum's head, dropping him like a log. He relaxed his left hand and Crum slid onto the weathered wood building's front stoop.

Standing over him, Ronin was beginning to remember who he was when Cobb began to whine strangely. "What the hell is wrong with you?" he said, turning to face the lake's most famous hotel proprietor when he realized that a much taller man had hold of Cobb by the hair.

"Mister Ronin! How nice to see you!" Smith said, hissing between gritted teeth. "I was just thinking of you and my not-so-old friend you dispatched a couple of days ago in Glenbrook."

"Smith, you need to let go of my partner there before I blow your damn head off!"

"I don't think you want to do that."

"Really?" he asked, drawing the long gun from his cross-draw holster and taking careful aim. It was 21 feet or so, and while he was capable of hitting Smith's rounded head without aiming, the sun was in his eyes and a miss wouldn't provide him with a clean second chance. And that's when he felt the sharp pain in his back.

Leonard Crum had taken his ceremonial dagger out of its wooden sheath, dangling from a 17-inch silver cord on his belt, and plunged it into Ronin's back, causing him to spin around and face his attacker. It stung like a dog bite. A big dog's bite, but not so badly or so deeply that it prevented the ex-priest from driving a left push kick, or *chassee* in French, into the short man's chest, knocking him over a pile of dirty pans and pots sitting beside the tender shack's door. Crum flew backward across the stoop and into the closest rail. "Son of a bitch," he yelled as he grabbed a handful of gravel and threw it Ronin's way.

Ronin was reaching at the knife, which had pierced his latissimus dorsi muscle, the larger muscle of his back, a good inch or two. But unable to reach the blade, he returned to a defensive posture facing the larger man as Smith threw himself forward over the front of the coach. Ronin's right jab collapsed for lack of muscular support, and Smith clinched around him, grabbing his friend's ceremonial blade and pulling on it. Ronin winced in pain, but not before he seized Smith's ear and twisted. Smith screamed and let go.

"Yeah," Ronin hissed, "that hurts, doesn't it?" With his other hand, he grabbed Smith's other ear, so that he now had control of both, and slammed his head into him. Smith slumped to the ground, unable to see, holding his face and crying. Ronin looked around for his gun.

"Looking for this?" Leonard barked, throwing another handful of gravel, this time hitting Ronin's eyes. He kicked the revolver over to Smith, who stopped crying long enough to grab it and stand up, bleeding. "Son of a bitch!" he yelled.

"Whatever," Ronin responded, clearing the dirt from his eyes. "So what's next, boys? You going to rob me?"

"We're going to kill you, friend," Leonard said, "but not before we get my brother out of jail." Crum picked up a large pry bar from the side of the shed and swung it hard, without warning, hitting Ronin in the neck and launching him tumbling, ass over ankles, onto the railroad tracks. "Grab him, will you Smith?"

Smith was standing, with one of Ronin's handguns in his hands, his eyes wide open in surprise. "Leonard, I don't think I've ever seen anyone hit like that before," he said, hoping not to be hit similarly by the enraged, stooped over, bushy eyed, uni-browed man.

"Nope. Gotta say, I'm pretty impressed with myself as well. Did you see him fly? Never seen anything like that in my life," he boasted, hefting the iron bar with his right hand. "I think I'm going to keep this stick."

Smith walked over to the tracks, grabbed Ronin's ankles and pulled him off the tracks. "What do you want to do with him, Leonard?"

"We're going to shut him and Mister Cobb here up in this shack, Smith. They'll stay good and warm there. And when Larry and I come back, we might jam this piece of iron up his ass." Smith shuddered. He'd never heard either of the Crums be so spe-cific before. It was time to find another line of work.

Chapter 64
LUNCH WITH EMMA

Emma pushed the cup of tea forward, thinking that too much time spent with the young doctor of Carson City might mean that church folks would start talking again. The lunchtime chatter at the Ormsby House Supper Club wasn't quiet enough to have a decent conversation about her concerns nor noisy enough to drive away the demons that had begun to nip at the corners of her mind.

Not that Amos Quinn was the person to go to. But who else was she supposed to talk to, when concerned about her friends Ronin and Dustsucker? And why weren't they home, wherever home was, save that it needed to be closer to her, particularly for the ex-priest who seemed to take up so much of her silent thoughtful time?

Emma excused herself from the table as Quinn rose from his chair, and indicated that she'd be back in just a few minutes. "I won't take long, Amos. And then maybe you'd be so kind to walk me up to the pastor's house?"

"Of course, Emma," he said, as he sat down wondering what pastor she was talking about. He watched her cross the room so as to ask where the indoor toilet and lavatory were. She always asked, even though she knew where it was, having been there so many times before.

Emma's mood seemed darker than usual, Quinn thought, striking a match and lighting his favorite pipe. It didn't seem as if he had much of a chance with the young woman, if her talking about Ronin was any indication. Sure, there were reasons to wonder how he was, what he was doing, whether he was safe, if he'd return unharmed and so on. He was about "the Lord's work," Quinn told her, though the words were meant only as a joke. Chasing crooks could hardly be considered church work, and he had never really gotten a good explanation from the man as to why he wasn't working in a church anymore. Or why so allegedly godly a man, as Emma put it, as Ronin should always be showing up in his office unannounced, bleeding from new orifices? None of the other pastors in town did, he explained to her, not that she listened. No really, he said.

Quinn was a Presbyterian. He liked explanations. If it wasn't for a need for good explanations, Presbyterians would probably be Quakers or Catholics, both of whom, it struck him, were more comfortable with mysteries.

"Miss Emma," he said, rising to pull the chair back from the table when she returned. She didn't sit. "Are we leaving already?"

"I don't know what else to do, Amos. I'm so upset inside with worry, and I can't talk here. But thank you for the lunch."

"Of course, ma'am. It's always my pleasure to see you. Is there any chance I might come calling on you later in the week, out at the mission?" he asked, holding his breath. Funny, how as a professional he could be doing the most intricate of surgeries and still have his heart stutter in front of a striking woman. And she was that, in a conservative, West Virginia, church lady sort of way.

"I don't think so, Amos, not this week," she said carefully, thinking that she shouldn't limit her options, should she change her mind someday. "It's already been a crazy week," she said.

"It's only Sunday, Emma."

"So it is," she replied, blushing. "Care to walk me to the Episcopal Church?"

"The Reverend Davis, then?"

"I'm sorry?" she asked.

"I was wondering which minister you were wanting to see?" he said, realizing that she had in fact already answered his question. It was the former Reverend W. W. Ronin that she wanted to see, minister or not. That was the only pastor she wanted to see. The rest of the ministers in town were simply ornamentation.

Chapter 65

ASH AND DUSTSUCKER

Cobb hadn't expected them not to be tied up. I mean, if you're going to imprison folks in a shed, you might give some thought to as to how prevent their escape. You might lock the door, for instance. You might even tie their hands or bind their legs. But Leonard Crum wasn't the highest card in the deck, and his companion, a simple emotional man named Smith from Sacramento, was so scared out of his mind that he'd be hurt by either of the Crum boys, that neither of Ronin's assailants were thinking. So when Ronin came to, W. A. B. Cobb, the proprietor of Lake Tahoe's second, but finest hotel, was sitting on the stoop of the cabin, waiting. "I was worried," he said, as Ronin stumbled out into the sun.

"Jesus, me too. I don't think I've ever been hit like that."

"No, I imagine not. I gave some thought at one point to returning to Glenbrook and wiring for a physician, you were pummeled so hard. But then I figured, if you needed something, if you started choking on your own sputum or blood, if your eyes rolled back in your head and you started spouting Bible verses and such, you might be happy to have me around."

"No kidding," Ronin said, blinking at the brightness of everything around him. "Is it me, or is everything a little more vivid than usual?" he asked. "I've just gotten the shit kicked out of me, but the sky is so blue! And the trees, what's left of them up here anyway, are greener than green!"

Cobb thought before replying. "I imagine it's the fact that we just barely escaped being killed by a very mean-spirited, slope-headed man with bushy eyebrows and an equally angry friend. That would do it for me."

"Yeah," Ronin responded, nodding. The two of them stood there for a few minutes looking out over the camp, until Cobb sat back down on the concrete steps in front of the shack and began to wring his hands.

"What are you doing?" Ronin asked.

"W., may I call you that?

"Sure."

"Something's got to be done about that man. I don't know who he is, or what he's doing up here or why he's so angry, but it's going to drive me nuts until I know he's in custody some place, somewhere distant or put away long. You said he has a brother?"

"I don't believe I did. But he does."

"Well then, that Smith guy must have said so, because they're headed to Carson City to spring a brother from the Ormsby County jail. And you know what?"

"No."

"They've got a three-hour start on us."

Ronin stood there for a few minutes, not knowing which hurt him more, his neck or his back. Cobb was looking over his wounds to see if there was anything they could do before locating the horses, turning the carriage upright and heading back to Glenbrook, when Slade and Ash rode up. It was nearly 4 o'clock.

"Yo, buddy! You look like you've had a tough time!" Slade shouted as they descended on horseback to the tender's shack. "Where the hell have you been?"

"That should be my question," Ronin replied. "Cave Rock for most of the day, then eight or so miles on my way up to Summit Camp with Cobb here, when that hairy-headed man, son of a bitch …"

"Leonard Crum?" Ash asked.

"… the same," Ronin continued, "jumped the two of us, toppled our carriage, stabbed me in the back and hit me in the neck with a square piece of iron! That's where I've been. How about you?"

Dustsucker stood there, stunned, as Ash jumped to their defense. "Summit Camp and then over to the graves of those two Washoe men with Little Wolf. We were just getting back when we ran into you."

Slade closed his mouth and then asked, "You okay?"

"Not hardly, but it'll do before I can get to a doctor, right?" he asked Cobb who nodded. Cobb had been to a dental school in Sacramento, before heading to the lake on his way to the gold fields. The hole in his back didn't look that much different than what he had seen in school, just longer and in a different place. Cobb began stuttering.

"Had that been a real knife, Ronin, and not, not, not … just a piece of shit toy dagger, you might be in real trouble," Cobb remarked, telling the story of how they made him pull the knife out of Ronin's back, bend it back in shape and clean it off before handing it back to their assailants.

"Here's the bad news, boys. Crum and that creep named Smith are headed to Carson City to break out the older brother, and they've got a three-hour start," Ronin said, looking at Ash for some guidance.

"It's a four-hour ride by stage. We can't catch up to them," Slade said, also looking Ash's way, who was thinking through the options.

"You've got a telegraph at the hotel, Cobb?"

"I do."

"Then you've got to send a message to Carson City. Have it expressed over to the Sheriff's office. We'll start riding right away." The marshal walked over to his horse, beckoning Ronin to follow.

"I'll not be going with you, Ash," Ronin said. "You and Slade can ride ahead, but I've got a score to settle with these men." He began walking over the carriage, where his four-inch Colt had fallen and for some reason not been picked up.

Slade jumped in. "I don't follow, Ronin. That's where we're headed, to Carson City. Where are you going?"

"I'm going to the same place you are, but hopefully sooner."

Chapter 66
HYRUM SMITH

Hyrum Smith was a black man, not that he was any man's Negro, and not that it precluded his being "a Mormon gentleman," he explained to the tall angry man who had a curious wound in his back. "Preclude" was the operative word, given that its use established his being a gentleman, though Hyrum wasn't sure what the word meant, except that he wasn't like the usual riff raff serving in the Sierras.

"I'm simply asking if you'll allow me to ride the slide to Carson City!" the tall man had said, before turning to express his annoyance to W. A. B. Cobb, the proprietor of the Lake House Hotel, who had once denied Smith a job, though he likely wasn't qualified for it. Still, he had hoped for a chance to prove himself.

"You don't know anything about liveries," Cobb had said and Smith had confirmed, before asking if there was anything else he could do on the property. Cobb had suggested the flume-tending job he was currently performing, in part because he was a large man.

"Size counts!" he heard himself say, before figuring that he might be hurting his chances saying such to a white man, a small white man at that. Over the last few years, he had proven himself, or his size had, anyway, though he worked now on Sundays only, when the regular crew was elsewhere, enjoying their time with their families, taking game, fishing — he had no idea what white people did, though he'd gained the friendship of a few Latter Day Saints in the valley who allowed him to fellowship with them.

"There's no reason you can't hear the Word of God," they said when he knocked at their door one afternoon unexpected and unannounced. "He just can't be an elder," someone had said, noting his color when he entered the front room of a small ranch house in Genoa, where a handful of well-to-do bearded white men and their women were gathered. "Nor an apostle," someone else said, not that he had ever wanted to be an apostle. That was for white people..

He simply wanted to testify to what he knew to be true: that Joseph Smith was God's witness, and that what he said was "truly true," he explained, a term none of the white folks had ever heard before.

"And Brigham Young," someone else responded, a name he remembered from Carthage, Illinois, "Joseph's successor," they explained, though he had lost track of the church when most of the Saints he knew moved to Utah. "A Mormon Moses," someone called Brigham Young, though he didn't know or really care. Smith had died while serving as Mayor of Nauvoo, Illinois. Having declared himself a candidate for the presidency of the United States, he was killed while sitting in a Carthage jail — though he couldn't imagine the Prophet ever sitting, not with God speaking to him and such. Word was that the Joseph was practicing polygamy (a term Hyrum had to have explained to him), so the *Nauvoo Expositor* said. Hyrum and his owner, and a few of his owner's friends, set fire to the newspaper whose first and only edition claimed such a false and slanderous thing as part of an expose on the church.

He'd been a proud Mormon ever since. And though moving west had taken him away from his family — his mother and brothers had remained in Monroe County, with a French family who was somehow related to the first family that owned slaves in Illinois, not that he knew anything about that — they were no longer slaves, of course. Lincoln's war had seen to that. They were free laborers, though the difference seemed insignificant. He'd stayed loyal to the family's religious tradition ever since.

"Nothin' wrong with being a Mormon," he said to the angry white man with two guns on his belt and a bible tucked into his vest.

"I'm not saying there is," Ronin explained. "I simply want your permission to slide down this wooden trough into Carson City — that's all I'm asking. Just look the other way. Don't tell no one. You can do that, right?"

"Mister, I don't have a problem with not seeing you do what I think you're settin' to do, I'm just trying to talk some sense into you," he said, gazing at W. A. B. Cobb, who could have hired him had he wanted to. "Mister Cobb, you okay with this?" He waited for the man's response.

Cobb, who had worked at the Lake House Hotel since its inception, put his fingers in his ears and shook his head, acting as if he couldn't hear what he was asking. Just like a white man, Smith thought. Doesn't want to know what's going on, particularly if someone is going to get in trouble or get hurt.

Slavery had been abolished in Illinois in the late 1700s. When Illinois was admitted into the union thirty-some years later, it declared itself "a free state," though the distinction was an empty one for blacks who couldn't vote and weren't able to own a weapon, serve in the state militia or gather in groups. It hadn't changed much since, if the testimony of travelers was to be believed. Hyrum put his fingers in his ears, parroting Cobb, then thought twice about it.

"Look, Mister Ronin, is that your name? You, sir, may have a screw loose," he said, though he didn't think the man had been drinking, so he put it tentatively. "This slide, you call it? It's got two switchbacks, 22 trestles and runs a dozen or so miles to Carson City. On a good day, and there aren't many good days on this mountain, you might be able to see what horrible thing is about to happen to you before it happens. On a day like today — a little dark and a little dense — you might die and not know it until you land in the hands of an angry God."

"Don't much believe in God, Mister Smith, not with the way my life has been going."

"Might as well call me Hyrum, Mister Ronin," Hyrum didn't much cotton to an angry white man misusing the Prophet's last name, "everybody else does. If you're going to be riding one of my logs, I want to encourage you to fix things between you and God, because if you ride this thing, you may meet him sooner than later!"

Chapter 67

THE V FLUME

"Twelve or so miles down Clear Creek Canyon there is a lumber yard," Cobb said. "It's about a mile south of town. You should be able to catch a ride from there, assuming you survive." Ronin's partner for the day had taken his fingers out of his ears, but was keeping his own confidences about the likely success, or lack of success more or less, regarding Ronin's choice of transportation to Nevada's capital city.

"You think this bandage will hold?" Ronin asked, while watching the tall Negro man tending the flume shake his head.

"I doubt it," Cobb said, swallowing hard. "I believe this is about the stupidest thing I ever heard up this way, Ronin, and I've been here a long while."

"That you have, Cobb," Ronin replied, regretting that he hadn't heard more from the man about his life at the lake or previous to it. Everyone had a story. He didn't even know the man's first name; W. A. B. is all the desk sign said. "I remember the first bill I saw for Benton's Stage Line. It had your name on it, Cobb. And I thought, why not 'take a luncheon,' as it suggested, 'at the Lake Shore House?' Emma would like that. I'm sorry it took so long for me to get up here. I should have come a long time ago."

"Let's hope you make a return trip," Cobb replied, looking over at Smith, who was posed to push the crudely made V-bottom boat onto the trestle work. "You sure you want to do this?" he asked. Over the years, the Lake Shore House proprietor had heard stories of boats, planks and so on, sailing down the flume at speeds up to 100 miles an hour. He assumed most, if not all of the tales, were braggadocio. It took a certain kind of men to match the mountains. But that didn't mean they weren't crazy.

Take James Finney, nicknamed "Old Virginny." Finney, one of the first placer miners in Gold Canyon in the early to mid-50s, Finney traded his share of a Comstock claim for a bottle of whiskey and a blind horse. He was a "charitable and honest man," someone said at his funeral in Dayton, Nevada a few years later, but he was crazy all the same. Or consider Henry "Pancake" Comstock, who ran away with another man's wife and, when the husband caught up with him, secured a bill of sale for the woman, trading her for a horse, a gun and $60 in cash. Both men had given their names to the area, though their lives left a great deal to be desired. Or Alvah Gould — Cobb often said when advising young men and women to save and to think conservatively about their futures — Gould sold his interest in the Gould and Curry mine for a measly $450 and spent it all in a single night's carouse. Now W. W. Ronin, too. "What will the newspapers say?" Cobb argued. He shook his head in disgust.

"Look, all I know is what I see," Ronin said.

"You've seen people do this?" Cobb asked, incredulously.

"A picture, Cobb, I saw two men in a picture running the flume in boats. Instead of packing tools and supplies on the rafts, they personally floated the flume down into the valley."

"Where did you see this, Mister Ronin?"

"In *Harper's Weekly*, a couple of years back in Reno."

"Oh, God," the Lake Shore House proprietor groaned. "Them's 'Go Devils,' Ronin! They're a tool carrier. And you'd be a fool to think that a man could fly down that flume, or any other flume, and survive."

"Fair did, according to the article!" Ronin prided himself on knowing things, having been "a professional smart person," he often said of his years as a parish priest. While he didn't believe everything he read — "some things aren't meant to be taken literally," a professor once told him when teaching him how to read the Bible, a point of view he suffered with ever since, as deciding what one should or shouldn't believe wasn't always easy — still, if there were words and pictures, he believed what he was reading to be more credible.

"You read an article in a magazine ..."

"... that had pictures," Ronin interjected.

"... that had pictures of a Comstock multi-millionaire risking his life in a 16-foot boat shaped like a hog trough. And you believed it?"

"Believe it still, Cobb. It's possible."

"Then you're a fool and you deserve your fate." Cobb turned his back and began fastening down the leathers on his buggy that had dumped earlier in the day. "Ronin?" he said.

"Yeah?"

Cobb turned back around to speak to a man he greatly admired. "Good luck to you. If anyone should survive such tom foolery, and it is that, you should. The world needs more people like you."

Ronin smiled appreciatively. He looked over at Smith for something similar, but found nothing. Hyrum Smith was no relationship to the man Ronin was going to kill or capture, or the Mormon prophet for that matter, though he was his namesake or, to be more accurate, Joseph Smith's older brother's namesake, not that it mattered.

"If you're going to do this, sit absolutely still," Smith said in all seriousness. "Shut your eyes. Say your prayers. Keep your hands to yourself. Good advice every day of the week." He took a breath and then spoke more sincerely. "Listen, Mister Ronin or whatever your name is. Take whatever the flume gives you in terms of water; there will be lots of it. And hope there's a God somewhere who will catch you on the other end, because that's what you're going to need."

Ronin nodded and then stepped into the crudely built craft. He stood there, thinking about lying down with his feet forward, as he had seen in the picture, so as to better endure whatever water the flume would bring, but he remained standing instead, his Yellow Boy rifle in one hand and his hat in his other, as if he was going to ride a bull.

"What the hell are you doing?" Hyrum asked.

"I'm not one to take a beating, Smith. I'd rather give one."

"I'm talking about your standing, Mister Ronin. There's every chance you'll be thrown from that plank if you hang your balls and brains so high."

"Let 'er go, Hyrum. I'm headed to Carson City. And death's angel is riding with me."

Chapter 68

DEAR LORD

It didn't take long for W. W. Ronin to see that Hyrum Smith's words were good ones. The boat, if you could call it that — barely two feet across, with the prow open and the stern closed — was roughly hewn out of two-inch planks and a handful of square nails. And while two seats were attached — only a fire-breathing demon from hell would think of such a thing, Ronin concluded — it was immediately clear that the only safe place in the boat, if a safe place could be had, was clinging to the boat's bottom.

The water rushed into the ex-priest's 16-foot mountain-hewn manger like nothing he had experienced before. It was as if the lake's stiffest night-time winds had determined that he'd have no facial features, or decided he'd have no future, if he didn't keep his head down. The speed and splash of the Marlette Lake water six miles north of Spooner pummeled him, as several small streams added insult to injury through feeder flumes along the way.

"It will take you less than an hour," the Mormon man had said, "if you survive."

He'd been an abolitionist during Lincoln's war, but served the Confederacy given his southern family and sympathies. Whatever racial bias he held — he figured there was little to it but wondered how he could escape having some, being a north-ern-educated white man and all — he repented of it as soon the boat hit its first bump, causing his hat to skim off into an awful void where devils screamed and angels stood in awe of a fool so perfectly foolish to float the raging stream from the top of Lake Tahoe to the Carson Valley floor.

The invention of the V-flume by Senator James Haines, of Genoa — whom he hadn't met yet but would surely kill if he did — and a steady, dependable water supply from the earthen dam at Marlette Lake, may have solved the mining industry's timber dilemma, but it would surely be his death he thought as he alternately grabbed the sides of the boat, or the front, until fears and fingers were pinched from his person, leaving him a heaving wreck.

"Dear LORD!" he screamed, though a man of God would never scream in such a way, not that he was much of one, cradling his rifle with his elbows pressed firmly against his stomach, its stocks skimming the rough sides of the flume to stabilize his ride. At times it seemed as if he would suffocate. "The LORD commands even the winds and waters to obey him," he remembered from his gospel readings, though no savior seemed present. Mountains and trees passed as visions before his eyes as he clung to the boards for dear life, 45-degree turns mere punctuation points there were so many of them. At times the pace slowed. He could open his eyes and drink in the scenery, as a man in the desert might an unexpected cup of water. It was proof he was still alive. But looking upward, he'd again see miles of flume and trestle ahead and realize that he could be moments away from the heavenly gates. Minutes morphed into hours (or so it seemed) and when the pace picked up, he clenched his hands and closed his eyes so as to deny the very real possibility that he was already passing into the great beyond.

He was compelled to go. There was no freedom ahead. If he didn't die, the men he was seeking, whom he was going to capture or kill, the latter being more likely, would know nothing of his suffering, if he could help it. But the sheer experience of it — many times worse than the gut twisters he'd endured when a stage's bolts and brackets had broken away, or a single goddamned horse had tried to chin the moon — would fuel the certitude of their certain demise. They were dead men, walking dead men, maybe, but dead men nonetheless.

All men died. Some good men sooner than others, he mused in the slower moments when the hunk of death he was riding permitted him to think. These men however, if he could endure — who had murdered simply to be more comfortable, who had killed so as to pad their possessions, who had frightened others into thinking they'd be better gone than giving — these men would die even sooner. And while the maintenance of the social order, he had once argued with his mother who initially believed he was leaving the ministry to become a lawman, was not his business, eradicating *their* evil stench from the earth was all he could think of as he plummeted toward the valley floor.

Listen to me, he thought, I'm hallucinating.

He was pleading with Saint Peter when the boat came to a sudden stop and he went hurtling toward the trees.

Chapter 69
AND IT CAME TO PASS

━━━━━━━━━━━━━━━━━━━━━━━━━━━━━━

"And it came to pass that an angel was sent by God unto a city of Galilee, named Nazareth, to a virgin espoused to a man named Joseph ..."

Emma wondered at those words from the *Gospel According to Luke*. She read them often and appreciated the thought that God sent angels to visit those he loved. She hoped that someday, she'd be visited by an angel as well, not that she was special, or that God had singled her out to do anything particularly important. Rather, all people were God's children. Everyone of them needed God's grace in some special way.

Her new responsibilities at the American Gospel Mission hadn't been nearly as difficult as she had believed they would be, given Henry's abandonment of her and of God's call on his life. She was surprised at how natural the new position of director came to her and looked forward to seeing what changes God would bring. But before she knew it, she was making changes.

The first adjustment she made was to keep better track of the children. Knowing *where* the children were was just as important as knowing *who* they were, she found out, a fact that had escaped her late husband, she figured, though she was still uncertain as to whether he had been complicit in the sale of the mission children to criminal interests or merely sloppy in his mission work.

"Not that it mattered," Ronin had once told her. "The results were the same."

She made other changes, as well. She involved Indians, for instance, in the decision-making. What was being taught, how the children were being asked to live and speak — it all went before the larger family. To everyone's surprise, Washoe men and women were now welcome in her house, as were Paiute, Shoshone and other tribes, though she noted it was often more difficult to mix these peoples together than it was to fold Indian folk of any variety into gatherings with her white friends. "You need to stop fighting with each other," she often scolded, not that saying so accomplished much. An angelic voice might be better listened to, she thought. Could she trust God to deliver such a message to her Indian friends? Had God chosen her to do that? Or would the peace of Christ begin only in a new generation of children?

She looked out the front window, at the mountains towering over Jack's Valley, rolling gently into the Mormon settlement around Genoa. How was it that God had blessed her and Henry, calling them to come to such a beautiful place?

Stepping away from the front window, she headed back to the kitchen. While walking through the front room, she crossed herself in the traditional Catholic manner, making the sign of the cross, touching her forehead first, then her chest, followed by both shoulders. "The forehead symbolizes heaven," a Roman Catholic friend had counseled her after her husband had left, "the stomach signifies the earth, the shoulders the places of power in our lives." She had seen a few of her friends kiss their fingers afterwards, though that seemed excessive and unclean. There was no reason she couldn't, she figured. She was a Presbyterian missionary, if she was anything. Her home church extended her and Henry a lot of latitude, though with Henry gone it didn't really matter what she did. She could do as she liked and probably could have always lived that way.

The Roman Catholic practice of crossing herself brought her peace after her daily devotional readings. The selection from *Luke* always stirred Christmas thoughts in her head and heart, as it announced the coming of the Savior to the world. She liked sharing it. "To people like you," she'd said often to the Indian men and women who had gathered at her house, "not to the powerful, not to the wealthy, not to the elite," she stressed, though she wondered if any of them understood what she was talking about. Power, wealth and status were important to white people, even in the back water burgs of Ohio and West Virginia, where she and her husband had made an initial go of things. Though she hadn't observed those traits to be important to Indians, she preached it anyway.

"To simple people, God has given extraordinary things," she told a stable man the week before and then, when he had asked, found herself stuttering over *what* things God had given him. It took her a few moments to find a decidedly Christian cadence: "the simple graces of Christian living," she replied, "faith, hope and love." Her friend had walked away, shaking his head, though she had learned to hold on to those gifts, knowing that God was working through her at the American Gospel Mission, and through the people toward whom she was most fond.

She crossed herself again and thought of Ronin, and then Quinn and other men, mostly ministers, in town. She prayed that God was blessing all of them. "This is the day the LORD has made," she said as she stood to clear the kitchen table, after the children had eaten. "Let us rejoice and be glad in it." She piled the plates a new pottery teacher had made into a single stack and began to take them to the larger of two sinks in her kitchen, when an angel whispered into her ear.

Chapter 70

A RICH INNER LIFE

Less than an hour later, Emma Nauman's carriage almost collided with Amos Quinn who, on horseback, was hurrying to the Carson-Tahoe Lumber and Fluming Company's lumber yard, about a half a mile from the mission.

"Whoa!" she shouted, pulling up on a new team of saddle horses that had just begun to work together as driving animals. One of the men at the mission had failed to sit on his lines a couple of weeks back, had lost one of them and been killed when the buckboard flipped over, dragging him down the gravel road outside the main house. Emma was nervous.

"Why Miss Emma, I didn't expect to see you today. How nice to run into you."

"I think I ran into *you*, Amos. Are you okay?"

Quinn stepped down from his horse and grabbed hold of Emma's reins to help calm her horses. His own horse seemed unperturbed. "I'm fine, Emma. Where are you headed in such a hurry?" he asked, becoming immediately aware that his question might be misunderstood. He cared for Emma and had continued to toss around in his mind the thought that the two of them might have a more intimate relationship, if Ronin would simply make up his mind and step away.

At the question, Emma lowered her head into her hands and lap and began to cry. "I was coming to see you," she sobbed, through a sudden tumult of tears.

Quinn, who had been attracted to Emma's strength, had never seen her whimper let alone cry, and wondered if he had imagined their courtship too quickly. His father had counseled patience with women, a quality he had failed to model with Amos' mother, though he'd seen his father offer it to others, particularly to his patients. Seeing her crying was unnerving.

"Emma! What's happened?" he asked. "Are you all right? Is everything okay?"

"I guess I'm fine," she replied. "I'm just so upset inside, carrying all this responsibility alone, and … now," she stuttered amidst the tears, "I think I'm hearing voices."

This is all I need, Quinn thought, another emotional female in my life.

Amos Quinn had moved to Carson City after finishing medical school, cutting short the time he had hoped to practice with his father and friends, in order to gain distance from his mother. Nevada's capital city was nearly 3,000 miles away from Philadelphia — it was about as far away as he could get — and yet his mother's emotional demands had continued, in daily letters and even telegrams.

"Brevity is the soul of telegraphy," the delivery boy had said quite proudly the day before, suggesting that his mother could better control the expense of her telegrams by eliminating unnecessary words and punctuation marks. "Every jot and tittle is being charged for," he bubbled. It was not his mother's inclination, judging by the length of her communications. Distance from his mother had solved little, and he did not want another needy woman in his life. He already had one.

"You're hearing voices?" he replied. Quinn knew that he was needed immediately at the lumber yard as a man had been injured while plummeting down the company's 12-mile 'V' flume from Spooner Summit. Though the companies generally forbade flume riding in the Sierra mountains, he'd heard of an occasional man fleeing the top of the mountain for the more intimate and pleasures found in the valley below. Serious injuries, even death, had resulted from such rides, though he neither seen nor treated any.

"You know me well enough to know that I have a rich inner life," Emma said.

Quinn smiled. He wasn't sure he agreed, but he was aware that Emma and Jesus seemed to have a continuous dialogue at times. "I am aware of that," he said, feeling for his watch in his right vest pocket.

"Then you know I pray a lot. I pray for you, for instance," Emma said, hoping that Quinn didn't take the admission too personally.

"I was not aware of that, Emma, but I'm pleased to hear that." He didn't care whether Emma prayed for him or not, though it seemed appropriate for him to say. "You said that you're hearing things?" he asked, looking at his watch.

Female hysteria was not an uncommon malady, though he'd never seen any symptoms in Emma. Shortness of breath, irritability, nervousness, faintness, sexual fantasies, a tendency to cause trouble — he checked them off in his mind as Emma nodded tearfully but appeared unwilling to say more. He'd been told by his father that hysteria was suffered by as many as 25 percent of all women, though the percentage sounded high in his experience. "It is particularly prevalent in virgins, widows and the religious," he'd said one afternoon, while speaking with a woman in his Philadelphia examining room.

"I don't know how to talk about it, Amos," Emma said.

He looked at his watch a second time. Pelvic massage was often called for, which was not something he was inclined to offer, given the complexity of their relationship and the availability of other remedies. There was a mechanical device now on the market, though he suspected mention of the device would seem offensive. He had read somewhere that Protestant physicians were more reticent to use or prescribe them, whereas Roman Catholic doctors felt it was their responsibility to do so.

"I apologize, Emma, I want to focus here," he said, stuttering. *A rich inner life, if she had any idea.* "But the fact is, I'm needed immediately at the lumber yard. Someone apparently rode the V-flume down into the valley this afternoon and is in pretty bad shape. They were going to put him on the spur and bring him up Stewart Street, but there was so much bleeding. I offered to ride there instead."

Emma's face grew immediately pale and she began to lean forward again in her seat. The horses grew more agitated. He tightened his grasp on their reins, as she began to swoon.

"Emma, are you okay?" He reached out and caught her as she began to slide off the carriage seat. "Emma!" he shouted.

He couldn't be in two places at once, and he didn't feel at all comfortable leaving Emma behind by the side of the road. "Emma!" he said, squeezing her forearm.

"I'm sorry, Amos." Emma muttered, "You said, bleeding?"

"Yes, a very stupid man went on a wild ride down the Clear Creek flume today. Rather that riding the flume until it came to a stop, he apparently fell off and is lying beside the flume. I need to go."

"I'll go with you," Emma said, pushing herself up and back onto the seat. "It's what the angel told me I should do," she said, wiping her eyes.

"The angel?" God, how he hated religious ideation.

"The voice, Amos. The angel said that Ronin was bleeding. Ride with me?" she asked, staring at him intently with those beautiful, though clearly crazy, brown eyes.

"Might as well," he said. *I can't escape the man and I can't seem to turn my back on his woman, either. God help me.*

Chapter 71

CHINESE JU-JITSU

"I sure as hell *am* ready to go," Ronin said to a Chinese flume tender, who was arguing with him while yelling at another Chinese man, who seemed to be in charge, not that he could be certain. "This is gobbledygook," he said, attempting to stand before being dropped again to ground. "God-damned gobbledygook," he murmured. Every time he went to stand up, the Chinese man would turn him by the shoulders, spin him around and push him down. Actually, it was his own body weight that was causing him to fall; the flume tender was trying to be kind. A small laborer in his mid-to-late-fifties, the Chinese man did little except to twist Ronin in funny directions so that he'd lose his balance and sit down. It was damned aggravating and Ronin was about done with it.

Given the ride he had endured, the fall he had suffered from the elevated flume as he entered the lumber yard in Carson City and the subsequent indignity of being man-handled by a boy-sized Chinaman, Ronin was exhausted. When Emma Nauman and Amos Quinn caught up to him, he was relieved. "Thank God!" he gasped, still swirling from the Chinese man's tumbling act.

"Mister Ronin, have you been drinking?" Miss Emma demanded, with her hands on her hips and her handsome physician friend looking on.

"Drinking? I don't drink! You know that," he said, standing for a third time before the Chinese man poked at his hip, spinning him around and dropping him on his ass. "I'm not drinking," he said, before remembering that Emma counted beer when asking that question, "at least not now," he added, "but I am hurt, and I'm about to kill me a goddamned Chinaman. Quinn, tell this man to stop ..." he droned before passing out mid-sentence, letting the two laborers and Dr. Quinn pull him out of the discard pile of timbers and planks and lay him across the seat of Emma's carriage. Seeing blood, Quinn lifted Ronin's shirt. "Emma, help me turn him over."

It didn't take much time for Quinn to find what he was looking for. "Vertically oriented stab wound on the right side of his back," he said aloud, "approximately 30 inches below the top of the head and four inches to the front of the body." The doctor placed his index finger at the top of the cut and his thumb beneath it, approximating the edges to be about an inch or inch and a half in length. There was no inferior or superior edge; the jagged wound was tapered at both ends, with no apparent residual, suggesting that it might have been made with a dagger. He pulled at it and watched it bleed. The cut was through the skin and subcutaneous tissue, entering the intercostal musculature. It did not appear to penetrate into the pleural cavity. Bruising was noted along the wound path. "The depth of penetration is 1-2 inches. Are you getting this, Emma?" It was a superficial stab wound or an incised wound, but he would be okay. "Emma?"

He turned around when she didn't answer and found her stroking Ronin's legs with both of her hands, her eyes closed, smiling. "Geez," he mumbled to himself, "Emma?"

It looked as if she was praying. He watched her lips tremble and wondered what she was saying when she opened her eyes and said, "He's on his way to Carson City, Amos. He needs to see the sheriff."

"He needs to take a trip to my office is what he needs to do, Emma. And you might come in and sit a bit, too. Neither one of you is doing all that well in my book. Here," Quinn said, "let's sit him up and get him some water. I want to suture this wound, though it's not much. Your friend is going to be okay, Emma. You probably will be, too."

He smiled as he assured her, something her former husband never did, God rest his soul, wherever he may be. But she didn't need the smile, not this afternoon anyway. She already knew he'd be okay. It was the others who were going to suffer, not that she could tell who they were or why or when. Ronin didn't let things like this go. And likely, the angel riding with him wouldn't let it go either.

Chapter 72
READY OR NOT

Sheriff Lloyd Hill was born in New York, City, which didn't make him a bad man, but it did give him a certain attitude toward people who thought they were bad men. Over the years, he'd grown intolerant of people who felt strongly one way at the expense of someone else feeling another.

Hill's ire was raised early on, growing up in New York City's Five Points neighborhood in lower Manhattan. Centre Street to the west, the Bowery to the east, Five Points was a cesspool of criminality. Pick-pockets, muggers, thieves and murderers accomplished what New York's frequent plagues and diseases could not. In short, it raised a man intolerant of bullies and a family anxious to escape the east coast for parts farther west.

"I'll not have some murdering son of a bitch tell me who should be sitting in my jail," Hill told his deputies when he received a telegram from W. A. B. Cobb at Glenbrook notifying him that Leonard Crum was headed his way to break his brother Larry out of jail. "I'll won't permit this kind of violence in my town," he added, though the power of a single lawman to keep a town's peace had been long overrated. The phrase "lawman" itself was nearly extinct.

Statehood had changed Carson City. What had once been a wooden town with a few thousand souls, little white frame houses and a sidewalk full of knot holes and loose boards, was now a much larger and more prosperous place. Homes, stores and government buildings boasted fronts of quarried stone and ornate fences. And there was talk of paving roads and gas lamps lining the city's residential neighborhoods.

Three train cars full of bricks were used to build Duane Bliss's home on West Robinson Street. The three-story Victorian boasted four chimneys and seven fireplaces, marble brought from Italy, Vermont and Georgia, gas-lighting and a telephone system linking the house to Bliss's hotel and lumber operation at Glenbrook. It was the proudest home in the state and Sheriff Hill would not see it, or others like it, ruined. "I don't care what that son of a bitch is thinking he is going to do," Hill said to one of his deputies. "We're going to stop him in the street, before Ash and Slade get here. He's a dead man, and anyone running with him."

"Sheriff, wouldn't it be better to wait for the others to arrive? I mean, there's only two of us, and if he's anything like his brother Larry, we may have our hands full."

Hill looked at the youngest of his deputies, a man noted more for his loud mouth than his physical assets or courage. "Son, you may not be the brightest candle in the mine, but I thought you had more stuffing in you. Leonard Crum is one man..."

"... one crazy man is what I hear," Spinnaker said.

"... and that's just fine." Hill finished. "One crazy son of a bitch and you're running for your knickers? I may be a damned Yankee to some of you here, but I'm not a running scared Yankee piece of shit! We'll stop him in the street, you and I, and when Marshal Ash gets here, he can collect the body. That's all I've got to say."

Fat chance of that, Spinnaker thought, remembering a shooting in the Chinatown section of the city a couple years before, when more than 150 shots were fired at one Chinese man, who was finally killed with a knife. Hill turned to take a rifle from the rack behind the desk and paused. "Spinnaker, how'd you get this job, anyway?"

"I'd hoped to be a teacher, sheriff. But old Miss Clapp didn't think I had the right stuff to be a part of her school. And Central didn't seem to be interested either."

"Did you try the South or North Ward schools, son? You would have been better suited, I believe."

"I did not."

"Not surprising, if you ask me," Hill replied, levering a cartridge into a .44-40 Winchester. "It takes a lot of sand to be a teacher, Spinnaker. Still, given that mouth of yours, you'd been a better teacher than a lawman."

Ronin had said something similar to him a while back, when prying him out of a chair that had collapsed in the jailhouse explosion. Maybe he ought to change his career, if galloping desperados were going to make Carson City their destination.

He hadn't signed up for any of that.

Chapter 73

A CLUMP OF GRASS

The pastor of the Presbyterian Church in Carson City looked up from his writing to watch a Mexican-looking man and his white companion cross Division Street. It was the ornamentation of the darker-looking man that struck him as funny. Too much silver, he thought as he put his pen back down on paper to complete his Sunday sermon. People just shouldn't ride around looking that way. The cow days are over and the gold rush as well, he mused as he re-inked the tip of his fountain pen.

"We are the oldest church in Nevada ..." the reverend wrote, pausing to make sure he was being honest. Well, not counting the Methodists, who organized the first congregation in Nevada but built no building, or the Roman Catholics who were the first to build a building but had to pick up the pieces when it blew down two years later.

"We inhabit the oldest church building in continuous use," he wrote, stopping when he realized it didn't have the same ring to it. He looked up again. He noticed that the two men were turning onto Musser Street, heading south toward the capital. He'd seen a great many people head up and down the Bigler Toll Road since its inception in 1863. No one charged to use it anymore, its use almost superfluous given there were so many other options to and from the lake. If there was any money to be made between Lake Tahoe and Virginia City, it had been made already. Folks heading to the Comstock were just fooling themselves.

"... so we should take seriously our place in things," he scribbled, "with a heart for the state and the state in our heart ..."

That sounds pretty good. What is it with those two? He watched the bushy-browed, stooped over Mexican-looking man pull at a string of horses that clearly didn't want to cooperate. One of the mustangs had found a patch of sweet grass, on the northeast corner of the church's front lawn, the sight of which made him smile. "The birds of the air will nest in our branches," he wrote, stopping to wonder if his people would recognize the words from Jesus' parables or if he should identify the quote. A tall, balding white man, also in tow, seemed embarrassed by the whole parade.

"Leonard, isn't the jail south of here? Why are we coming in so far north?"

"I don't remember where it is, Smith. My brother knows that kind of stuff and he says they keep moving it. But he's here, I can tell it! We'll just ask about him and go on from there."

Smith dismounted, and grabbed a handful of green grass and pushed it into his mount's mouth. He wasn't at all happy to be in Carson City. If Leonard didn't hurt him any, other folk certainly would once they found out who they were and why they were here. He looked over at a house, which sat beside the Presbyterian Church. A man looked out from a desk in front of a first-story window. He nodded. The man smiled.

It had been a long time since he had seen anyone smile. When his partner was alive, they'd often joke about the day's marks. And though it struck the two of them as cruel to be laughing so, it wasn't nearly as harsh as the crimes they had brought upon unsuspecting folk who might have been friends in another life, had their luck been different. A hungry man is a desperate man, they used to say to each other. When the Crums picked them up, they were both hungry. With nothing to collect on the Comstock's silver and gold fields, they were on their way back to California when the Crums had offered them something to eat. And when it became evident that they could cast in with them — robbing and pillaging folks who had so much more — it didn't take much to choose. They could always leave, they figured though they soon found out that wasn't the case. Now Jones was dead. Smith swatted at the flies around his horse's eyes, but was careful not to hit too harshly.

"Leonard, we could stop at the courthouse and ask there. They'd likely know if your brother was in the jail or in the prison."

"I hadn't thought of that," the younger Crum said. Leonard hadn't heard from his brother directly. He only knew that Larry had been picked up on the toll road after the killings. "I don't much trust sheriffs and such, but maybe we ought to." The whole thing made Leonard's stomach turn. It was getting so that you couldn't even kill an Indian without people asking questions. It wouldn't take much for people to put things together once they began asking about his brother. "Get back up on your horse and let's get going," he said, as Smith looked over at the church house again, hoping to somehow connect with the man in the window, whoever he was.

At this point, anyone could be helpful. Anyone other than Leonard or Larry Crum, he figured.

Chapter 74

TAKING UP

Ronin rolled off of the back of the carriage and raised his Yellow Boy to say thanks. "You all need to get off the street, Emma. I don't know when this lunatic is coming but it's bound to be ugly."

"Does he ever stop?" Quinn whispered as he flicked the reins. The horses began to trot north on Carson Street toward Quinn's office.

Emma looked over, surprised. "It's not a novel, Amos. This is real. What's wrong with you?"

"I'm just saying it never seems to stop, Emma. If it's not one thing with him it's another. And before you know it, someone is getting hurt or killed. I just don't get it. It's not like he's a deputy or something."

Emma swallowed hard as she watched Ronin sprint toward the Ormsby County sheriff's office. Life was too precious to see the man she cared for in danger again. But someone had to stand in between the dark and the light. A couple daytime deputies or a nighttime guard couldn't do it all, and Marshal Ash was often hundreds of miles away when things went terribly wrong in the capital city. What of the poor Washoe men and their families? And the children who had been taken from the mission months before? She was grateful for what Ronin did, standing in the gap and keeping people safe, occasionally earning a dollar or two to do so. "There ought to be more people like him, Amos, not fewer. And if you search your heart, you'll know that I'm right."

Quinn paused. "I'm just saying, Emma, there's nothing wrong with letting professionals take care of this sort of thing. It's a different time now. Modernity is coming! There will be street lamps soon, and a broader tax base, and a stronger sheriff's office. Before you know it, the Virginia and Truckee railroad will run a car straight from Carson City to Reno, where a person will be able to do their shopping and still be home before nightfall. The west, as Mister Ronin knows it, is over. Civil society doesn't need this sort of man anymore. In fact, a man like Ronin — running around with all of his guns, taking the law into his own hands — well, it makes all of us less safe, not more safe."

Emma sat silently, as a chorus of carriage springs and horse's hooves echoed rhythmically against the wood and stone buildings on Carson Street. Quinn's office was only a few blocks away. No matter what he said about examining her, she simply didn't feel like it. In fact, she wasn't sure she wanted any kind of attention from Amos Quinn anymore. She and he were too different to spend time together, however professional, intimate or well-intended. She would have to tell him.

As they passed the Ormsby House, she turned so as to tell him what she was thinking, as two men came around the corner of Musser and Carson Street. A short, bushy-browed, stoop-shouldered man pulled at a string of horses and barked orders to a fearful-looking man, telling him to tie up to one of the courthouse posts. She pulled her brown-knit wrap tight against her shoulders. "Amos, get us out of here. Quickly."

"Not there, here!" Leonard yelled, as Smith began to tie the reins of his horse to a small cottonwood tree. "If people meant for you to tie horses to a tree there'd be a sign saying so! Obviously, they want us to tie down here," he gestured to a post by a worn concrete bench.

"Right, Leonard. I'm sorry." Smith grabbed the reins of his horse while slipping two lines around the hitching post. He didn't get down.

"You coming with?" Leonard snarled.

"I thought you might want me to stay here and watch the horses."

"Good idea," Leonard smiled. "I like a thinking man. My brother does, too."

Smith rubbed his jaw and smiled back. *People don't beat other people they like.* "I'll wait right here," he said, looking about. It wouldn't take much to untie the horse and head for the hills, he thought looking over at the long gun attached to Leonard Crum's saddle. *Maybe that's what I need to do.*

Crum tumbled back out of the door, just as a thin, frail, gray-haired woman was attempting to push her way in. She held a pile of papers in her hand. "Excuse me ma'am, I didn't see you there."

"I don't imagine you did," she retorted.

"He's still in the county lock-up," he shouted toward Smith, who was edging his horse closer to Crum's. "Really, ma'am, I don't think I deserve that," he responded to the woman, who was now standing in the door frame looking his way.

"None of us get what we deserve, mister, not enough of us, anyway."

He looked at her and growled. It really didn't matter how nice he was. People treated him poorly. Maybe it's as simple as how I look, he thought, slicking his hair back with his right hand while holding his hat in his left, attempting to give a respectful nod. "Let's get a move on, Smith. It's time we go see my brother." Looking back at the woman in the doorway — who could have been his mother, or Smith's, if their mothers were still alive — he yelled, "I'll not let some ugly old lady keep me from my business."

"Well!" the woman said, pushing the door open with an audible *harrumph.* And that's what did it for Timothy Edwards Smith, from Sacramento, who was so scared out of his mind he couldn't imagine staying with Leonard Crum another five minutes. Right there, right then, Smith decided. He'd take no more of the Crum's unkindness. He would change his life. When Leonard Crum wasn't looking, he'd begin his new life by looking for something good to do. There'd be no more nastiness in his life. He was ready for a change.

Chapter 75

SHERIFF'S OFFICE

"Hello? Anyone here?" Ronin waited a minute by the door, so as not to surprise the deputies, and then entering, shouted into the jailhouse, thinking someone might be there. "Sheriff?"

"That you, Ronin?"

The voice was taunting and familiar. Larry Crum was sitting, smiling in the third cell to Ronin's right, a big, fat stogie between his lips. He was all prettied up, as if he had somewhere to go.

"I thought the sheriff didn't allow you boys to smoke back here?" Ronin said tentatively, looking around and curious as to why the jail appeared empty.

"I don't smoke, Mister Ronin. I'm celebrating."

Ronin looked in each of the cells and then returned. "You're celebrating? Tell me what you're celebrating, you dim-witted piece of shit."

"Settle down, reverend, that's no way to speak to one of God's children." Ronin winced. Sometimes his anger got the best of him. Prayer hadn't helped and working out on a heavy bag hadn't helped much either.

"I'm celebrating that my brother is coming to town."

"You know this?" Ronin asked, now more curious than ever.

"The sheriff said he was going to prepare for a special visitor. Santa Anna is coming, my friend."

"Yeah, the sheriff told me you were babbling about that."

"He is. And he will cut your heart out."

"Listen, you piece of garbage. I've already met your brother," Ronin said, grinning. "And he's a back-stabbing son of a bitch, if you ask me." Ronin turned to show the tear and blood stain on his vest. "And while he gave it his best, his best wasn't good enough, Larry. And your best isn't good enough either, Larry. You're boy is a dead man walking, Larry."

"I doubt it."

"You go ahead and doubt what you want to doubt, my friend. You're headed to prison and your brother, if he isn't killed this afternoon by the sheriff or me, will be headed to prison with you. Won't that be cozy?"

"Got a light, cowboy?"

Ronin moved to the cell door, quicker than expected, and grabbed hold of the prisoner's vest when he heard the sheriff calling from outside. "Ronin, get the hell out of my office, son."

Ronin pushed Crum onto his bed and ran to the front door, where he saw Sheriff Hill peering out a second story window in a house across the street. "What are you doing up there, Hill?"

"It's a mouse trap, son, but you're standing in the middle of it. Spinnaker is up the street with a rifle. We hope to catch them in a cross-fire. Get the hell out of my way, son!"

"You got the back door covered?" A barely-audible "oops" crossed Hill's lips.

"Not to worry, sheriff. I've got it."

"You sure, son?"

"It's what I do," Ronin grinned.

It was then, right then, with the two of them yelling at each other across Ormsby Street that Larry's Crum's brother and his friend appeared, on Curry Street between Seventh and Eighth Avenue. A stoop-shouldered, bushy haired, uni-browed man named Leonard and his balding companion were pulling a string of horses when they heard Ronin shouting. Leonard Crum knew that voice, because he had heard it before, in the village of

Glenbrook at Lake Tahoe. Crum kicked his horse into a gallop, and then yanked their reins in a manner that would make his brother Larry proud, right in front of the jail before the sheriff could get off a shot. Bounding from the horse, he barreled into the ex-reverend standing in the doorway and knocked him inside the door, slamming the door shut.

The sheriff swung wide with his rifle for a secondary target. Where was the other guy? Where Timothy Edwards Smith once was, two horses were now standing, their rifle scabbards empty, right in the middle of Curry Street.

Chapter 76

KNIFE FIGHT

Leonard Crum had failed to bring a gun to a gun fight, something his brother would never do. But the bigger of the Crum boys was close enough that it really didn't matter. Ronin was picking himself up from the floor when he boot-kicked the wheel gun out of his hands. Both guns were still sliding across the floor when Leonard threw himself on top of him, pinning Ronin's already injured back to the floor, his rifle beneath him. Leonard began slapping the ex-reverend with his open palms. Once, twice, three times across Ronin's face, so quickly and harshly that the blood Leonard's hands produced didn't allow Ronin to feel or see past his nose.

Leonard Smith's huge ham-sized fists beat at the ex-preacher so fiercely that Ronin had no option but to cover up and bridge with his feet, hoping to throw his attacker over the top of him. His clipped his elbows close to his face, and suddenly folded his head as high up as he could go and roared! Then just as suddenly, he threw his head backward and, arching upward with his stomach and pushing off with his feet, launched Leonard Smith up and over into the desk behind him. A loud crash confirmed that he had succeeded. The heavy oak desk — which had endured years of abuse in the sheriff's office, including a significant explosion, having once shielded a younger deputy from losing his life in that blast — caused his attacker to briefly lose consciousness. Ronin pushed out from beneath him, wiping away the blood in his eyes with his sleeve, only to catch a glimpse of the man rising again.

Crum pulled his Masonic dagger from its silver sheath and slashed at Ronin. *What the hell?* Left and then right. Right and then left. Ronin threw his backside toward the windows in an odd maneuver that pulled his stomach away from the blade, his hands flapping wildly like a bird trying to leap from its nest. He tried to regain balance, though precious little could be found as a diagonal cut went sailing past his right ear, then another past his left. He drew his hands back close to his chest and waited for Leonard's cuts to end, and then anticipating his next — straight in and up — he caught Leonard's arm with both of his hands in an awkward block, an "X block," his Savate teacher used to call it. "You'll know when you need it. It will come naturally. If it doesn't, good. Because it's garbage," he had said one Monday morning, emphasizing the second syllable of the word as if to suggest it was originally French. When the blade came in, Ronin dropped his arms in an X, so as to protect his torso, and kicked at Leonard's knee. The stooped man screamed.

Ronin grabbed the knife hand. There wasn't any technique to a knife fight, the fur trader had said. If he was lucky, he'd find his way to a doctor's office while his attacker was dropped off at the morgue. He twisted Leonard's powerful right hand sharply, his wrist and fingers so that they pointed to the ceiling, and dropped back suddenly with his right leg bending Leonard's knife hand forward with such force that he heard the ligaments tear. Both men screamed as Leonard dropped his knife at Ronin's feet.

Ronin clipped his right boot tip into Leonard's ribcage, and then snapped it again at Leonard's neck. An odd, guttural sound caused Leonard's older brother to begin shaking his cell door. "What have you done to my brother? Stop it! You'll kill him, you rebel son of a bitch!" Leonard, unable to answer, grabbed his throat as Ronin threw two right hooks to the side of his head and a left upper cut to his chin. Leonard Crum crumpled to the floor, spitting and heaving and cursing and bleeding, on his hands and knees but still very much alive. "Son of a bitch!" Larry Crum whined from the back room. "What have you done to my little brother?"

Ronin bent over and grabbing his knees to rest, glanced about to make sure Leonard was out for the count. He was exhausted, having been stabbed in the back, beaten into a mindless frazzle riding the Clear Creek flume and now nearly getting stabbed again by the same bushy-headed jingle-bobbed jackass who had cut him in the first place. He was stumbling about when Sheriff Hill blew through the door with his rifle at the ready. Hill lowered it and asked breathlessly, "Are you okay, son?" having slid down a slate second story roof into some holly bushes in his attempt to rescue a man he could now clearly see didn't need rescuing.

"Yep," Ronin quipped, still trying to catch his breath. "Where are your deputies?

"Spinnaker should be up the street. He's not here yet?"

"Not that I've seen," Ronin said, glancing toward the back door, which still appeared to be locked.

"What about the other little shit — Smith, was it?"

"The tall guy? Up the street, too, I guess." The sheriff pushed his rifle into a corner and reached toward Ronin, so as to help.

"Let's hope they're together, sheriff," Ronin began to breathe easier. "Because I'm going to finish both of them if one doesn't have hold of the other. This back-stabbing son of a bitch nearly killed me again."

"I can see that," Hill said as he guided Ronin to a chair. "Take a break, son. Let me look after this rodeo clown," he said as he grabbed Leonard Crum by his collar, tossing him into the thick, wooden door that separated the jail from his office. Leonard crumpled onto the floor. "I believe the stage is getting in. And if your friends are on it, they'll clear the street on their way down to the jail house. We'll figure out where to go from there."

"What's going on in there?" Larry Crum bellowed from the back room.

"Shut the fuck up," Ronin and Hill said simultaneously, and then began laughing.

Chapter 77

TIMOTHY EDWARDS SMITH

Seeing Leonard Crum's rifle just sitting there in the scabbard was too much to resist, Smith figured when Leonard went barreling through the sheriff's office door. And given that all eyes were turned toward the jailhouse, Timothy Edwards, as his mother called him, decided there and then that this was his lucky break. Climbing down from his horse, he grabbed the rifle and then ran west toward Ash Canyon. Though the sandy, sage-covered hills took a little getting used to, he dug his heels in when the upward climb became difficult, side-stepping his way into the scrub juniper bushes and trees and lying flat on his back so as to wait for night fall.

He had no idea what he was going to do, other than to get away and do something different. No one had ever treated him as badly as Leonard Crum, not that it was necessarily his fault. The man was damaged, deranged or something. While his older brother could be counted on to keep him in check, with Larry in jail there had been no end to the physical and emotional abuse Leonard had unleashed on him. Simply said, he was finished and not having a forward-looking plan was the least of his troubles if the law or Leonard caught up with him.

He rocked his back deep into the sand, twisting left and right so as to deepen the hole he was in and better blend with the sharp shadows of the Sierra's late afternoon sun. It would be only a matter of minutes now, he thought, looking at the sun over his right shoulder. Assuming they didn't search for him quickly, darkness would ensure his escape, and running close to the mountains, he could gather what he needed from homes and ranches along the tree line. Perhaps he'd hike to the lake, or to Reno, though either walk seemed extreme. Maybe it was better to trek eastward across town toward Dayton and make the 17-mile climb into Virginia City. Given the hoopla in Carson City, it would be days before Marshal Ash was back in his Virginia City office. Given a month or two more, Smith believed he'd be unrecognizable among the thousands of laborers still trying to make a living on the Comstock Lode.

Thinking the latter made better sense, when nighttime fell he hugged the first set of hills, using Leonard Crum's rifle as a crutch at times, and headed northwest back through town until he came to a small saloon on Carson Street. Not being a sober man when the opportunity to imbibe presented itself, he stopped for a drink.

"Set me up, barkeep."

"That'd be 'Please, set me up, barkeep,' cowboy!" a tall. thin man barked from behind the bar. "I'm Jack. And you?" The man stood there with his hand outstretched, smiling.

"I'm not anybody worth remembering, Jack. And please, if you would."

He slid onto a stool and looked around the room as men emptied into the street to see what the ruckus was about down by the jailhouse. A bottle and a glass were set in front of him when he turned back, and Jack was still standing there, smiling.

"Everybody's worth remembering, son, and tomorrow will always be a better day than yesterday."

"I doubt that," Smith huffed, brushing the dust from his pants and onto the floor. He looked up and found his new friend frowning. "Sorry," he said, bashfully. "I should have done that outside."

"No problem," Jack said, grabbing a broom. "Doesn't look like we've got a whole lot going on right now. I've got a little time," he said, pushing the broom and sweeping some of the dust at Smith's feet toward the door. "How is it you've stumbled into my humble establishment, son? You look troubled."

"No more than anyone else," Smith said, as he looked for just the right table to sit at as the bar seemed a little too friendly and inquiring. "I'm wondering what I'm going to do, now that my ... um ... former line of work has worn out. That's all."

"Seen a lot of your friends over the last couple of years, heading back from old Virginny to ... where'd you say you were from?"

"Sacramento last, old man."

Jack winced. He hadn't been called an old man since he lost his saloon on Ormsby Street. Despite Ally calling him that, he still missed her. Though sharp-tongued, she brought a lot of smiling faces into the place. When she left, both he and the bar aged. He guessed it was true. Sooner or later, even a man who stayed out of the Nevada sunshine was sure to get wrinkles.

"I'm sorry, friend. I've got no reason to mistreat you," Smith said. "The name is Smith, Timothy Smith, and I'm not quite sure where I'm headed yet."

"I hear there's work south of here, if you can get there."

"Bode, right?"

"Yup."

"That's a ways. And to be frank, I'm thinking of heading north instead."

Jack finished up with the broom and grabbed a hand cloth. He began wiping down tables, in the general direction of his only customer. "Nothing much north, except for Reno. You got a job in Reno?"

"No job. Still looking," Smith replied.

"I'm not much for the city. Hell, Carson City is big enough. And with the railroad, there will be plenty more people there in the next few years." He shook his head. Enough people and you had a business. Too many people, and your business has become a big bother. "This place is a pretty quiet. I like it that way."

Smith looked around and didn't have to wonder why. Where many of the establishments in Carson City were well appointed, with brass, wood paneling and wall paper, this bar didn't have any of that. "You just open, friend?"

"The bar, yes. The business, no. I used to be over on Ormsby, maybe they call it Curry Street now. Maybe you've been there? Had a girl named Ally working there, pretty auburn-headed girl, a big bosom and an even bigger smile." He paused for a moment, remembering. "She's gone now ... and the clients with her."

Smith thought of a big-breasted server named Ally in Glenbrook and wondered if they might be the same gal, but kept his mouth shut. He couldn't disappear, if pieces of his life kept reappearing, particularly women, who when they discovered he wasn't interested made a point of telling others that. Disappearing was at the top of his list. "Never met her, Jack ... you seem to miss her."

"Nah. I just miss the familiar, friend. You?"

"Working on finding a new familiar, I guess."

"It ain't easy."

"Jack," the bald-headed man said, "nothing's easy, friend, particularly something righteous and good."

Chapter 78

MORT SPINNAKER

A wheezing Mort Spinnaker hit Jack's front door like the building was on fire and it was up to him to bring water. But the building wasn't, and Spinnaker wasn't after water as much as he was seeking a small shot glass filled with liquid courage. He was headed to Virginia City and had decided he was going to be a teacher instead of a lawman, given that the Fourth Ward School was looking for a new teacher and things in Carson City didn't seem like they'd be slowing down anytime soon.

"Whoa, buddy!" Jack exclaimed, looking up from the table next to his new friend. "Slow down, Mort. Let me get you something for your breathing."

Despite being a young man, and a lawman in Carson City, Mort Spinnaker was known to have suffered from childhood asthma. Over his twenty-some years as an adult, he had yet to find a cure. The doctors told him there was little they could do when he was short of breath, other than to offer steam or chest massage. And while both were relatively pleasant, he coveted a morning and evening dose of mash to help relax his lungs.

"I'm fine, Jack," he gasped. "Just ran from the sheriff's office. Apparently, they've caught the brother of that bandit we've been holding for some time, and there's one more guy loose on the street somewhere."

Jack looked over at Smith, who was stirring his whiskey with his jackknife. The two men's eyes met before Spinnaker realized that Smith might be the man he was talking about. It made his chest seem even tighter.

"You got some medicine for me?" he asked, looking away.

"Sure 'nuff, son, here," Jack said, setting a shot glass in front of him at the bar.

"Who's the bald guy?" he whispered. Jack shrugged. It didn't pay him one way or the other to stick his nose in other people's business.

"'Endeavor to be quiet. Keep to your own business,' the Good Book says, Mort. Man's heading out of town is all I know."

"Well, that makes two of us," Spinnaker mumbled, picking up his glass.

Jack raised his voice so as to continue speaking with his new friend in the corner of the saloon. "So the way I figure it, every day is a new day, son. And most days are better than the one before it."

"Think so?" Smith said, looking over at the wheezing man seated on the stool. "How about you, sir?" he asked, trying not to raise his voice, like he was challenging the man. "Do you think tomorrow is going to be any better than today?"

Spinnaker threw his head backward and downed the shot. "Another," he said, looking over at Jack, before he looked toward the stranger and replied. "I'm counting on it."

"How so, Mort?" Jack asked. He didn't yet have a mirror up, nor could he afford to break any tables or chairs. It was important his new clientele got along.

Mort swallowed a second shot of whiskey before replying. "I'm headed to Virginia City, Jack. Going to become a teacher, I think. I made a few contacts. It seems like there's some interest. And with the mines closing, there ought to be plenty of places to keep warm. I'm done with ..." he looked over at the man in the far corner ... "I'm done with what I was doing."

Jack was a man who had learned to keep mouth shut, all those years on Curry Street across from the capital complex. Ally kept a good trade going and folks didn't need to know who was visiting whom and when. His recently becoming a Roman Catholic had only confirmed things. "I'm glad to hear that, Mort. You look happy. Happy's good." Jack smiled.

"I am. How about you, stranger?" he looked back over to the corner of the saloon.

"Well ... I've been thinking the same thing. Virginia City sounds as good as any place to start over. And a school is a hell of a lot better than most places I've been. Mind if I sit?" he said, pushing his chair back and standing, so as to take a seat at the bar.

"Long as you ain't a lawman or a loser, I guess!" Spinnaker picked up his rifle from the stool next to him and propped it against the bar on his opposite side.

"Definitely not a lawman, friend. And a loser? Well ... it's something I'm working on."

The two men smiled at each other as Jack went about his business. Starting a new life may not be easy, he mused, but it was often a lot easier than living the life one was leaving behind. And it was a hell of a lot easier if you had a friend.

Chapter 79

I'LL BE DAMNED

"Well, I'll be damned," Ash said, as he stepped off of the stagecoach and found W. W. Ronin standing there with his rifle, smiling.

"I hope not, marshal. Eternity is a long time, if you believe that sort of thing," Ronin said, pulling his hat down in an attempt to hide his battered face.

"You don't, reverend?" Ash asked, surprised.

Ronin grimaced, having never liked the word "reverend." He liked it even less now that he wasn't one. "Used to," he said. "Don't anymore."

"Oh, my!" Dustsucker interrupted, as he stepped onto the street. "What happened to you?"

Ronin turned, his grimace changing to a grin. "I caught up to the slower of the two Crum brothers, I guess, or with his hands anyway. There I was, standing in the doorway of the sheriff's office gabbing, minding my own business, when that bushy-haired braggart comes riding hard up to the porch and slams himself through the doorway. I'm afraid the surprise and scuffle left things pretty broken up inside, the office that is."

"I imagine so," Dustsucker laughed, as he put his hand on his friend's shoulder. "Let me see your back," he asked. Ash watched the tall, ex-preacher wince as he turned slightly to show the stab wound, where Smith had attempted to plunge his Masonic dagger clear through his back so that it came out the other side.

"You're lucky it was a piece of shit that stabbed you, Ronin. A better knife would have taken your lung!" Dustsucker shook his head. "I don't see much to matter on your back, except for a lot of dirt and a little blood. Doctor seen you yet?"

"I'm supposed to head up that way at some point, Dusty. But right now, I'm hoping to find Crum's bald-headed accomplice."

"Smith?" Ash asked.

"I think that's his name," Ronin answered, turning to face the marshal. "I left Leonard all busted up on the sheriff's floor, if the two of you don't mind hurrying that way. I was hoping to find Smith running up the street."

"I'm surprised he's still with riding with that sadist," Ash offered, chambering a round into his rifle.

"I'm assuming so," Ronin responded, rolling his shoulders frontward and backward to see if he couldn't alleviate some of the pain he was in. "They were together in Glenbrook. That's all I know. Sheriff says he saw another man with Leonard before he ran through the jailhouse door."

"So, you're serious about how you got ... so beat up?" Ash asked, hesitating to draw attention to Ronin's swollen face and bruises.

Ronin glared in response. "Marshal, I've got a good amount of respect for you and your office," he mumbled. "But having been in a few scrapes together, you sure as hell don't seem to know when to keep your mouth shut, if you don't mind me saying."

Slade laughed and then felt the tension.

"I don't say things twice," he continued. "And I don't often lie when I'm saying them once, friend." He held his gaze.

It was the word "friend" that caused Dustsucker to pay attention, as Ronin's gaze wasn't one a man would give a friend unless he was touching his woman or poke.

Ash spoke first. "I'm just saying, Ronin ... I don't know how you got here so fast. And if you took a ride down that river in a box, well, a reasonable man might think you got banged up a bit on the flume. That's all."

Dustsucker stepped in between the two men. "That'd be three times, marshal, if he chooses to explain again. I don't think I've seen a man survive asking Ronin the same question three times."

Ash snorted and took a step away to look north on Carson Street. Ronin relaxed.

"We'll head down to the jailhouse," Dustsucker offered. "One of them two sons of bitches killed those men at Lake Tahoe, or at least they know who did."

"Thanks," Ronin smiled. "I'll be down in a few minutes. I'm going to take a look around to see if I can find Spinnaker or Smith."

"Spinnaker's not there, either?"

"Nope."

"I don't get it," Dustsucker said, hiking his gun leather up so that it sat higher on his waist. He drew one of his revolvers, opened the loading gate and placed another cartridge in it so that it held six not five as was customary.

"The sheriff said they got into a discussion earlier in the day that led him to believe that maybe Spinnaker didn't want to be a deputy anymore. Big surprise there."

"I don't understand," Dustsucker said, returning one revolver to its holster before grabbing the other.

"Spinnaker's always been a wind-belly, if you ask me. He's fat in the middle and a bit poor at both ends."

"Ah, come on Ronin, can't blame a man for being a youngster. He's barely twenty. He'll shape up," Dustsucker said, pulling another cartridge from his belt.

"I doubt it, Dusty. The sheriff says he wants to be a teacher."

"No kidding."

"Yup. Bill sent him up the street with a rifle to wait for Crum and Smith. It's been about half an hour. Smith's nowhere to be seen. Spinnaker neither."

"I'll be damned," Ash muttered looking up the street toward the mint.

"That's the second time you've said that, marshal," Ronin quipped, looking his way. I'm beginning to think it's a religious preference."

"Nope. Haven't got one, Ronin, though with all the gun play, I've been thinking about it. I'm just wondering, isn't that Smith there, stepping out of the saloon? And who's that with him? My eyes aren't what they should be."

"There's your youngster, Dusty," Ronin said, levering a .44-40 cartridge into his Yellow Boy, "wearing a wedding ring and looking all friendly with each other."

"Well, I'll be damned," Dustsucker exclaimed.

"Neither of you will be, if I can help it." Ronin shouldered his rifle and began striding north along the boardwalk on Carson Street. "Not today, anyway," he mumbled, "though there's a good chance one or both of these men may get to meet their maker."

Chapter 80

SHOOT OUT ON CARSON STREET

Ronin broke into a run as soon as he was away from his friends. And while he generally didn't mind running — it was a rare capture or kill that didn't necessitate a quick skip or scurry along the way — it wasn't as if he was at the top of his game, given the beating he had just endured a couple blocks south in the sheriff's office.

He ran along the west side of the road, as it gave him the best cover. Two men were crossing Carson at Telegraph Street. Their pace was quick, and while he couldn't make out the second man, the first was clearly Spinnaker, the young Ormsby County deputy sheriff who, with nighttime deputy Jim Garrett, had allowed Larry Crum to escape a few days earlier.

Despite the Spinnaker's breathing difficulties — Ronin kept a soft spot for folks with respiratory illnesses, because of his father having inhaled hot gasses in a wartime explosion — he had never regarded Spinnaker highly. He remembered a certain difficult exchange he had had with Spinnaker and another deputy just prior to the jail's explosion the previous year that had so severely injured his leg.

His ribs began to ache as he jogged between busy customers and merchants. A tall, busty woman in a purple hoop skirt, with a lace umbrella and yellow blouse, yelled for him to get out of the way as he brushed by her already barking poodle. What the hell would a woman need with a poodle on Carson Street, he wondered as he hurried north toward the men, one of whom he believed to be wanted for murder. Poodles are retrievers, not lap dogs. His breathing began to labor and his legs grew heavy. He found himself yelling to Spinnaker to stop, despite thinking it wasn't the brightest of moves, given Spinnaker's clear comfort with the other man, whom he now recognized as Timothy Edwards Smith, Leonard Crum's accomplice. Both men spun around, surprised, Smith firing a lever-action Winchester at him, waist high. *Thank God, who could hit anything that way?* And what the hell, why didn't Spinnaker do anything? Why was he just standing there?

He listed into a Carson Street store front, his left shoulder crashing through a pane of window glass that said, "Jewelry and Loan, Great Deals on New and Used Merchandise, Cash to Buy or Loan on your Valuables." How odd that he could read the sign so quickly, he thought, as a man — or men, he didn't know — were shooting at him. The glass shattered above and around him, a larger piece falling into his left thigh and cutting it. He shouldered his Yellow Boy, pressing his right cheek against the walnut stock, and slammed two shots north toward the corner of Carson and Telegraph streets, before realizing that he didn't know if he had a clear site picture. There were people everywhere, some of whom were scattering for safer streets and cover, while others seemed to be simply holding their mouths agape that anything so unbelievable could be happening around them.

"Sheeple," he mumbled, shaking his head and wondering how anyone could be so out of touch to believe that their community was safe simply because there were lawmen living nearby. "Deputies are minutes away when seconds count," he'd told Emma once, when explaining what he did and why he did it.

He suddenly felt cold. Looking down, he noticed that his pants had changed color. His favorite pair of canvas riding jeans now appeared red instead of tan, the piping on them — which held a much heavier brown seat in place — seemed wet. On better days, he liked how they almost formed a side crease, adding contrast and color to an otherwise droll appearance. He missed wearing the nicer clothes he used to wear as a clergyman. Looking up again, and struggling once more to breathe, he discovered the two men were gone and that a pile of women and men were kneeling or lying prone in their place.

Ronin stood to get a better look when a rifle shot split the wood in front of his face. *Marshal Ash was shooting at me? No, he's gesturing, pointing across the street to a rifleman crouching behind a tree stump.* Another shot pinged off a metal sign above him. *Deputy Spinnaker is crouched there as well, with a Colt in his hands!* He watched him thumb a cartridge into place and point it his way. *What the hell is happening?*

Ronin took aim at the stump and sent a pile of splinters into Smith's face, pushing the two men into an attorney's office on Telegraph Street. He noticed that Ash and Dustsucker were running his way when he stepped out onto the street and stumbled.

"That's all I remember," Ronin said, looking up into Emma's round, brown eyes. "I have no idea how I got here." His friend sat silently, smiling in a paneled physician's office next to the Ormsby House. A parlor clock was ticking rhythmically, at a faster pace than his heartbeat. Emma's lips were moving; her eyes were closed. It was if she was saying something, but he couldn't hear her for the buzzing in his ears.

The room seemed familiar, with Amos Quinn looking studiously at his left leg and Emma standing by his side. She was holding his hand, he noticed, and smiling, which didn't seem all that bad except for Quinn's reaction, though he couldn't tell if it was the leg or the lady that was bothering him most.

"What happened?" he asked. His mouth was dry and his throat felt as if he hadn't anything to drink for days, as if he'd been sick or something.

"Hell if we know," Marshal Ash answered. Ronin looked to his left and noticed Dustsucker and the marshal, the two of them standing there instead of at the sheriff's office, as he had earlier asked. "Last thing either of us saw was Smith and Spinnaker shooting and you falling into the street."

"I don't remember falling into any street. Seriously?"

"Don't make me repeat myself," Augustus Ash said, chuckling. "You know I don't like repeating myself."

Dustsucker laughed. Ronin couldn't tell what was so funny.

"It's not bad, reverend. It's a bruise, if you will. It nicked your head, threw a lot of blood I suspect. But lucky for you it didn't enter your cranium."

Quinn wasn't a bad man, though he was sure he had told him not to call him that. Maybe it was the doctor thing that bothered him most. When the hell did doctors get so stuffed-shirt? The world was better when bleeders were best handled by barbers, though he didn't expect medical experts would agree. He grinned. Emma looked at him curiously.

"You're going to need a new rifle, Ronin. Had it not been for the brass receiver on your Yellow Boy, you might be a dead man. And had the receiver been made of steel instead of brass, the pieces might have been worse."

"What are you saying, Dusty?" he heard himself ask, as the buzzing began to clear.

"I'm saying you were standing out in the middle of the street, levering your Yellow Boy like a mad man, until it was empty. You stood there looking at it, as if looking at it would load it, when Spinnaker stood up and took careful aim, busting your rifle to pieces. It all happened so quickly that neither Ash nor I could get a shot off."

"What happened so quickly?"

"Spinnaker, dude! Aren't you listening? Spinnaker grabbed Smith's gun, of all things, and put a bullet right into the receiver of your rifle, a piece of which hit you in the head."

"Deputy Spinnaker? I never liked that man." Ronin tried raising his right hand to his head to explore the wound, but couldn't as Emma was holding it.

"Don't move so much," Emma said.

"I've got a hard head, I've been told," Ronin said, looking up into Emma's eyes. "What about my leg?"

"It's fine," Quinn interrupted, annoyed with all the talking. "Nothing nearly as bad as the last time you were here."

"I don't imagine," Ronin replied, looking up at Quinn and then to Dustsucker, who was smiling at Emma. Ash seemed irritated. He grinned and noticed Emma looking at him again, curiously.

"The Crum brothers?"

"Well, that's an interesting story," Happy Hands said, as he entered the room, pulling the door closed behind him.

"My brother!" Ronin shouted, attempting to sit up, but grabbing his side and coughing instead. Emma looked at the doctor, mouthing the words, "My brother?" Quinn shrugged his shoulders.

"Might have hit his head when he fell, I guess, who knows?"

"How are you, my brother? I am sorry I couldn't wait any longer for you by the rock. It was nighttime and I was cold." Happy Hands smiled. "And ... I didn't feel as if I was welcome there."

"The Standing Grey Stone does not like just anyone sitting there too long, my friend. But do not worry. It was no bother." Happy Hands stood at his feet, gazing at him.

"Well, isn't this nice," Ash said impatiently, "we're all together."

"What happened to the Crum brothers, marshal?" Ronin asked, before catching Emma's glance at Ash and wondering why she seemed so annoyed.

"I'll let Happy Hands explain. It was his discovery," Ash replied, looking over at Emma and raising his eyebrows as if to say, "Stay out of this."

"We'll say no more, marshal. My patient needs his sleep."

"I agree," Emma said, pulling a blanket up over her patient, who suddenly felt so warm that it was wonderful lying there. Was it the blanket that Happy Hands had laid across his feet? Was it the gathering of his friends? He closed his eyes.

"We'll have supper together, William, in a day or two. Happy Hands can explain then," Emma said, as she bent forward to plant a kiss on Ronin's forehead. But Ronin never noticed, because he was already asleep, dreaming.

"Discoveries come slowly, my friend," Happy Hands said in his dream, "every seven or eight years or so. You can't know, or become, everything at once, William. A good life takes time."

Ronin picked up a rock and threw it into the clear blue water of Lake Tahoe. It skipped, once, twice, three times before it sank to the sandy bottom. He could still see it, maybe ten or twenty feet deep, a dozen feet from the shore from the gray rocks scattered along the shoreline. The surface current — driven by the near constant late afternoon winds at the lake, so much so that Tahoe's uniquely blue water was beginning to be covered with white caps — had carved gentle ridges in the sand. It was clear enough that Ronin thought he could see little grey fish, with teeth, smiling back at him. "When a spirit helper first comes to a man, he becomes ill. Horrible things often happen. If he is not careful, he can lose his life in times like these. That is when a man needs his spiritual friends most..."

Chapter 81

SUPPER

Emma began to clear away the dishes. Her guests, U.S. Marshal Augustus Ash, deputy Marcus T. Slade and Happy Hands, had gathered to celebrate the end of a troubling mystery, and to be thankful — to the extent that they could, as generally irreligious people might — for Ronin's survival in the gun battle on Carson Street. "You've all been so kind," she said, to bless our mission this way."

Ash squirmed. He had promised himself not to set foot on the mission grounds unless it was for professional reasons. He didn't understand the woman and hardly appreciated what the mission was attempting to do for the Washoe, Paiute and Shoshone tribes in the area. "An Indian will always be an Indian," he'd told Emma when she approached him for money last spring.

"Things have been real tight after the kidnappings," she'd replied. "My husband truly screwed the pooch." He laughed, before realizing that Emma was making, what he considered to be, an inappropriate comment about one of the women in her former husband's life. Still, the phrase seemed silly, coming out of the mouth of a so conservative a gal that he could hardly contain himself as she went on about the budget and revenues of Carson City's first Indian school, and how difficult things had been since Henry Nauman's disappearance. Religious people, particularly supporters, loved a good and scandalous story, but would hardly support one with their finances.

"Emma, I have as little to do with Indians as I can, ma'am. And I sorrow over your condition; I really do. But there's no improving an Indian's life without making him a white man," he said, before being interrupted.

"Or white woman," she said fiercely, causing him to feel judged and to feel even more uncomfortable. Did the American Gospel Mission really think what they were doing with the nation's aboriginal tribes was a good thing? Not that he was a religious man, or had read much about it, but prior to heading over the Sierra Mountains to the Comstock gold fields, he had acquainted himself with the history of the Indians in the area so as to appreciate what had gone on before him and, perhaps, to benefit from it.

"Your presence here tonight honors what we do in this place," Emma continued, standing in the kitchen doorway. Ash noted that no one at the table was looking at Emma as she stood speaking. Not a one of them. No one here had anything to do with church, or Christian missionary efforts or the American Gospel Mission for that matter, except for the matron who ran it. This must certainly ring harshly to Happy Hands' ears.

"Ma'am, you bring out the best in people, to be sure," Ash said standing, hoping to bring the gathering back to its original purpose, having begun to wonder if he was attending a fundraiser. "If I may," he said, looking over at Emma, "I'm hoping we can help Mister Ronin understand what happened those couple of days he was languishing in Doctor Quinn's office. And where is Doctor Quinn, anyway, if I may ask?"

"I didn't think to invite him. I'm sorry," Emma said, wringing her hands with a towel. Ronin smiled. *It would appear as if Doctor Quinn is no longer in the running.*

"Well, I've been thinking," Ronin interrupted, appreciating the opportunity. "You've all been so considerate and kind. But it is I who owe everyone a debt of gratitude. I had no idea what I was missing, laying there on Carson Street as Spinnaker and Smith got away," he said, winking at his friend Dustsucker.

"Ouch, Ronin," Dustsucker replied.

"How about you let us tell you the story first, before you jump to judgment?" Ash continued.

"Of course, marshal," Ronin laughed, "I meant no harm."

"We caught up to you, having to choose to run one direction or the other ..."

"... and with you laying in the middle of Carson Street," Dustsucker added, hoping his friend would understand, "we thought it best to check on your condition, my friend, instead of the prisoners."

"Of course," Ronin nodded.

"Quinn was already on the run up the street and, seeing that you were still breathing, we made a search of the lawyer's office they had run into, and the surrounding businesses, and could find nothing."

"Nothing good comes out of an attorney's office," Ronin said, laughing. "Most lawyers offices, anyway."

"Whatever the case," Ash continued, "we figured that they were headed to the railroad depot, so we posted there until the last train left, but saw no one." Ash looked around the room to see if everyone understood what he was saying. "If you ask me, Smith and Spinnaker apparently continued north and east by American Flat into Virginia City, or doubled back so as to head to Reno. But they're gone, without a trace, and that's just how it is."

"You're assuming they're together?" Ronin asked, pushing his plate away so that he could lean his forearms on the table.

"We have no evidence for or against," Slade chimed in, "though a barkeep on Carson Street indicates that they met in his saloon and seemed friendly to each other."

"We imagine they'll turn up someday," Ash said, "and maybe you'll be the one to find them. The charges are attempted murder, for both of them of course, with some additional ones on Spinnaker's side. And once we catch up to Smith, I imagine there will be a few more his way, as well, assuming that we get one of the Crum brothers to break."

"What's happening with the Crums at this point?"

"Well, that's Happy Hands' story, I suspect, short of pointing out they're both headed to the new prison on Fifth Street, until we know something more damning. Happy Hands?"

Ronin's Washoe friend sat smiling at the head of the table. Even though called on, he did not seem anxious to speak. After a few moments, he stood. "I don't often get such attention," he said finally, putting his knife and fork down on the table in front of him and folding his napkin securely at the side of his plate. His dinner etiquette was now exemplary, Dusty had related earlier, given the opportunities he was enjoying with townsfolk once it became known that he had contributed to solving the Washoe murders.

"Well?" Ronin asked.

"Do you remember the pebbles in the mouths of my dead friends?"

"I'm sorry, Happy Hands, I didn't realize they were your friends."

"The Washoe are all friends, Ronin. It is I who am sorry. I thought we had spoken of this before."

"We had, *I'm* sorry. Please go on."

"Well, shortly after you left the sheriff's office, I arrived on horseback. I assisted Sheriff Hill in making an inventory of Leonard Crum's possessions when I found that Leonard Crum had a pocket of rocks, apparently, the same sort of rocks, or rather pebbles, as those found in the mouths of the dead Washoe men. And as they are particularly rare at the lake …"

"I had no idea."

"… yes, they're found only in certain areas, having been deposited during a time of great ice, I am told. It was very odd to find some in his pocket. Most white men do not know where to find these rocks."

"I don't understand," Ronin said, gesturing for Emma to sit down beside him.

"Not that it matters, my friend. Leonard made such a fuss about our taking 'his treasures,' he called them — he apparently cleaned his dishes with them when camping without water — that no shushing or cell banging on the part of his brother could keep him from speaking about them at length."

"You mean, he admitted placing them in the mouths of the dead men?"

"Yes, William. It was all most odd. How is it that white men can make so much fun of our holy place, the Standing Grey Stone, and value such smaller stones as their personal treasures?"

"I imagine such distinctions will make lawyers a lot of money someday," Ronin chuckled, until he noticed that Happy Hands was not laughing at all.

"Exactly," Ash chimed in. "We are fearful that Larry Crum's Masonic connections in Washoe City will afford him and his brother a very good attorney, Ronin. It's likely to be seen as circumstantial evidence, or a forced confession, given how dim-witted the uni-browed brother seems. But there are enough charges to put both of them in prison for a very long time."

"Well, I'll be damned," Ronin said, "caught because of a pocket full of stones. Who would have guessed?"

"I trust you'll not be damned for some time, my friend. You have a new adventure ahead of you," Happy Hands continued, with so ominous and prophetic a tone that Emma looked up from thinking her own thoughts about Ronin's future.

"A new adventure for Mister Ronin? Is there no end to Mister Ronin's adventures?" she asked with visible frustration. There were tears in her eyes. The table was silent for a moment, so much so that Dustsucker's intermittent, but still audible wheezing caused everyone to turn his way instead of looking at the still-lingering tears in Emma's eyes.

"I'm not speaking of Mister Ronin and Dustsucker riding off together, my friends." Happy Hands looked at Emma, and then at Ronin, who sat opposite him at the other end of the table. Dustsucker smiled. "This adventure has to do with a woman, my friends, not a man."

"Oh Jesus," Ash exhaled, "I can't take any more of this."

"Not at this table, marshal. I'll not have such speech at my table, sir," Emma scolded, picking up her napkin to wipe her eyes. "It's bad enough that you feel comfortable saying the 'd' word in my house. I'll not tolerate your taking the LORD's name in vain."

"I'm sorry," marshal Ash said, looking contrite. Ronin felt his face redden and looked over at Dustsucker, who seemed suddenly distracted.

"A woman, my brother?" he gulped.

"A number of women, my friend — and you'll not hear the end of it until it is over."

Chapter 82

MOUNTAIN CATHEDRALS

"You know this church was built in 1868, parts of it anyway. A lot of it burnt down in the Great Fire, not that I could tell you which part did or didn't," Spinnaker said to his new friend, Timothy Edwards Smith, previously of Sacramento but most recently delivered from the hands of the Crum Brothers, who had beat him regularly like a runaway slave.

"And not that I would care," Smith said, "I mean, not that I would have cared, prior to Jack leadin' us in the prayer of salvation a couple of days ago."

"Exactly, my friend," Spinnaker nodded, anxious to get on with his narration. Spinnaker loved visiting Virginia City, on his days off and particularly coming by Saint Mary's Church. "It's the mother of all Catholic Churches in Nevada," he said, practicing what he hoped would be the high-toned voice of a school master at the Fourth Ward School before the week was out. "The first church was erected in 1860, but as you will find out, the winds up here in Virginia City are pretty amazing. I mean, they'll blow the shit right out of you," Spinnaker continued.

"I'm not sure we should talk that way, Mort. I mean, there's got to be better words, now that we're saved and all."

"It's just between friends, Timothy. It doesn't much matter, I don't think, unless you're talking to children. Anyway, the wooden church blew down, just like the wooden church in Carson City did, where Jack is a member, Saint Teresa of Avila."

"Right."

"So the next church was built with bricks."

"One brick upon another," Smith said, "just like our new lives, right? And the wolf blew and the three pigs and all that."

"Exactly," Spinnaker smiled. *The tall, balding man seemed teachable. What fun all of this was going to be.* "The arches and pews are made from California redwood. You see the moldings there? That's pine. Where they found wood to build with, I don't know. There's nothing in the mountains anymore, but it's beautiful, don't you think?"

"I imagine they got it up here on the railroad, Mort, don't you think?"

Spinnaker nodded.

"I hope our lives will turn out the same way, Mort. I mean, it may take us some time and all, but what God doesn't do quickly, we'll do with some effort, right?"

"Exactly," the former Ormsby County deputy said. The two of them — Mort Spinnaker, who had no middle name, except for the nicknames others friends and deputies assigned him when making fun of his being so opinionated and all, and Timothy Edwards Smith, the former partner of the late Mister Jones who, as a team, helped the Crum brothers with their reign of terror prior to their becoming prisoners of the Ormsby County sheriff's office in Carson City — sat right in the first pew of Saint Mary's Roman Catholic Church. "Saint Mary's in the Mountains, Father Manoque likes to call it. You'll meet him," Spinnaker said. "Paddy Manogue loves the Irish, but he loves the English, too."

"That's good," Smith said, wondering if he had any Irish blood in him at all, but looking at Spinnaker's pale features, figured that English was good enough, at least for the two of them, and not that they could change that anyway. "What are we going to do, Mort? I mean, to blend in and all?"

"Well, I know a couple women, who have a house a block or so south of the Colombo Restaurant on B Street, who hold meetings where fortunes are told, good and bad."

"I never put much stock in in crystal ball gazing, Mort. I don't imagine the Catholic Church does either," Smith said. "I know Larry didn't trust them anymore than he did ministers."

"Well, I don't know anything about that," Spinnaker replied, "but I read a couple years ago that Paddy attended some meetings. I don't imagine it'd be a problem our attending a few, then."

"No I suppose not." Smith got up from the pew — it was the first time he'd ever sat so far up in church, folks of his status generally taking to the back pews, not that he frequented churches all that much, save to sleep in them when traveling.

"Word is," Spinnaker continued, "some of these women can reveal secrets no mortal man or woman ever knew, including a man's destiny. Eilley Bowers has the call, from what I hear, though I wouldn't know how to find her."

"Seriously?"

"Yup. Ever since the mansion failed — you ought to know all about that, given that you and the Crum brothers lived in the valley for a time — that's what she's been doing. According to the newspapers, Eilley can find missing persons, stolen articles, gold, silver, whatever it is you're looking for. I think she's over on C Street, though I don't rightly remember, and it may be that she lives in Reno. I don't know."

"Well, whoever you're thinking of, Mort, will be fine with me. Maybe we can get something to eat at the same time. And you know, it might be good to get a handle on whether or not Ronin survived all that shooting."

"What I know about that guy, Timothy, is that if he isn't dead there will come a point where we surely will be."

"That doesn't seem at all Christian, Mort, given that we're trying to change our lives and all." Smith patted his chest pockets, looking for tobacco and matches as they walked away from the church toward a special dinner being held by the Daughters of Charity to benefit the Saint Mary Louise Hospital. The new hospital complemented a small boarding school and orphanage but depended on the contributions of folks who used the sixty-bed facility. Mort was hoping that if the school didn't want him, he'd find work assisting the sisters with something. There was no better way to undo a lifetime of gunplay and guilt than to do good to those who most needed it. Jack had said that orphans and widows were those who needed it most, but that sick people might come close.

Spinnaker pulled some papers from his vest pocket and handed one to his friend. The two began to roll their own smokes as they headed to the supper being held at the Mackay mansion. "I don't imagine it will matter, Smith," he said, working to get a tight wrap on the tobacco his new friend had shared with him. "If Ronin is still alive, it won't much matter for either of us."

AUTHOR'S NOTE

Mid-way through reading my first novel in the W. W. Ronin series of Westerns, *East Jesus, Nevada*, a clergy friend asked me, "Where did you get the idea of Ronin?" She and I had been pastors in Nevada, she in Wells and Wendover, I in Carson City. And while I hadn't pressed her to buy my book, she had read it, perhaps out of friendship but ending in curiosity.

Truth be told, "W. W. Ronin" is an alias I use in two cowboy shooting organizations: the Single Action Shooting Society — the largest western shooting group involving multiple guns, real ammunition and steel targets, sometimes at lengthy distances — and the Cowboy Fast Draw Association, where wax ammunition reigns at a much shorter and faster pace. Both groups tolerate me as Life Members, though I spend most of my time now enjoying the World Fast Draw Association and my home club, the Portland Fast Draw Club in Saint Helens.

I like things Western, which is probably why I write Westerns.

Historical fiction may be a popular genre in the United States — with sales in the millions, even billions of dollars, depending on where you draw the lines — but Western fiction demands a certain hardiness. Simply said, there's very little money in it.

Years ago, a favorite professor introduced me to the role of power, prestige and wealth in America and his hopes, I suspect, that each of us would find some place in it. The Ronin novels may achieve some level of popularity — I hope they do, *Lady of the*

Lake being the second in the series, *The Pinkerton Years,* a nearly finished third — but writing them will likely never propel me into the kind of reward my sociology professor was hinting at, despite my first editor's question, "Wouldn't it be nice if you were the next Louis L'Amour?"

I write what I write because it brings me pleasure. But given that it's historical fiction that I'm writing, you have a right to expect something other than "I'm just writing this out of my head." So here's the disclaimer: everything in this book is fiction, except for those characters, places and events that are not.

You should know, for instance, that I've attempted to be accurate to the characters, times and places in the W. W. Ronin series of Westerns. Where *East Jesus, Nevada* shares an history of the Comstock Lode — one of the most important mining finds in American history — *Lady of the Lake* offers a story settled in the challenging history of nearby Lake Tahoe and, perhaps Nevada's most ancient people, the Washoe Indians.

Significant effort is spent in each of these books to make sure the geography and history is accurate enough to provide a reliable and entertaining tale. In this second book, for example, please excuse (or enjoy) the fictional tale where real Nevada characters like A. B. Cobb, the proprietor of the Lake House Hotel (parts of which still stand as a private home in Glenbrook, Nevada) and Augustus Ash, a Virginia City resident and the state's real U.S. Marshal, interact with characters significantly less real: W. W. Ronin, Marcus T. Slade (called "Dustsucker" by his friends) Emma Nauman and Happy Hands. These latter characters are simply figments of my unrestrained imagination.

Back to my clergy friend's e-mail. "William Washington" was the name of my paternal great-grandfather. A farmer and minister in the Pentecostal Nazarene Church, he rode with Biffle's 13th Calvary (Confederate) during the Civil War. Details of his life (he settled just south of Reelfoot Lake in northwestern Tennessee) are source to much of the backstory of the upcoming and nearly-finished third novel in the series, *The Pinkerton Years.* My protagonist's last name, "Ronin," simply describes where I've ended up in my 61st year as a human being and writer.

You may already have guessed, if you're a reader of my blog at www.greggtownsley.com, that much of my writing is autobiographical. Good writing is always about what the writer knows or is willing to learn during his or her life journey. Having said that, if reading the books in this series leave you better acquainted with the history of Nevada, particularly at the close of the Comstock mining period in the late 1870s and early 1880s, I'm happy. If they've helped you to live a more reflective life, I'm glad for that too. If my "parenthetical writing style," as a reviewer of my first book called it, provides you the space to wonder, I'm even more pleased. Life is too long and complex not to sit a bit and cogitate. So it goes...

I want to offer a few words of acknowledgement before the story begins.

To the late Victor Goodwin, my longtime friend and parishioner in Carson City, Nevada: I rarely had the better of Vic, in the frequent back and forth of things during Rotary meetings at the Ormsby House and even in church. You were always an education and inspiration to me, Vic, even though both of us would have been embarrassed to admit it.

Similar gratitude is due former Nevada State Archivist Guy Rocha, who granted me a phone interview while he was soaking in his Carson City bathtub. I asked whether anyone had ever ridden a Comstock V-flume and survived. Guy doubts it, but let this book (and its unstated research) serve as argument. Should we meet in person someday, I'll be more specific.

My appreciation also to anthropologist Don Handelman, whose oral history of the Washoe Tribe, and in particular its most famous shaman, Henry Rupert, was invaluable in helping me to understand what it might have meant to be a Washoe holy man in the late 19th century.

To the folks at the Nevada State Museum in Reno and the Silver State National Peace Officers Museum in Virginia City, my profound thanks. Despite reading dozens of volumes of Nevada history, historical clippings and personal interviews over a period of more than a dozen years, I wouldn't have been able to dial-in the history of these books without you.

But most of all, to my wife, who is always my cheerleader and who remembers my song when I've forgotten even where I've placed my keys: you are my muse, my best editor, critic and friend. It's to you that I dedicate this book.

ABOUT THE
AUTHOR

Gregg Edwards Townsley is a reflective, free-thinking ex-pastor, martial artist, writer and western fast draw enthusiast living in St. Helens, Oregon. No strange to the places his characters inhabit — Reno, Carson City, Virginia City and Lake Tahoe — he raised his children in northern Nevada, from 1984 through 1993, as pastor and head of staff of the First Presbyterian Church in Carson City.

Gregg enjoys hearing from his readers, posting updates and background to his work on his website and blog at www.gregg-townsley.com.You can find him on Facebook: www.facebook.com/GreggEdwardsTownsley, or subscribe to his Twitter updates at http://twittter.com/greggtownsley.

The author encourages your review of this book and his others at www.amazon.com.

www.ingramcontent.com/pod-product-compliance
Lightning Source LLC
Chambersburg PA
CBHW061306170626
46817CB00001B/72